I've travelled the world twice over,
Met the famous: saints and sinners,
Poets and artists, kings and queens,
Old stars and hopeful beginners,
I've been where no-one's been before,
Learned secrets from writers and cooks
All with one library ticket
To the wonderful world of books.

© JANICE JAMES.

CHANTAL

Torn from the dazzling salons and glittering balls of aristocratic London, the beautiful, beguiling Chantal found herself caught into a gathering maelstrom of wild and dangerous adventure. From an evil château and a debauched French nobleman, to a deserted tropical island and a bold Portuguese pirate, she was swept into a whirlwind of passion and scandal, anguish and ecstasy. This saga pulses with the vivid legacy of Chantal's stepmother, the incomparable Mavreen, and her bewitching 'sister', the untameable Tamarisk.

CLAIRE LORRIMER

CHANTAL

Complete and Unabridged

CHARNWOOD
Leicester

First published in Great Britain in 1980

First Charnwood Edition
published 1996

British Library CIP Data

Lorrimer, Claire, *1921 –*
Chantal.—Large print ed.—
Charnwood library series
1. English fiction—20th century
I. Title
823.9'14 [F]

ISBN 0–7089–8907–1

Published by
F. A. Thorpe (Publishing) Ltd.
Anstey, Leicestershire
Set by Words & Graphics Ltd.
Anstey, Leicestershire
Printed and bound in Great Britain by
T. J. Press (Padstow) Ltd., Padstow, Cornwall

This book is printed on acid-free paper

For my children,
IAIN, NIKKI, and GRAEME

Foreword

Of necessity historical novels are a blend of truth and fiction. It is remarkable how frequently the adage 'Fact is Stranger than Fiction' proved to be the case while researching. It was intriguing to discover a book in the British Museum by a Major W. Stirling relating to the fate of the HMS *Tiger* in 1836 in which her survivors did reach the safety of the Seychelles island of Astove. The survival of members of the fictitious frigate HMS *Valetta* is based on fact.

The story of Chantal is based on the following true facts:

The town of Compiègne with its Roman ruins, Palace, Forest, Châteaux all exist, although Boulancourt itself, is imaginary.

The existence of the convict ship, *Surrey*, the Pulteney Hotel, Prince Esterházy de Galántha are facts as are all the incidents relating to history, politics, politicians, royalty, the arts, industry and the law. The laws relating to divorce and legitimacy in France in Chantal's day are also true. Strange though they may seem, so are the mishaps at Queen Victoria's coronation.

The island of Coetivy, named after the Chevalier de Coetivy who first sighted it in 1771, exists as does Mahé, these being two of over ninety islands in the Seychelles Archipelago. Place names prevailing on Mahé during the period of the story have been used in preference to those currently in use. The existence of pirates in the area, the trading of slaves and their treatment are historically correct. The names of slaves in CHANTAL are taken from an original slave register.

The incarceration of Antoine de Valle's prisoner in CHANTAL is similar in nearly every respect to that of a lady who lived in England in the ninth century. There are documents recording her imprisonment and death. The interesting point here is that when the *real* prisoner was discovered, she was naked, wearing only a red wig! This is fact and not fiction, but to have included such details in *Chantal* may have stretched the reader's credibility too far.

I am greatly indebted for help received from:
Croydon (Reference Section), East Grinstead and Edenbridge Libraries.
M. Lucien Mourgeon (Avocat).
Mr. Gilbert Pool (Tourism Director for the Seychelles).
Mr. Nirmal Kantilal Shah (Mahé).
British Maritime Museum (Greenwich).
British Museum (Library).
Institut Français du Royaume Uni (Bibliotèque).
Joy Tait, Sandra Clifton (Research).
Penrose Scott, Gill Ayr (Secretarial).
Mr. Malcolm Paisley (Photographer) for family documents.

Cast Of Characters

1831 – 1840

Chantal (*natural daughter of Sir Peregrine Waite*)

John de Valle (*son of Mavreen*)

Mavreen, Lady Waite (*stepmother of Chantal*)

Sir Peregrine Waite (*(alias Gideon Morris), her husband*)

Dickon Sale (*Mavreen's childhood friend and servant*)

Rose Sale (*his wife*)

Antoine de Valle (*natural son of Mavreen's former husband Gerard de Valle, deceased*)

Stefano (*Antoine's servant*)

Tamarisk von Eburhard (*Mavreen's daughter*)

Charles von Eburhard (*her husband*)

Richard
William
Lisa
Clarissa
} *their children*

Baroness Lisa von Eburhard (*Charles von Eburhard's aunt*)

Anne Lade (*friend and sister-in-law to Mavreen through her second marriage*)

Julia Lade (*her daughter and Chantal's friend*)

Dorothy (*Chantal's maid*)

Dorcas (*Mavreen's maid*)

Elsie (*Tamarisk's maid*)

Duc Dubois (*French aristocrat and friend of John's*)

Duchesse Dubois (*his wife*)

Fleur Dubois (*their eldest daughter*)

Aimée
Rose
Jeanne } (*their other daughters*)
Suzanne
Noelle

Luke (*John's servant*)

Princess Camille Faloise (*alias Marie Duval*) Antoine's guardian and wife)

Captain Anson (*Captain of HMS* Valetta)

Thomas Lovell (*1st Lieutenant of HMS* Valetta)

Kaftan (*Lascar sailor on HMS* Valetta)

Dinez da Gama (*Portuguese pirate and captain of* O Bailado)

Miguel (*First mate of* O Bailado)

Zambi (*African slave-girl*)

Siméon St. Clair, (*Plantation owner on the island of Mahé*)

Narcisse (*Siméon's African housekeeper*)

Tobias (*her husband and Siméon's foreman*

Rose Printanière (*their daughter*)

Mathias (*her fiancé*)

Jerome
Fabies
Gaspar
Moses Bemba
Figaro } (*freed African slaves on Siméon's plantation*)
Joliecoeur Justin
Zephir Volant
Azor Lafleur
Babet

Jack Clifton (*Captain of* Jason, *a Convict ship*)
Admiral Pentell
(*British Naval officer at Admiralty House*)
Smithers (*his clerk*)
Hamish McRae (*Captain of* Seasprite)
Paul Mylius (*younger brother of the Civil
    Commissioner on Mahé*)
Janet
Phoebe
    (*his daughters*)
Pierre (*young French messenger*)
Blanche Merlin (alias Marianne Antoine's
    mother)
François Noyer (*a prisoner*)

Prologue

March 1821

ON the 8th of March, 1821, the woman died. The four-month old child in her arms wailed fitfully as her mother's body froze in the bitter night air, waking the exhausted man huddled beneath his cloak nearby.

Gideon Morris, known to all but a handful of people as Sir Peregrine Waite, was roused from sleep to the bitter discomforts of cold, hunger and a renewed awareness of the throbbing pain of the half-healed wound in his leg.

"Maria," he called gently, "the child is hungry and needs feeding!"

He reached out a hand to the hunched figure of the young woman lying beside him in the bitter night air.

The stiffness of her body brought him fully awake. As the baby's crying intensified, a sudden fear that the mother was dead made him hesitate to touch her a second time lest that fear was proved justified.

"Maria!" he called again, this time urgently.

He was deeply shocked and distressed to realize she was dead although this tragedy was not altogether unexpected. He had never loved the young Neapolitan woman in the way he knew a man could love the woman of his dreams, but he had nevertheless felt a deep

1

affection for Maria. For all she was but a simple peasant without breeding or education, her loving devotion to him these past twelve months had earned his gratitude and respect. Not only had she proved courageous and loyal, but her nature was essentially passionate and caring.

As the child's wails became weaker Perry's stunned immobility gave way to action. With difficulty he prized the baby from her mother's stiffened arms. The minute face was pinched and blue with cold. Hurriedly he unbuttoned his thick cape and the jacket beneath, and removing his pistol, pressed the small body close to his chest where his own body heat might impart some warmth to it. At once the tiny hands began to search instinctively for the mother's breasts, the hunger in her little body of over-riding concern.

With a renewed sense of shock Perry realized that the woman's death would almost certainly result in the death of the child. It had not been weaned and the chances of his finding a wet nurse here in the mountains of Italy were highly improbable, even had he the money to pay for such services.

It was now over a week since they had left the comparative safety of the encampment in the hills above Potenza. They had lived there with other members of the resistance force called the Carbonari ever since he had led them into hiding after an uprising against the Government in Naples nearly a year ago. The uprising had failed and they had been chased into the hills.

Perry was so severely wounded that had it not been for the care of these poor peasants he would certainly have died. The men, driven by poverty and a burning sense of injustice, were in war-like mood and anxious as soon as he, their leader, showed signs of recovery, to renew their resistance. But most had lost their weapons and there was no money to buy more. From his sick bed, a straw palliasse on the floor of a shepherd's hut, Perry dispatched a messenger to Pisa with a written request to his friend, the poet Percy Shelley, to send funds. He had given Pietro his last remaining valuable — his gold watch, with which to guarantee his authenticity to the Shelleys.

For several months the small band of Carbonari waited, living on the meagre rations supplied by the poor people in Potenza who were themselves close to starvation. Maria nursed Perry, attending to his dreadful wound as best she could. She was a dark-haired, comely young woman approaching thirty and already widowed, her farmer husband having been killed in an earlier uprising. The intimate bond between nurse and patient deepened as Maria's passionate nature revealed itself. When in an unguarded moment, she shyly declared her love for the handsome English aristocrat, the essence of their relationship changed and they became lovers. She was never in doubt about the true nature of their association.

"I know we cannot be married — it would not be right for a titled Englishman to wed a Neapolitan peasant girl!" she had said in her simple, direct way. "But I love you — *io t'amo* — and I know that you need a woman. I want you to take me even if you cannot love me."

Perry had not resisted her for long. He had come to Italy for the very purpose of forgetting the one woman in his life he could ever love or marry — Mavreen, now the wife of the Vicomte Gerard de Valle.

Not a night passed that he did not think of her, long for her, wonder whether she was happy now that she shared her life with the man she had loved for so long. He hoped that perhaps with Maria's soft arms enfolding him, his dreams might at last be haunted less often by his memories of the passionate love he had once known with Mavreen.

When Maria told him she was with child he had received the news with deepest misgivings. The privations of their lives in hiding in the hills were extreme and in any event he had no wish for a child, far less an illegitimate offspring for whom he could not disclaim responsibility. But for the sake of the woman who cared for him so selflessly, he tried to hide his reaction. Maria was clearly proud and delighted to be bearing his child. When the babe was born in the early hours of a chill November dawn, he had allowed her to believe that he, too, was delighted as she placed the tiny girl in his arms.

"We could call her Maria after me or Lucia since she was born at break of day," the proud mother had whispered. But Perry was unable to share Maria's pride or radiant joy and gave no thought to the baby's naming.

4

One by one the men began to return to the farms which they had left to join the Carbonari, for it was becoming clear to them all that the messenger, Pietro, had never reached the Shelleys and no funds would be forthcoming. Word came from other members of the Carbonari that resistance was weakening and that their cause no longer justified the neglect of their farms and families. By the end of January all had left the encampment and Perry, too, would have departed but for the unhealed leg wound which forbade walking any but the shortest of distances.

For a while he contemplated sending Maria into Naples to see the British Consul, Sir Henry Lushington, to ask for aid since he was, after all, a British subject. But he feared for her safety should she be recognized as an associate of the Carbonari. Her former husband had been well known to the authorities and he dared not risk her recognition.

"We will remain here a while longer," he told her. "You, too, need to regain your full strength. By March the weather will be better. Then we will make our way north where my friends are living. They will care for you and the baby."

But he had underestimated the seriousness of his leg injury which, despite Maria's care, had not healed properly, for splinters of bone were still buried deep within his thigh. With unwelcome frequency abscesses occurred and he was seldom without fever and pain.

The child thrived on her mother's milk, but Maria tired quickly and was clearly losing weight as they began their travels northward. They survived on the rabbits Perry snared, a skill he had learned in his youth when he had first had to live on his wits. Occasionally a farmer would give them milk, but often they were turned away because they had no money to pay for their requirements. The milder Spring weather was late in coming, and the bitterly cold nights with only the roughest of shelters to keep out the winds, added to their misery and ill health.

To Perry it was clear now that Maria had kept from him the true state of her weakness. Rather than be a burden, she had walked beside him uncomplainingly until he, himself, had given in to weariness and pain. With the child needing food every four hours or so, Maria's strength ebbed and unrecognized by her, she had developed milk fever.

Perry's self-condemnation was acute as he closed the lids over her eyes and covered her drawn, beautiful face with her cloak. But for the child, he thought bitterly, she might have survived; and he felt a moment's anger as the baby began to wail its frustration within the warm confines of his jacket. There seemed little doubt that it too must die for he had no means of feeding it. Perhaps, he thought wearily, it would be for the best. There was no great future for an illegitimate girl, motherless and with a father who cared not whether she lived or died. Death might be the best solution and the kindest for the baby, since to die slowly of starvation could only prolong its misery.

With a feeling born partly of exhaustion, partly of despair, Perry reached for the small moist bundle and withdrew it from his jacket. The shock of the cold air silenced its cries. With miraculous rapidity the crumpled red face paled, uncreased and became a tiny replica of its mother's, the petal-smooth, creamy-olive skin curving gently over delicate cheekbones. The long dark lashes, wet with tears, lifted suddenly and two beautiful almond-shaped eyes stared up at him in mute appeal. From beneath the rough-spun shawl in which Maria had wrapped the child, one small clenched fist appeared, and as the minute fingers uncurled, Perry noticed for the first time the dainty perfection of the pearl-pink nails.

For the rest of his life, Sir Peregrine Waite was never to forget the magic of that moment when first he felt the full force of fierce paternal love for his daughter. The awareness of her perfection, of her dependence upon him, of the fact that she was part of him, overwhelmed him. Tears that he could never have shed for her mother, now filled his eyes as he realized the baby's helplessness and frailty. In that same moment, he knew that he could never again contemplate her death; that somehow he would find a way to save her. He determined that insofar as it was within his power, his love would be large enough and strong enough to ensure that she would never miss her mother.

As the baby's cries were renewed Perry faced the need for immediate action. He knew they could not be too far from La Spezia for they had left the outskirts of Livorna behind them two days since. He should soon find a hill farmstead where hopefully he could obtain milk for the child.

Lack of food and the poisoning of his blood from his leg wound had brought Perry almost to the end of his strength. Although it tore at his heart to leave Maria unburied, he knew he must now conserve what energy he had left for the sake of the child.

Limping awkwardly, Perry began his slow journey over the hills. The sun was high in the sky, imparting a small measure of warmth to his aching limbs, before he first heard the bleat of goats and knew that help was not far off. The baby was silent now — a fact which increased his anxiety for its hunger pains must be even more acute than his own, and a healthy child would be protesting volubly. With renewed effort he strode forward and a moment later he saw with a sigh of relief a herd of goats browsing on the hillside. A lad of twelve years or so was guarding them.

"*Buon giorno!*" Perry waved from a distance and shouted his friendly greeting a second time. To his dismay the boy neither returned his greeting nor the wave of his hand but jumped to his feet and menacingly raised the stout stick he was holding.

Perry was well aware that bands of brigands, robbers and outlaws, often starving and very dangerous, attacked such isolated farmsteads in order to obtain provisions for themselves. Doubtless the goatherd mistook him for one such, ragged and disheveled as he must appear to the boy. Cautiously, he walked forward but now the boy took fright altogether and, abandoning his herd, ran like a young hare towards his home.

Wearily Perry followed him the half mile downhill to the farm only to find the stout wooden door of the little cottage heavily barred against him. For half an hour he banged upon the door, alternately shouting and pleading for assistance. Either the occupants did not understand his excellent Italian, which doubtless differed considerably from their own dialect, or they were too frightened to risk confrontation with a man carrying a pistol.

Perry's spirits flagged alarmingly as the hopelessness of his position struck him. With the child in his arms, he could not shoot his way into the house. The next farmstead might be many miles away and even if he could find the strength to walk there, the baby must be fed soon if it were not to die.

Staring down into the dark eyes, so large in the tiny pinched face, he knew that he could not permit himself to collapse, leaving them both to the mercy of the farmer. There must, he thought desperately, be something he could do.

As if in answer to his thoughts, the faint bleat of a goat reached his ears. A sudden, secret smile spread across Perry's exhausted face. It would not be for the first time in his life if he were forced to resort to theft in order to survive, he thought. He had but to steal one of the unguarded nanny goats for the child to be certain of nourishment however long it took him to reach Pisa.

Knowing that suspicious eyes were regarding him fearfully from the grubby windows of the farmstead, he walked away in a different direction to that of the grazing herd. Making a large detour, he came upon the animals from the far side of the hill. Laying the baby carefully on the ground, it took him but a few cautious moves to approach the nanny of his choice, secure it with his belt and lead it away from its companions.

Surprisingly the animal neither struggled to resist him nor called a warning to the herd. Clearly it did not consider Perry's gentle handling a danger. He remembered well from his youth how to milk an animal, but the task of feeding the baby with the liquid he had channelled into Maria's cooking pot presented a more difficult problem. Necessity aroused his natural resourcefulness. He dipped his 'kerchief into the warm milk and placed a corner of it into the child's mouth. It was not long before the starving baby began to suck. Each time Perry removed the kerchief to soak it once more in milk, the wails increased in volume and despite the gravity of the moment — for this was her last chance of survival — Perry grinned, marveling at his daughter's tenacity and at the huge force of anger contained in so tiny a frame.

Only when she had fallen asleep, totally replete, did Perry take a long draught of milk himself. Far more easily digested than cow's milk, the stolen nourishment revived both man and child. Perry watched her for a while, anxious lest she might have overfed or that the new type of milk might not suit her. But the color had returned to the baby's cheeks and she slept quietly and happily, not stirring when he lifted her into his arms. He resumed his walk, the nanny goat trailing behind him.

In such a manner Perry and his daughter reached the safety of Rome where he was able to seek assistance at the British Consulate. There he was given fresh clothing for himself and the child, money to suffice for his needs, a carriage to take him to Pisa and a wet nurse to accompany them. The goat was left at the Embassy. To the secret amusement of the residents, Perry insisted that it should not be sold but be allowed to live out the rest of its life in the Embassy gardens.

"After all," he told his host, "the animal saved my daughter's life!"

As April drew to a close, the small party arrived at Pisa to he greeted by the astonished but delighted Shelleys.

"We had word that you were dead, my dear fellow!" Percy said, looking curiously at the nurse and then at the bundle in Perry's arms.

"This is my daughter and this woman is her nurse!" Perry said smiling. "I am hoping that Mary will care for her, for the child's mother is no longer alive."

"As if you could have any doubt upon it!" Mary cried, peering at the child in his arms. She gave a small cry of wonder. "What a beautiful baby, Perry! How old is she? What is her name?

Who was her mother?"

"Let our friend rest a while before you ply him with questions!" her husband suggested, noting Perry's pallor and guessing correctly that he was far from well.

He led Perry into the salon where he sank wearily into one of the comfortable chairs, still clasping the child in his arms. His leg was paining him almost beyond endurance and he was alternately shivering and burning with fever. Yet he gave no thought to his health as he smiled at Mary.

"My daughter is twenty-two weeks old today. But as to her name, she has none as yet. Her mother suggested we might call her Maria, or Lucia because she was born at break of day. But during our adventures of which I will tell you presently, I have been thinking a great deal on the matter." He turned to his friend and said eagerly, "This is no ordinary child, Percy. Even at her tender age, she is showing the most astonishing eagerness for life. She has survived where other infants must surely have died. And unless she is cold or hungry, she is the happiest little skylark in the world." He turned once more to Mary.

"She warrants a more unusual name than either Maria or Lucia," he said softly, "something that expresses her joy and enthusiasm for life; her individuality. Even allowing for the fact that I am her father and you may judge me prejudiced in her favor, I swear to you she is like no other child!"

"Then we will think of a very special name

for her!" Mary said. "But Lucia will suffice for the present. Now I can see you are sorely in need of rest and care, Perry. Leave the child to me, my dear. I will take good care of your beautiful daughter!"

Reluctant to release his burden, Perry said:

"'Tis a miracle she has survived, my friends. I am forced to the conclusion that destiny has some special design for her since few so young can have suffered so poor a start to life and yet smile so confidently at the future."

Neither he nor his companions realized at that moment how prophetic were Perry's words and how greatly his child would one day need that confidence to survive the physical and moral dangers that lay in wait for her.

Happily unaware of the future, Perry allowed the kindly woman to remove from his arms the little girl he was eventually to christen Chantal.

1

August 1837

AT the head of the thirty-foot-long oak dining table sat a young, fair-haired man. He was smiling enigmatically as he surveyed the scene before him, his dark eyes narrowed speculatively, his brows raised slightly as if in scorn or boredom.

From the far end of the table, a young Parisian blood lurched forward across his female neighbor, oblivious to etiquette as he called out in a high, shrill tone:

"Antoine, *mon ami*, is it not time to let us see tomorrow's contestants?"

A burst of clapping from forty pairs of hands echoed upwards to the ceiling some thirty feet above their heads. Goblets of wine were knocked over by waving arms. As the dark red liquid ran from the polished oak surface and stained their clothes, shouts of protest mingled with cries to their host to satisfy their demands.

Antoine de Valle remained silent, his beautiful aristocratic face impassive as the noise and disorder at his table increased in volume. Only the imperceptible curve of his finely shaped mouth betrayed a hint of distaste as his eyes went from face to face, noting the heightened color of those who had already over-imbibed. Many of the women were as drunk as the men. Every one of them was young and liberally endowed with feminine appeal. Demi-mondaines, they were paid companions of his friends — the young bloods who could afford to pay for the luxury of smooth, white shoulders, invitingly curved breasts and tempting mouths.

Their host seemed oblivious to the fact that the morals of these females, like their manners, were as out of place in the banqueting hall of the Château de Boulancourt as was the disorder of half-eaten foods littering the great table. There were no servants in attendance. Later, when the diners adjourned to the *salle à jeux* to enjoy the delights of the gaming tables, servants would be permitted to return to the huge dining-room to clear up the debris. Antoine de Valle was not, as he might appear to a stranger, impervious to his reputation and once the food had been brought to the table, no servant who might carry tales was present to witness the orgy of such banquets as these.

"Do not keep us in suspense, *mon vieux!*" another of the male guests pleaded. "Let us whet our appetites for tomorrow's entertainment."

Roughly the man detached himself from the clinging arms of the woman beside him.

"You have not forgotten that proverb you so often quote, Antoine? 'Satiety of what is beautiful induces a taste for the singular.'"

A roar of laughter from the men greeted his words. Their female companions shrieked in shrill protest. The noise was deafening.

Smoke from the guttering candles in the many candelabra stretching the length of the table

16

curled slowly upwards, stinging the eyes of the two young kitchen boys concealed in the gallery high above one end of the room. Both knew that were they caught espying their masters, they would be thrashed within an inch of their lives and instantly dismissed from service. But curiosity had this night got the better of them. The scene they surveyed was in no way disappointing. Both were simple-minded village lads who had heard their elders speak of 'ladies' such as these. But no gossip had prepared them for the sight of a bare bosom exposed to view as if it were of no import; far less of a man's hand idly fondling it whilst he drank from a goblet, or engaged in conversation with the painted beauty seated on his other side.

Their master suddenly raised his head and spoke. Fear overcame their fascinated curiosity and the boys scuttled off noiselessly as Antoine de Valle said:

"Since you insist, *mes amis*, I will have the gladiators brought in!"

A vast cheer greeted his announcement. He rapped loudly upon the table top to summon his personal servant, Stefano. The man, swarthy and Italianate in feature, hurried into the room. He bowed and bent his head close to his master's.

"*Vous desirez, Monsieur le Vicomte?*"

"The young men may come in — but not the prisoners!" The last words were emphasized but so softly that none other than the servant could hear them.

Whilst waiting for his orders to be carried out, Antoine de Valle allowed himself to dwell for a moment upon the thought of tomorrow's pleasures. In the morning he and his house guests would rendezvous at the hunting lodge in the heart of the great forest of Compiègne. The dogs would be assembled and *la chasse au sanglier* would commence. Hopefully the animals would scent many of the wild boar grovelling in the thickets, rooting for acorns, beechnuts or other food. They would send them fleeing towards the riding party waiting to kill them with their half-stocked sporting guns. Later in the day the best of the beasts would be roasted whole for the evening repast. But before that, the party would repair to the Roman amphitheatre for the real sport of the day.

Antoine's dark eyes glowed in his somewhat surprisingly pale face. The amphitheatre was one of the few pleasures of life, he reflected, that could still stir his senses. He had discovered the old Roman ruins when he had first returned to Compiègne five years ago. One of the young assistants to the stone mason who was working on the restoration of the Château had unearthed a great stone slab carved and grooved so beautifully that Antoine had been called to see it. He had at once recognized its archeological origins and set a group of laborers to careful digging of the mound from which the blocks of sandstone had been retrieved. One by one the old slabs had been dragged from their earthy graves, the mud washed from them and the broken pieces placed in rows for careful matching. It was nearly two years before the complete circle of the old Roman amphitheatre was exposed to the naked eye.

It was then Antoine conceived the idea of restoring it as nearly as possible to its original entity. The cost of employing masons to hew and carve new sandstone from the nearby quarry was enormous; but once begun, he could not bring himself to abandon the project. A year ago it had been completed and Antoine was able to realize his private dream — to recreate within the walls of the amphitheatre the same atmosphere as in Roman times.

He had ordered that a twelve-foot-high fence of beech palings cut from the forest be erected around the old ruins to give total privacy. None but a few of his most trusted servants and, of course, his guests knew exactly what nefarious events took place in the Boulancourt amphitheatre. From time to time, peasants from neighboring villages or from the town of Compiègne itself wandered too close to the fence for their own good. Since the ruins were on the Boulancourt estate, they were shot at by guards for trespassing. Some lived to tell the tale of savage dogs and guards with shotguns; but others were not seen again and fear now kept all but the most curious and adventurous at bay.

Antoine smiled, his dark eyes humorless as he congratulated himself upon his well-kept privacy. Not for him the boring round of social niceties common to the members of the aristocracy and gentry who lived in the surrounding countryside. He had rapidly earned the reputation of being a recluse and the invitations that had at first poured in when it became known that a de Valle was once more in residence at Boulancourt, were no longer forthcoming. Matrons with marriageable daughters ceased leaving their cards and such were the rumors circulating as to the company Antoine de Valle entertained at the Château, that he was now politely ignored by those who had sought earlier to include him on their calling lists.

His thoughts were halted by the entrance of the twenty young athletes who were to take part in the morrow's performance. Dressed like Greek gods in togas and thonged sandals, their bronzed young bodies glistening in the candlelight, they ran in pairs the length of the oak panelled banqueting hall. Here they halted briefly, bowing and smiling at the assembly. Amidst the noise of applause, there came cries of admiration from the women, some so suggestive in content that the men burst out laughing. One woman stood up and sauntered over to the group of athletes, running her hands over the muscles of a blond lad, feeling him as she might have adjudged the condition of a race horse. The boy's face, glistening with sweat in the heat of the room, turned a fiery red. The men near enough to notice, laughed and called to him to make the most of the lady's admiration and enjoy the favors she seemed anxious to bestow upon him. Others joined in with cries of encouragement.

Excited by the attention she had drawn to herself, the woman deliberately ran her hands over the boy's chest and pulled teasingly at the soft golden hairs. Still standing a little apart from him, her hands wandered downwards to his slim hips and her fingers moved towards his groin whilst the men applauded with ever increasing eagerness.

Laughing, she reached up and undid the buckle on his shoulder. His white toga fell at his feet leaving him naked. Desperately the young athlete looked in appeal towards his master seated with impassive face at the end of the long table. He and his companions had been kept apart from women whilst their training for tomorrow's sport continued for weeks on end. The woman's scent, her bared breasts and the touch of her hands were undermining his self-control. His pride was powerless to fight the wild tempo of his blood as his body responded to her caresses.

"*Mon petit amour!*" she crooned as her body curved toward him.

The shouts of laughter and further encouragement were deafening but suddenly Antoine's voice, sharp and penetrating, silenced everyone.

"Enough tomfoolery!" he announced. "My gladiators must reserve their energies for tomorrow's games. Afterwards . . . well, *nous verrons!*"

The woman moved back to her place at the table. The boy, covering himself with his hands, joined the other athletes as they ran back up the room, their sandaled feet making little noise on the polished oak parquet floor. They stopped only to bow to Antoine before leaving the room.

"Where do you *find* them, Antoine?" one young man asked enviously. "In Paris there are no such Greek gods for hire for whatever purpose. *Mon Dieu*, you have all the luck!"

"It is not a matter of luck!" Antoine replied. "I do not believe in luck. As to how I accomplish what others do not — that is a matter of using one's intelligence. I am not so stupid as to search for my gladiators in Paris. I arrange for them to be sent here from other countries. Anything is possible if you are prepared to pay for it — as you should know!" he added pointedly, nodding in the direction of the slim, dark-haired beauty clinging to his guest's arm with all the outward appearances of loving devotion.

A shout of laughter greeted his words for there were few men present who were not cognizant of the price demanded by the dark beauty for her favors. Most of those present had money. Sons of the aristocrats who had fled France during the Revolution, they were now back in their own country restored to favor by the return of the monarchy. Louis Phillippe sat firmly on the throne and the revolts against his predecessor Charles X were troubles of the past. An attempt last year to assassinate the King had failed and there was amity with a peaceful England ruled by their new young Queen, Alexandrina Victoria.

It was generally assumed by Antoine's acquaintances that he, too, was a very wealthy young man. It was well known that his father, the former Vicomte Gerard de Valle, had left him his estate and they judged from the lavish restoration and furnishing of the Château de Boulancourt, that the twenty-nine-year-old heir had not counted the cost. The Château was even more richly adorned than the Royal Palace in Compiègne!

Paintings by artists such as Corot, Turner and Constable adorned the rooms. The Château de Boulancourt was now not only a museum of art but a work of art in itself.

"But then Antoine is an artist *manqué!*" someone had once remarked. "Had he been born in other circumstances he might well have become a great painter!"

"*Monsieur le Vicomte!*"

Antoine was startled out of his reverie by the urgent tones of the servant, Stefano, standing at his elbow.

"Well, what is it?" he asked impatiently.

The man held out a silver salver on which lay a letter written in perfectly formed script. It was addressed not to the Vicomte de Valle, but to Monsieur Antoine de Valle.

Frowning, Antoine took the missive and began to read. As his eyes quickly scanned the page, his frown deepened to a scowl. Suddenly he stood up and held up his hands, calling for silence.

"My apologies, *mes amis*, but the party is over. You will all have to return to Paris immediately!"

There was a chorus of protests.

"It is but ten of the clock, *mon cher.*"

"Are you crazy? It will take us five hours to drive back to the city!"

"The horses are tired!"

"We shall be set upon by brigands!"

23

"What of tomorrow's sport? You cannot mean to dismiss us in so cavalier a fashion."

Their host's face had resumed its customary immutability.

"I regret the inconvenience but you must leave!" he said quietly but with an authority that brooked no change of opinion. "I would not demand this untimely interruption to our planned enjoyment were it not absolutely necessary. Stefano . . . " He turned to the servant and said firmly: "Order the carriages to be brought round at once. Tell the visiting servants they must be packed and ready to leave in half an hour!"

The cries of protest dwindled to murmurs of discontent as the guests staggered out of the room. Finally only Antoine remained, seated alone at the head of the great refectory table.

He picked up the letter which had been brought by a messenger from the Hôtel de France in Compiègne. His lips tightened as he began to read it for the second time.

'My dear Antoine,

'It was with the utmost surprise that I learned from the landlord of this hotel that you are in residence at the Château de Boulancourt.

'I arrived here this evening with my husband, Sir Peregrine Waite, his daughter, Chantal and your half brother, John. With no expectation of seeing you, it was our intention only to visit the grave of your dear father

24

which I have not seen since I last came to Compiègne six years ago for this same purpose. On that occasion, I was informed by Monsieur Mougin, the avocat, that you were somewhere on the great continent of America but that he had no knowledge of your exact address. I was most gratified, however, to see that all was in good order at Boulancourt.

'Had I known where to write to you, I would of course have done so long since for I promised your father that I would watch over your welfare. Alas, circumstances proved it impossible for me to keep that promise since your guardian, Princess Faloise, left no forwarding address when she closed up her London home the year your father died, and removed you to a foreign country.

'My pleasure in learning of your current proximity is therefore of the utmost and unless it should prove inconvenient, it is my intention to call upon you tomorrow morning. It will then be possible for us to exchange intelligence as to our ways of life since last we saw each other.

'Please be so kind as to return word to me via my messenger.

'Your affectionate stepmother,

'Mavreen.'

Antoine leant his elbow on the table and rested his chin on the palm of his hand. He stared thoughtfully into the smoky distance of the furthest end of the room.

"*Zut alors!*" he swore softly. And then with controlled violence, he added: "*Sacré Dieu!*"

But even as he used the profanity, he knew that there was no way he could refuse to receive the one woman he hated above all others — Mavreen de Valle; or now, so it seemed, Mavreen, Lady Waite!

He took a decanter of wine and filled his glass, then downed it in one gulp. It must be seventeen years, he thought, since he had last set eyes on his stepmother. He had been eleven years old and certainly not too young to realize that it was she alone who had stood between him and his father; she who had watched him with her penetrating gaze, waiting for him to make a mistake, waiting always for the chance to poison his father's mind against him. And his father, poor doting fool, had been clay in her hands. She had mesmerized him with her beauty, her brilliance, her force of will. And when the moment came and he, Antoine, had committed the stupid, unnecessary little crime of theft from a fellow scholar at Eton, she had persuaded his father to turn him out of her home. *Her* home! But she had not been able to turn him out of *his* rightful home. His father, Gerard de Valle, had made it clear beyond any doubt in his Will that the Château and the Boulancourt estate were to be his absolutely.

He put down his empty glass and picked up

the letter, scanning the lines a third time. His eyes paused as he found the sentence for which he was searching . . . *'your half-brother John.'* He had no knowledge of such a brother and wanted none. He could but presume that when he and his guardian, Princess Camille Faloise had left England, his stepmother was with child by his father. If this were so, then his father had a fully legitimate heir — a legal contender for the title Vicomte de Valle.

"Not whilst I live!" Antoine muttered darkly. "I may have been born out of wedlock but by God my father recognized me. I and I alone am the Vicomte!"

He stood up so suddenly that the chair on which he had been sitting overturned with a crash upon the parquet floor. Stefano came running into the room.

"Fetch me quill, paper — at once, man!" Antoine ordered. "And tell the messenger who brought the letter not to leave until he has my reply. Hurry now!"

His mind made up, he was now no less anxious than Mavreen for tomorrow's rendezvous. It had always been part of his policy for success in life to make himself aware of the dangers that lay in wait. Then and then only, could he be certain of overriding them.

2

"LOOK, Papa! Are the trees not even more beautiful than those at home!"

Sir Peregrine Waite surveyed his daughter's rapt young face with affectionate indulgence. This child of his, he thought, was proving an everlasting joy to him. Chantal seemed only to see the good things of the world and her enthusiasm for life and adventure were sufficiently infectious to encompass all who met her.

Mavreen leant out of the carriage window and called to her head groom, Dickon, to slow the horses to a walk. The hot summer air was stifling even at this early morning hour and the shade cast by the giant oak and beech trees was a welcome drop in temperature for the occupants of the four-in-hand.

Mavreen, still beautiful in her late fifties, looked fondly at her husband Perry and smiled at her stepdaughter, Chantal. She thought how pretty the child looked in her rose pink silk mantle with its wide cape-like collar trimmed with pink beribboned flowers. Her face was framed by a silk bonnet, the matching ribbons of which were tied under her chin like a posy of rose petals. At seventeen the girl gave every indication of becoming a beautiful woman.

A convent education had been an excellent choice, Mavreen decided. Chantal was no milk-and-water child and needed the discipline the nuns insisted upon. She had inherited a volatile, emotional, impulsive character from her Latin mother. Combined with her father's adventuresome spirit, such a nature, if misdirected, could all too easily lead the young girl astray.

Mavreen's eyes moved from Chantal to the young man seated beside her and who, secretly, she held dearest to her heart. Her darling John was a son to be proud of, she reflected. Physically he resembled her and bore little likeness to his father, her former husband, Gerard de Valle. But by nature he possessed all Gerard's most worthy attributes. He had inherited his father's strong sense of duty, his integrity, his love for the past and regard for the importance of history. As well as being a keen sportsman, John also enjoyed the pursuits of the mind and studied history, architecture and archeology for pleasure. He exhibited a warm, loving regard for his family with all of whom he was on excellent terms. At nineteen he was still very young and a little unsure of himself but he had a strong measure of determination which resulted in a will of his own. He was not easily swayed by others despite his youth, and only his propensity for tolerance saved him from being too dogmatic once his mind was made up.

Mavreen turned once more to look at her husband. Perry was grey-haired now but remained exceptionally handsome. Although she remembered her former husband with deep affection, she knew she made a far better wife for Perry than ever she had for Gerard. Theirs had proved the perfect union in every way, she decided. Perry knew exactly how to handle her. He could laugh her out of the doldrums, coerce her into love when she imagined herself too tired to enjoy such pursuits. He was patient when she was unreasonable but never permitted her to get the better of him in an argument unless he believed her in the right. They were not only the very best of friends but they were still lovers after fifteen years of married life. She had so much to thank him for. His generosity of heart in bringing them here to Compiègne was but one facet of the many aspects of his thoughtfulness. He knew that the fact of Gerard's grave being unattended on the anniversary of his death always preyed on her mind.

The discovery that Gerard's son had returned to France and was in residence at the Château de Boulancourt had been totally unexpected — and only in part welcome. Neither she nor Perry had ever liked the strange, morose boy Gerard had brought home to England at the age of five.

Mavreen had tried to make allowances for Antoine, not only because he was Gerard's son but because she did not wish to be prejudiced in any way against him because he was not *her* child but had been begotten by a farm girl on Gerard's estate. In those days, when Gerard had first brought Antoine home to

England, John was not yet born and Gerard passionately wanted a son to succeed him. He had idolised the boy and indulged him in his every wish despite all Mavreen's warnings that Antoine needed severe discipline if ever he was to overcome his baser nature.

It had come as a great relief to her when Gerard decided to put the boy in the care of a Frenchwoman, although she regretted the choice of the Princess Faloise for Antoine's sake. The Princess was known to have a penchant for young boys — a rumor Gerard refused to accept. He was insistent upon sending Antoine to her. He visited the child regularly even after their own son John was born and continued to do so until he died. Mavreen herself had not seen Antoine since the day he had left her household.

As if divining Mavreen's thoughts, Chantal lent forward and laid her hand lightly on her mother's arm.

"Mama, will you tell me more about the man we are so soon to encounter? Ever since I learned that we were actually to meet John's half-brother I have been consumed with a curiosity which John will not satisfy!"

"I know as little as you do about this Frenchman," said John calmly. "I was but three years of age when he left England and never had occasion to meet him since."

"There is very little to be said about him!" Perry broke in, his voice sharper than was customary when addressing his family. "In appearance, when last your mother and I

31

saw Antoine, he was very fair and resembled his paternal grandfather, I believe, but he had his father's dark eyes. The boy was a remarkably beautiful child, I recall — but abysmally spoilt."

"Like you, Chantal!" John said. Although he was teasing there was more than a grain of truth in his accusations. People found it hard to deny Chantal any whim or fancy.

"Even if you and Mama and Papa spoil me just a little, I was of a certainty not spoilt at my Convent!" she remarked, adding: "Is this not exciting, John? On my very first sojourn abroad, I am to be the guest of a French Vicomte who sounds so much more interesting than an English Viscount."

"I am certain that Antoine is *not* the Vicomte de Valle!" Mavreen broke in. "As far as I have been able to ascertain under French law, a natural son may not inherit his father's title. So Antoine has no claim to the *vicomté*. It is John who holds the title."

John's face showed no less amazement than Chantal's.

"But I never knew that, Mama!" he said. "You never mentioned the fact to me, I had assumed that when my father died, his first son inherited both estate and title!"

"We were not *absolutely* certain that you had indisputable right to the title, John," Perry intervened. "As you know, your father died unexpectedly. It appeared that he had left no Will. The documents relating to Antoine's birth and your father's subsequent acknowledgement

32

of him were believed to be at Boulancourt. Unfortunately, a detailed search of the Château and subsequently in England provided no trace of them."

"I am convinced Gerard did not bring them to England!" Mavreen said to Perry. "But it was of no great importance for I was well aware of your father's wishes, John. He wanted Antoine to be his heir — not because he loved you less but because Antoine was his first-born son. But he could not give him the title. Since he was not legitimate, Antoine by law could only inherit one-sixth of the estate. However, knowing how dearly your father wished Antoine to live at Boulancourt and assume responsibility for the de Valle properties, I took it upon myself to write to the *avocat*, Monsieur Mougin, and advise him that you were unlikely ever to challenge Antoine's right to live there should he so desire."

"You were far too young at the time to be consulted upon the matter!" Perry added.

"I was concerned in the main for your father's purpose," Mavreen continued, "although naturally I would not have deprived you of your subsequent right to claim Boulancourt even had it been possible for me to do so. I knew you would, upon coming of age, be an extremely wealthy young man in any event. Your grandfather left his entire fortune to you, John — a very considerable one which included properties of increasing value in Yorkshire as well as in London. I felt satisfied that once you were of an age to be consulted, you would agree that your half-brother should not be left comparatively penniless whilst you laid claim to a second fortune."

"Then you know me well, Mama!" John replied without hesitation. "This half-brother of mine was deprived of much by virtue of his birth and he is welcome to our father's home. Nevertheless, is it not wrong that he should use the title of Vicomte since neither the law nor I can bestow it upon him?"

"Quite wrong!" Mavreen agreed. "I will speak with Antoine when we meet, although it may not be necessary. It is not unlikely that the peasantry assume him to be the rightful Vicomte. Antoine himself may make no such claims. We shall have to see."

Round-eyed, Chantal looked from her mother to John as she absorbed this fragment of the past.

"Suppose that you had no other fortune, John, and wished to claim the de Valle estates for yourself, you would not want to live in *France*, would you? Your home is in England."

"Since I have not yet seen Boulancourt, I cannot say if I would want to live there or not," John said in his quiet voice, his eyes serious. "But when all is said and done, Chantal, I am half French by virtue of my birth and if Boulancourt is only half as beautiful as Mama describes it, I might well have enjoyed a second home there."

"Well, I am glad that the estate belongs to your half-brother," Chantal announced. "I would not be at all happy to think of you living so far away from us, John. I cannot imagine a home you did not share with us!"

John's face softened.

"Surely you do not think I would consider living in France without you, do you, you silly little goose?" he said. "You would accompany me as my housekeeper were I to take up residence at Boulancourt."

Chantal laughed.

"You might need a female to run your home until you marry," she said, "but when Julia is your wife, you will not want your little sister playing the gooseberry!"

John's face flushed. His eyes looked stormy.

"I do not know how many times I have to tell you, Chantal, I have not the slightest intention of marrying Miss Julia Lade — even if she is your best friend, not to please you and certainly not to please her!"

He was impatient for the day to come when his parents considered Chantal sufficiently mature of mind to be told that she was not his little sister, as she supposed, but the natural child of his stepfather. Then and only then could he advise her that one day they could be married and live happily together for always. That was John's secret wish. He could not imagine that he might ever want to marry a different girl or that he could love another as he loved Chantal.

Chantal looked downcast.

"I know Julia is only sixteen years of age," she said, sighing, "but she is already very pretty and will become more so. Mama agrees with me, do you not, Mama? Besides, Julia positively dotes upon you, John, and would make you the most loving wife!"

"Perhaps that is why John has so little interest in your young friend!" Perry said wisely. "A man enjoys a little hunting, m'dear, before he catches his quarry!"

His eyes turned to Mavreen and they both smiled, remembering how many years had passed before *he* had caught his quarry. When he had first met her thirty years ago, she had refused to marry him because although her second husband James Pettigrew was dead, she held an obsessional belief that Gerard de Valle was still alive despite the fact that he had disappeared in war-torn Europe.

It had come near to breaking Perry's heart when Mavreen's conviction proved to be right and she chose to marry Gerard when he returned from Russia. It was a further nine years before Mavreen became his wife, the year after Gerard was tragically killed in a carriage accident.

It was a story Chantal loved above all others to hear her father tell. She never tired of hearing him relate how he had journeyed to England to visit Mavreen and discovered her free at last to marry him. It seemed like a fairy tale ending of 'happy-ever-after' when finally they were wed.

There were times when Mavreen confided to Perry that to her too their marriage seemed like a fairy tale so contented was she. As for her feelings for Perry's daughter, she admitted that there were many occasions when she felt closer to Chantal than she had ever felt to Tamarisk who was her own flesh and blood.

Such comments always brought forth a smile from Perry.

"You and Tamarisk were far too alike to be able to live under the same roof in peace for long!" he vouchsafed. He had always had a deep affection for Mavreen's daughter which was in no way diminished by the arrival of his beloved child, Chantal. The child was a constant delight to him. She was as daintily built as a Dresden china figurine; her voice was musical and perfectly pitched, and her manners and sentiments betrayed an instinctive refinement and breeding. As for her laughing, singing moods and quick flashes of fiery Latin temper, he loved that part of her too!

Chantal was not yet aware of the fact that she was his natural child. Believing Mavreen to be her real mother, she knew nothing of the Neapolitan girl who had nursed him when he lay wounded in the hills behind Naples years ago; or that she was the result of his union with this kindly girl who had cared for him so devotedly.

This was a story he would tell her when she was older. For the time being, he and Mavreen wished to keep her ignorant of life's sadder and less savory side. One day perhaps, he would tell her of his own childhood and how he had been forced to steal to support his mother who had been branded as a witch.

He might even tell her of his years as a highwayman when he was known as Gideon Morris, a man with a price upon his head; of how eventually his spoils had made him rich enough to claim his rightful heritage as a gentleman and take his place in Society under the assumed name of Sir Peregrine Waite.

But looking at his daughter's innocent face and bright, trusting eyes, he knew that time was not yet come. "Let her live with her fairy tale illusions a few years' longer," he had cautioned Mavreen. The child had never known anything but love and kindness. She was not aware that evil stalked the world or that there existed people with characters like Antoine de Valle's hidden beneath the appearance of such beauty as to catch one's heart strings. Pray God, he thought, that she would one day marry a decent, kind, loving boy like John and never know the depths to which some men could sink.

Neither he nor Mavreen realized that Chantal was already aware of the existence of Antoine de Valle due to the fact that Elsie, Tamarisk's maid, had gossiped a little too freely.

Elsie had recounted how, late one January evening, John's father, the Vicomte Gerard de Valle, had arrived from France in the middle of a snowstorm, bringing with him the most beautiful little fair-haired boy whom the servants were informed was the child of his first marriage to an Italian princess.

"That there French boy were anything on God's earth but the angel he looked!" Elsie warmed to her story. "Neither your Mama nor Lady Tamarisk's governess, nor no one could control him. But the Vicomte could see no wrong in the boy! Proper little devil he were and we were all that glad to be rid of him when

38

he went off to boarding school!"

But the subsequent whereabouts of the boy Chantal could not discover for Elsie did not know what had become of him and as for John, he appeared as ignorant as herself.

Now her half-forgotten curiosity was newly aroused for she was about to meet the young man, Antoine de Valle, who was John's half-brother.

"In a little while I will be able to discover for myself if he was even half as beautiful to look upon as Elsie described or as a person even half as bad," she thought as the tall, shady trees beneath which the carriage was passing seemed to become less numerous and Mavreen announced that it would not be long before they reached the perimeter of the de Valle estate.

She gave a cry of delight when first she caught sight of the magnificent Château de Boulancourt.

"Oh look, Mama! How beautiful!"

Built originally in the thirteenth century, the Château was sited on raised ground so that its occupants could more easily espy the advance of an enemy. Surrounded by a deep moat, the steep stone walls glowed a soft golden sand color in the morning sun. The dark waters of the moat surrounding the outer walls of the Château sparkled in the sunlight. As they drew nearer, Chantal could see the water lilies, yellow, white and pink, floating on the surface.

"'Tis more like a castle than a château!" John commented, as his keen artist's eye surveyed the architecture of the huge mansion. "I had no idea that Boulancourt was so large!"

"Nor I!" Mavreen confessed "There have been several major additions since last I was here. How beautiful the gardens look!"

The circular beds of massed geraniums, marigolds, begonias and calceolarias made islands of brilliant color in the ocean of finely cut grass. Backed by ornamental walls covered in wisteria and within a framework of beech, oak and chestnut trees, the effect was superb. The visitors stared entranced.

With fond amusement, Perry regarded his young daughter's excited face as their carriage rattled across the great wooden drawbridge and was halted by the servant in the small guardhouse.

They were obviously expected, for the man on hearing their names at once waved them on, pointing their way up the steep cobbled road leading beneath a great stone archway into the courtyard.

Chantal was leaning out of the window, her eyes bright with interest as she watched the mélée of servants busy about their work in the courtyard. There was a groom leading a spirited black horse to its stable. Maidservants were filling their iron pails with water from curious serpent-shaped pumps from whose open mouths gushed a somewhat rusty-looking liquid. Despite the huge basket of freshly laundered linen on her head, a washer-woman bobbed a curtsey as the carriage passed by her. Two lads in green aprons paused in their sweeping of the hot dusty cobblestones, leaning on their birch-twig brooms to stare at the four-in-hand as the coach-man, Dickon, brought the horses to a standstill.

At once the twelve-foot-high oak front door swung open and a liveried servant hurried toward them.

Chantal bent her head close to John's and whispered wickedly:

"By the look on that man's face, I do not think he is much impressed by our hired carriage!"

"And I do not care much for his countenance!" John whispered back. "I never did see so grim and unwelcoming a visage!"

But Chantal was no longer listening. As she alighted from the carriage behind her mother, she had caught sight of a tall, slender young man descending the steps with outstretched hands.

Impeccably dressed in dark blue tail-coat and matching close-fitting trousers, he bowed gracefully.

"Welcome to Boulancourt!" he said, with only the faintest trace of French accent. He assisted Chantal from the carriage. As she dropped a curtsey, his handsome, serious face broke suddenly into a smile of such beauty that Chantal felt her heart miss a beat. "You are *more* than welcome, Mademoiselle!" he said, putting out a beringed, perfectly shaped hand to raise her to her feet.

Chantal found herself looking directly into his eyes. They seemed blacker than any eyes she had ever seen, dominating his pale, thin face with its aquiline nose and finely cut mouth.

She suppressed the impulse to turn to her mother and enquire why no one had advised her of their host's exceptional handsomeness. The bone structure of his face, she thought, reminded her of the picture of the Angel Gabriel which hung on her Convent wall.

Her admiration was total, but no less than that of Antoine de Valle for the golden skinned, dark-eyed young girl smiling so shyly as he stared down at her rapt, glowing face.

3

August 1837

AS Antoine shook hands with Chantal's father and John, his eyes returned swiftly to Sir Peregrine's daughter. He had not expected the dandy he had once known to be capable of producing such a charming little filly. He was quite captivated by the pink blush that stained her cheeks as he raised her from her curtsey. The women of his acquaintance had long since forgotten how to blush — if ever they had been smitten by such maidenly attributes, he thought wryly.

"You have no servants with you, Madame?" he asked Mavreen. "No maids? No valet?"

Mavreen looked surprised.

"We scarce need personal servants in attendance for one day!" she replied.

"*Mais qu'est ce que c'est, donc?*" Antoine lapsed into French. "Is my home not large enough to accommodate you? Or perhaps not grand enough for your taste? Would you not agree that it is most unseemly for you, members of my family, to reside in a hotel in Compiègne whilst Boulancourt is at your disposal?"

Mavreen caught Perry's eye and finding no decision therein, said doubtfully:

"I was not aware that your invitation to luncheon was intended to include a sojourn

43

with you, Antoine. In any event it was our intention to return to England tomorrow after we had paid our visit to your father's grave."

"Oh, Mama, please may we not stay longer in France?" Chantal cried. "It is all so beautiful and . . . "

"Hush child!" Perry broke in not unkindly as he surveyed his daughter's bright eyes and heard the suppressed excitement in her voice.

"It might be possible, I suppose . . . " Mavreen began when Antoine interrupted her. Turning to Sir Peregrine, he said:

"There is excellent hunting in the forest, sir, and I do not doubt that you, too, enjoy *la chasse!*" he added, glancing at John. "If you will stay a few days, I can arrange a boar hunt for Monday morning and can offer you the very best of mounts. You do still ride, Sir Peregrine?"

By now Antoine had led his visitors into the *grand salon* — a magnificent high-ceilinged room with ornately carved pillars and cornices. The white painted walls were hung with huge oil paintings by old Masters. Chantal, who was greatly interested in art, noticed them instantly and longed to study them more closely. The chairs on which they were invited to seat themselves were covered with beautifully worked tapestries from the town of Beauvais. A liveried footman came in with wine and freshly-made lemonade. Over the rim of her crystal goblet, Chantal eyed her parents anxiously.

"Have you decided that we need not return to England tomorrow?" she burst out unable to contain any longer her impatience to know their answer.

Mavreen smiled.

"We shall be delighted to enjoy your hospitality, Antoine!" she said. "I know that Sir Peregrine and John will much enjoy the hunt you have kindly offered to arrange for them. Mayhap Chantal and I might also join in the sport for an hour or two!"

Chantal turned to Antoine with shining eyes.

"My Papa is the best horseman in the whole world!" she announced proudly.

"Forgive my boast, Mademoiselle, if I tell you that I, too, am considered an accomplished *ecuyer*!" Antoine replied smiling. "Perhaps your Papa and I should have a challenge and discover who really merits most your high regard!"

"You have the advantage of youth, my boy!" Perry interrupted. "But then I have the advantage of experience!"

Sensing an undercurrent for rivalry, Mavreen said quickly:

"I remember on your first meeting with my husband, Antoine, you were both upon horseback. You were riding with Tamarisk and me in Hyde Park. You were on your very first pony, do you recall? And none too sure of yourself, either. Do you remember, Perry?"

"How could I forget, m'dear!" Perry replied with a glance at Mavreen that did not escape their host.

Antoine's face flushed an angry red although his expression gave no hint of his feelings. He was unlikely to forget that day nor the humiliation he had suffered at Sir Peregrine's hands.

"I was living at my home in Harley Street in those days," Perry continued, not intending Antoine's discomfort but for Chantal's and John's benefit. "The weather was so cold we abandoned our ride and repaired to my house to partake of hot chocolate!"

Antoine needed no further reminding. Even now he could relive the moment of fury that had engulfed him when Sir Peregrine had discovered him guilty of the theft of his gold watch. How gauche and ignorant was the Antoine de Valle of those days! Newly arrived in England, he had been too young to know that gentlemen like Sir Peregrine were not of the same ilk as the ignorant dolts of his previous experience who were too slow and stupid to recognize a thief, let alone catch one.

In France, living with his mother and grandfather on a farm, Antoine had spent the first five years of his life observing how his mother stole from the stall-holders on market day in Compiègne. Sometimes she took a length of velvet to fashion him a new suit, other times a ball of lace for the edging; or perhaps a pomade for his hair. Sometimes she stole food — delicacies which she thought he might fancy. Daughter of an impoverished farmer, his mother could never have afforded to buy the riches she insisted were due to him, her only son. From the day of his birth she had determined that he should have only the best of everything, since ultimately he would leave the farm and live like a real aristocrat.

How right she had been, Antoine thought wryly, in her unshakeable assumption that one day his father, the rich, important Vicomte de Valle, would return from the wars to his home and acknowledge his natural son! The neighbors — even his grandfather — had thought her expectations crazed but she never doubted the future. Her thefts were fully justified as she always vouchsafed they would be. But shrewd though she was in this matter, she had not known enough about the ways of gentlemen to warn him that thieving offended their code of etiquette. Nor was his theft of Sir Peregrine's gold watch necessary. He had stolen it not from need but merely because he fancied it; and he had had no thought of detection.

Fortunately, as it transpired, Sir Peregrine had not reported the transgression to his father and had seen fit only to thrash him. But Antoine had never forgotten that hand upon his buttocks; nor had time lessened his resentment against the man who was the first ever to chastise him. After all these years, he thought he might now find a way of revenging himself. The seduction of Sir Peregrine's pretty little daughter could prove an interesting way to even the score.

Chantal was very inexperienced, he surmised, and unquestionably a virgin. It would be no difficult task for him to render this young girl as clay in his hands, for he could charm any woman if it pleased him. Moreover, such dalliance might help to pass an hour or two less boringly than were he to confine himself to the company of his silent, serious half-brother.

He turned now to John and said:

"Although we share the same father, sir, methinks we do not resemble one another in our appearance in any single respect!"

"We all think John is just like Mama!" Chantal broke in. "Do you not agree, sir?"

"Perhaps!" Antoine replied, glancing at his stepmother with grudging admiration. This woman would always have the power to attract men's gaze, he thought, remembering as if it was yesterday, the jealous resentment he had felt towards her for diverting his father's attention from him. She alone had stood between him and his father's total love, for his father had never had more than a mild affection for his elder child, his daughter, Tamarisk.

"How is Tamarisk these days?" he asked curiously. "She showed promise of great beauty, I recall!"

"Which promise was indeed fulfilled!" Perry said.

"You must come to London and visit with us all!" Chantal cried. "Would that not be nice, Mama, Papa?" She laughed gaily, her eyes teasing. "And you cannot refuse to be our guest now that we have agreed to be yours!"

Without understanding why, John had taken as instant a dislike to his half-brother as Chantal had taken a liking to him. Furthermore, he decided, he had no wish to reside in the Château as Antoine's guest. He felt a quite unjustified resentment towards his mother when she instructed Dickon to ride back to Compiègne and order their servants to pack and bring their boxes to Boulancourt.

But strongest of all John's emotions was his anger at Chantal. He told himself that she was behaving in the most childlike and annoying way, talking too much and with more enthusiasm than was proper for a young lady to evince. So rarely critical of her, John's disapproval now disturbed him.

He decided that his mother must caution Chantal. She was no longer a convent schoolgirl but a remarkably pretty young woman with all the budding charms of a newly fledged butterfly. It was strange, he reflected, that he had never thought of Chantal in such guise before. How was it possible that she had changed so suddenly from child to woman?

It did not occur to John that for the first time be was seeing her through the eyes of another man who was now staring at Chantal with a look that in no way hid his interest in her. Moreover this rival for Chantal's attention was better looking than himself, and with the suave manners and sophistication of an older man. At this very moment, Antoine was smiling with great charm as he replied to Chantal's invitation to visit them in England.

"I would be enchanted!" he was saying. And to John's further irritation, he lightly touched Chantal's bare, softly-rounded arm, his long, tapering fingers lingering there a fraction of a moment too long. Afraid that he might reveal his jealousy, John announced abruptly:

"I shall return with Dickon to Compiègne!"

Seeing the look of astonishment on his mother's face, he added: "Someone will be required to settle our account with the landlord who may not be too happy with our precipitate departure!"

"Then pray let me lend you one of my horses, my dear brother!" Antoine interposed gracefully. "The carriage will be uncomfortably overcrowded with your servants and boxes!"

Unable to find adequate excuse for refusing such a sensible offer, John allowed himself to be conducted by Stefano to the stables where he was given the choice of some of the most beautiful horses he had ever seen. As he swung himself into the saddle of a magnificent bay mare his spirits lifted. Riding away from the Château towards the forest he felt as if he were not leaving a domicile of exceptional beauty and magnificence, but a place of oppression and malevolence. By the time John reached Compiègne his normal good humor was quite restored and remained with him as he paid off the hotelier and saw Dickon, the servants and the boxes safely upon their way.

Traveling more quickly on Antoine's excellent mare than Dickon with the heavily laden carriage, John reached the forest several leagues ahead of the servants. His self-confidence had returned and his thoughts dwelt happily on the long years of companionship shared with Chantal during their childhood. He knew that she loved and respected him, albeit as a brother three years older than herself, but with a passionate affection second only to that she held for her father. So enduring a relationship must stand him in good stead when his mother permitted him to declare himself. Then Chantal would see the Frenchy dandy who was his half-brother in his true light, he reflected. He had no real cause for jealousy.

The sunshine was warm across his back and his mood of cheerfulness increased. He hummed cheerfully as he rode into the dappled shade of the trees.

Suddenly he glimpsed what he thought to be a young deer darting amongst the tree trunks. Almost at the same instant two shots rang out, followed by a third and then another. Not more than a minute later, John's 'deer' broke from cover and came running towards him.

It was after all no animal as he had supposed but a young lad of approximately ten years of age who fell exhausted in a heap dangerously close to the mare's hooves. His face, hands and legs were bleeding profusely from the scratches of brambles; his clothes were torn in shreds; his face beneath the dirt and blood was scarlet.

"*Aidez-moi! Aidez-moi!*" he gasped.

John dismounted. Hitching the reins of his horse over a low hanging branch, he took the boy by the arm.

"*N'ayez pas peur!*" he said, sensing the child's terror but still unaware of the cause of it.

There was a sudden crash from the thickets. The startled horse shied nervously as two men, each carrying a gun, came into view.

Both giants in stature, the men were dressed

51

in the loose brown jackets and rough leather breeches common to the woodcutters who lived on the edge of the forest. They were bearded and red in the face from the exertion of running. One of the two stepped forward and doffed his hat perfunctorily before saying in a coarse argot:

"We want *le chenapan!*"

"Ruffian?" John translated sharply, laying his hand on the boy's shoulder. "This is no ruffian. He is but a child!"

"He was trespassing!" the man said rudely. "Hand him over!"

John stepped forward, his face angry as he said:

"How dare you order me in such fashion! You would do well to remember to whom you speak!"

The man's eyes narrowed.

"It matters little to me who you are. I am carrying out my master's orders. I am instructed to shoot all trespassers on sight!"

The boy broke into a storm of tears, clinging to John's legs with the tenacity of one who believes his life hangs in the balance.

By now John was very well aware of the precariousness of his situation. It might be half an hour or more before Dickon arrived upon the scene. If the men chose meanwhile to murder both him and the boy and conceal their bodies, the faithful Dickon would find no trace of any disaster. In such a vast forest as that of Compiègne, it would be easy enough for people to disappear. The scoundrels looked bloodthirsty enough to commit any crime.

It crossed his mind fleetingly that were he to hand over the terrified child as the men wanted, his own life would no longer be in peril. But such cowardly action was not, nor ever would be, in John's nature.

"The 'master' to whom you refer is, I presume, Monsieur Antoine de Valle?" he enquired in a cold authoritative voice.

"He be the Vicomte, though that's naught to do with you!" one of the woodcutters replied rudely. "Hand over the boy else we'll take him from you!"

"'Tis clear you are unaware of my relationship to your master!" John said quickly, tightening his hold upon the boy who was now trembling so violently that his small legs barely supported him. "I am his half-brother, the Vicomte John de Valle. When he hears of this incident he will have you both flogged for such outrage!"

To his dismay, the surly expression on the men's faces gave way to sardonic laughter.

"So you be the Vicomte de Valle, my fine gentleman!" one of them said sarcastically. "We know better, don't we?" he said to his grinning companion. "Do you take us for fools that we don't know who our master is?"

John's heart sank. It appeared that Antoine had in fact laid claim to the title which was not rightfully his. Anger now lent him additional courage.

"Enough of this badinage!" he cried. "Lower your guns and be on your way or I will order you both to be flogged within an inch of your lives! *The boy stays with me.*"

53

The two men looked at one another and then, in sudden doubt, at the young Englishman confronting them so fearlessly. It was true they were not at the moment on the Vicomte's estate but in normal circumstances that would have made no difference. Anyone caught trespassing, especially near the fences surrounding the Roman ruins, was not permitted to go home alive with their tales. The instructions to shoot regardless of the culprit's age or sex were quite implicit. Yet the Englishman's voice was authoritative and both men felt a strange reluctance to attack him.

Reasonably certain now that his life as well as the boy's hung in the balance, John assessed his situation. The man nearest to him was a great brute of a fellow, heavily bearded, low skulled, coarse featured. His massive shoulders and forearms would enable him to crush a man merely by embracing him too forcibly. His companion, though slighter in stature, had a mean, cruel face, its lopsidedness lending him an air of cunning and menace. Unarmed, John knew he would have no chance were he to try to fight his two aggressors. But if he could disarm them . . .

He felt a swift thrill of excitement as a plan formulated in his mind. He suspected that the men were dolts for all their physical strength else they would long since have wrested the boy from him and ignored his protests.

With a calmness he was far from feeling, he said:

"You are obviously unaware that my servants

are following behind me with my baggage. You did not imagine, surely, that a guest at the Château Boulancourt would travel without retainers? In point of fact, I think I can hear the carriage approaching."

He turned his head to stare back down the path with a well simulated look of relief and cupped his mouth with his hand.

"Holla! Dickon. Here, to me!"

So well did he play his part, even the boy turned his head as did both woodcutters. On the instant, John took a big stride forward and wrenched the gun from the man nearest him. Raising it to his shoulder, he pointed it at the second fellow.

"Lower your gun, man, else I will shoot your companion first and then you!"

Fear rather than courage prompted the woodsman to cling to his weapon. His finger hovered over the trigger and he might, indeed, have pulled it had his attention not been diverted. The child realizing in that instant that he might make his escape, promptly took to his heels like a young deer, his thin legs carrying him swiftly into the tangled undergrowth.

Once again, John acted with remarkable promptitude. As the second woodcutter turned briefly to aim at the boy, he knocked the weapon from his hands. Now both men were disarmed. Despite the seriousness of the moment, John grinned at the look of surprise and dismay on his prisoners' faces. It was clear they were unable to comprehend how exactly when they outnumbered John two to one the tables had been turned on them.

It was nevertheless with a feeling of relief that John heard in reality the sound of a carriage approaching through the trees. Within a few minutes, Dickon stood at his elbow. Briefly, John explained what had transpired and instructed Dickon to bring a stout rope from the carriage and secure both men to a tree.

"They can cool their heels whilst I ride on to the Château and inform my brother as to their dastardly behavior," John said. "'Tis to be hoped he will deal with them appropriately for I cannot believe they are in truth his servants and acting upon his orders!"

But when he reached Boulancourt, Antoine was not immediately to be found and when he related his adventure to Perry and his mother, they cautioned him to broach the matter tactfully. If Antoine de Valle, the man, was an adult version of the boy they had known, his anxious mother told him, it would not be stretching the imagination too far to suppose he *might* give orders for a child found trespassing to be shot. As a boy, Antoine had seemed to lack the normal emotions of love, tenderness and sympathy for others. One of his best favored pastimes had been to torment the young servants, knowing that they could not answer back for fear of losing their employment. It was not such a big step from such sadistic pleasures to the persecution of children.

John regarded Mavreen with astonishment.

"You mean you would wish me to consider

56

such behavior as tolerable?" he demanded aghast.

"Of course not, my love!" Mavreen replied. "But the Boulancourt estate is Antoine's, John, and those men *his* servants. It is not for us to question his authority. Intervention has already proved dangerous for you. I am quite anxious enough thinking of the peril you were in."

"Nevertheless John has every right to question Antoine." Perry intervened. "He may well have saved that boy's life and is entitled to demand on whose authority those men dared hold a gentleman at gunpoint."

By the time John found occasion to question his half-brother, Antoine had had the incident reported to him by his servant, Stefano. He was well prepared therefore with an evasive reply, saying he would investigate the incident.

There was nothing more John could do to substantiate his suspicions.

★ ★ ★

"Why can I not like Gerard's son?" Mavreen sighed as her elderly maid, Dorcas, fastened the buttons of her evening gown.

"I understand your sentiments, my love!" Perry said. He crossed one long, tightly clad leg over the other and lent back in his chair the better to admire the curve of Mavreen's back and the small waist which he still loved to encircle with his two hands. "I like Antoine no better than you do, although I must concede

57

that he has grown into a most personable young man!"

"I do not deny that he is excessively handsome!" Mavreen agreed. "But I do not trust him, Perry. Why should he want us to stay here at Boulancourt? The servants here all refer to him as the Vicomte, and he must know that I will raise the matter of his assumption of Gerard's title ere long. One cannot imagine he is anxious for such confrontation."

Perry frowned, deepening the lines furrowing his forehead.

"I confess that puzzles me!" he agreed. "Antoine must know the Civil Code of France. The *vicomté* is clearly John's."

Mavreen took the necklace of emeralds Dorcas held out and fastened it about her throat. It matched perfectly her exquisite low-necked evening gown with its small puffed sleeves and delicate embroidery of fine gold thread decorating the lustrous green silk.

"I am concerned about John!" she said. "He has been behaving in a manner quite unlike himself — in fact as any gauche boy on leave from school! John is nineteen and most accomplished in matters of etiquette. Yet he neither spoke nor made attempt to join in our conversation this afternoon. Mayhap he is sickening for some ailment?"

Perry laughed.

"I doubt that very much, my dearest. 'Tis a deal more likely that he is resenting the manner in which Antoine is charming my innocent little daughter."

Mavreen swung round and stared at Perry, her eyes searching his face to see if he were serious. Finding him so, she dismissed Dorcas and as soon as the maid had left them alone, said forcefully:

"You cannot mean that John is jealous! Why, Chantal is his sister. He has no interest in her as a pretty young girl to be wooed!"

Perry sighed.

"I think the time has come when 'twould be best for us all if we faced the truth, Mavreen. John is not Chantal's brother and Chantal is not his sister. They are related by our marriage only and in no other fashion. If John and Chantal were ever to wish to marry, there is nothing against such a union."

Mavreen's expression was one of astonishment.

"But that is an absurd notion Perry!" she said. "I cannot conceive of such a likelihood. Related or not, they have grown up together as brother and sister." Mavreen's eyes portrayed her uncertainty. "You know that I love Chantal as much as if she were my own daughter, Perry. I have nothing against her in any single respect. But her devotion to John has always been that of adoring sister for an elder brother."

Perry stood up and gently put his arms around his wife.

"There is no cause for worry, my love!" he said firmly. "The jealousy I sensed in John's attitude might spring from the protective instinct he has always shown towards Chantal. Let us not worry our heads about contingencies which may never materialize. We should concern ourselves

59

instead with the possibility that my innocent little Chantal may have her head turned by the handsome Antoine. I fancy she is finding it an agreeable novelty to be so obviously admired. The fellow must seem to her both debonair and worldly and doubtless she is flattered that a man of his age should find her interesting. He must be more than ten years her senior.

"I would like to think his character was as flawless as his appearance," Mavreen remarked.

"Let us leave Chantal's affairs aside for the moment," Perry said, "for we have yet to decide how to approach Antoine this evening regarding his right to use the de Valle title."

"'Tis best we discuss this matter with him privately!" Mavreen commented. "I would prefer that John is not present. I will instruct him to take Chantal for a walk in the gardens after dinner."

John was more than content, when the long meal was finally over, to remove Chantal from Antoine's attentive company. Walking with her down the stone-flagged path leading to the rose arbor, he decided to take this opportunity to warn her of the dangers of appearing too friendly with strange men.

"I am sure 'tis not your intention to play the coquette!" he said, his voice gently reproving. "Nevertheless even the most innocent flirtation such as you are enjoying with Antoine, could lead to misunderstanding."

Chantal's dark eyes clouded instantly with surprise and distress. John so rarely corrected or criticized her. She was the more hurt because

60

she could see no reason why she had incurred his displeasure.

"I am truly sorry if I have upset you by my behavior!" she said genuinely contrite. "But truly, dearest John, I cannot see why you should accuse me of flirtation. Is it that I talked too much at dinner? Mama is always telling me I am an incurable chatterbox!"

John looked down at the trusting young face raised anxiously to him and wished desperately that he had curbed his tongue and left his mother to explain such matters to Chantal. It was obvious to him now that when she had laughed at Antoine's sallies, replied so gaily to his conversation, smiled at him so disarmingly, she had had no understanding of the encouragement her eager enthusiasm must give the man.

"Perhaps you were monopolizing the conversation just a little too much," he said, putting an arm around Chantal's soft shoulders. He hugged her as was his wont when in childhood they had been in dispute and harmony had been restored. At once Chantal leant her head upon his shoulder, relaxing against him in content that he was not seriously displeased with her.

"Doubtless 'tis my mistrust of my half-brother which makes me anxious lest you become too friendly with him," John continued unwisely.

He felt Chantal stiffen and she removed her head from its resting place.

"You cannot seriously believe he would have allowed that boy to be harmed, John?" she questioned.

Although secretly impressed by the courageous manner in which John had intervened to rescue the hunted boy, she was still of the opinion that his interference had been unnecessary. When her father had related the incident to her earlier that evening, praising John for his presence of mind and daring, she had been horrified by the immediate thought that her dearest John might have been killed. But whilst filled with admiration for his reckless disregard for his own life, she nevertheless doubted that the woodcutters were acting on Antoine de Valle's instructions. As for Antoine de Valle himself . . .

"How *can* you dislike so delightful and friendly a brother?" she enquired. "No one could have made us feel more welcome, nor shown us greater courtesy."

John bit his lip in an attempt to stifle his desire to repeat his opinion even more forcibly. He was quite convinced the woodcutters had intended the child's death and were in truth acting on Antoine's instructions. But he had no proof and Chantal could all too easily declare him unjust in condemning a man for no better reason than that of instinct.

"We know very little about my brother!" he replied vaguely. "I suspect that Mama never had any real affection for him but she will not be questioned about those days when Antoine lived at Barre House. Tamarisk once told me that he was an odious child and greatly spoilt by my father."

Chantal sighed.

"It is therefore understandable that Mama

might have had cause to resent the arrival of a small boy who rivalled her for her husband's attention!" she commented thoughtfully. "But that was twenty years ago, John! With time's passing the child has become the most delightful of men. I, for one, find the Vicomte charming and I am sure others must think so, too!"

John remained silent, gazing down at Chantal with eyes that were all too painfully aware of her. He supposed, uneasily, that it was the Latin blood inherited from her mother that gave her skin that delightful golden glow; that caused her dark eyes to flash so brightly in laughter or anger; that suggested the fires of passion dormant within her young virginal body.

"Be certain of one thing, Chantal," he said sharply. "Antoine is not the Vicomte de Valle. He has no right to use the title. The title is mine!"

To his surprise, Chantal's laughter rang out bright and clear.

"So *that* is the cause of your ill-natured attitude towards your brother!" she cried. But she added more seriously: "I do understand your feelings about your title, John, if they are based on truth."

"The servants, the woodcutters, the landlord at the hotel all referred to my brother as the Vicomte!" John muttered.

"But they might have assumed, since he lives at Boulancourt, that he really is the true Vicomte!" Chantal argued. "He has not so called himself in my presence."

"My father's coat of arms is everywhere in

evidence!" John retorted. "The bed linen and silverware — even the stationery is crested."

Once again Chantal's lips twitched with laughter.

"You are building a vast mountain from a tiny molehill!" she reproved him. "Of course your father's crest and coat of arms are everywhere. Boulancourt was his home. It is still the home of the de Valles."

John plucked one of the long-stemmed pale yellow roses lining the stone path leading to the sundial. He broke off the thorns and handed it to Chantal. The bloom was touched with the evening dew and Chantal buried her face in its petals with a little cry of pleasure.

"Everything is so beautiful here at Boulancourt!" she said. "Why must you spoil our sojourn, dear John, with your suspicions and ill temper?"

"I apologize if I appear boorish!" John replied. "But you might as well know, Chantal, that I am by no means alone in my mistrust of the handsome Antoine. Mama is even now questioning him as to my father's Will. It is for that purpose she asked me to bring you out here to the gardens so that they might discuss these matters in privacy."

"I am sure by now it will all have been satisfactorily explained!" Chantal said unconcernedly. "I have been awaiting a chance to tell you, John, how greatly I admire your bravery this afternoon. Papa told me that but for your intervention, the boy might have been severely punished and that you showed great courage."

Mollified by Chantal's flattery, John's mood lightened. As they continued their stroll together, he found himself sharing Chantal's optimism that Perry and his Mama would by now have resolved the matter of his right to the de Valle title.

But matters indoors were far from being satisfactorily resolved. Antoine stood with his back to the mantelshelf, his dark eyes unfathomable as he faced his stepmother and Sir Peregrine who were seated opposite him on the two beautiful *fauteuils*. His stepmother's face was taut with suppressed anger. Her husband's was impassive. Antoine imagined that he, himself, was concealing his emotions; but the two tiny spots of red staining his high cheekbones were indicative to any who knew him well enough that he was keeping his true feelings under the tightest control. He spoke quietly, his tone icy but polite.

"I repeat, Madame, at the risk of boring you, that I am my father's heir in every respect and have proof of it. Moreover I cannot accept that my father's intentions towards me before he died are any concern of yours."

Mavreen's eyes flashed dangerously.

"And I repeat that they are very much my concern!" she said, her tone rising ominously. "My son John is not yet of age and I, as his guardian, must consider his interests. Moreover, Antoine, you are overlooking the very important fact that I was married to your father and therefore owe it to his memory to see that his wishes are carried out."

Perry spoke for the first time. Rising to his feet, he went to stand behind Mavreen so that he could rest his hands restrainingly on her shoulders. Addressing Antoine, he said smoothly:

"If you are acting quite within your rights, sir, then pay my wife the courtesy of producing the proof you say you have. It can only take a matter of minutes to fetch this document which can scarce be said to inconvenience you. Why continue to aggravate this otherwise pleasant family reunion by a refusal to set our minds at rest?"

For a long minute Antoine stared at the man he hated more than any other in the world, as he assessed the danger were he openly to make an enemy of him. Suddenly the tension in his body relaxed. He had remembered that he need never fear Sir Peregrine Waite, no matter how strong, brave or influential the man might be. He knew enough about Sir Peregrine's past to put his life in jeopardy were he, Antoine, ever to reveal the information. He surmised he was one of the few who knew Mavreen's husband's true name was Gideon Morris, that he was once a notorious gentleman of the road.

Antoine's lids dropped over his eyes, concealing the satisfaction it gave him to think that be held this trump card. But he had no intention of playing it for the moment. Clearly Sir Peregrine and his stepmother had forgotten he knew all about that part of their lives.

He bowed to Mavreen with apparent indifference.

"It seems that you are intent upon forcing me to speak of matters which would be far better unmentioned," he said sighing. "So it is against my wishes that you will now hear facts that cannot fail to distress you. I am sorry!"

Mavreen frowned. There was a pitying tone to Antoine's voice that did not escape her. Her head lifted proudly.

"I am adequately cautioned!" she said pointedly. "So pray continue!" She was strangely glad to feel Perry's hands resting protectively on her shoulders.

Antoine ran his fingers lightly over his blond curls and sighed meaningfully.

"Then to be blunt about it, Madame, I use my father's title because I alone have the right to do so!" he said. "It is clear to me that you are unaware that my father married my mother on the day he learned that she had borne him a child. He was not obliged to marry her, of course, and he did so for the sole purpose of legitimizing the son he had always wanted. I do not wish to speak ill of the dead, but I readily admit that he did wrong not to inform you of this marriage when subsequently he met *you* again. It must have seemed a cruel twist of fate to discover you were at last free to marry him when he, for the second time, was unable to make you his wife. But he lacked the courage to tell you the truth and took the risk of embarking on a bigamous marriage to you trusting that no one would ever know of his earlier wedding to my mother. I regret that I am the one who has now to confess this ugly truth to you for

I am aware how deeply such intelligence must distress you."

Mavreen's hand covered her mouth as if to stifle the cry of horror that trembled on her lips. Perry's grip upon her shoulders tightened as he said:

"You have proof of this, I suppose?"

Antoine's eyes smiled back at him disdainfully.

"I am not given to lies, Sir!" he said.

"Then you will show us this proof?" Perry persisted.

Antoine shrugged.

"I could do so! However, the relative documents are in the safe keeping of my *avocat* and it would be impossible to put my hands upon them for several days. Besides which I am sure that you, Madame, would not doubt the word of a de Valle?"

Mavreen bit her lip. Her hands, now clenched together, lay trembling on her lap. Her thoughts whirled in confusion. Antoine's story sounded quite convincing. She searched her mind for memories of the past. She recalled clearly Gerard's amazement when he first learned that he had a son. Could it have been feigned? She had been at Boulancourt the day Blanche Merlin arrived with Antoine seeking recognition for him. She, Mavreen, had never before doubted that Gerard's surprise, delight and astonishment when first he saw the boy were no more assumed than the peasant woman's anxiety to see justice done for her child. Even now she could not seriously doubt the genuineness of Gerard's emotion.

"*I do not believe Gerard married your mother!*" the words burst from her.

Antoine shrugged his shoulders.

"I did not expect that you would, Madame!" he replied coldly. "I did my utmost to warn you that such unfortunate news would come as a shock to you. When you have given the matter more consideration, you will come to accept it as the truth."

"Never!" Mavreen cried. "You must first show me proof of your parents' marriage, Antoine. You forget that I was here in France when your mother brought you to meet your father for the first time. I know how many hours your father spent with the *avocat*, Monsieur Mougin, trying to find a way by which you could be legitimized. It would none of it have been necessary had he been married to your mother!"

Antoine's face registered no concern.

"What else could he have done in the circumstances?" he pointed out inexorably. "He must have realized that you would never tolerate a position as his mistress. He prearranged that meeting with my mother and myself, persuading her that it was in her best interests to play the part of the wronged servant for *my* benefit. My mother would do anything that was for my advantage as I am sure you know. Father then played his part in convincing you, pretending visits to the *avocat* for one purpose whilst in fact he was making legal financial arrangements for my mother to move far away from Compiègne, where you would be unlikely to encounter her again."

Mavreen fell silent. She had begun to doubt her own senses. Antoine's story was hideously plausible. Everything could have happened just as he described.

'Oh, Gerard! Gerard!' she thought, remembering bitterly how from childhood to middle age, he had always put his love for her second to his sense of duty to his family, his heritage. 'How could you have so deceived me?'

Yet Antoine had explained even this. Gerard knew she would never have lived with him as his mistress. She had told him so years before. And loving her, he could not bring himself to risk losing her again.

Afraid of the tears now threatening her, she turned to Perry.

"Come, my dear!" she said with difficulty keeping her voice from trembling. "Let us retire for the night. I have heard sufficient unpleasantness for one evening. We will discuss the subject again on the morrow!"

"My regrets, Madame!" Antoine said courteously, coming forward to open the door for her. "It is a matter of great sadness for me that your first evening beneath my roof should fail to be the joyful occasion I had planned."

He bowed formally to Perry, who spake an uneasy 'goodnight' as he returned the bow. For a split second, their eyes met. Antoine's brooding gaze seemed to radiate triumph.

He enjoyed every minute of that encounter, Perry thought as wordlessly he followed Mavreen out of the room.

70

4

August 1837

THEY talked far into the night, Mavreen lying with her head against Perry's shoulder, his hand stroking her cheek or her forehead as he tried to soothe her restless spirit.

"I came to Compiègne to honor Gerard's memory!" she gave voice to her bitterness. "Am I to leave despising him for his deception?"

"I know 'tis hard for you to accept," Perry replied gently. "But you must try not to think badly of him, my darling, for he was normally a man of integrity. There was no other way he could resolve his predicament, torn as he must have been between his great love for you and his duty to his heritage. I am sure he acted as he thought best in such difficult circumstances."

"Best for Antoine!" Mavreen cried. "But never best for me, Perry. If only he had been honest enough to tell me of his marriage to Blanche Merlin! He could have obtained a divorce — the *avocat* even suggested divorce to him. We could then have been legally married and John . . . " her voice broke as she added wretchedly: "What of John, Perry? Have you considered that these facts must render him illegitimate?"

"Let us not concern ourselves too much with that," he murmured, kissing her with deepest affection. "After all, my love, he will be in excellent company, will he not? You! Me! Tamarisk! Chantal! I think our little family must hold a monopoly upon bastardy. 'Till now, young John was in reality if not legally, the only exception."

"You make it sound an honorable state!" she said. "Oh, Perry, I am so glad you are here beside me. Am I being very silly to care so much?"

"I do not think so!" Perry replied without hesitation. "You loved Gerard very deeply and it is only reasonable you should feel hurt by the discovery that he deceived you. But have you considered, my love, that we have no *proof* of this? We have only the word of a man neither of us trusted as a child and know nothing whatever about since he became adult. I, for one, do not believe that cold, calculating boy can have grown so sensitive and kindly with the years that he tried to withhold from you the knowledge of his rightful claim to nobility in order to safeguard your feelings!"

Mavreen sat up, her hair tumbling about her shoulders as she bent to look at Perry's face in the darkness.

"You really believe he was lying? That Gerard never married Blanche?" she asked. "I wish I too thought likewise. Besides, Antoine has not attempted to conceal his claim to nobility, Perry, for he is openly addressed here in France as the Vicomte de Valle. Though 'tis true he showed reluctance to give me the facts when I demanded them."

"Perhaps for a less savory motive than to spare your feelings," Perry suggested thoughtfully. "He might not wish you to look too deeply into his claim. Remember, my dearest, we have still not seen proof of the marriage!"

"But we can obtain it, if it exists, without Antoine's complicity!" Mavreen cried, her eyes shining with sudden excitement. "We can call upon Blanche Merlin and demand she show us proof of her marriage to Gerard."

"Better still, we can enquire at the *Mairie* and ask to see the register!" Perry suggested. "Which confirms our decision not to return at once to England. We will need to remain here for several more days if we are to clear up these points once and for all."

A silence fell which lasted but a few minutes before Perry said:

"I am trying very hard not to be prejudiced by past memories of Antoine but with the best will in the world, Mavreen, I cannot feel trust in him. Call it an instinct if you wish. There was something strange in his manner when we spoke to him about that child John rescued who was in such terror of those men in the woods. I cannot exactly describe Antoine's expression. It held anger, as if he resented our interference, but something more. I felt he would have preferred that boy to die. I disliked the cold tone of his voice when he said: 'The penalty for trespassing is death, you know!' — although he corrected himself swiftly when John protested we were discussing a lad of but ten years of age."

Perry put his arms around Mavreen and drew

her down upon his chest. His fingers traced the outline of her mouth and suddenly she felt his heartbeat quicken.

"It is not unusual for us to share our sentiments, is it?" he remarked, his voice making clear to her that he was smiling, although she could not see his face. She understood his meaning very well, for they were always in accord in the act of love. Her face softened with tenderness as she caught his hand and held it against her lips. At once his arms tightened around her. His mouth found hers as their limbs entwined in familiar intimacy.

Suddenly Mavreen drew back. To Perry's surprise, she whispered hesitantly:

"Perry, you do not think we are . . . too old for . . . this?"

"Too old for loving one another?" he questioned. "What is this, Mavreen? What put such nonsensical an idea into your head?"

She relaxed at once against him and laid her cheek against his.

"I was just wondering!" she murmured vaguely. Although it was very rarely she did not confide in her beloved husband, her thoughts involved a memory of Gerard which belonged to him only. She felt it would be disloyal were she to speak to Perry of her honeymoon with Gerard. Though it was twenty-four years ago, her mind had sharply recalled his condemnation of poor old Lisa von Eburhard. 'She is far too old for that kind of thing!' he had said, referring to her current affair. And they had had a fierce argument upon the matter, Mavreen protesting that such intimacies were only ways of expressing love; and that love itself should not die with age. Gerard's attitude had distressed her then as now Perry's pleased her.

"I love you, my darling!" she whispered, "far more now than when we were first married. I do believe that with every year that passes, I love you more!"

"You are stealing my words from my lips!" he teased her between kisses, "although I had been about to declare that I love you more with every *minute* that passes, my Mavreen."

They were not the only wakeful personages in the Château de Boulancourt. In his large gold and white bedroom in the east wing, Antoine de Valle had dismissed his servant and clad only in a silk banyan, he was pacing the room with the slow padding of a restless lion. His excitement was intense . . . too intense for sleep to be possible.

Antoine had been immensely stimulated by his handling of a confrontation he had long known must take place some day. He had prepared for it with his usual care for any undertaking, giving every detail the most minute consideration. And nothing had gone wrong!

He had no regrets for the curtailment of his weekend plans. His Roman games could wait. Playing cat and mouse with his relatives was just as stimulating. In the meanwhile, he must not let this night's success cause him to relax his guard. Neither must he underestimate his stepmother or Sir Peregrine. The plausibility of his story might momentarily have convinced them of its truth. But by morning, he thought, it would be more than probable that they would have begun anew to doubt his word. He must assume that they would not leave for England until he had given them adequate proof.

He walked across the room, his feet making no sound upon the soft pile of the Persian rugs, and stood by the gothic-shaped, diamond-paned window staring down into the moonlit courtyard below. It was empty now of people and animals. Shafts of silvery light reflected off the rounded cobbles, sparkling like a thousand tiny glowworms. Towering upwards, the great stone walls of the Château covered with vines and clematis seemed to shimmer as the night breeze stirred the leaves. Around and beneath his own window he could smell the scent of the roses and lonicera that clung to the stonework in massed profusion.

His eyes took in the beauty of the Château's silhouette against the moonlit, star-studded sky; and his mouth hardened. This was *his* home, *his* heritage. It mattered not to him how many narrow-minded legal administrators pontificated that his father should have married his mother, that he had no rightful nobility. No law would change the fact that he was the elder son and should by birthright take his father's title. Let the law be damned! He was the law at Boulancourt and he had claimed the *vicomté*.

His carefully laid plans had not taken into account a legal heir for he had been ignorant of the existence of his half-brother, John de Valle.

Why, he wondered, had his father not told him the child was born?

His lips curled derisively. John de Valle was English despite the fact that his father was French. He looked and behaved and doubtless thought like an Englishman and bore no more resemblance to a French aristocrat than had he, Antoine, to an English milord. Antoine had not the slightest intention of allowing John to disinherit him. He blamed the Princess Camille bitterly for not having advised him that his stepmother had suddenly in her late thirties produced a son after twenty childless years.

Camille! He must soon pay her another visit. One day she would have to succumb to his wishes. He was growing impatient with her stubbornness.

Normally so controlled in his emotions, Antoine could not think of the Princess Camille Faloise without the gall of bitter loathing rising in his throat and threatening to choke him. She was the only human being that he had ever allowed to outwit him since he had grown to manhood. But he had been lulled by her obsessive devotion to him in his youth. When he had decided upon offering marriage to her as a means of securing her vast fortune, he had assumed mistakenly that she believed his declaration of an undying love so great that it transcended the disparity in their ages.

At twenty-two he had been unversed in the various aspects of French law and had paid little attention when Camille took it upon herself to arrange the marriage. How many hundreds of times had he subsequently berated himself for not checking upon those details! He had been so certain that Camille trusted him absolutely that it had not crossed his mind she suspected his motives. But the silly old woman had not been quite so stupid as he had supposed. He had expected that they would enter into a marriage-without-contract which would have entitled him to practically all power over her property. But Camille had arranged a *régime de la séparation de biens*. Too late Antoine discovered that there were share certificates and jewelry worth more than half her fortune that even as her husband he was unable to touch.

At first Camille had been generous to a fault, denying him nothing that he asked. But as his demands increased, so she began to suspect the true facts underlying their marriage and her generosity ceased. Antoine was then forced to realize that he had bound himself for life in marriage to an elderly woman from whom he could expect very little more than she had already given him. She refused to inform him whether or not she had made a Will naming him as beneficiary. He had known then that either he must spend his life kow-towing to a wife he neither loved nor desired in the hope that she would eventually die and leave him her fortune; or else he must find a way to force her to give him what he intended to have.

Whilst their relationship was still outwardly intact and Camille only suspected his true motives for marrying her, he persuaded her to return with him to his estate in France.

Making certain that she would not have the opportunity of announcing her return to her homeland to any of her friends and relatives still residing there, he had removed her at once to Compiègne and imprisoned her in a suite of rooms in the east tower of his Château. By placing totally trustworthy guards at her door and allowing only two trusted female servants to attend her, he had ensured that no one else knew of her existence.

He had anticipated that it would not be long before she gave way, signed the documents releasing her shares and informed him where she had hidden the fabulous collection of jewelry left her by her first husband. Her resistance had been remarkable and not even the near starvation diet he imposed had made the slightest impression on her. With the bitterness of a woman who knows she has been married solely for her money she insisted she would rather die than reveal the facts he wanted. Her hatred of him was equalled only by his hatred of her.

Now her mind was beginning to weaken with solitariness and the approach of old age. It disturbed him to think that if she lost her reason altogether he might never succeed in making her reveal the information he was utterly determined upon getting. He had already waited six years and could, if needs be, wait longer still. His capacity for patience was enforced by the certainty that he would surely win in the end.

Thoughts of victory over one woman merged with speculation as to his chance of victory over another — the little golden-skinned Chantal!

How ravishingly pretty she had looked at dinner that evening, her dark hair curling around her face in ringlets each threaded with tiny pearls. Her white silk dress was demure yet ravishing, the embroidered bodice and full skirt enhancing her delightful figure. Antoine was in no doubt whatever that the girl was a virgin but without the irritating coyness and simpering manner of very young girls which he found so tedious — as tedious as the knowledgeable tactics employed by women well versed in the arts of love.

For Antoine de Valle, the very word love was an enigma. He had heard it spoken, read about it; listened to songs of love; owned many valuable works of art depicting love; but it was meaningless to him in that it had never found an echo in his heart. Such stirrings of emotion as he felt had always been desires for material possessions, for *objets d'art*, for the Château de Boulancourt, for delicately-made fabrics, tapestries, embroideries, for jewelry, finely cut glass or hand-wrought silver and gold. His heart, if that was the center of feeling, remained unmoved by human beings.

Antoine understood all too well the sensuous delights of the body. At an age when he should have had no knowledge of such primitive passions, he had been corrupted by the woman his father had chosen as his guardian. The Princess Camille's penchant for young boys must have been known to most of Society, he now reflected. Only his father's absence from the London scene for so long could have kept him ignorant of the Princess' reputation.

Long before Antoine attained the age of majority, he was sickened by the perfumed caresses of women, by their indiscriminate kisses, by their white, wandering hands and their insistence upon pressing his golden head to their soft, smothering bosoms, declaring inevitably that he resembled nothing so much as a Botticelli angel.

At the memory, Antoine's mouth curled in scornful derision. No woman lived, he had long since decided, who was worthy of a man's respect or devotion. They were all predators, greedily taking their foolish little pleasures without regard for a man's dignity or pride. They were too stupid to guess at his thoughts when he had submitted to their embraces, succumbing only because he had known that he would be well rewarded for his apparent compliance!

At first when he was very young, Camille and her friends had rewarded him with sweetmeats, playthings, bonbons and picture books. As he grew older, the gifts became more lavish — gold chains, a silk cravat, rings for his fingers, an enamel snuffbox, a gold tinderbox. It had not been long before his room was filled with such possessions, many of which he disposed of, thereby realizing large sums of money. His greatest need was for money — not because he did not receive a generous allowance from his father, but because for the first five years of his life, he had watched his mother hoarding every sou. The main topic of her conversation had been her hatred of the poverty which gripped them and the security which money alone could guarantee. He had derived an even greater satisfaction from the knowledge that it was not sous he hoarded but gold guineas.

When Camille took him to the New World, he soon discovered that there, too, life was only easy for the rich; that only the rich received unquestioning respect. He learned that money opened the gates to freedom. As his wealth increased and he ceased to be entirely dependent upon Camille, he could when he so chose, free himself from her house for a few days and exchange her smothering attentions, and those of her woman friends for the companionship of men.

With his extraordinary good looks it was not long before Antoine was courted by gentlemen with the same preference as Camille for the company of young boys. He welcomed their attentions, infinitely preferring their companionship to that of females. They were at least open in their desires and there was a kind of honesty in their dealings that made no pretense of love. The romantic, poetic nonsense employed by Camille and her friends to disguise their secret cravings was willingly exchanged by him for the straightforward approach of men who offered certain rewards for certain favors.

It was not only the growing size of his bank account that made Antoine moderately content with his life. He had always enjoyed the sense of power the women had given him when he learned how enslaved they could become by his smile, his kisses, his pretense of affection. That sense of power was magnified a hundred times when he discovered that noblemen of wealth and prestige would humble themselves to beg for his favors. For a long while, he had savored the knowledge that young though he was, he had importance for men and women of great influence and sometimes even fame. He had derived endless hours of amusement playing one admirer against another until he could call whatever tune he pleased. This, above all others, had been his favorite pastime with Camille. Over the years, as she witnessed his growing popularity, she had come close to dementia in her insistence that he confine his favors to her alone.

It was Camille and not he who had first conceived the idea of marriage. And Camille was not the fool some thought her. She had been well aware that marriage to a woman over thirty years his senior was unlikely to appeal to him. But she did have a very tempting wrapper for the acid sweetmeat she offered him — her vast wealth. She had accumulated a fortune in her youth from the Prince Faloise to whom she was married. But within a few years he died leaving his widow riches beyond Antoine's imaginings. All these would by French law be his, she had informed him, in exchange for his vows to be a faithful husband to her always and never to leave her side.

Antoine, greatly tempted by her offer was still pondering upon it when word arrived from the French *avocat*, Monsieur Mougin, that now he had come of age, the de Valle estate and the Château de Boulancourt were his by virtue of his late father's Will. The silly fool had made no mention to Antoine of the existence of his half-brother, John de Valle; but merely informed him that according to French law, he could not inherit his father's title despite the fact that it had always been the late Vicomte's wish that he should do so.

That wish Antoine had decided, would be honored somehow. And as he now stepped back from the window and drew the heavy brocade curtains, closing out the moonlight, he recalled how he had devised a plan he believed to be foolproof. He had married Camille without further delay, for although he had not yet attained the age of thirty, life had long since taught him that there was nothing beyond the grasp of those who would pay any price, go to any length or take any risk to achieve their goal.

Antoine smiled in secret satisfaction. He *was* the Vicomte de Valle and let those who questioned it prove otherwise.

5

August 1837

JOHN regarded his half-brother with an admixture of admiration and dislike. Try as he might, be could not belittle the handsome figure Antoine cut in his violet silk tail coat, matching trousers and primrose yellow, frilled shirt. He looked every inch the Vicomte he professed to be.

John was plagued anew by his uncertainty. His mother was regarding him with a look of loving concern. This afternoon she had informed him that Antoine claimed not only his father's title but his own legitimacy. It had come as a great shock to learn that he might have been born out of wedlock. That he might have no claim to his father's title was a lesser blow for he had never greatly concerned himself with his French heritage.

But the real reason for his disquiet was fear that Chantal would pity him. His feelings for her were adding to his confusion. He admitted to himself that they had undergone an extraordinary metamorphosis. He no longer loved her as a dear little sister, but as a man loves the girl he hopes one day to marry. He had spent a sleepless night considering the consequences of this discovery and had been greatly comforted by the belief that there was no impediment of his marriage to Chantal if ever she should agree, when they were both older, to become his wife. In a year or so he would be twenty-one and Chantal, his adorable, enchanting, lovely Chantal, would be a young woman, her schoolroom days far behind her. Perry, whom he respected and loved, was unlikely to refuse him as a son-in-law. He held John in high regard and knew him to be rich enough to keep Chantal in luxury. Moreover, so John believed, he had a title to offer her. If Chantal married him, she would become the Vicomtesse de Valle!

Now in the space of a few minutes those expectations had been dashed when his mother had pointed out to him that the very foundations of his life might have been based on a falsehood; that his father might have committed bigamy. His mother had brought him up to revere the very name of Gerard de Valle, a man John scarcely remembered for he had died when he was but a child of three years. "Your father was a man of great honor and integrity," she had so often told him. "Do model yourself upon him, John, for he was truly noble!"

The bile rose in John's throat. Only his mother's and Perry's suggestion that the veracity of Antoine's claim was questionable prevented him from returning at once to England where sanity and honesty still prevailed. He had even contemplated wildly the idea of joining the Royal Navy to escape the disgrace he now felt lay heavily upon him. As for Chantal — he now felt unworthy to speak of love to her. His only salvation lay in the possibility that his half-brother was lying. Yet the man seemed so self-assured, so completely master of himself, John feared he did indeed have the proof be claimed.

He looked up at Antoine and met those searching dark eyes with a courage he was far from feeling, although he had requested this interview in order to quiz him further.

"Since my good name is in question," he said quietly but with dignity, "I feel you owe it to me, sir, to offer *written* proof of your mother's marriage to my father. If you will oblige me by showing some document to prove your own legitimacy, I will give you my word never to trouble you again with my own claim to our father's title!"

Antoine shrugged his shoulders indifferently.

"That is a reasonable request, I think," he said quietly. "I will obtain the document relating to my mother's marriage within the next two days so that you may examine it. Meanwhile may I suggest that we try to put this unpleasant matter out of our thoughts so that you can all enjoy your visit to Boulancourt, as was indeed my intention. I realize that my revelations must have come as a severe shock to you, but unless we allow it to be so, I see no reason why it should become a disaster."

"What is your meaning, Antoine?" Mavreen asked. Until now, she had allowed John to conduct his own interrogation She sensed some wily stratagem behind the kindly tone of Antoine's voice.

Antoine gave the faintest of bows in her direction.

"I mean only that these unfortunate scandals need not be known outside these walls. I, for one, have not the slightest wish publicly to discredit my young brother in any degree. On the contrary, I am more than content that my own legitimacy should remain in doubt whilst his remains unquestioned."

John flushed a deep red. He was much moved by the generosity of Antoine's gesture and ashamed of his own mistrust of his half-brother. He was shocked when his mother said in a cold, hard voice:

"And the price of your silence, Antoine?"

There was a faint narrowing of Antoine's eyes but so fleeting that none observed it. He maintained the friendliest of expressions as he said with a hint of sarcasm:

"I regret, Madame, if anything I may have said has given you cause to suspect me of having an ulterior motive. I do assure you that I have none but the most worthy of motives. It was not my intention, as you already know, ever to reveal my father's past indiscretions. It was unfortunate that you, Madame, felt it necessary to look into the past although I quite understand your concern for your son's right to the title. However, if you and John both feel content with the proof I shall be giving you, I require nothing for myself other than to be the acknowledged Vicomte de Valle."

"Antoine is being very considerate, dear Mama!" John said. "He is offering to protect

88

both your reputation and mine — not to mention that of my father. I think we should act upon his suggestion and forget these matters for the present."

"Very well, if that is your wish!" Mavreen said reluctantly. "So let us now speak on another subject, Antoine. Will you not tell us of the years since I lost touch with your life? What has become of the Princess Camille Faloise? I have heard nothing in England of her since your departure abroad. Is she living now in France?"

"I regret to inform you that my former guardian died some years ago!" Antoine replied coolly. "As you may well imagine, Madame, her passing was a sad loss for she had always acted as a mother to me!"

Mavreen's lips curled in disbelief, for she knew Princess Camille had not a maternal streak in her body.

"May she rest in peace!" she said. "And your own mother, Antoine, she is still living, I hope?"

"Alas, no!" said Antoine. "The years of deprivation during the wars took greater toll upon her than upon those of similar age who enjoyed better circumstances. She died within a year of my father."

"Will you please excuse me?" John broke in, for he had heard Chantal's laughter in the gardens beyond the open French windows of the *salon* and guessed that she was walking with her father.

But Antoine too had heard the girl's laughter

and like John was drawn towards its light-hearted promise of gaiety and fun.

"Let us all repair to the gardens!" he suggested. "I have yet to conduct you round the rose walk. I think you will find a stroll there most rewarding. We will invite your little sister to join us, John."

John's cheeks flushed. It was on the tip of his tongue to respond fiercely that Chantal was *not* his sister. But some inner caution made him bite back the retort. Filled with angry resentment at the thought that Antoine was likely yet again to monopolize Chantal's attention, he followed his mother and his host into the garden.

His mood was not improved when it was to Antoine and not to him that Chantal came running, her hands cupped together to support some private treasure.

"You must look at this beautiful flower, Sir!" she said, "and inform me of its name. Papa has not seen its like before and it is so very pretty!"

"But not so pretty as the hands that hold it!" Antoine replied with exaggerated gallantry as he smiled down at Chantal. "It is a godetia I believe. I will have one of the gardeners gather a bouquet to put in your room!"

Chantal's face grew pink with pleasure.

"You are very kind, sir!" she said shyly. "I had not intended to ask for a bouquet!"

"Now will you not do me a kindness in exchange?" Antoine enquired. "'Twill not be in the least difficult to enact. It is simply to consider me as a friend and call me by my

Christian name. The formality of your address makes me feel a stranger."

"Then it will be my pleasure to call you Antoine!" Chantal said without hesitation. She turned to her father and John who had silently observed this interchange — Perry with amusement, John with ever-increasing jealousy. "Is this not the most wonderful of days!" she exclaimed. "The sun is shining so brilliantly and I feel so happy!" Impulsively, she took John's arm and in a teasing manner shook it in gentle reproof. "How can you look so glum on such a perfect morning?" she remarked. "You are not ailing, dearest John?"

He withdrew his arm and did his best to smile as he replied:

"I am perfectly well, Chantal. I apologize if my visage has spoiled your contentment even in the smallest degree!"

At once Chantal stood on tiptoe and reaching up, kissed John's cheek as if it were the most natural thing in the world for her to do. Watching her through narrowed lids, Antoine noted the gesture and felt no jealousy, for it was quite clear to him that the girl's affection was no more than that of a loving sister. It was equally obvious to him that John's reactions were far from brotherly as with reddened cheek he detached himself from Chantal's embrace.

Perry too had watched the interchange. Later that day, when he and Mavreen were alone in their bedchamber changing their attire before the evening meal, he recounted the episode to her.

"I think you should prepare yourself for what

91

seems likely to come about!" he said. "I am of the belief that young John is in love for the first time in his life, not with little Julia Lade as we had once thought probable, but with Chantal. And I fear that John is going to suffer as a consequence. Chantal loves him — but only as the dear, familiar companion of her childhood. If her romantic interest in anyone has been aroused, then it is by Antoine."

Mavreen's face revealed her distress.

"That is bad news on two counts!" she said. "If you really believe Chantal is attracted by Antoine, the sooner we remove her from his influence the better. As for John . . . I must talk with him and explain that he must put all thoughts of Chantal out of his mind."

"Why so, m'dear?" Perry asked, his face registering his surprise. "All is fair in love and war, so 'tis said. John and Chantal are both very young so John has time on his side to woo the girl if that is what he wants!"

"You mean you would really have no objection if they wished to marry?" Mavreen's tone of voice expressed her disbelief.

"Indeed not! They are well matched." Perry replied immediately.

"But it would be most . . . unseemly!" Mavreen cried. "To me they are brother and sister and will always be so!"

Perry's face took on a look of firmness.

"You must not think it, for it is not so!" he said. "'Tis not often you and I are in disagreement, my love, but I am in no doubt whatever that your sentiments regarding our two children are quite mistaken. As I have said before, they are not related in the smallest degree and there is no legal impediment to their marriage should they desire to wed. Will you not bow to my judgement in this instance and leave matters to resolve themselves? It can do naught but harm for you to express your opinions to John. Your opposition might serve merely to consolidate a possibility and turn it into a fact. Moreover you will antagonize him quite unnecessarily."

"John is too young to know his own mind!" Mavreen muttered, her eyes clouded with uncertainty.

"But not too young to love!" Perry replied. "Love must run its course, Mavreen, as well you know."

He walked across the room and took her in his arms. She responded at once to his kiss for throughout the sixteen years of her marriage to Perry, she had never been able to resist him for long when he chose to be the lover. But her mind could not accept his advice, and she was convinced that she could not give her blessing were Chantal and John ever to ask for her agreement to their marriage.

★ ★ ★

When the Monday morning dawned heralding yet another cloudless day, the household was early astir. Antoine, true to his promise, had arranged a hunting expedition in the forest. In the bustling courtyard of the Château, grooms were busy saddling mounts from his well-stocked stables. Decked in a saddle and bridle of the palest leather with engraved silver embellishments, Antoine's beautiful white stallion snorted and pawed the cobbles in restless impatience to be on the move.

Chantal was in a fever of excitement. Dressed in a red riding habit, perfectly tailored to fit her slim young figure, she seemed to glow like a magnificent ruby.

Perry, observing her with amused affection, said:

"You must really curb your impatience, Chantal, since nothing is achieved by it. It is but a twenty minute ride to the hunting lodge and Antoine has already stated that the hounds will not be marshalled before half past nine of the clock!"

Exactly on time, the handlers arrived at the rendezvous with the pack of hounds and the boar hunt was under way. The dogs were well aware of what was expected of them. Soon, baying furiously, noses to the ground, they were searching out the thickets, frightening birds and beasts from their hiding places and sending them fleeing into the clearings in the forest, where the gentlemen on horseback could ride in pursuit until close enough to shoot their quarry.

Several of the grooms were also mounted and rode behind Antoine, Perry and John. Chantal and Mavreen rode a little way off, preferring not to be too close when the beasts were killed.

"'Tis very like our fox-hunting in England!" Perry remarked to John, "save that here we are chasing boar, deer, pheasant . . . anything that runs or flies, 'twould seem!"

By the hour for dinner, Mavreen was feeling the effects of the morning's exercise and professed herself too weary to continue the hunt in the afternoon. Chantal's face fell although she at once volunteered to accompany her to the Château. But Mavreen smiled her refusal.

"There is no necessity for you to forgo your sport, my dear!" she said. "As it happens, I have several purchases I wish to make in Compiègne and when I have changed my clothes, I will take the carriage and Dickon shall drive me to the town."

Even Perry was unaware that this had been her intention from the day's start.

Some three hours' later, Dickon halted the carriage in front of the *mairie* in Compiègne. The *maire* was summoned by the *secrétaire de mairie*. Awakened from his lengthy afternoon *siesta*, he hastily donned his black dress coat, tried to straighten his crumpled linen shirt and presented himself to the English milady.

Mavreen announced the reason for her visit and after obtaining his promise of total discretion, she said:

"Although I now address you as Lady Waite, *Monsieur le Maire*, I was formerly married to the Vicomte de Valle — the late Gerard de Valle. It is therefore a personal matter about which I have occasion to enquire, a matter of family history."

Her companion bowed several times in a flurry of nervous anxiety. It was not every day he was called upon by a person of such consequence.

"Any service at all that I can render, Madame . . . " he murmured, spreading out his hands significantly to show his willingness to oblige.

"I wish to be given access to your register," Mavreen said simply. "There are certain details I require to check concerning a marriage of a member of the de Valle family."

"But of course, Madame!" the mayor replied, glad to hear that the demands of his illustrious guest were so simple. "If you will tell me what year this marriage took place, I will have the *secrétaire* find them for you as speedily as possible."

"That may prove a little difficult!" Mavreen interposed, "since I cannot be exact as to the year of the marriage. I can tell you only that it most likely took place in 1807 although it may have been in 1808 or even 1809."

"It would take some time to find one marriage amongst so many," the mayor said thoughtfully. "If you could tell me exactly whose marriage you are concerned with, I could ask the *secrétaire*?"

"I fear you will have to take my word for it, Monsieur, that it is necessary for me to search for myself," Mavreen interrupted. "I will not trouble you longer than is necessary."

But as the mayor had forecast, it was no simple task to look through all the marriages registered during the three years she believed most likely to include a wedding between Blanche Merlin and her husband, Gerard. Her eyes were sore with straining as she painstakingly deciphered

96

one record after another, the spidery script in the register proving at times almost illegible. She could not discover the names for which she searched.

It was growing late when she closed the cover of the last book.

She rang the bell and the mayor came hurrying back into the office.

"You have not found what you are looking for?" he asked anxiously. To his surprise Mavreen smiled.

"I am delighted to say that I have not!" she said. Seeing his expression, her smile deepened.

"It was a marriage which would not have pleased me!" she explained as best she could.

"Could the wedding not have taken place elsewhere?" the mayor enquired as he helped Mavreen to rise from her chair. "If the marriage was undesirable, as you infer, Madame, is it not unlikely to have taken place so near to the family estate?"

Mavreen considered the logic of the mayor's remark. She said thoughtfully:

"I suppose the couple may have traveled further afield although I had supposed, since the lady's home was near Compiègne that the wedding would have been here — or close by."

"If it is of such importance to you, Madame, perhaps it would be as well to enquire at Beauvais, for example. Maybe also at Clermont and Noyon — although there is no knowing how far away from home they may have traveled to accomplish their intention. Did I understand you to say that you do not know for certain if this marriage took place at all?"

"No, I am not certain!" Mavreen admitted thoughtfully. "But I thank both you and your clerk for your assistance — and for your suggestions, *Monsieur le Maire*. Now if you will be so good as to summon my servants, I will be on my way."

As Dickon drove slowly back to Boulancourt through the forest, Mavreen said:

"I learned nothing, Dickon. I am no wiser as to the truth than when we left Boulancourt earlier this afternoon." Suddenly she smiled as she added: "'Tis the greatest pity you never learned to speak the French language, Dickon, else you could have related to me the gossip from the servants' hall!"

Dickon shook his head regretfully.

"'Tis a muddling tongue for the likes of me, surelye!" he agreed.

Since they were quite alone, they spoke not as mistress and servant but with the easy familiarity of old friends. It was Dickon's parents who had given Mavreen a loving home on their farmstead in Sussex when she had been left penniless and motherless as a tiny girl. She had grown up with Dickon and his brothers and sisters, her life identical to theirs except that she regularly attended the house of a tutor her father had engaged for her when he discovered her existence. When she was fifteen, her father, Sir John Danesfield, had taken her to live in London, eventually launching her in Society and finding her a husband with a fortune and a title. But Mavreen had never forgotten her foster home and family, and Dickon, whilst acting as her head groom whenever she chose to travel abroad, had in private remained her trusted friend.

He said now in the rough Sussex dialect she well understood:

"You should ought to be queered, for there be sing'lar goings-on in that there Château, surelye!"

"In what way strange?" Mavreen asked. "Of what should I be suspicious?"

"I cannot rightly say!" Dickon replied, pulling one ear in perplexity. "But every marnin and night, there's an old Frenchy woman as comes down to the servants' dining room and fetches a tray of food what's been put ready for 'er. She doant never say nothing but teks it off somewheres else. It doant be servants' food 'cos the platters and such be a deal bettern' what we be eating from. I done kept my eyes open liken you said to do!"

Mavreen gave a long, deep sigh.

"Does it not seem wrong to you, Dickon, to harbor suspicion as to the character of the Vicomte's son? How upset Gerard would be were he to know that I am seeking to discredit Antoine!"

Dickon, without hesitation, answered firmly:

"The Vicomte was an unaccountable good man and never had no dishonor in his heart nor head. A noble man he were and 'tis his name his sons do carry. If'n this Frenchy son be a bad 'un, then 'tis right he be discounted for the sake of the Vicomte's memory!"

Mavreen regarded her servant's grey head with respect as well as affection. Dickon was no scholar but he had a countryman's simple understanding of right and wrong.

"It be a shame, surelye, the Vicomte beant alive to see Master John growed to manhood!" Dickon went on. "Mayhap he'd not abeen so taken with his eldest if'n he'd knowed what an unaccountable fine gentleman Master John 'ud grow to!"

Chantal, however, was not painting such a favorable picture of John as seated at a table in her bedchamber, she composed a letter to her friend, Julia. She commented on the strangeness of John's behavior.

'You would be hard put to recognize the John you know! Even this day when we have enjoyed the most magnificent of sport in the nearby forest, John has been scowling and short-tempered and I have to confess, did not put up a very creditable performance. Papa said he has never known him so poor a marksman.'

She leant back in her chair, her small white teeth biting the end of her quill as she pondered how best to express herself to her confidante. Momentarily, her concentration wandered and she smiled as she considered that she was supposed to be lying upon her bed resting after the long day in the saddle, refreshing herself before the evening meal. But she was

100

far too stimulated by the events of the past few days to be able to contain her thoughts in quiet composure.

Returning to her letter, she continued writing:

''Tis my belief poor John's nose is a little out of joint. At home he is always considered second only to Papa in importance but out here, it is his half-brother who steals the limelight. And small wonder at that, Julia, for Antoine de Valle is truly the most fascinating of men. I will confess (to you only knowing you have given me your promise never to reveal our secrets) that I am much taken with him — so much so that I think of little else.'

And that was the truth, Chantal considered as she paused to dip her pen once more into the inkwell.

'Oh, Julia! I do believe I am in love. Why else should I blush when he pays me a compliment or tremble when he touches my hand? If only I could be sure what love is, I could advise you better of my feelings. All I can tell you is that I have never before enjoyed such confusion of emotion. When I am not in his presence I lie on my bed imagining that we are together. I daydream in the most wicked fashion. Last night I pretended that I was lying quite naked on my bridal couch and that Antoine was my bridegroom and I awaiting him on our wedding night. I pictured

101

how the door would open and he would come to the bedside and take me in his arms. But there, as you will realize, dear Julia, the dream ended for we have not yet discovered how married people love each other, have we? Why will no one tell us? I asked Elsie, as I told you was my intention, but she gave me no satisfactory answer but said I would be the happier for not knowing "nor experiencing neither!" she added in the most warning tones. Mama, when I questioned her, smiled and said I would discover "this most perfect aspect of nature" all in good time, by which she meant when I was betrothed. So I am no wiser and unsure if the experience be unpleasant, as Elsie suggested, or beautiful, as Mama inferred.'

Chantal drew a third sheet of paper from the drawer and sighing, returned to her task.

'I have yet to tell you that I believe my interest is returned and that despite the fact that he is approaching thirty, Antoine (as I am to call him) has professed himself "charmed" by me — a girl but newly out of the schoolroom. Is that not hard to credit? I am the happiest girl in the world . . . '

Chantal would not have written those words had she been aware that at this very moment, Mavreen was confronting Antoine and informing him that she intended to leave Boulancourt with the minimum of delay.

6

August 1837

MAVREEN regarded her son's unhappy face, her heart aching at the knowledge that she could not protect him from the blow she had been forced to inflict upon him.

"I wish I could offer some hope that I am mistaken!" she said. "But I have seen the record of your father's marriage to Blanche Merlin with my own eyes. When I told Antoine I had discovered no record of it at the *mairie* in Compiègne, he gave his copy to me reluctantly but without preamble. I fear there is no further room for argument! The marriage took place in Toulon."

John drew a long, deep breath. It seemed there was no further doubt that he was the offspring of an illegal marriage, a bastard with no claim on his father's name and with no heritage of nobility to pass to his sons.

"I cannot ask her to marry me now!" The cry was wrenched from him. Mavreen stared at John in perplexity.

"Marry?" she echoed. "Of whom are you speaking, John? Of Julia Lade?"

John's face flushed an angry red as he turned away from his mother and paced the room in restless frustration.

"Of course not of Julia, Mama!" he said irritably. "I have no love for the girl as well you know. It is of Chantal I am speaking. I love her. I want . . . wanted . . . to ask her to marry me. Not yet, of course, but when we were both a little older . . . " He broke off, looking at his mother's anxious face uneasily.

"What is so wrong that you should regard me as if I had taken leave of my senses?" he asked defensively.

Mavreen controlled herself with an effort as she recalled Perry's words. He had advised her that John's feelings for Chantal had changed. He had further informed her that there was no impediment to the union should the young people desire it. Yet she herself still thought of them as brother and sister.

"Does Chantal know how you feel?" she asked tentatively.

John shook his head, his eyes bitter.

"I doubt Chantal has had time to give me a single thought since we came to France!" he said harshly. "She is bewitched by that noble half-brother of mine. And he makes no bones about the fact that he finds her enchanting — as any man might, I dare say!" he added with renewed bitterness. "I had supposed that *I* would one day make Chantal the Vicomtesse de Valle. Now my half-brother may enjoy the privilege!"

"Enough of this nonsense!" Mavreen broke in, her green eyes blazing with sudden anger. "I have no intention of listening to such ridiculous notions. Whether or no you love Chantal is one matter but that she should entertain such feelings for Antoine de Valle is quite another. Even were Chantal herself to wish it, neither your stepfather nor I would consider such a marriage. I do not wish to hear you speak of this again, John, for of a truth 'tis quite absurd. In any event we shall all be returning to England within a day or two. I have already informed Antoine of this intention. Your father has sent one of the servants ahead to Dieppe to book cabins for us on the packet to Newhaven. We hope to embark the day after tomorrow. Once we have left Compiègne, Chantal will not see Antoine again. Perhaps this intelligence will make you happier!"

John's face softened instantly. He did as he had wished earlier to do and put his arms around his mother's shoulders, hugging her warmly.

"I am sorry if I have been boorish!" he said. "Please forgive me, Mama. And for my selfishness. You too, must be suffering, for I know how greatly you respected my father's memory. Now . . . "

"Now I prefer that we should not speak of your father again!" Mavreen interrupted. "I loved him . . . and I think he loved me — too much perhaps, to be able to risk losing me. He must have suffered a great deal in the knowledge that he had deceived me — for he was an honorable man. I prefer that he should be remembered as such. And now we must both go to our rooms to change our attire. The hour is late and we shall of a certainty be in retard for dinner."

The fact that Mavreen, John and Perry were all late in appearing downstairs that evening, afforded Antoine the opportunity he needed to speak alone to Chantal. The moment she appeared in the *petit salon*, he hurried forward to greet her. Discovering him alone save for the footman who had opened the doors for her, Chantal smiled shyly.

For once Antoine did not immediately comment upon her appearance although she looked ravishingly beautiful in her low cut dress of white satin with its silver lace overskirt looped on either side. Her hair was arranged in a multitude of ringlets. Around her creamy neck was a fine silver chain from which hung a silver filigree flower with a diamond heart, nestling between her breasts. Matching droplet earrings gleamed through her shining dark hair, in which was a flower made of silver lace with a diamond brooch for its center.

"It is most important that I should speak to you quite alone!" he said, taking her white gloved hands in his and leading her gently through the open casement into the garden. "I do not know if your parents have already advised you of the situation but we may not have much time left!"

"I have not seen my parents since we returned from the forest!" Chantal said, her forehead creased in perplexity at the ambiguousness of his statement. "Is anything wrong, sir?"

Antoine walked the length of the terrace, descending the stone steps to the lawn before he replied to her question. Stopping beneath a giant copper beech, he once again took possession of Chantal's hands.

"I am afraid that there is a great deal amiss," he said, "and since your family have not told you what is afoot, then I must do so. I would have preferred to break the news more gently but time will not permit delay."

Seeing that he had her full attention, he quietly but in firm tones told her of his unwillingness to cause distress but despite this, her stepmother had insisted upon seeing proof of his claim to the *vicomté*. He had been forced therefore to reveal the unpleasant facts of past history and show her a copy of his parents' marriage particulars. Naturally enough, Antoine continued, this had come as a great shock. Understandably she and John felt hurt and bitter and not least, antagonistic towards him as the cause of their present feelings of humiliation. They had therefore decided to return at once to England.

Chantal's face registered her dismay and indignation.

"But that is most unfair!" she cried. "I certainly have no wish to leave Boulancourt! 'Tis not your fault that you and not John are your father's heir."

Chantal's words gave Antoine all the encouragement he needed to pursue his intent.

"I too, am heartbroken at this sudden curtailment of your visit," he said, "for it means that our newly discovered friendship must come to an end before it has scarce begun." He looked directly into her eyes, holding her gaze by the intensity of his own. "Had we the chance to spend the next few weeks together," he said in a low vibrant voice, "I would not have presumed to speak as I am now about to do. I would have waited until I was more certain that you had some small regard for me."

Chantal's eyes widened. Her pulses racing, she said honestly:

"You must know that I do already hold you in high regard, sir!"

"Antoine!" he corrected her, smiling. "It seems you are intent upon denying me the happiness of calling me by my name." The smile faded. "Or do you too resent me for being the true Vicomte de Valle?" he added with pretended bitterness.

Chantal's eyes flashed.

"A title or lack of one is of no import to me whatever . . . Antoine!" she added the last word shyly. "What matters to me in a person is his character, and . . . and I have found in you only that which is to your credit!"

Antoine drew closer to her so that their bodies were almost touching.

"And I have discovered in you all that is purest, sweetest and most charming in your sex!" he said, the genuine sincerity in his voice leaving Chantal in no doubt as to the honesty of his compliment. "Therefore I am in despair lest on your return to England you forget my very existence. Chantal, 'tis my intention to come to London next year when your new young Queen is crowned. There will be much celebration which we could enjoy together. May

I call upon you then or will you have forgotten me long since?"

Chantal let go her breath. She was so happy she could not speak her thoughts for fear of betraying her feelings. Before she could answer, Antoine went on:

"Meanwhile, we could write to one another but I fear your parents would not allow the passage of letters between us!"

Chantal caught her breath.

"What harm would there be in our correspondence?" she asked. "And since there would be no harm in it, you could, if you wished, send me a letter in the care of my friend Julia Lade!" she added tentatively. "I can trust her absolutely."

"You would not feel it wrong to deceive your parents in this manner?" Antoine asked curiously, for such deceit seemed out of character.

"I would never deceive them in other matters!" Chantal replied thoughtfully. "But in this instance I consider them at fault for blaming you for a situation that you could not avoid. 'Tis unjust that they would resent your — our friendship — for having prior claim to your father's title. You have not robbed John for 'twas never truly his, was it? If wrong were done, 'twas by your father and not by you."

"Perhaps it was wrong of me not to advise them of the truth when I myself first became aware of it. But I had no wish to hurt either of them and I saw no reason to do so when I came of age," Antoine said.

109

"You acted most kindly!" Chantal replied, her sympathies, as Antoine had hoped, entirely with him. "I am certain that once my mother and John become accustomed to the truth, they will cease to make you the butt of their bitterness."

"With you as my champion, I cannot fail to succeed in my hope to restore family unity," Antoine said, delighting in the color which stole into Chantal's cheeks at his compliment.

With her promise to reply to his letters fresh in his ears, it mattered not to Antoine that John glowered his disapproval when with Chantal on his arm, he returned to the *petit salon*; nor did he feel the slightest pang of jealousy when Chantal ran to the younger man and with her natural affection, took his hand and said:

"Dearest John, do not look so glum, I pray you, for your scowls quite mar the beauty of this lovely evening!"

With shrewd awareness, Antoine was convinced that he had already won the first part of his campaign; that ultimately, this girl would be his. The seeds of victory were well and truly sown and the harvest was all but certain to be reaped.

He was even more certain of himself when later that night, Stefano brought him the letter Chantal had written earlier to Julia.

"Mademoiselle gave this to one of the footmen requesting that it should be dispatched as soon as possible on the next post-chaise!" the servant said. "I thought, Monsieur le Vicomte, that you might like to see . . . "

"Thank you!" Antoine broke in. "You did right, Stefano. You may go!" he added as the servant backed hesitantly away from him.

Alone in his bedchamber, Antoine studied Chantal's neat, beautifully formed script before finally breaking the wax seal with a thin paper-knife. Unhurriedly he read the letter, then carefully, with practiced skill, folded it so that the recipient would never know it had been perused. The seal he repaired with the painstaking care of an artist.

There was no doubt now, he thought, that the girl was succumbing to his charms. If he had any doubts to trouble him, they were on account of his own feelings rather than hers. The knowledge that Chantal had assumed far too much importance in his life made him uneasy. Since her arrival he had had thought for little else — his Parisian friends, his gladiators, his prisoner in the tower — the two men in the dungeons. He felt disarmed; at an unaccustomed disadvantage in this unfamiliar situation where he had almost feared her rejection of him. He had never before cared whether a woman had a good opinion of him or otherwise. He had taken what he wanted as and when he wanted. But with Chantal, her pleasure came before his own. Her regard for him mattered in a way that had no bearing on her authority. She was but a child, without influence, without title or fortune that he knew of. She had nothing he might want — except herself.

It was this above all, that most worried him.

"Can it be that I love her?" he questioned

himself with nervous cynicism. "I, who despise all women?"

But Chantal was unlike the others — unlike any human being he had met. She was without guile, without cunning, without avarice, without coquetry. Yet with his vast knowledge of females aided by his instinct, he knew that deep within, Chantal was no milk-and-water Miss but a creature of fire and passion, of ideals and enthusiasms. He sensed that beneath the convent-bred meekness was a strength of character that would take her to the stake for her convictions as readily as Jeanne d'Arc. If there was weakness in her, it was due to her inexperience of life — and of men. Her childlike trust in humanity might prevent her from foreseeing the evils that encircled her.

No one would have been more surprised than Antoine to know that he was determined at all costs to protect her, not just from others who would seek to despoil her, but from himself. He no longer desired her seduction. He wanted to possess her for all time and to this end, he intended she should become his wife.

Antoine, self-styled Vicomte de Valle, was for the first time in his life in the grip of love. So disturbed was he by this unaccustomed emotion that it entirely escaped his mind that he was not free to marry. He, Antoine de Valle, already had a wife.

7

December 1837

CHANTAL'S cheeks were pink with pleasure as she and her friend Julia Lade sat in the privacy of her bedchamber.

The two girls were perched upon the edge of Chantal's bed, their pastel-colored muslin dresses spread around them, revealing glimpses of white silk stockings and dainty ribbon-sandals. In her excitement, Chantal had disarrayed her dark hair. Normally parted in the center and smoothed behind her ears, it now hung over her flushed face in a mass of ringlets. In her hand, she clutched a letter.

""'Tis four months since I left France!" she said to her companion, her eyes bright as they scanned the pages. "Yet Antoine still misses me! He says none of the females he encounters can hold his attention. Do you not find that astonishing, Julia?"

Julia nodded solemnly. A year younger than Chantal, she still had the round plump cheeks of childhood. Although her eyes were remarkable — a deep violet blue fringed with long curling lashes, she did not at once turn the heads of men as did Chantal.

The youngest of thirteen children, born late in her parents' middle age, Julia's life at home in Worthing could not bear comparison with

Chantal's carefree existence. She loved nothing better therefore, than to visit with Chantal. There was always some bright, amusing social event to enjoy with her friend; or distinguished visitors from the world of politics, art or literature to be met at Lady Waite's soirées and at Home's.

Chantal climbed down from the bed and knelt at Julia's feet, resting her chin on her friend's knees. Staring with wide open eyes, she said in hushed tones:

"There is something even more astonishing I have to tell you! Last night Mama called me to her room and informed me that now that I had reached my seventeenth year, I was old enough to know about my forbears!" Chantal's eyes widened still further with excitement. "Julia, Mama is not my Mama at all! My real mother came from Naples. Papa met her when he was fighting with the Carbonari. Papa, who was leading the revolt, was wounded in the unsuccessful uprising by these men. The young widow of one of the fighters nursed Papa back to health and . . . and because she was so beautiful and kind, Papa loved her!"

Chantal watched Julia's face for some sign of her reactions. She was by no means certain yet of her own. Her first feeling of dismay upon discovering that she was not the person she had always believed, had changed to excitement. Deep down within her, she had always felt different. Moreover she and her elder sister, Tamarisk, looked so unlike each other that the dissimilarity had oft been remarked upon. Now she understood why, for not only did they have different fathers but different mothers as well!

"My real mother died whilst Papa was taking us away from Naples to safety in northern Italy!" Chantal continued her story. "So you see, Julia, John is no more my brother than Tamarisk is my sister, and Papa is my only real relative!"

Julia's eyes were round with wonder. Yet she was not in the least surprised to hear that Chantal had such a strange, romantic background. Like Chantal herself, she had always believed her friend to be someone special.

Chantal tugged at Julia's hand.

"Do you understand all I have said, Julia?" she asked. "It means that I am born out of wedlock. Mama says I must not feel in any way disgraced, for my arrival upon this earth was an act of God and in no way my doing. She said I must be grateful to Papa for having proved himself so loving and devoted a father to me. Nevertheless Julia, the fact remains that Papa did not marry my real mother and Mama would not explain to me how they came to have me, a child, if they did not enjoy married love!"

"Perhaps children can be had by other means!" Julia said thoughtfully. "After all, Chantal, 'tis everywhere known that Lord Byron had a daughter by Claire Clairmont; and what of Horatia Hamilton? She had Lord Nelson for her father and the late Lady Hamilton as a mother."

The girls stared at one another questioningly.

"Tamarisk will be arriving in England soon!" Chantal said. "I will ask her to explain matters to me, Julia. After all, she has had four children so she should know exactly what occurs. I am certain she will tell me for it was she who answered all our questions that day we thought I was bleeding to death!"

Both girls giggled at the memory of their former ignorance, forgetting that they had been seriously frightened at the time by the unexpected onset of Chantal's womanhood.

With one of her quick changes of thought, Chantal put away the pages of Antoine's letter and pulling Julia to her feet, waltzed her friend around the room.

"Would it not be splendid, Julia, if we could one day have a double wedding — you to John and me to Antoine! What kind of wedding dress would you choose? I should like . . . "

The remainder of the morning passed in pleasurably romantic daydreams. Downstairs, trying to concentrate upon the day's edition of The *Times*, John was aware of his exclusion from their female companionship and resented Julia's monopoly of Chantal. He would have resented it still more had he heard the part he was designated to play in their plans, for nothing was further from his mind than marriage to Julia.

Sighing, he rang for one of the servants and sent the maid upstairs with a message to the two girls that he would take them riding in Hyde Park if they so desired. He knew that Chantal would not be able to resist such an outing for she enjoyed an hour or two's canter in Rotten Row as well as he did. As for the faithful Julia, he must resign himself to the fact that where Chantal went, she too would go.

John's sense of frustration increased as the weeks passed. Both Perry and Mavreen had forbidden him to speak to Chantal of his growing love for her and the enforced concealment of his true feelings was becoming ever more irksome. In one way he could understand his stepfather's reasoning. Chantal had only just left the seclusion of her convent school and had no experience of the adult world. Perry had felt she should be free to meet and enjoy the company of other young men before being asked at such a tender age to consider marriage to John whom she had known all her life.

"Give her one year at least, to explore the pleasures of growing up without ties or obligations!" he had reasoned with John. "On her eighteenth birthday, you may declare yourself if you so wish!"

His mother's reasons were far less acceptable. They were based on the belief that any sentiment between him and Chantal would be a continuation of the brother-sister affection they had always enjoyed.

"Fondness is not sufficient grounds for a happy marriage!" she insisted. "Love is essential, dearest John — the deep, passionate, all-consuming love of a man for a woman. You and Chantal are but children and have yet to discover the deeper vortex of emotion that can pale all other of life's experiences to insignificance."

How could he explain to his mother that a

passionate desire to possess Chantal was as great a facet of his love as his adoration of her? His mother seemed convinced that love itself was an appurtenance of mature men and women and could not be experienced by youth. Yet he could have argued with her that *she* had been but fifteen years of age when first she fell in love with his father, Gerard de Valle!

"You would soon forget this folly if you would but occupy your mind with other pursuits!" she said. "It is not good for you to be so often in Chantal's company."

It was Chantal herself who finally brought about his departure from the family home.

"I do not know what has overcome you these days, John!" she admonished him. "You used to be such excellent good company but nowadays your face is as long as a country-man's mile and you are forever glum and boorish. Why even Julia, who adores you, has commented upon your sullen conduct and your everlasting scowls!"

Hurt, mortified, yet knowing Chantal's accusations justified, John accepted an invitation from a schoolfellow to go grouse shooting in Scotland and he did not return until Christmas. By then, the family had repaired, as was their custom, to their country house, Finchcocks, for the festivities and he wished to see his half-sister, Tamarisk. She and her husband Charles and their four children were home on long leave from Malta where Charles had been stationed. John liked his brother-in-law and adored his young nephews and nieces.

Tamarisk quickly assessed the trite reasons for the tension within the family circle. Her mother, as always, was totally content in her relationship with Perry. But John and Chantal were ill at ease and it was not long before Tamarisk received their confidences. As she confessed to Charles, she was not a little concerned to discover the current state of affairs.

Charles, in middle age, had changed little from the young midshipman who had proposed to Tamarisk some twenty-three years previously. His sandy hair was only very slightly tinged with grey at the temples. His body remained strong and supple and only the lines about his mouth and eyes gave him the look of maturity required of a naval captain with all the attendant responsibilities.

He regarded his wife with his customary complacency. Tamarisk too, had changed little during the fifteen years of their marriage. Like her mother, she had retained her slim, lithe figure despite the birth of four children. She still enjoyed the healthy outdoor activities that kept her youthful, riding whenever the opportunity arose, taking long walks with the children and joining in their favorite sport of cricket.

Such was the steadfastness of his love for her that it encompassed all her relatives, and his devotion to Tamarisk's family was no less than hers. He considered himself happily married and only on the rarest of occasions did he regret that his wife failed to love him with the same passionate intensity as he loved her. But he never allowed such thoughts to undermine his conviction that he was the luckiest man in the world to have such a beautiful and intelligent companion.

He never forgot that she had endured unimaginable horrors at the hands of the dastardly Genoese merchant who had viciously raped her. He was unfailingly gentle and forbearing in his marital demands upon her. If it seemed as if she were permitting him the pleasures of her body from kindness rather than from need or passion, he put such thoughts firmly from him. He knew he had no cause for jealousy since she gave no encouragement to other men. As for her childhood adoration of Perry — that was a subject for talk and astonishment between them. Tamarisk professed that it was impossible for her to believe that she had ever been silly enough to suppose that Perry would interest himself in her whilst he had her Mama to love and cherish; and that her love for him had been no more than hero worship.

Charles listened patiently whilst Tamarisk told him of her anxieties. She was preparing for bed with the help of her devoted maid, Elsie, as she recounted the details of the family's visit to Compiègne and their reacquaintance with Antoine. When Elsie had departed, she climbed into bed beside Charles and informed him of Chantal's confession that she was secretly receiving letters from Antoine — letters expressing love and devotion.

"Chantal seems to find him unbelievably handsome and quite the most charming of men!" she sighed. "The first I can believe, for Antoine was a very beautiful little boy and could never have grown up to be other than a remarkable man. But charming . . . that is indeed less easy to imagine. Moreover Charles, I do not at all like their secret exchange of letters. Chantal herself is uneasy about the deception and would prefer to inform Mama and Perry if Antoine were not so set against it. I understand that he will be coming to England for the new Queen's coronation next year. I have told Chantal that she must not meet with Antoine behind Mama's back. I do not trust him, Charles — nor ever had occasion to do so in the past!"

"Perhaps Chantal will meet with someone else to engage her affections before he arrives!" Charles said comfortingly. "Young girls do not often remain steadfast at Chantal's age!"

"I think she is more attracted by the romantic notion of love than by the feeling of love itself!" Tamarisk commented shrewdly. "But that is not all my concern, my dear. I am much more seriously worried about our poor John. I think he genuinely loves Chantal and he is utterly miserable because he knows that she still looks upon him purely as a brother."

"Did you not tell me earlier that they are both now aware they are not related and could marry if they chose?" Charles asked, putting his arm around his wife's smooth white shoulders as she snuggled down beneath the warm coverlet beside him.

Tamarisk nodded.

"Chantal is still far too young to judge wisely

121

for her future!" she said. She looked fondly up at Charles, her green eyes gently teasing. "Why at her age I fancied myself in love with that feckless young actor, Leigh Darton. Do you recall him, Charles? And all the time you were patiently waiting for me to come to my senses!"

"And a long wait I had too!" Charles mocked, blowing out the bedside candle and preparing for sleep.

Beside him Tamarisk lay wakeful, her thoughts uneasy as she remembered John's unhappy face; and Chantal's ecstatic one as she confessed to her excitement in receiving yet another letter from Antoine.

"Beware, Chantal, lest it is the very secrecy of this correspondence which lends it so romantic an aura!" she had cautioned.

Chantal had flushed a deep pink, her eyes filling with indignation.

"Why is everyone against poor Antoine?" she asked rhetorically.

Not twenty-four hours later, she was asking John the same question. Antoine's name was raised during the evening meal when Mavreen recounted to Tamarisk some of the details of their visit to France. Without warning, John suddenly burst out in a low angry tone:

"Chantal was quite captivated by my half-brother's smooth charm and Frenchy manners! But then she is far too young to see through him, Tamarisk, as I am certain you would have done."

Chantal rushed to Antoine's defense.

"Could it be that I am less prejudiced than

you, John, or Mama? You choose to forget that he tried to prevent your discovery of past events in order to spare your feelings. He only revealed the facts when you and Mama forced the truth from him. Is that not so, Papa?"

Perry looked at his daughter's pink cheeks, saw the flash of anger in her dark eyes and felt a moment's misgiving. He did not want her to champion Antoine's cause for that might change a mere susceptibility to the young Frenchman's flattery into something more dangerous.

He tried to joke away the seriousness of the discussion, quickly changing the topic of conversation. Although Chantal was willing to let it drop momentarily, upon finding herself alone in the library with John later in the evening, she raised the subject again — but this time with a genuine desire for understanding.

"You know that I have always respected your opinions and your judgement, John!" she said. "Yet now I find myself in total discord with you over your half-brother. It seems so unfair that you should condemn a man whom you cannot prove guilty of any misdemeanor. If you could give me but one proof of Antoine's duplicity I would allow you your criticism of him without argument!"

John looked away from Chantal's questioning gaze, his eyes bitter as he said:

"I cannot give you proof, as you know very well. But one day I shall reveal my half-brother to you in his true light and you will know that I am right in my judgement of him."

Chantal tossed her head.

"Until then, John, allow me to keep my own opinion, for a man is surely innocent by our English law until be is proven guilty!"

"Chantal . . . " Her name, wrung from his lips, held such a note of anguish and longing that the girl forgot the argument in her curiosity.

"Is something wrong?" she prompted, her tone now gentle where a moment before it had been defiant. "You spoke so strangely, John. Is aught amiss?"

He made no move to touch her, for he dared not trust himself to keep from sweeping her into his arms and declaring the agony of his love for her. His sojourn in Scotland had in no way lessened his feelings but rather were they increased by absence. She seemed to him to have grown even prettier and more desirable whilst he had been away. He longed to cry out his love for her but his promise to his mother kept him silent. He turned away from the sight of her sweet, upturned face; from the temptation of those softly parted red lips; from the kindness in her dark eyes.

"'Tis but a wish that you were older!" he muttered.

At once the fire flashed back into Chantal's eyes.

"You think because I am two years younger than you that I am still a child!" she said crossly. "Well you are wrong, my dear John. Although you may see me as a child, there are others who see me as a woman; who find me desirable and enchanting and witty and amusing . . . "

Hurt beyond bearing, John broke in:

"Doubtless you refer to Antoine's opinion. Oh, I dare say he paid you many pretty compliments; that he found it quite diverting to amuse himself with an inexperienced schoolgirl. In a minute you will be boasting that he kissed you!"

It was the first serious quarrel they had ever had and Chantal was aghast. She stared at John wide-eyed.

"I do believe you are jealous!" she said. Suddenly her anger was gone and she felt strangely happy. Her mood changed, her eyes crinkled with mischievous laughter. "Confess the truth, dearest John. You do not want me to like or admire anyone but you! You are cross because I have admitted to finding another young man interesting and amusing."

"It is of no matter to me whatsoever!" John lied, flushing at the nearness of her guess. "It is your privilege to flirt with whom you please and no concern of mine!"

"Indeed!" Chantal retorted. "Then you will not object if I meet with Antoine when he comes to London next year for the Coronation? For he has promised to come . . . and to visit me."

Her words were a far greater shock to John than he permitted her to realize. Shrugging his shoulders with well-feigned casualness, he said:

"If Mama and Papa raise no objection, I have none. But do not expect me to receive him kindly for I have no liking for the fellow nor ever will have!"

"And that is both unfair and uncivil of you, John!" Chantal said. "I shall tell Julia that you are not half so nice a person as she and I always believed. I shall tell her on no account to consider marriage to such a bigot and a boor. And that reminds me, it was most unkind of you not to kiss her beneath the mistletoe when she called to wish us a merry Christmas. You know very well how happy it would have made her!"

John's face was now taut with anger and frustration.

"I will not be forced by you or anyone to attach myself to your adored Julia!" he said furiously. "It may amuse you both to treat me like some puppet on the end of a string to be manipulated for your joint amusement. But understand this, Chantal, I will kiss whom I please when I please and I will never, ever marry Julia even if I have to remain a bachelor for the rest of my life."

He had at last effectively silenced Chantal. She spoke no word as he turned away from her and walked out of the room On her face was a look of bewilderment coupled with dismay. John had not been joking. He had meant every word he said. Were Julia to know it, it would break her heart. For as long as Chantal could remember, she and Julia had planned her eventual marriage to John. They had never taken seriously his flirtation with blond, blue-eyed Miriam, for instance, who made no secret of her adoration of him; or with Joanne, who was pretty enough never to be at a loss for a dancing partner. Could he be interested in either of them she now wondered.

Chantal sighed. Growing up was not quite so

simple as she and Julia had supposed. Choosing a life partner looked as if it might prove a lot more perplexing than choosing a best friend at school.

It never occurred to Chantal that if John did not wish to marry Julia it might be because he wished to marry *her*. If she were to marry anybody, she had made up her mind it would be the handsome young Vicomte, Antoine de Valle.

8

June 1838

CHANTAL'S heart beat with an excitement so intense she was unable to remain still for an instant. Antoine was in London. This very morning a messenger had arrived bringing Mama and Papa a formal announcement of his arrival and a request that he might call upon them at Barre House at the earliest opportunity.

Mama had looked far from pleased.

"I suppose I cannot refuse to receive him since we are his only relatives!" she had said to Papa across the breakfast table.

"At least he is not expecting to reside with us!" John remarked scowling. "I suppose we should be grateful he is lodging at the Pulteney Hotel, though doubtless he is anticipating an invitation from us."

Chantal had last week received a letter from Antoine informing her of his intended visit, so the news came as no surprise to her. Holding her breath, she looked from one to the other of her family.

"Why not invite him to your dinner party tomorrow, m'dear?" Perry suggested to Mavreen. "With so many illustrious guests present he can not expect us to pay him much attention. Moreover we can seat him near the American

128

Ambassador. Antoine has lived in Andrew Stevenson's country and can engage him usefully in conversation about the New World."

"Very well, if you think it advisable!" Mavreen agreed, albeit reluctantly. "I suppose like everyone else Antoine has come to London for the Coronation and we must expect that he will remain here until after the event next week."

Only John noticed the sigh of relief Chantal permitted herself. He noted too her heightened color and his heartstrings tightened. He had always decried jealousy as an ugly trait and he fought hard against giving way to it. But try though he did to subdue his resentment, the fact remained that it hurt him whenever he saw Chantal so much as smile at another young man. To observe her waltzing in the arms of an admirer was such intolerable pain that whenever possible, he declined invitations to the many parties Chantal and Julia attended. He knew that Chantal was puzzled by his anti-social behavior and she openly accused him of turning into a dull, boorish individual lacking all charm.

"You were such good company once!" she reproached him sadly. "Now you do nothing but scowl at me and you seldom escort Julia or me anywhere as was your wont. Were it not for Tamarisk, we would have no chaperone to take us abroad to parties. You have become most selfish, preferring to read your dull old books in the library to being with us."

Perry, knowing very well the reason for John's churlish behavior, pleaded with Mavreen to permit the boy to declare himself.

"'Twould be far better for all concerned if Chantal knew the truth!" he said. "I am convinced that she would not take a proposal of marriage from John seriously. Were she to refuse him, he would have to turn his thoughts elsewhere."

Mavreen regarded her husband curiously.

"I thought you were not against an eventual marriage between them?" she said.

"Which indeed I am not!" Perry replied. "But the secrecy you have imposed upon John is hardly fair either to him or to Chantal. She is growing to resent if not dislike John without just cause. Let him declare himself! Even were Chantal to accept him, we can impose a year or two's engagement before they marry if you feel they are too young to be certain of themselves."

Mavreen sighed.

"I am anxious that neither of our children should make the mistake of marrying without love!" she said. She smiled suddenly and putting her arms around Perry, hugged him to her. "Perhaps I am prejudiced concerning love!" she said softly. "Many marry without it and live contentedly enough. But you have shown me how perfect marriage can be if one has the right partner. I want no less happiness for our children, my darling."

"Let us trust to their instincts!" Perry suggested. "I do not think Chantal is romantically inclined towards John as yet. Were he to turn his attentions elsewhere, she might well begin to see him in a different light."

"Very true!" Mavreen agreed. "But let him wait until after the hubbub of the Coronation celebrations. Their lives can continue calmly until then."

Chantal however, was far from calm. She was laughing excitedly as she twirled herself around to the exasperation of the young maid, Dorothy. The girl was attempting to fasten the tiny buttons of her white foulard gown which was painted with delicate clusters of lavender sprigs and tied with ribbons. Matching ribbons decorated the shoulders of the dress and her dark hair.

Julia felt obliged to whisper a caution.

"Your Mama will guess that something is afoot!" she warned. "Do try to stop fidgeting, Chantal. And stop . . . stop glowing!"

"I cannot be still!" Chantal admitted. "How could I, dearest Julia, with *you-know-who* coming to Mama's ball! I shall see him in less than an hour's time!"

When both girls' toilettes were completed to Dorothy's satisfaction, grasping Julia's hand, Chantal led her along the upper landing to the head of the staircase and they gazed down at the guests arriving in the hall below.

Chantal's eyes searched for one figure only — that of the fair-haired young Vicomte. But Julia, blue eyes wide with interest, stared in fascination at the famous personages whom she was to have the honor of meeting.

"There is the Duke of Wellington!" she gasped to Chantal, espying the slightly bowed

131

but still soldierly figure of the Field Marshall in his splendid dress uniform, bedecked with jeweled sash, brilliantly-colored cummerbund and elegant dress sword. The high gold collar exaggerated the prominence of his eagle-like features.

Chantal nodded. She was not particularly interested in the Iron Duke whom she had met before.

Julia sighed, by no means for the first time envying Chantal her exciting life. Aunt Mavreen, she considered, was as different from her own conventional, matronly mother as was she herself from the sparkling Chantal. According to Julia's mama, Aunt Mavreen was a law unto herself. She had always disregarded the prevailing fashion and instead created her own. Because she was so delightfully different Society often ended up copying her ways and modes. Not for Lady Waite the strictures of social convention. She made her friends where she pleased, inviting to her home those she found amusing, unusual, clever, quite regardless of their standing. In her circle, aristocrats mingled with artists, politicians, musicians, poets, playwrights, soldiers and professional men less socially acceptable but whom she deemed interesting.

"I think Aunt Mavreen succeeds so well in flaunting convention because her unusual guests are *never* dull or boring!" Mistress Lade had commented shrewdly. "She herself is very well connected — and rich and beautiful enough for those with more snobbish regard for class distinctions to hesitate to criticize her. At all events, invitations from Lady Waite are seldom refused and more often are greatly coveted."

True to her reputation, Mavreen's guest list this evening was as varied and unconventional as could be conceived. Because she herself loved music, she had invited the young Hungarian, Franz Liszt and his friend and contemporary, the Polish composer, Frederic Chopin. She had encountered the latter at a musical soirée which he had attended with Baronne Dudevant, the notorious novelist who had taken the *nom de plume* of George Sand. Mavreen had been immediately interested in the younger woman who had confided that two years previously, she had fallen in love with the young Polish composer. When she confessed that the rumor was true that she often chose to wear men's clothing, Mavreen admitted that there had been occasions in her youth when she, too, had gone disguised as a man. But she made no mention of the fact that such occasions had been part of a secret life she had once led with Perry, making sorties with him upon the highways of Sussex in the days when he had amused himself by assuming the role of a gentleman of the road. Were Perry's former exploits ever to become known, his very life could be forfeit, since he was wanted by the Law as the highwayman, Gideon Morris.

Chantal however had no interest in the arrival of any of her mama's friends, for the great doors of Barre House had opened yet again and there at last in the hall below stood the slim, elegant young man she had been so longing to see, Antoine de Valle. As she gazed down at him, her heart beat suffocatingly. He seemed to her to be more handsome even than she remembered from the previous summer.

Formally attired in a dark blue kerseymere tail-coat over tightly fitting matching trousers, Antoine de Valle looked perfectly proportioned and even taller than the six feet he boasted. His velvet waistcoat, shot with silver, red, and blue, was very much *à la mode* as were the trousers which were short enough to reveal shapely stockinged legs and beribboned evening pumps.

Chantal grasped Julia's arm.

"That is *he!*" she whispered. "Oh, Julia, do you not agree with me that he is the *most* handsome man you ever saw?"

The girl beside her nodded silently. The Frenchman's good looks were undeniable. Even her beloved John could not compare in comeliness with this fair-haired foreigner. How different the two young men were in appearance, she thought, for all they were half-brothers with the same father.

"We must go down at once," Chantal said urgently, smoothing her skirts and lifting her head in an attempt to compose herself. "I do not want to miss one moment of this magical evening."

But as the girls slowly descended the wide staircase, some of Chantal's carefully assumed composure deserted her. She clutched Julia's arm nervously.

"Do you think Antoine will still find me pretty?" she asked. "I think I should die if he was disappointed in me!"

"Fiddlesticks, Chantal!" Julia replied fiercely. "How could he be disappointed. I have never seen you look more radiantly beautiful!"

Entering the huge salon arm in arm with her less comely friend, Chantal drew the admiring gaze not only of the man she hoped to fascinate, but of John too. His heart somersaulted as he caught sight of her and in that single moment of time, he knew that he would never love another as he loved this young girl, that he could never marry another. No matter what befell, he thought, he must openly defy his mother's wishes with regard to Chantal. He could no longer bear to keep silent as to his intentions towards her. He *must* declare himself — even if his proposal were to prove unwelcome. It could not harm Chantal to know of his love for her and at least she might begin to regard him as other than a surly brother!

He moved forward with the intention of joining the two young girls. But before he could reach them, a man stepped out of the throng of people surrounding them, and whilst John was still some yards distant, approached Chantal and bowed low over her hand.

Even without seeing the man's face, John recognized his half-brother. There was no mistaking the pale blond hair or the innate physical grace with which the Frenchman moved. Momentarily John had forgotten that Antoine de Valle was to be present at tonight's dinner

135

party. Now his resentment returned in full. Rooted to the spot he watched whilst Chantal presented the newcomer to Julia.

Her cheeks pink, Chantal's eyes were sparkling with unmistakable pleasure. John could not hear above the hubbub of conversation in the room the fulsome compliment Antoine had just paid Chantal, but he could see her blushes, the sudden shy droop of her lashes and he guessed accurately that the man had been flattering her.

His mouth tightening defiantly, John walked over to them. Antoine bowed, his eyes narrowing imperceptibly as he recognized the younger man.

With apparent affection he said:

"So I have the pleasure of renewing your acquaintance too, my dear brother! I was but this very minute telling Mademoiselle Julia what happy memories I have of your visit with your sister to my home last summer!"

John's expression changed to an angry scowl as his eyes met Antoine's mocking stare. "*My home!*" Antoine had said as if to remind John that he was the rightful heir. "*Your sister,*" when Chantal was no such relation. "*Happy memories!*" They were very far from happy for him, John thought, as he made the most cursory of bows good manners would allow.

"I do so wish I too could have visited Compiègne!" Julia broke in. She was aware of the undercurrent of emotion between her three companions and hoped to bridge the silence that had befallen. She sensed John's silent

136

anger and hoped for his sake that he would not show himself in too unfavorable a light on this occasion. The wish was totally unselfish. Her quiet observant eyes had noted these past months how John had looked at Chantal and she had been forced to realize that the man she had hoped one day would love her had fallen under Chantal's spell.

Julia was saddened — but not in the least surprised. Not only did everyone love Chantal, herself included, but her friend had blossomed from awkward, angular schoolgirl into a beautiful, exciting young woman in the year since they had left the Convent. Chantal's was no delicate, dreamy, reposeful beauty. She had the fiery, colorful exciting loveliness that bespoke her Latin origins. She stood apart from the pink-and-white complexioned English girls who were her contemporaries. Judging by the eager queue of young men always awaiting the opportunity to dance with her or sit next to her, it was obvious they admired Chantal's unusual beauty no less than did her female friends.

Until this meeting with Antoine de Valle, Julia had questioned how Chantal could find any man more handsome and attractive that John. But five minutes in the Frenchman's company were enough to answer her puzzlement. The young Vicomte was as comely as Michelangelo's David. His features were chiseled with perfect symmetry, the extraordinary dark eyes set wide apart, the nose neither too long nor too short, the mouth softly curved yet somehow determined in expression as if seeking to belie any hint of weakness.

In figure too he was perfectly proportioned, shoulders wide yet not burly; hips and legs slim and shapely. If there were any single fault in such perfection, Julia pondered, it lay in his hands. Though exquisitely tapered, the white beringed fingers ended in nails that had been so sadly bitten that not even the most careful of manicures could conceal this unfortunate habit. But this tiny imperfection was quickly over-looked, discounted by the Frenchman's charming looks, his perfect manners and amusing conversation.

Mavreen had seated Antoine between two beautiful women at the dinner table. From Chantal's placing at the opposite end of the huge table, it seemed to her that both women were as susceptible to Antoine's charm as Julia had been.

Chantal tried not to feel jealous and it was with great relief she saw Antoine's dark eyes continually turning to her. It seemed he was smiling at her in secret intimacy, perhaps reminding her of the letters they had exchanged.

Across the vast candlelit table, the hum of conversation mingled with the gentle clatter of silver knives and forks upon the Sèvres plates. The glittering assembly, well used to the delicacies of the rich man's table, paid little attention to the innumerable extravagant dishes served by the liveried footmen. It was Mavreen's policy to have one servant behind every chair so that no guest was kept waiting for

138

wine or food nor had his conversation disturbed by ill-attendance to his needs.

Glancing down the length of the table Mavreen could see the two great Field Marshals, Wellington and Soult, arguing animatedly. Her dear old friend, Mary Wordsworth, seated between them, seemed to be enjoying their discussion, she thought with her usual concern for her guests' pleasure. Her eyes moved slowly round the table. There were plenty of interesting men to keep the ladies amused — politicians such as the up and coming Tory, William Gladstone; the fiery young Benjamin Disraeli; Henry Brougham, that tireless law reformer; and Perry's good friend, Lord John Russell, Leader of the House of Commons and Home Secretary.

Those ladies not interested in politics, she had placed beside men of different concerns — the author and poet, William Wordsworth; the promising new young writer, Charles Dickens, who was already making a name for himself in the literary world, and that equally interesting French playwright, Alexandre Dumas who was a protégé of his King, Louis Phillipe. And to add variety to her guest list, she had invited the engineer Marc Brunel and his son, Isambard. She herself, particularly admired Marc Brunel for the brilliant inventions which had enabled him to achieve recognition and climb above his lowly origins. Mavreen was not surprised to see Tamarisk listening with interest to his conversation nor was she surprised by the man's obvious pleasure in his table companion.

Her daughter had no cause to question her

comeliness, Mavreen thought with pride. In the candlelight Tamarisk could pass for a girl of twenty. Her fair hair curled softly about her face, which despite her age, was quite unlined, unlike that of Madame Dudevant, Mavreen reflected. It was interesting to ponder why one woman aged and another retained her youth. Was happiness the key to youth, she wondered? For Tamarisk was perfectly content, married to her doting Charles. Her life as a naval officer's wife was too varied to be dull and she enjoyed the years she had spent in Gibraltar and Malta. In another month she would be on her way with Charles to India — a posting which would have delighted both of them entirely but for the fact that they must leave their young children behind under Mavreen's guardianship. The Far Eastern climate was not suitable for them at their ages.

Mavreen's face broke into a secret smile as she considered herself as a 'grandmother.' Her darling Perry would have none of it when she told him that it was more than high time she assumed her allotted rôle.

"You are no older in looks or spirit than on the day I first set eyes upon you!" he insisted whenever she made mention of her advancing years. "You are as beautiful, as desirable, as fascinating now as ever you were then. And you do not have to take my word for it, my love. You cannot be blind to the way in which men's heads turn to take a second glance when you enter a room. Were I unaware of the faithful love you bear me, I would be most heartily jealous of your many admirers!"

Mavreen sighed in quiet satisfaction remembering Perry's compliment this very evening.

"With so many of your would-be lovers in attendance tonight," he had vouchsafed, "I shall feel obliged not to allow you out of my sight. You look ravishing, my dearest, and I would lay no blame were one of them to overstep the bounds of propriety!"

Her glance went to one of the 'would-be lovers' to whom her adored, ridiculous Perry had referred. The Prince Esterházy de Galántha was the Austrian Ambassador in London. Now forty-two he was a man even richer than herself, with family estates that included twenty-nine lordships with twenty-one castles, sixty market towns, four hundred and fourteen villages in Hungary besides titles in Austria and a county in Bavaria. Always outrageously dressed, he tended to display his extreme wealth in his attire. He was erudite and amusing; and despite the ten years disparity in their ages, flirted harmlessly but quite openly with his 'Firebird,' as he chose to call Mavreen. She was never quite certain whether to believe him when he insisted that the liabilities of his vast estates were such that he had only a modest yearly income upon which to survive.

But her glance did not linger long upon her admirer for at the opposite end of the table sat the only lover she desired — her beloved Perry. On his right hand sat Mary Shelley, widow of his dear friend, Percy. Both Perry and Mavreen admired this woman deeply for her

141

energy. Despite time taken by her own writings, she was currently editing four volumes of her husband's work.

Fate was a strange thing, Mavreen mused. Perry had once lent the late poet some money. As a result, he had been asked to be godfather to one of Percy's children. The death of that boy in Italy had been the deciding factor that made Perry leave England to visit the bereaved Shelleys and at the same time, make a final break with her. In those days, her marriage to Gerard de Valle was uneasy; and her husband was violently jealous of the fact that Perry had once been her lover. At the same time, Tamarisk, then a girl in her teens, had believed herself in love with Perry. When he went to Italy, Tamarisk had disappeared on a wild escapade in search of him and in so doing, nearly lost her own life at the hands of a Genoese rapist.

Her daughter's terrible experiences were all long in the past; yet even now Mavreen sometimes wondered whether, if Tamarisk had not undergone that frightening experience, she would ever have married the quiet, unexciting but ever faithful Charles. She doubted if the marriage was founded on the same passionate basis that had swept her and Perry into each other's arms. In fact she doubted if Tamarisk had ever given way to that delirium of the senses which could drive men and women to such heights and depths of emotion. Her daughter was always calm and controlled. Instinct told Mavreen that Tamarisk was capable of great passion, yet she seemed perfectly content with a marriage that appeared more of the mind than of the body.

Mavreen's eyes turned again to Perry. How lucky she was to have a husband who satisfied her physically as well as emotionally and intellectually, she thought. How right he had been when all those years ago he had warned her that she could never fulfill herself with Gerard; that Gerard was not a child of nature, as were they. The inhibitions, reserves and traditions of Gerard's heritage had indeed formed a barrier which did not exist between her and Perry.

Her eyes turned finally to Gerard's eldest son. Try though she might, she could find no pleasure in Antoine's presence in her household, nor ever had. Coldly she could admit that in appearance, no young man could be a greater credit to his father. He assumed the rôle of Vicomte de Valle with all the appearances of nobility. Yet she could not convince herself that Antoine was noble in character. She would never trust him, although there were no real grounds for mistrust. Only a primitive instinct prompted her misgivings and strong though this was, she could not justifiably reject Antoine on so little evidence. As for John's dislike of his half-brother, this might well be equally unfounded, as Perry suggested, and be based on jealousy of Chantal's admiration for Antoine.

That same primitive instinct which made her keep Gerard's son at arm's length, now warned her that she could not much longer prevent John from openly declaring his love for Perry's daughter. Although she had told Perry that she wished to protect Chantal from choosing a life partner before she was old enough to judge her needs, this was not the only reason which dictated her unwillingness for John to propose marriage to the girl. She sensed that Chantal did not hold any feelings of romantic love for him, and loving John so deeply herself, she desired to protect him from hurt.

Had Mavreen known of the letters that had passed between Chantal and Antoine and with what pleasure and excitement the girl received these missives, she would have realized her instincts were well justified. John, himself, was far from unaware of the situation as he noted how frequently Antoine and Chantal were exchanging glances and smiles. He could be in no doubt as to Chantal's feelings and Antoine was scarcely troubling to conceal *his*. Not even the fascinating conversation flowing freely around John could subdue the bitter thoughts that raged in his tortured mind.

Matters did not improve as the evening wore on. During the musical interlude when Franz Liszt played several of his compositions, Antoine managed to seat himself beside Chantal and from time to time, John could see their hands touching. Occasionally Antoine bent his head and whispered in Chantal's ear.

Antoine de Valle was not, as John rightly supposed, commenting upon the beauty of one of Monsieur Liszt's new Études. With an urgency that was quite contrary to his usual dispassionate attitude to women, he was urging Chantal to agree to a secret assignation at his hotel on the following day.

"Bring with you your friend, Mademoiselle Julia, if you must!" he whispered. "But I *have* to see you alone, Chantal. If you but knew how often I have thought of you these past months, longed to be near you! It is nearly a year since I last saw you and I have been desolate without you. Now that I am once again in your presence, I am even more deeply enslaved by your beauty. Have you no heart, *ma belle* Chantal? Do you care nothing for me?"

For once in his life, Antoine was telling the truth and the conviction of his tone assured Chantal of his sincerity. She wondered if it was his intention to declare himself at this proposed secret meeting and the possibility both excited and frightened her. If he were to ask her to marry him, she was unsure what reply she would give. To leave England, marry Antoine de Valle, perhaps against her parents' wishes — and most certainly against John's — was too big a step to contemplate lightly and would need careful consideration.

Antoine's letters had given no hint of marriage. Indeed the word love had not so far passed between them. Events were moving too swiftly for her comprehension. Yet if it were not his intention to ask her to marry him, what other reason had be to demand so passionately to see her alone? She could not believe that he would ask her to meet him for a dishonorable purpose.

Chantal's cheeks flushed at the thought. True to her promise to Julia, she had asked

Tamarisk to tell her how children could be begotten outside of marriage. And Tamarisk had explained that men and women did perform the act of love without the blessing of Holy Matrimony, warning Chantal of the temptations of passion and repeating Mama's caution to preserve her virginity for her future husband.

"If a man truly loves you, Chantal," Tamarisk had ended her discourse, "he will not offer you less than marriage. And if you truly love him, you will want to marry him."

Yet now on this first occasion when she could put such a yardstick to the test, she was not sure if Antoine did truly love her; and more importantly, whether she loved him! Yet she was sure that she *must* do so. Why else should her heart beat so suffocatingly whenever he touched her? It seemed to lurch inside her breast and she trembled each time he smiled at her.

"Will you not call upon me here at Barre House?" she pleaded for the second time. "I am certain I could persuade Papa to permit you to call even if Mama and John are against it."

Antoine's lips tightened, but he restrained his anger and said softly:

"Your Papa will of a certainty do as your Mama wishes. Have courage, *ma petite*! You know that you can trust me. I swear that you will come to no harm, that no breath of scandal shall touch your reputation. I will tell them at the hotel that you are my sister. It is not so far from the truth since your Mama was once my stepmother!"

146

Later he furthered his persuasions.

"Consider the alternative!" he said. "I must call here at your house perhaps to be scorned, humiliated and worse still, refused the opportunity to see you. If we are forbidden openly to see one another, then my heart would break!"

Hers too, Chantal thought! Antoine was justified in desiring a secret tryst. Were he openly to declare his love and if she decided to accept a proposal of marriage, this would be the time to do battle with her family. Then, once her mind was made up, it would be for Mama and John to realize that Antoine's intentions were entirely honorable. Unless they could discover an impediment to the marriage, then she would be ready to defy them.

But first she must decide if this was the man she wished ultimately to marry. She must decide if she really loved him or merely found him fascinating. Only this morning she had eagerly accepted Tamarisk's invitation to accompany her and Charles to India. If she were truly in love, why then was she not regretting a commitment that would separate her from Antoine for two whole years?

If she could only be certain how one recognized love, she thought, as the concluding bars of the Étude in B Minor drifted across the room. Mama had always maintained that when Cupid's dart found its true target, she would know it instantly.

Why then, was she still unsure?

9

June 1838

OUTSIDE the front door of the Pulteney Hotel the two girls paused. Now that the moment had come, both were equally dubious as to the wisdom of this adventure.

They had left Barre House on foot not ten minutes since, professing an innocent desire to purchase a sheet of music from one of the many new shops lining the streets in Piccadilly. As was customary, Mavreen had instructed one of the footmen to accompany them to carry their packages; but once out of sight of home, Chantal had dispatched the man upon an errand to Regent Street with instructions to call for them at Aubert and Company, the watchmakers, in an hour's time.

Mavreen was not surprised at their desire to walk, for driving a carriage in Piccadilly was far from easy these days. The road had become hopelessly congested since the opening of so many shops. Many of them had carriages and handcarts which plied to and fro in the street outside advertising their wares.

"'Tis nearly noon!" Chantal commented, regarding the little enamel fob watch attached to her promenade dress. "Antoine will suspect that I am not after all keeping my promise to meet with him."

Julia sighed, her round, childish face creasing with anxiety. She tried not to think of Aunt Mavreen's wrath if she discovered they were keeping a secret assignation with the Frenchman.

"Perhaps it would be best if . . . " she began, but Chantal interrupted her, her dark eyes taking on an expression of determination.

"I intend to keep my promise!" she said, and taking Julia's arm firmly in her own, walked through the doors of the hotel before her resolve could weaken.

Chantal felt an immense relief when she caught sight of Antoine standing by one of the marble pillars in the hall, for it had crossed her mind that he might have given up waiting for her and gone elsewhere. Only with difficulty did she restrain herself from running towards him.

As always Antoine presented an impeccable appearance. His violet sateen trousers were strapped beneath the instep so that they were perfectly unwrinkled. Over the pale mauve frilled shirt, he wore a single breasted tail-coat with close fitting sleeves, the collar and cuffs edged in velvet. His silk cravat was fastened with a pearl tie pin. In one hand he held pale pink doeskin gloves and an ivory topped malacca cane.

Smiling his strange beautiful smile, he bowed low over Chantal's hand, inclined his head to Julia, and for the benefit of the manager of the hotel he said in a raised voice:

"My dear sister — and Cousin Julia! How good of you both to call! I have refreshments awaiting in my rooms. Would you care to accompany me upstairs?"

149

So with practiced ease, he made their daring escapade to his private apartment sound perfectly respectable and both girls were less nervous as they preceded him up the wide staircase. Antoine put them further at their ease by speaking smoothly and easily about the preparations the hotel was making for the coming celebrations on Coronation Day. Still apprehensive, Julia was relieved to note that neither the footmen nor the page-boys appeared in the least surprised to see two young ladies ascending the staircase with a man and without a chaperone in attendance. She had spent a wakeful night wondering what Chantal's Mama and Papa and John would say if they knew what had been planned for the morrow, for she feared above all the withdrawal of their affection for her. Had the decision been hers, she and Chantal would not be here.

Antoine had taken a pleasant sunny suite of rooms overlooking Green Park for the duration of his sojourn in London.

"I fear they do not have quite the same elegance as one enjoys in one's own home!" he apologized, indicating a sofa where they might be seated. "But now that they are transformed by your presence, Mesdemoiselles, I can no longer find fault with them!"

The two girls accepted the glass of Madeira wine Antoine offered them. Tactfully Julia went to sit by the window, leaving Chantal and the Vicomte in comparative privacy. Charmed by Chantal's ill-concealed nervousness at what she clearly considered was wicked behavior, Antoine sought to put her at ease.

With a gentleness he would have employed with a nervous filly, he removed her glass of wine and replaced it on the table. Then he sat down beside her upon the brocade sofa and took both her hands in his.

"We may not have much time alone together!" he said in a low urgent voice. "So you must try to forgive me, my sweet Chantal, if I appear too hasty in what I have to say."

He raised one of the small gloved hands and turning back the lace cuff of her sleeve, pressed his lips upon her warm, smooth skin.

"Last evening at your house," he continued, watching the flutter of her eyelashes with renewed delight at her shy innocence, "there was no opportunity for me to speak of the many passionate concerns that have consumed my heart and mind this past year. I dared not write of them in my letters to you lest you should misconstrue my meaning and determine that our correspondence should cease."

He observed the heightened color in her cheeks and encouraged by the knowledge of her physical awareness of him, be proceeded with confidence:

"You cannot be unaware of my sentiments, my lovely Chantal. Before I first set eyes upon you, I had no thought of love. I believed such passions were for other mortals and that they would pass me by. Now I know why I have never before truly loved a woman. It is because I was waiting for you. Believe me, Chantal, for I am speaking the truth that is in my heart. *Je t'aime! Je t'adore!* I want you for my wife."

His declaration, whilst not entirely unexpected, nevertheless unnerved Chantal by the very intensity of feeling with which it was made. His sincerity was not in doubt, and she felt she owed him as honest a reply as she could formulate in the light of her confused emotions.

"I am honored by your proposal!" she said. "But I fear I cannot be as certain of my feelings as you profess to be of yours. I do not know if I wish to marry you, Antoine. I think I do love you but . . . "

"But you have not known me long enough to be sure," Antoine finished the sentence for her. He was far from disappointed by her reply. At least she had not refused him so he had every reason for hope.

"I am the first to appreciate that neither of us has had the opportunity to learn of our compatibilities," he added reassuringly. "But would you not agree, my lovely Chantal, that this is one very good reason why we should enter into a formal betrothal? If you will seriously consider marriage to me, we can obtain your parents' approval. This would ensure that future meetings between us could be as frequent as we desire. If after all you concluded that you did not care sufficiently to become my wife, it would be a simple matter for our engagement to be broken, would it not? But I believe you will learn to love me, *ma bien aimée* — even if you care nothing for me now."

"I do care . . . I care very much!" Chantal cried. "But marriage is a most serious undertaking and I cannot be sure my affection for you is akin to the love a woman should feel for her future husband."

With a swift glance at Julia to make certain that he could not be overheard, Antoine lent closer to Chantal. His voice was low and vibrant as he murmured:

"You are too young and innocent to be the judge of passion! But I could arouse you to such transports of delight and pleasure you would not doubt your feelings for me."

Chantal trembled as she felt the pressure of his hands on hers. Strange sensations were coursing through her body and her heartbeat quickened even faster as she felt his lips brush her cheek. Were it not for the presence of Julia, she knew that she might have succumbed to the strange desire within her and permitted him to kiss her mouth.

Her companion watched the flutter of her eyelashes as her taut young breasts rose and fell in agitation. With apparent nonchalance he let his fingers trace the curve of her soft arm and sensed the passion dormant within that virgin body. Seduction would be no hard task, he thought grimly. This girl was ready for love even if she were as yet unconscious of it. But this was neither the time nor the place even were he himself to wish her submission. It was a matter of amazement to him that in point of fact he would not have taken her in lust even were she to desire it. He wanted the surrender, total and absolute, of her spirit as well as her body. He wanted her love.

"We must be leaving!" Chantal said with a

sudden anxious glance at her timepiece. She looked at Antoine with renewed uncertainty.

"Can you not call upon me at Barre House?" she pleaded. "I am sure you are mistaken in thinking that Mama and Papa will not be happy to receive you. Were they to know how . . . how you feel . . . how I feel . . . " She stumbled over her words but then continued: "My parents could not find fault with the honor you have paid me in proposing marriage!"

Mistaking his cynicism for lack of confidence in himself, she smiled at the expression on Antoine's face.

"You do most surely underestimate yourself, sir!" she said. "I am convinced they would welcome so eligible a suitor!"

Releasing her hands Antoine stood up, his face now inscrutable as he said quietly:

"'Tis you, *ma petite* Chantal, who underestimate their resentment of my very existence. 'Tis natural, after all, that Lady Waite should feel bitter about the accident of birth that gave me rather than her son the right to my father's title. And were that not sufficient to ensure her antagonism towards me, she must resent even more bitterly my father's marriage to my mother which invalidated her own."

Chantal drew a deep sigh as she accepted the logic of Antoine's reasoning.

"Nevertheless," she argued, "Papa has no reason to blame you for something which was not your doing. And Papa has great influence with Mama. Will you not permit me to tell him of your desire to call upon me and of my wish

154

that you should do so? He cannot refuse us the opportunity to become better acquainted, for surely he will wish me to be certain of my feelings for you before we enter upon a betrothal!"

It was on the tip of Antoine's tongue to remark that he had little love for Sir Peregrine Waite, the man who had humiliated and chastised him nearly twenty years ago and upon whom he had sworn to be revenged. For the sake of winning Chantal's hand in marriage, he was now prepared to forego that revenge but he abhorred the prospect of having to go cap in hand to beg favors from him. Antoine was convinced that Sir Peregrine too, remembered that childhood incident. Might he not now regard him as the erstwhile pickpocket who wished to steal his daughter from him? Moreover he doted upon his only child and would scarce wish to see her married to a Frenchman who would take her to a foreign country far from his loving protection.

Doubtful although he was of the outcome, Antoine nevertheless said:

"Very well, if it is your wish, Chantal, then speak to your father! But for the time being, it might be best to make no mention of marriage knowing he would consider my proposal unreasonably hasty. If we were to admit to our closer acquaintance, he might condemn us for the secrecy we have enjoyed!"

Chantal nodded understandingly.

"Have no fear, Antoine!" she said softly. "I will keep our secret. And I will do everything possible to persuade Papa to make

155

you welcome. I will be so happy if you are permitted to call upon me. We can enjoy so many things together. I will show you the garden for it is quite a picture now with the roses in full bloom. And I will show you my paintings and play to you upon the pianoforte if you would care to listen and . . . "

She broke off as Julia came across the room to stand beside her.

"'Tis growing late, Chantal!" she said anxiously.

"Dearest Julia! We have neglected you quite shamefully!" Chantal cried, hugging her friend excitedly. "But to a good purpose, I assure you. I am to speak to Papa this very afternoon and obtain his permission for Antoine to call upon me as often as he wishes. So hopefully there will be no more clandestine meetings, and you will not again have to act against your conscience."

Unwilling to pour cold water on Chantal's happiness, Julia forebore to express her own reactions to this excited announcement. Like Antoine, she too doubted that Chantal's parents would make him welcome. Julia knew from Chantal that Antoine's existence had now been proved to render poor John illegitimate and she could not believe that the family would place their loyalties anywhere but with John. She herself had felt unhappily disloyal in abetting Chantal's involvement with Antoine. Now with this new turn of events, she could relinquish her rôle and the responsibility that went with it.

"Come, Chantal!" she said with a sigh of relief. "It is high time we returned home."

It was Antoine's assumption that in the

156

absence of the Barre footman, he would accompany the two young ladies to their front door. Chantal however declined his offer to escort them.

"We have but a very short distance to go," she said, "and to be frank, sir, I fear that Mama or Papa might look from a window and deduce that Julia and I had not after all been upon a shopping expedition!"

"Then I will call a carriage for you!" Antoine said determinedly for he was well aware of the impropriety of two young girls walking unchaperoned in the streets of London, albeit fashionable Piccadilly.

"Perhaps that would be for the best!" Julia vouchsafed nervously. But Chantal laughed.

"'Tis broad daylight and we cannot possibly be in any danger," she said, "lest it be that of meeting an acquaintance who might report us to Mama. We will keep our heads discreetly lowered so we are not recognized."

But rightly, Antoine would have none of it and accompanying them to the door of the hotel, hailed a passing cabman.

Julia gave a sigh of relief as their driver — an elderly, white-haired, hunch-backed old fellow — urged his equally decrepit old horse in the direction of Barre House.

But her relief was short-lived. Behind them sounded the urgent clanging of fire bells. Along with the other carriages and carts, their driver urged his horse to the side of the road as pedestrians stopped to stare at the approaching fire engine.

As Chantal peered curiously from the window, the big red contraption drawn by four huge horses came racing towards them, the firemen in their helmets ringing the brass bells to warn those ahead of their approach.

Despite its weariness and age, the old nag pricked up its ears nervously as the noisy engine approached and edged away from the pavement as the crowd fought to get closer to the road for a better view. Accustomed though the animal was to the London streets, the din and the press of people were too much for it. As the engine sped past on its urgent mission, the horse plunged forward after it, its terror lending it a strength beyond the control of its elderly driver. Helplessly, the old man hauled on the reins but to no avail.

Inside the cab, the two girls were flung from side to side as they clung to one another in fear and excitement. They fully expected that at any moment the old cabby would be toppled from his driving seat. It was fortunate that the fire towards which the engine was heading was not too far distant since the old nag was bent upon following the galloping horses in front of it. It came to a halt outside a warehouse in Blackfriars. Its coat was steaming with perspiration, its chest heaving and its legs trembling as the cabby stumbled down from his seat to hold its head.

Julia was near to tears but Chantal's cheeks were pink with excitement as she, too, alighted.

"Come quickly, Julia!" she urged her friend. "The firemen are unrolling the hoses."

She stared in horrified wonder at the blazing warehouse where men, women and children stood in a chain passing buckets of water from one to the other in a hopeless attempt to douse the fire. The narrow street was filled with smoke. A second fire engine arrived from the opposite direction and the firemen lowered their hoses into the river.

It was a half hour before the fire seemed under control, by which time Chantal — and a less eager Julia — had mingled with the watching crowds. When at last they turned away to look for their carriage, it was to discover the old man and his horse had disappeared.

"Oh, Chantal, what will become of us now!" Julia cried, close to tears.

"We shall quite simply find another cab!" Chantal replied with a confidence that waned rapidly as she stared around her. The sight of Julia's face, blackened by smoke, caused her to look down aghast at her own begrimed arms. Unless they could find somewhere to wash before returning home, there would be no hiding *this* escapade from Mama, she thought uneasily.

As if in very answer to her thoughts, she heard a voice at her elbow.

"Got yerself lost, dearie?"

The accent was pure Cockney and Chantal turned to look at the woman who had addressed her. A dirty pink feather boa hung round her neck, only partly concealing a nearly bared bosom above which a heavily painted face smiled grotesquely at the two girls. Chantal at once assumed from her unladylike appearance that the woman was an actress of doubtful quality. She knew that in normal circumstances she would not be allowed to speak to this stranger but for the moment, any woman seemed a safer friend than the dirty, unkempt circle of men who now surrounded them.

"Our cab driver has vanished and we wish to go to St. James's!" she said with as much authority as she could command. "Can you assist us? I will pay you, of course!"

The woman grinned. She had never been in doubt that Chantal had the means to reward her.

"Corse I'll 'elp yer, ducks. Lawd only knows wot yer Ma 'ud say if she seed yer all on yer ownsome like and in such a state, too. Given 'er the slip, eh?"

"That's none of your business!" Chantal retorted sharply, uneasy at this woman's shrewd perception of the truth. "Nevertheless, my friend and I would like to clean ourselves before we go home. Is there a hotel nearby to which you can conduct us?"

Again the woman grinned, the leer stretching her scarlet lips in an ugly grimace.

"Ain't no 'otel, dearie!" she cackled. "But yer can 'ave a wash in my room down the street a bit — cost yer a bob or two but it's clean enough, I dare say."

Chantal hesitated, far from certain that she should take advantage of this offer. Julia tugged at her arm.

"Let us go home, please Chantal." In a

whisper she added: "I'm so frightened. I'm certain she is a woman of the streets!"

"Then she is not likely to harm us!" Chantal whispered back. "Besides, I have no intention of confessing our adventure to Mama. She will of a certainty forbid us to leave the house alone and I am quite determined to see Antoine again, no matter what!"

Nevertheless, she could not ignore Julia's fearful warning that their companion might indeed be a woman of the streets — which meant that she sold her body to men for money — or so Tamarisk had told her. To go to this woman's room was to take untold risks. She and Julia might even find their bodies being offered for sale.

Horrified by her own imagination, Chantal shook off the dirty hand tugging at her sleeve.

"Find us a cab, my good woman. I wish to return home at once."

She took a gold coin from her reticule which the woman quickly grabbed.

"Carnt leave you two little ladies all alone 'ere, now can I, whilst I goes fer a cab," she said craftily. "Give us another sovereign, lady, and I'll stay 'ere and guard yer both whilst I send a kid to get yer a cabby!"

Chantal was certain she was being overcharged but however disreputable the female, at least she offered protection from the men, now leering and grinning as they listened to the discussion. Suddenly her protector turned and screamed at the men in a shrill unintelligible Cockney and slowly they drew back.

161

Chantal was unaware that they were obeying their own jungle laws and respecting the woman's insistence that the two young girls were her catch, to be exploited as best she could. Nor did she realize that by the time the cab arrived, both she and Julia would have been robbed by pickpockets who would later share their booty with the harlot. Their losses were only discovered as they sank back in the cab's interior in grateful relief at their escape.

"'Tis of little consequence," Chantal comforted the tearful Julia. "I will replace your bracelet and Papa will give me money if we need it. What matters now is that we should go in to the house by the servants' entrance and that it is Dorothy and not Mama's Dorcas who sees us."

She knew Dorcas would certainly report their filthy state to her mistress whereas Dorothy would secrete them up the back stairs and help them to wash and change their attire before they were noticed.

Fortunately for the two adventurers, it was nearing three of the clock and Cook was busy dishing up luncheon when they crept in by the area door. Dorothy, who had been hoping to catch sight of the postboy who was her approved caller, was hovering by the door.

"Lawks a-mercy!" she gasped as she caught sight of their blackened faces.

Chantal put a cautionary finger to her lips, her fear now gone and an admixture of relief and excitement making her eyes sparkle.

"Cause a commotion in the kitchen, Dorothy,"

she commanded, "whilst we slip up the back stairs!"

As the grinning young maid went off to do her mistress' bidding, Chantal grabbed Julia's hand and like two black gazelles, the girls darted swiftly to the sanctuary of Chantal's room.

There the faithful Dorothy found them sprawled upon the bed laughing like naughty little girls, now that the danger was past and there was nothing to fear.

★ ★ ★

Two amongst ten thousand, Tamarisk and Charles sat at the back of Westminster Abbey awaiting the arrival of the young Queen for her coronation. But Tamarisk's thoughts were not upon the coming ceremony.

"'Tis not to be wondered at that Chantal believes Perry and Mama to be unfairly prejudiced against Antoine!" she commented. "She was not even born when my father arrived suddenly in London with a son we had not even known existed. Mama and I tried to like the boy but you must recall Charles, how unlovable he was!"

Charles, looking hot but most distinguished in his baronial robes, regarded his wife affectionately. Her constant concern for the happiness of others was one of her most endearing qualities.

"I do not remember the boy well," he replied, "although I do recall the occasion when he was expelled from Eton. I believe your parents insisted that he was dismissed unjustly but my Aunt Lisa had no doubt as to his guilt. It seems she knew the wife of the headmaster who informed her that the offence occasioning de Valle's expulsion was by no means the first time he had been caught thieving. A nasty affair!"

Tamarisk sighed.

"I suppose 'tis possible the boy could have changed with time!" she said. "But nothing is known of his life with Princess Camille nor what pursuits they engaged upon in the New World."

"Doubtless he will return to his own country once the Coronation has taken place!" Charles said reassuringly. "And 'tis but a month now before we depart to India."

"You are quite certain, my dear, that you have no objection to having Chantal go with us?" Tamarisk asked.

Charles repeated his earlier assurances that he thought it an excellent idea. He considered that since their children were to be left behind in England, Chantal would provide company for Tamarisk whilst he was busy with his duties at sea. Moreover, unmarried pretty young girls were at a premium in so remote a part of the Empire and Chantal could expect to enjoy unlimited attention from the young bachelors stationed out there.

"Your little sister will not have time in India to brood over Master Antoine!" he commented dryly.

Their discussion ended abruptly as the noise

outside the Abbey rose to a crescendo, heralding the approach of the grand procession. The vast congregation within the church turned their heads to stare at the great open doorway, the whispers and murmurs of excitement all but drowning the fanfare of the trumpeters.

Charles standing nearly a foot taller than Tamarisk, commanded a better view and identified for his wife the approaching dignitaries now preceding the Queen into the Abbey.

"The Dean of Westminster is foremost," he told her. "Those immediately behind him are the Queen's Household Controllers. The elderly man holding the crimson bag is her Treasurer."

"That must be Her Majesty's Vice Chamberlain next in line," Tamarisk, standing now on tiptoe, whispered back. "See how the ruby ring and the sword on his cushion reflect the light!"

Between him and the Archbishop of Canterbury walked a number of officials. Close behind this dignitary came the Princesses of the Blood Royal — Mary and Sophia, sisters of George IV.

"I have not seen the Princesses before," Tamarisk whispered to Charles. "But I saw King George several times when I was a child. He used to attend Mama's soirées. Of course he was only the Regent in those days."

Following the Princesses came the Duchess of Kent, the young Queen's mother, and the Duchesses of Cambridge and Gloucester magnificently robed — all with their attendants.

This show of female finery was closely followed by the Princes of the Blood Royal, the Dukes of Cambridge and Sussex in equally colorful regalia with their attendants; behind them came the Earls of the Realm.

"Do you recognize the Earl of Minto?" Charles asked. "He is a trifle more splendidly dressed than at your Mama's dinner party last week!"

Viscount Melbourne carried the heavy Sword of State, his page close behind him. The Duke of Wellington followed sedately with his pages, carrying Staff and Baton; and after him came the Duke of Somerset carrying the Orb.

Now, at long last drawing all eyes to her, came the eighteen-year-old girl who was about to be crowned Queen of England. Only four foot ten inches in height, Victoria looked touchingly childlike but nonetheless beautiful. Her robe was velvet, crimson in color, trimmed with ermine and bordered with gold lace. She was wearing the collars of her Orders and on her head was a simple circlet of diamonds.

"How lovely she looks — and so composed!" Tamarisk remarked admiringly. Suddenly she drew Charles' glance to the eight young girls bearing the Queen's train. The trains of their own white and silver rose-trimmed dresses were so long that they were having some difficulty in managing that of their Sovereign without tripping themselves up.

Charles returned her smile.

"'Tis obvious that Coronation ceremonies are held but seldom," he said dryly, "else those participating would be better rehearsed."

The service commenced, the young Queen

bearing herself with great dignity throughout the long ritual. It seemed to those watching her an omen of good fortune when at the moment the crown was placed on her head, a ray of sunshine fell upon her, reflecting off the mass of brilliants and colored stones with which her new diadem was festooned.

The voices of thousands of her subjects broke into massive cheering which finally gave way to the strains of the National Anthem. The congregation cheered and waved their handkerchiefs with such enthusiasm that their crowns and coronets wobbled precariously on their heads — a fact to which Charles drew Tamarisk's attention with an amused smile.

Suddenly the Earl of Surrey, Treasurer of the Household, threw a quantity of silver Coronation Medals about the choir and the lower galleries. There followed an undignified scramble as choir boys, Peers and Generals wrestled with one another on the Abbey floor in an attempt to secure one of the souvenir medals. Order was not restored until the boys resumed their places and the choir broke into the one-hundred-year-old processional hymn, '*This is the day the Lord hath made!*'

It was but one of the incidents Tamarisk and Charles related to an attentive audience when they dined at Barre House later that evening. Chantal and Julia were agog with eagerness to hear every detail for they had seen only the returning procession as it passed by their vantage point in Pall Mall on its way to Buckingham Palace.

"Near the end of the ceremony," Tamarisk related patiently, "the Bishop of Bath and Wells turned over two pages at once but failed to notice his mistake. He must have told Her Majesty that the service was finished for she returned to St. Edward's Chapel for some refreshment and had to be fetched back!"

"Poor old Lord Rolle caught his foot in his robe when he was paying homage to the other Peers!" Charles said. "He rolled to the bottom of the steps leading to the throne. But all praise to him — for he is nearly ninety years of age, you know — he made a second attempt. The crowd, including ourselves, cheered him noisily as he took each step!"

"And the Queen, showing us all the sweet compassionate nature she has, leaned down to prevent the risk of a further tumble by the poor old gentleman!" Tamarisk told a delighted Chantal.

"It has been a day for many different emotions!" Charles added. "Not least has our British sense of humor been to the fore. I heard from Lord Minto that the foreigners present when Lord Rolle took his tumble, were informed that it was part of the *droit de seigneur* to demand 'a roll' in addition to their homage from this particular noble family!"

"Oh, I wish I could have been there!" Chantal sighed. "One day I will be invited to the Abbey. I will marry a Prince or a Peer and . . ."

She broke off, her cheeks turning a bright pink as she remembered that she was contemplating marriage to a French Vicomte and could not therefore select a Prince or a Peer for a husband.

"And have you such a Prince or Peer in mind?" Perry asked teasingly, noting his daughter's blushes. He was surprised when her color deepened and she did not return his teasing smile with one of her customary pert rejoinders.

Without a word of warning, John stood up, the glass of wine before him tipping over and spreading in a dark stain over the white damask cloth.

"I think I can answer your question, sir, as the cat has clearly got Chantal's tongue," he said in a harsh voice. "She is hoping to marry a man of lower rank than either a Prince or a Lord. Am I not correct, Chantal, in supposing that you are anticipating a proposal from a mere Vicomte?"

Julia's nervous gasp passed unnoticed as Chantal sprang to her feet and faced John across the table.

"And even if I were, John, 'twould have naught to do with you!" she flared.

"It has everything to do with me . . . " John began but Mavreen held up her hand demanding silence. She looked directly at Chantal as she said coldly:

"'Twould seem there are events taking place in this house of which your father and I are in complete ignorance. We will repair to the withdrawing room where you will be so good as to explain what this nonsense is all about, Chantal!"

Not a little frightened now that the moment had come when she must confess that she had met Antoine in secret, Chantal followed her stepmother's upright figure, her own head held proudly erect in an attempt not to betray her nervousness.

Behind her walked John. His temper had abated and his eyes expressed his misery at the knowledge that he had inadvertently betrayed Chantal. Julia, following in his wake, looked even more unhappy and felt guiltily aware of her part in the secret rendezvous.

But it was not Chantal's purpose to involve her friend if she could avoid it. No sooner were the family seated and the servants dismissed than she said in a cool, level voice:

"It was my intention to speak to you and Papa in due course, Mama, when the moment seemed auspicious to discuss my future. But I realize that it would be wrong to keep secret any longer my encounter last week with Antoine. I was supposedly shopping in Piccadilly whereas in fact I was taking refreshment with Antoine in his hotel!"

She took a deep breath and unhappily aware of Mavreen's scowl at the mention of Antoine's name, she continued defiantly:

"I would have told you before now but you and Papa have made clear to me your dislike of Antoine — a dislike I have always felt to be quite unjustified. Whilst not desiring to go against your wishes, nevertheless I saw no harm in speaking with him. Indeed, I felt it would have seemed churlish for me to refuse his invitation. You have no need to be alarmed. Antoine behaved with the utmost circumspection, as did I. I think you malign him," she added with renewed defiance. "He has no wish to deceive you and has begged me to approach you on his behalf. He wants your permission to call upon me." She saw Mavreen's eyes turn to her father and the look that passed between them. Her defiance gave way to dismay.

"What reason have you to deny him?" she cried out. "None that is valid in so far as his character is concerned. You object because he has displaced John ... but that is not Antoine's fault. As for his intentions towards me — they are perfectly honorable. He wishes to marry me!"

Mavreen was about to speak but Perry quickly intervened.

"And you, Chantal? You wish to consider this young man as a possible husband?" he asked, his voice carefully controlled lest he aroused Chantal's antagonism.

Seeing the uncertainty in her eyes, he stood up and walked over to her chair, placing his hand gently upon one of her shoulders.

"You cannot know him well enough to be certain that you love him!" he said softly. "So I will assume that for the moment you seek only to know him better so that you may correctly judge your feelings for him?"

Chantal jumped to her feet and threw her arms around her father's neck, hugging him.

"I should have known you would understand, Papa!" she cried. "Antoine intends no wrong, I promise you. He is not even resentful that you and Mama dislike him — only sad that it should be so for he admires you both greatly. Please may he call upon me, Papa? Please?"

"*If he sets foot once more in this house I shall leave!*"

John's voice startled them all. Julia's cry of dismay was lost in Chantal's exclamation.

"That is horrible of you, John!" she cried. "You must know that I am as anxious that *you* should like him as that Mama and Papa should approve of him. He *is* your half-brother . . . yet it would seem you consider him an enemy!"

"Perhaps I do!" John replied, avoiding Chantal's eyes as misery engulfed him. "But I will not retract my opinion of him even were you to beg me to do so. I neither like nor trust the man and were I in a position to refuse him the pleasure of paying court to you, I would consider it my duty to do so!"

"Then I am glad that you have no control of my destiny!" Chantal flared. "You are cruelly prejudiced against an innocent man!"

"Oh, Chantal," Julia protested weakly. "You cannot mean that. Besides, you would not be at all happy if John were to leave home!"

"Would I not?" Chantal retorted. "Then you do not know my feelings very well, Julia. I care not what becomes of such a bigot!"

His heart heavy but his pride now uppermost, John bowed to his mother and with one last agonized look at the girl he loved, he turned on his heel and left the room. Julia burst into tears and ran into the garden. Mavreen, silent but with a look of anxiety, followed in John's wake. Sighing, Perry took Chantal's arm and led her to the sofa.

"You seem to have plunged us all into a nice mess of pottage!" he said with a quizzical smile. "I do not remember such disturbance in our midst since you were in the nursery and threw the chamberpot at poor John because he would not kiss you good night!"

Despite the gravity of the moment, Chantal smiled.

"You do not think John really intends to leave home, do you, Papa? Julia was quite right when she said I would be most unhappy if he did!"

"As I well know!" Perry told her. "But 'twould seem the moment has come when, if you are to understand what is happening, you must be made aware of a small deception that has kept you in ignorance of certain facts. John loves you, Chantal — not as a brother but as a young man loves the girl he wants to marry. Have you not suspected as much?"

Seeing his daughter's eyes widen and hearing her gasp of astonishment, he continued quietly:

"He wished to tell you of his feelings last year when he himself was first aware of them. But your mother felt you were too young to be concerned in such a serious matter as matrimony and that you should be permitted to enjoy your youth without fetters of any kind."

"My poor John!" was Chantal's first comment before she added thoughtfully: "I had thought my joyous childhood companion was turning into a dull and boorish man when all the time he . . . "

173

"Yes, he was languishing with a love he had been forbidden by his mother to express. So you see, my little skylark, growing up is not always so simple an experience as it might appear; and when deciding your future, you must take into account John's love for you and what affection you may possibly have for him!"

Chantal stared at her father, her eyes bewildered and uncertain.

"It is so hard for me to consider John as . . . as a suitor!" she said hesitantly. "He has always been my dearly loved brother. And of course I do love him, Papa, but . . . "

"But not as you think you could love Antoine? Is that it?"

Chantal blushed.

"My feelings for Antoine are quite different!" she said guilelessly. "I cannot explain it very clearly, Papa, but when he holds my hand, I find myself trembling with an admixture of fear and excitement. Moreover, I have to confess that . . . that I greatly enjoyed being kissed by him." She touched her cheek reminiscently. She was relieved to note that her father appeared unshocked by her statement.

"It is not unnatural for you to have such feelings," he said quietly, "and I do not deny that Antoine is exceedingly handsome. Nevertheless, my darling, to feel attracted to a good-looking admirer is not necessarily to love him and I would want you to know a great deal more about this young man before you reached any conclusion. Marriage is a most serious undertaking."

Chantal hugged her father yet again.

"I should have spoken to you sooner, Papa," she cried remorsefully, "for you understand everything quite perfectly. As yet I have no inkling as to whether or no I wish to be married to Antoine. I know only that I want to see him again . . . and not secretly without your agreement. May he call, Papa? And if he does, will you try to like him, for *my* sake?"

"I will do my utmost to see him anew through your eyes!" Perry promised. "Now I must go and see if your Mama and John have reached any decision with regard to John's future. Meanwhile, my love, must I remind you that you have promised to go to India with Tamarisk and Charles and that it would be wrong to dishonor this undertaking. 'Twill mean a separation of a year or two from this young man who has taken your fancy, but if true love exists between you both, then it will grow all the stronger for your absence. If you will give me your promise that you will go with Tamarisk whatever proposal Antoine may suggest, then I will persuade your Mama to allow him to call here to see you as often as is convenient."

"Then I give you my word!" Chantal cried without hesitation, her eyes shining. "As for India, I am agog with excitement at the prospect of traveling to such a faraway country and not even Antoine could keep me from such an adventure! So you need have no fear that I will abrogate that decision, Papa."

Well satisfied by her promise, Perry went in search of Mavreen. Not least, at the back of his mind, was the knowledge that he could comfort John with the fact that Chantal was not yet ready to commit herself to Antoine de Valle and that hopefully she would be on her way to India before her heart was lost beyond recall.

10

July – August 1838

THE heat of the fierce July sunshine forbade the exertion of walking. Antoine removed his bottle-green tail-coat. He spread it on the lawn beneath the welcome shade of the great lime tree that grew beyond the rose garden at Barre House and drew Chantal down beside him. Far from the house itself, he knew that they were beyond the view of watchful eyes. Whilst realizing that it was unlikely his stepmother or Sir Peregrine would spy upon them, he suspected that the household servants might gaze out of windows and gossip if they could discover some intrigue for their tittle-tattle.

Taking Chantal's hands in his, he lifted them and pressed kisses upon the petal smooth skin. She leaned against him and through the thin covering of his shirt, he felt her body tremble. Slowly, as if by accident, he let his fingers travel up her bare arm until his palm touched her breast through the white muslin of her dress. Even had he not heard her tiny gasp, he would have known she was sensitively aware of him for her cheeks had colored in a charming blush.

"Chantal!" he murmured. *"Comme je t'adore!"*

Impulsively, she caught his wayward hand and pressed it against her hot face. Her eyes were dark with unhappiness. In a low tense voice she said:

"Antoine, I have some exceedingly bad news to impart." She paused before adding miserably: "We cannot after all continue to enjoy each other's company for a further month."

Only with difficulty did the man beside her hide the anger that swept over his face.

"Are you telling me that your parents have renewed their objections to me?" he asked, drawing his hand furiously from her grasp.

She looked at him in dismay, his anger new and disturbing to her.

"Oh, no, no, Antoine. 'Tis not my parents' fault. 'Tis that the boat taking us to India must now sail four weeks ahead of the listed date. We leave . . . next week."

"*Next week!*" Antoine repeated, stunned by this announcement and revealing his genuine anxiety. "But that is insupportable!"

"I know!" Chantal whispered, tears stinging her eyelids. "I have been so happy these past weeks and I was looking forward so much to the days ahead. But the matter is beyond Papa's control. Charles says that there has been trouble of some sort on an island called *Mauritius* — something to do with the slave trading — and our ship has now to take out an Aide for the Colonial Governor together with urgent dispatches for him from the Government. Charles says 'twill be but a minor diversion from the normal route to India but it necessitates an earlier departure than was planned."

"Then you cannot sail with your sister and her

178

husband!" Antoine said violently. "I cannot lose you now, my adorable Chantal. I beg you, do not go with them. We will be married at once and I will take you back to France."

Chantal lowered her gaze so that she should not be weakened by the ardent longing expressed so eloquently in Antoine's eyes and voice. She comprehended only vaguely the violence of his passion although the faint stirring of bodily desires that he had aroused in her on their first secret encounter had become increasingly disturbing this past week. In the music room when she played the pianoforte to him, he would stand behind her, his hands resting innocently upon her shoulders and yet his lightest touch sending shivers through her body, setting her nerves alight to sensations that were thrilling yet strangely frightening.

It was as if Antoine had some magical ability to affect her body by a mere glance, a touch, his breath upon her cheek. No matter where they sat, or stood, he was at her side, a compelling shadow that she could not ignore. On each of the two occasions he had kissed her upon the mouth, she had come near to fainting, so strange and wonderful were the feelings that encompassed her. She could not understand why the touch of his mouth upon hers should cause even her legs to tremble and her whole body to be consumed with the desire to melt against his.

"Do you not love me — even a little?" Antoine had asked again and again. Each time she had responded with a greater assurance that she believed the feelings she had for him were indeed those of love.

"Chantal, you have not given me your answer!" his voice now interrupted her reverie. "Tell me that you will not leave me; that you will consent to be my wife. You cannot doubt that I love you. I will give you anything in the world you want. I desire only to make you happy. *Je t'aime, je t'aime, je t'aime!*"

Slowly a tear spilled down her cheek, and another and another until she was crying quietly. He put his arms around her.

"Why do you weep?" he asked, his voice angry with fear. "Does it make you unhappy to know how much I love you?"

"Oh, no, indeed not!" Chantal whispered through her tears. "But I must go with Charles and Tamarisk, Antoine. I promised my father that I would and I cannot break my word to him!"

With a frightening abruptness, Antoine released her. Jumping to his feet he stood looking down at her, his eyes narrowed, his lower lip jutting forward as he muttered:

"So he has outwitted me after all! And I was stupid enough to believe that he was permitting my courtship of his daughter. Fool that you are, Antoine de Valle. *Imbecile!*" He stared at the weeping girl and felt strangely disturbed by her distress. With an effort he controlled his anger. "Come now!" he said. "There is no need for tears, Chantal. Despite everything, I do not think there is need even to consider parting. You must realize that your father extracted that promise before he realized that you loved me. If you explain matters to him and tell him that you wish to marry me, he will surely release you from your vow."

Chantal ceased crying as she stared up at Antoine with renewed hope. But his words, though momentarily seeming like a miraculous solution to their joint unhappiness, soon brought further anguish as doubts re-assailed her.

"But Antoine, I do not know if I wish to marry you!" she blurted out with a childlike frankness. "How can I be certain that I love you the way a girl should love the man she is to marry? I know only that I do not want to be parted from you for two whole years! As for Papa, he will repeat what he said to me before — that a two year separation is an excellent test to discover if our love is real or false!"

"So he has safely covered all contingencies!" Antoine thought, his hatred of Perry intensifying.

"Your father would have made an excellent General!" he commented bitterly. Seeing Chantal's uncomprehending gaze upon him, he fought once more for self-control. All was not yet lost, he told himself. Even as far away as India, this girl would not easily forget him. And he would ensure that she did not.

He took from his left hand a gold signet ring. Bending down, he put it in Chantal's palm, closing her fingers over it.

"With this ring I plight thee my troth!" he said solemnly. "I pledge my everlasting love. I will never take another woman to wife, even if I have to wait fifty years for you to come back to me, my Chantal. Each time you gaze upon my ring, *remember that I am waiting for you*. You are destined to be mine, as I am to be yours. One day you will love me, marry me, even if you do not know it yet!"

Chantal stared at the ring and then at Antoine.

"I will keep it with me always!" she cried in a fierce agony of uncertainty. With one part of her she longed to throw herself back into his arms, declare her love and agree to become his wife. Yet deep, deep within her, she knew she could not make such a vow in total honesty.

Perhaps if she knew what love really was she could be certain, she thought wretchedly. But was anyone ever certain as Tamarisk suggested? She had vouchsafed: "You will know it beyond a doubt when true love comes to you!" Did John love her in such a way — beyond all doubt? Surely if John truly loved her, he would not have carried out his threat to leave home, abandoning her to Antoine's attentions as if he did not care whether she submitted to another or not. If he had truly loved her, she decided, he would have stayed and fought for her hand. But without a care for her feelings, he had left without even a farewell, oblivious to the hurt such action inflicted upon her. How different was Antoine's way of loving from John's, she reflected. *He* never lacked in the giving of fine compliments, of endearments and now, to comfort her, he had given her his ring.

Longing now to comfort him, she reached up and kissed his cheek.

"As soon as I am able, I will write to you!"

she promised. "I will keep a journal, Antoine, so that I can relay faithfully to you everything that happens to me. If you will do the same and write to me, we shall not feel the parting so terribly; nor will we be strangers when we meet again. Oh, if only I had a miniature with your likeness to take with me! There is no time now to have one painted."

"I need no physical reminder of you, Chantal. Your image lives upon the edge of my consciousness day and night and I can conjure up your beloved face at will!"

Yesterday, when their impending separation had seemed a long way off, such a compliment from Antoine would have brought Chantal nothing but joy. But now his loving words increased her uncertainty and distress. For all his words of love and fidelity, she thought, there was no guarantee that he would not forget her once she was far away in India. It was only to be expected that he would meet many girls far prettier than herself. No one could deny his eligibility; nor that his exceptional good looks had the most devastating effect upon the female sex. Many of her mother's friends had commented quite openly upon Antoine's charm and fascination. Nor was there a servant in Barre House, so her maid Dorothy had told her, who did not come near to swooning if the Vicomte so much as said 'thank you' to them.

"Why am I so faint hearted?" Chantal asked herself, tormented once more by her doubts. "I, who prided myself that I never lacked for courage, seem now to be quite without it!"

She looked at Antoine's face and felt weak with longing to throw herself into his arms in total surrender. Beneath his frilled lawn shirt she could glimpse the bare skin of his chest. Her hands ached to touch him and quite unconsciously her body strained towards him. Perhaps if Antoine had spoken further words of love, she might even then have weakened and told him she would marry him if her parents would agree. But Antoine's mind was concerned only with this unexpected reversal to his plans and how he might overcome it. He was unused to having his desires gainsaid and the knowledge that he no longer controlled his destiny made him both angry and uneasy.

Momentarily his agile mind pursued the possibility of abducting Chantal; of taking her to France by force before she could board the boat for India. He knew that money would buy all the physical help he needed to carry out this direction of Chantal from her parents' control. But he could not count on her deeming such action as romantic or desirable. He would risk incurring her fear and dislike of him. Since above all it was her love he craved, he dared not take such a risk.

His feelings greatly perturbed him. He could not accept that he, Antoine de Valle, who had never yet in thirty years cared more for another human being than he did for himself, should actually fear losing the trust and respect of a young girl. It was not even as if she professed to love him! Yet he dared not risk offending her, upsetting her, frightening her lest he lose that slight affection she did profess for him. He no longer contemplated her seduction nor desired her submission. He wanted her total surrender. And for this he must wait now for two long years. The fact was intolerable yet so far as he could see, inescapable.

In a sudden agony of despair, he drew her into his arms and kissed her with passionate longing. Briefly he felt her soft warm body melt against him as she returned his kisses with matching fervor. But her weakening was only momentary and she drew back from him, her eyes clouding with uncertainty.

"No, Antoine! 'Twill only make our parting the harder to endure!" she whispered, instinct guiding her where her lack of experience in such matters failed. "Since we must say goodbye, let us do so quickly and not prolong our torment!"

Regaining his composure, Antoine released his hold upon her.

"Come then, *ma petite*!" he said as he took her arm to lead her slowly back towards the house. "'Tis clear I must resign myself as best I can to our separation. Fate has been cruel to us, has it not, by curtailing our opportunities to further the course of our love. But perhaps she will be kind in bringing us together again before the two years have passed. They seem an eternity to me!"

"Oh, I will pray for it!" Chantal cried. "Even now some miracle might occur that will prevent our sailing so soon. We may yet be reprieved!"

On the day prior to sailing, it indeed looked

as if the miracle would take place, for there was a storm so violent that windows of houses were broken by the hailstones. The *Times* reported that 'pieces of ice had fallen from a sky so dark it might have been a winter's night.'

"Let us hope it is not an ill omen!" little Dorothy remarked anxiously as she packed the last of Chantal's clothes into a bulging valise.

Despite the fact that Chantal had cried herself to sleep the previous night believing herself heartbroken at the parting from Antoine, she was agog with excitement when the moment came for her to set foot on HMS *Valetta*, great wooden ship with furled sails and busy crew.

In deference to Charles' rank of Rear Admiral, the Captain personally met his passengers as they boarded. He effected introductions to the officers and then led the party to his own cabin which he had allocated to Charles and Tamarisk for the voyage. This cabin, though small to their eyes in comparison to their own bedchamber, was comfortably furnished, the guns discreetly hidden under chintz covers.

The two maids, Elsie and Dorothy, were accommodated next door in the Captain's day cabin and Chantal in the still smaller cabin usually allotted to the First Lieutenant.

Mavreen and Perry, who had boarded with the departing passengers in order to pay their farewells, looked about them with interest.

"But for the fact that I am certain the climate of India would not suit me," Mavreen said, "I might wish that we were sailing with you, Charles!"

She glanced at Chantal's excited face with quiet satisfaction. The girl's tears the previous night had disturbed Perry who had begun to fear that his daughter might genuinely be heartbroken by this separation from Antoine.

"'Twas an excellent scheme to send Chantal on this voyage with Charles and Tamarisk!" she whispered now to Perry in a low voice. "'Twould not surprise me if she very soon forgets all about Antoine and transfers her affections to that nice young Lieutenant whose cabin she has usurped!"

Perry looked a deal happier.

"God grant you all a safe journey and a happy one!" he said as Charles came up to him. He could give no logical explanation for it but he still felt uneasy at the thought of his only child leaving home to cross the oceans to the other side of the world.

"Captain Anson is an excellent fellow and I have every confidence in him," Charles said reassuringly. "'Tis not every captain in our Navy who is as popular with his crew!" he added thoughtfully. "These poor devils who serve under him are entirely at his mercy. A less humane Captain can make life hell for such men — allowing his officers to bully them and flog them for the slightest fault."

"We need have no fear for our children's welfare!" Mavreen tried once again to reassure Perry as they bade their farewells and drove slowly homewards. "The Captain seemed a very pleasant man."

As Charles had forecast, Captain Anson

did indeed prove to be a charming traveling companion to his passengers and to be greatly loved by his men. When he discovered that a dishonest chandler had sold the mess officer meat that was little more than lumps of bone and fat, the officer was severely reprimanded for his lack of supervision.

For the first few weeks at sea the passengers and officers did not fare too badly. There was plenty of live stock aboard and there had not been time as yet for the butter or cheese to turn rancid. Food assumed an unnatural significance to the travelers for they had little else to do but eat and walk the deck for entertainment.

Chantal went frequently to the quarterdeck to observe the helmsman steering the great vessel across the ocean. Sometimes she stood with Dorothy watching the sailors climb the rigging of the main mast, feeling dizzy to see the men clamber along the spars to furl the huge billowing sails high above their beads.

Tamarisk kept a watchful eye upon her. They had been at sea a month and yet another month must pass before they reached the island of Mauritius where they would disembark whilst HMS *Valetta* was freshly provisioned. In the meanwhile, she decided, Chantal could come to no harm for the eyes of one of the young Lieutenants were nearly always upon her.

"Thomas Lovell is an extremely pleasant young man, Chantal!" she observed shrewdly. "And clearly much taken by you. Do you not return his admiration just a little? Charles says he is a most able officer and personally I find him quite charming."

Chantal's brow furrowed as she let her mind dwell momentarily on the blue-eyed, sandy-haired young officer who seemed ever at her elbow.

"I like him very much as a friend," she admitted. "But I cannot welcome his attentions. He is so young, Tamarisk — at least, he seems so to me since I enjoyed Antoine's company. Thomas Lovell, by comparison strikes me as sadly gauche — and as awkward as a schoolboy!"

Knowing full well her mother's and Perry's hope that Chantal would soon forget Antoine once she was far distant from him, Tamarisk sighed regretfully. Still young enough herself to appreciate Antoine's attraction for a girl of Chantal's age — or indeed for a woman of any age — she understood Chantal's romantic leanings towards him.

"Do you think ever of our dear John?" she asked Chantal curiously. "I had hoped that he might return home before we left England in order to wish us a safe journey. But of course, he had no way of knowing that our date of departure would be advanced."

Chantal let drop the velvet waistcoat she was embroidering for her father.

"I have thought much about John these past few weeks," she admitted. "It was never my intention to hurt him, Tamarisk, as you must well know. I have loved and admired John for as long as I can remember. But how could I have surmised that his feelings towards me had changed from those of a brother to those of an . . . an admirer!" she said frowning. "'Tis so hard for me even now to think of him as such."

"Perhaps Mama was mistaken in keeping from you so long your true identity and the knowledge that John was not your brother," Tamarisk said. "I believe she felt it might upset you to know you were born out of wedlock!"

Chantal sighed.

"Perhaps it would be more seemly of me if I were shocked by the circumstances of my birth," she said. "But to be quite truthful, Tamarisk, I am not at all put out by this intelligence. Papa tells me that my natural mother was both lovely to look upon and of a rare sweet disposition and that I can respect her memory. I think I always felt instinctively that I was a little different from other girls. Once I knew I had a Neapolitan mother it seemed to explain quite satisfactorily my apartness. Would it have disturbed or shocked you, dearest Tamarisk, were you to be told that like me, you were a bastard?"

Tamarisk was silent as if pondering the matter. She did not feel it right for her to inform Chantal that she was not the true daughter of the elderly Lord Gilbert Barre as everyone supposed; or that her mother and Gerard de Valle had been lovers years before they had finally married and that she, Tamarisk, was the natural child of their union. Chantal believed her stepmother to be completely virtuous and to have led a blameless life. It was Mavreen's opinion that were Chantal

190

to know differently, it might encourage her to choose a less virtuous life for herself.

After seven and a half weeks at sea, Chantal's embroidery had to be set aside as *Valetta* sailed into the tiny harbor of Port Louis on the island of Mauritius.

By now the temperature of the air had considerably increased, so close were they to the equator. Tamarisk and Chantal dared not venture into the hot sun without the protection of their parasols, for they were cautioned to take the greatest care lest their fair skin should blister. One of Tamarisk's young midshipmen had already contracted sunstroke and when they disembarked she insisted that he be taken with them to the Colonial Governor's house where she could look after the boy.

Unfortunately the Governor, Major General Sir William Nicolay, was far from well. It therefore fell to his wife to make their visitors welcome and the good lady made no secret of her relief at the timely arrival of the Governor's new Aide.

The Governor's house was built of stone and seemed immensely spacious after the confines of the ship. Chantal and Tamarisk were delighted to have fresh water once again to bathe in and to look out from their windows upon the green palm trees and the brilliantly hued flowers that grew in such profusion on this tropical island. They were both impatient to make a tour of the town which teemed with the strange foreign faces of the Chinese, Indian, Portuguese and African inhabitants.

"'Tis like the Garden of Eden!" Tamarisk enthused to Charles as she stared beyond the colorful garden to the blue skies and turquoise sea.

But at dinner that evening the Governor's wife poured cold water upon their enthusiasms.

"Since the abolition of slavery," she told them, "it has been one of my husband's main duties to try to enforce the edict. But our old enemies the French, whilst giving token agreement to abolition, nevertheless turn a blind eye when it suits them. Positioned as we are on this island only some five hundred miles from French Madagascar and about the same distance again from the east coast of Africa, the Indian Ocean around us teems with privateers and slavers. The efforts Sir William has made to keep this island free of these slavers has aroused much ill feeling towards the British. Quite frankly we shall not be sorry to leave here."

Charles nodded understandingly. He already knew that a large part of the British Navy was committed to anti-slavery patrols; indeed that a great many officers and ratings were never employed in any other pursuit.

For two days whilst they drove around the island in Sir William's carriage, the sun shone brilliantly from a cloudless sky. The heat and humidity became oppressive. But on the third day, when they were ready to board HMS *Valetta*, a soft wind sprang up, rustling the palms and the sails. Small clouds gathered slowly on the horizon.

"We shall have rain before long," announced

Sir William who had recovered sufficiently to bid them farewell at the quayside. "But this wind from the south will speed you upon your way. Safe journey!"

After consultation with Charles, Captain Anson decided to set sail in a north northwesterly direction. It would not be long before they could expect to cross the equator and but a further few weeks before they reached Bombay.

Although the best speed *Valetta* could achieve in normal conditions was eight knots, now running before the strengthening wind they were soon racing at twelve knots across the turbulent sea. But on the second day out of Mauritius, the wind suddenly changed and they encountered cross currents that worried both Charles and Captain Anson. They reduced sail, watching the sky anxiously. They were both aware that hurricanes were not unknown in this hemisphere and that to be caught in winds of one hundred miles an hour was to risk capsizing in horrendous seas.

"We are already off course," Captain Anson said, studying his charts. "But there is little we can do other than ride before the wind!"

Whilst Tamarisk and Chantal tried to calm the hysterical servant girls below decks, Charles with the Captain and crew fought to keep the ship steady as the winds increased in velocity. The mizzen topsail was furled and the main topsail reefed. Charles went below to warn the women that there was a deal of water on deck and imminent danger of it entering their cabins and penetrating the hold.

Tamarisk looked at her husband's drenched oilskin-clad figure and knew from the tenseness of his body and the lines around his mouth that he was far from happy about the prevailing conditions.

"Take care, my love!" she said, kissing his salt-wet cheek before he went on deck again. "And do not worry about us. We will manage."

With Elsie moaning that the end of the world was nigh and Dorothy weeping, sleep was impossible. Tamarisk and Chantal took turns reading quietly from the Captain's Bible. In the early hours of the morning, a huge wave washed away one of the helmsmen. The cry of "man overboard" was only just heard above the crash of the waves on deck and the screaming of the wind in the rigging. Three hours later, another heavy sea stove in the deadlights and frames, broke the cabin woodwork and flooded the floor to a depth of two feet.

Aghast, Tamarisk and Chantal clung to one of the wooden bunks as their personal possessions were washed around the cabin.

Two seamen, drenched to the skin and near the point of exhaustion, came splashing into the cabin with orders to assist the four women as they strove to secure the remaining windows. In answer to Tamarisk's questions, one of the men replied that *Valetta* was indeed caught in the center of a hurricane; that the holds were flooded; that the mouldings, lead, carvings and deck decorations had all been swept away. Even whilst he listed these disasters, another took place as the starboard bulwark was smashed,

194

followed by the main bulwarks.

Charles appeared briefly, his eyes dark with worry as he announced that the damage to *Valetta* was beyond repair.

"Never before in my life at sea have I seen waves of such enormity," he told Tamarisk quietly. "All hands are pumping the flooded holds."

He handed her the leather bundle he was carrying over one arm.

"Take this!" he said. "It is a Daniel's life preserver!"

He demonstrated briefly how the waterproofed leather contraption could be inflated by blowing air through a silver tube.

"It is quite simple to don!" he explained, showing her the two leather straps through which she must put her arms and a third which must pass between her legs to hold the preserver in place around her waist.

"'Tis Captain Anson's!" he said. "But he insisted that I should give it to you. It will keep you afloat in the water for some hours."

White-faced, Tamarisk stared at her husband. She made no move to try on the strange contraption.

"You must give it to Chantal!" she said. "She is younger than I and if only one of us is to survive . . . "

"No, Tamarisk!" Charles broke in sharply. "You and not Chantal have the greater responsibility to live. You have four young children who would be orphaned were the worst to happen."

"Charles, I could not . . . "

"I have never demanded anything of you throughout our married life!" Charles interrupted again. "This time I am not requesting, Tamarisk, I am insisting — for the sake of our children. If the order is given to abandon ship you are to put on the preserver."

Before Tamarisk could reply, one of the oil lanterns fell from its hook on the wall behind her, crashing into the water still covering the floor and plunging the cabin into darkness. Tamarisk, disregarding her shoes and stockings, jumped down from the bunk and paddled towards Charles.

"Is all lost?" she asked quietly. "Are we about to perish, Charles? I am not afraid to hear the truth."

"I fear the situation is very serious!" Charles replied, his voice lowered so that neither the maids nor the seamen would overhear his pessimistic prognosis. "'Tis quite impossible in this weather to ascertain the full extent of the damage but I think we are beyond hope of saving the ship."

As he turned to leave the cabin, Tamarisk caught his arm.

"You are not going up on deck again, Charles? If we are to drown, then let us be together!"

Gently he detached her restraining hand.

"Be sure that I shall not leave you and Chantal down below if we have to abandon ship," he said with a smile. "You will have good warning, I promise you."

That warning was all too soon in coming.

One of the young midshipmen, his drenched white face a mask of fear, burst into the cabin with a message from Charles to tell them to don their cloaks and come up on deck as speedily as possible.

"We are trying to launch the longboats!" the boy said tremulously.

Elsie burst into tears and was sharply reprimanded by Tamarisk.

"We have no need for floods of tears with so much salt water already about us!" she said in an attempt at humor. "Now get your cloak at once, Elsie and follow me."

Dorothy was suddenly found to be missing. Chantal discovered the girl in her cabin packing a valise.

"You must leave everything!" Chantal commanded, hoping her voice did not betray her inner fear. "If we are to take to the longboats, Dorothy, we shall not require my evening dresses nor my nightgowns, shall we?"

Seeing the girl's terrified eyes, Chantal took her firmly by the arm and forced her to move ahead along the swaying passageway and up the steep wooden stairway. The bitter cold of the sea water rushing to meet them, all but swept them off their feet. Mingled with the shouts of the sailors, they could hear the fierce screech of the furious wind as it tore at the rigging. As they reached the tilting, rocking deck, Chantal caught sight of Tamarisk and Elsie, already drenched to the skin, clinging to a trailing rope. Obedient to her husband's command, Tamarisk had donned the life preserver but there was no sign of Charles.

Holding Dorothy by her arm and keeping a secure grasp upon any handhold she could espy, Chantal edged nearer to Tamarisk. But before she could reach her sister, a gigantic wave swept over the starboard gunwale. Horrified, Chantal saw the young midshipman standing beside Tamarisk swept off his feet by a wall of green water. The boy rolled helplessly about the deck as the ship listed heavily. As she righted herself, *Valetta* then swung violently to port and the boy was washed back over the gunwale into the boiling ocean.

Still too shocked to be able fully to appreciate this horror, Chantal was aroused from her immobility by Tamarisk's scream.

"Charles! Take care! *Charles!*"

Her voice barely rose above the howling of the wind and was unheard by Tamarisk's husband who stood on the mizzen deck above them. Neither did he seem to have heard high above their heads, the ominous crack as the mainmast split.

As if in a dream Chantal saw the massive mast with its sails furled tightly to its spars come crashing towards the stern. It was obvious that Charles was unaware that he stood in the path of mortal danger. Tamarisk screamed once again before one of the great spars came swinging diagonally towards him. As it struck him, he toppled sideways beneath the rigging; the ship lurched to starboard and the mass of sodden canvas, swinging ropes and broken wood swept him ruthlessly into the sea.

There was now no doubt that the ship would not survive the storm. With every inch of canvas lost, wallowing with the broken masts weaving a fantastic pattern against the leaden sky, HMS *Valetta* swung once more to starboard. Now broadside on, the white-topped walls of water crashing onto the decks, she was beyond assistance. Men, animals, guns, woodwork were swept away, those living creatures who were not already crushed to death by the heavy flotsam, drowned within minutes in the raging sea.

Stunned by the manner of Charles' shocking death, Tamarisk was all but unaware of the sailor who now crashed into her, knocking her off her feet and tearing her icy hands free from the rope to which she had been clinging. Together, in a dance of death, they rolled across the deck, arms and legs entangled until a wave of salt water swept them away.

Chantal watched disbelievingly, numbed by the horror, the noise, the screams, the total confusion, as the tattered broken ship sank lower and lower into the water. She was aware that Dorothy had disappeared; that a dark-skinned Lascar was tugging at her arm. But her mind could not grasp that he was attempting to point out to her one of the longboats washed overboard and upright in the sea. He shouted once more in a language she did not understand; then scooped her up under one arm as if she were a child. Holding her thus, he leapt from the deck.

The shock of the cold water stunned her

mind to total oblivion. When next she became fully conscious, the sailor was hauling her into the boat and she was briefly aware of pain as a rowlock grazed the skin of her arm. She collapsed onto the bottom of the boat, her cloak and skirt so heavy with sea water that she could not stand. Pulling herself to a kneeling position, she grasped the rough edge of the boat and peered out with horrified eyes. *Valetta* was sinking into the maelstrom, Captain Anson clearly visible on her half submerged deck.

Frantically the sailor attempted to row the longboat away from the suction he knew would follow the sinking of the vessel. His bare back streamed with water as his muscles strained with his efforts. The fear on his face was sufficient in itself to make Chantal aware of the danger they were in even had she been ignorant of the height of the waves tossing them around like a cork and threatening to capsize their tiny boat.

"God have mercy upon us!" she whispered, closing her eyes as death approached. But when she next opened them, *Valetta* had disappeared and the Lascar, breathing heavily, had eased his oars. Without warning the wind dropped and Chantal could hear the waves slapping almost playfully against the side of the boat in which she lay.

Mercifully, she was unaware that this was but the eye of the storm. The worst was yet to come.

11

September 1838

JOHN sat astride his horse, allowing the beast to make its own pace through the quiet French countryside. Several paces behind him rode his servant, Luke, with a pack horse carrying their baggage. John had chosen this method of travel rather than a hired carriage, preferring the gentle motion of the animal beneath him and the clean fresh air to the stuffy confines and bumpy interior of a post-chaise.

A somber mood had engulfed him since on his return to Barre House he had discovered that Chantal had already departed for India with Tamarisk. He was bitterly disappointed to learn that he was not in time to bid her a safe journey and to be reconciled after their angry exchange of words. But this morning his mood changed and he was feeling comparatively cheerful. The day was bright with autumn sunshine and he had just left a delightful *auberge* where he had spent the previous night in comfort and in excellent company.

John's face broke into a smile as he thought once more of the charming French family whose path he had crossed at the inn. His fellow guest, the Duc Dubois with his wife and six daughters had upon his arrival welcomed him into their midst and the Duc had insisted that he share their table. Later that evening when the ladies retired, the Duc admitted with a whimsical smile that he would make welcome *any* eligible young man of good family.

"With six unmarried daughters, would you not do likewise, *mon ami*?" he had asked with commendable honesty. "One daughter is a blessing, two a joy but six a calamity!" he added with a smile.

The girls' ages ranged from sixteen to twenty-five and they were far from uncomely. Indeed they were all pretty enough not to lack for suitors, John complimented their father.

"But alas, I can give them no dowry!" the Duc Dubois told him with a Gallic shrug of his shoulders. "I lost most of my wealth during the Revolution; and although we were able to return to France and reclaim our Château outside Beauvais, the farms from which my family prospered had been allotted to the peasants during the Napoleonic regime. The Château itself was in ruins. We therefore live quietly without ostentation or extravagance and I fear I cannot afford to entertain for my daughters as befits a gentleman of my background. Even if I were to do so," he added, "I could not afford to buy them the clothes and finery that they need if they are to keep up appearances in the right circles. *Mes pauvres filles!*" he lapsed into French. Then with a broad smile that belied his chagrin, he said cheerfully: "*Tant pis!* We are a devoted and happy family!"

Which seemed to be the case, John reflected as he rode towards Compiègne. The girls had flirted with him and giggled amongst themselves as if they cared not one jot if they never found husbands. He had told the Duc he might well have set his cap at one or another of them had his sentiments not been engaged elsewhere.

Chantal! The thought of her stirred his heart to a new and fiercer resolve. He was even now upon his way to Boulancourt to renew his acquaintance with his half-brother. It was his intention by some means or other, to discredit Antoine de Valle so that never again would Chantal consider him a worthy suitor. John doubted no less than did his mother that Antoine was not the paragon of virtue that he seemed. There were too many dark areas in his life. Where, for instance, had he been between the years when he left England and returned to Compiègne? Why had he never attempted to visit his relations in England until this summer? Was he really so rich that he could afford to lavish untold luxuries upon Boulancourt without regard to the cost? The family fortune had been lost during the Revolution and Antoine de Valle could have inherited from his father only that wealth which he had acquired from his first wife, Faustina.

"Her father was a Prince from Naples!" Mavreen had told John. "Faustina was his only child and he gave her an exceedingly handsome dowry when she married your father. But it was not a fortune! Much of it was spent by your father in his lifetime on Boulancourt. There could not have been a great deal left to pass on to Antoine."

"Perhaps Antoine's guardian, the Princess Camille Faloise left him her money when she died," John suggested, "if indeed she did die in America as Antoine stated. We have no proof of it!"

Perry had laughingly accused John and Mavreen of becoming obsessional in their refusal to believe anything Antoine told them. But Mavreen insisted that her instinct was seldom wrong and no matter how far-fetched it might seem, she was convinced of Antoine's innate amorality. When John chose to support his mother, Perry pointed out shrewdly but not unkindly, that John must naturally have a bias against his half-brother even were he not conscious of the fact.

"Not only has he stolen your title, John, but he has tried to steal your sweetheart!" Perry had remarked, adding softly, "and so far, John, you have left him unchallenged. Your absence allowed him many hours alone with Chantal to pursue his cause."

His stepfather's comment had convinced John that it was time he ceased to run away from his problems. So he had planned this visit to Boulancourt hoping that he and his mother would be proved right and that he would unearth some dark shadow in Antoine's life. He would demand to see once more the proof of his father's marriage to Blanche Merlin. The document could have been forged. If it were genuine, Antoine would not object to its comparison with the official record of the marriage which his lawyer had told him would have been registered at the *Mairie* of the town where the ceremony was performed. John told his mother that he would not leave France until he had verified the marriage beyond doubt.

He did not expect his half-brother to welcome him despite the fact that on leaving London, Antoine had stressed his desire to stay in contact with his English relations and had invited them to visit him whenever they should find occasion to go to France.

If Antoine de Valle was displeased at John's unexpected visit he gave no outward sign of it when John and his servant finally arrived at Boulancourt. He made no secret of his surprise, however, as he took John to the library to partake of refreshment in the cool shade of the book-lined room.

"I was of the opinion, my dear brother, that you had no feelings of affection for me," he said, pouring wine into a goblet. "May I assume you have had a change of heart?"

John prevaricated. He had felt it was time they got to know each other a little better, he murmured. Moreover, he added truthfully, the study of architecture was one of his favorite pastimes and the Château de Boulancourt fascinated him.

"Perhaps I may make some sketches," he said. "Though by no means a creative artist, I am reasonably proficient at copying what I see. I have a portfolio of beautiful houses to which I would like to add this magnificent Château."

Antoine's eyes narrowed. He doubted very much that an interest in Boulancourt was the real reason for John's visit. Certainly he had no wish for John to look too deeply into the interior of the Château. There were at the moment two men confined in the dungeons. Though it was highly improbable that John would find a way to them past the vigilant guards, Antoine had no desire to risk arousing the slightest hint of suspicion as to his private activities. In addition to these prisoners, he was equally concerned lest John should discover the presence of the third prisoner concealed in the East Tower.

He glanced at his young English relative, trying to assess John's true motives so that he was not caught unawares. In Antoine's experience, few men were without vice. With some it was easy money, with others women, drink, gambling or not infrequently, a particular perversion. He had but to discover John's weakness to be certain of taking control of him.

"Though an admirable pursuit, I cannot think sketching is an exciting hobby for a young man of spirit!" be said. "As it happens, I have been thinking of arranging some entertainment for myself. It was my intention to invite here a few — shall we call them acquaintances — from Paris. Some of the women are exceedingly handsome and without doubt very free with their favors. It might amuse you, my dear brother, to observe a less conventional dinner party here at Boulancourt, than you are used to at home in England."

At twenty-two, John was far from being a prude. Together with the young bloods of his acquaintance he had followed the usual custom of the times, frequenting the noisy coffee-houses and enjoying the favors of any light-o'-love whom he encountered. But such harmless indulgences had lost their enchantment since he had discovered his love for Chantal and he could no longer savor the delights of a woman's body without feeling that he was somehow sullying the girl he loved. But now that Chantal was thousands of miles away and he would not set eyes upon her for many, many months, he wondered if he could remain faithful to her memory.

"Be it as you wish!" he had told Antoine non-committally. "I would not want my presence here to disrupt your normal way of life, so please do not alter your plans on my account. For my own part, I am neither for nor against such entertainment."

They were like two dogs, warily circling one another, mistrustful of each other's motives. Outwardly the half-brothers maintained the formalities of friendship, taking meals together, riding in the forest, playing chess or backgammon of an evening, but each reserving any true pretensions to intimacy.

On the fourth day of John's visit, Antoine announced his intention of going to Paris. He had decided that John was after all every bit as guileless as he seemed. His interest in architecture appeared genuine enough for he spent many hours with his sketching materials or in careful study of the masonry of the Château. He was harmless, Antoine decided, and he suspected John would also prove to be a gullible prey to the lascivious Parisian females he would select to corrupt his prudish morality.

"Whilst you are absent, I will pay a visit to the palace in Compiègne!" John told a satisfied Antoine who was well pleased to learn that John would not be poking into too many crannies at Boulancourt whilst he himself was away.

John had no intention of conducting a search of the Château. His interest was centered in Antoine's papers where he hoped to find the key to his half-brother's past. He therefore observed with satisfaction from the window of his bedchamber Antoine's departure in his cabriolet. When he was convinced that there would be no last minute reversal of plan and the cabriolet had disappeared over the drawbridge he decided to begin his search in the library.

He closed his bedroom door behind him and made his way along the stone passageway leading to the main stairway. The passage seemed deserted with no sign of footman or servant girl hurrying about their business. It therefore came as a considerable shock when a dishevelled, wild-eyed old woman stepped out from her place of concealment behind the brocade drapes of one of the tall casements.

At first John believed he had encountered a lunatic as the woman grabbed his arm with surprising strength and like a witch, beckoned him to follow her back into his bedchamber. He observed her appearance with misgivings. Her long grey hair straggled across her gaunt wrinkled face in wild abandon. Her fingers, gnarled and crooked, the nails broken and dirty, clutched feverishly at his arm. Her eyes, red-rimmed, brilliant with fear and urgency, increased his conviction of her insanity.

No sooner had she dragged John inside the bedchamber than she swiftly turned the key in the lock. Now suddenly she began to speak. Her pure diction and her perfectly phrased English came as a second shock to him for her voice was that of a lady of distinction, utterly at variance with her slovenly appearance.

"I am Camille, Princess Faloise!" she announced in firm clear tones. She peered short-sightedly into John's face. "I know who you are," she said. "My wardress informed me. You are Gerard de Valle's younger son, John!" Her voice took on a new forcefulness as she added: *For the sake of your father who was my friend, you must help me.* Do you understand what I am saying? For the love of God, you must help me to get away from here."

"Pray be seated, Madame!" John said, for the old woman was now trembling so violently that he feared she would lose her balance. He felt a thrill of excitement stir in his veins. If this were in truth the Princess Faloise, why was Antoine keeping her a prisoner?

"We may not have much time!" she said. "It will be only a matter of minutes before my wardress returns to the tower with my midday repast. When she finds me missing she will give the alarm and all the servants in the Château will search for me. They will find me here and . . . "

"Be calm, I beg you!" John broke in soothingly. "No servant shall enter my bedchamber without permission. I assure you you are quite safe here with me."

The old woman pursed her lips in a cynical smile.

"My guards have master keys to all the chambers!" she said. "They will force their way in whether you wish it or not. Now listen to me whilst there is still time, for my very life depends upon it!"

John listened with increasing incredulity to the extraordinary story she now related to him. Despite the lucidity of her speech, reason rejected the fantastic tale she was unfolding. Yet gradually the quiet persistent melodious voice with its trace of French accent altered his opinions yet again and he became convinced of the authenticity of her identity whilst still doubting her story.

Shrewdly she judged his reaction.

"I can see by your face that you find it hard to believe Antoine would have married a woman old enough to be his mother!" she said dryly. "But he wanted money — *my money*. That is all Antoine ever wanted from the days of his youth and he would steal — even kill, to amass the fortune he craved. When your father died he left Antoine his estate but insufficient means to live at Boulancourt as Antoine desired. Half Gerard's wealth was bequeathed to his only daughter, Tamarisk, and although Antoine wrote to the lawyers disputing the bequest, he had no grounds by which to dispute the Will."

Her face took on an expression of acute bitterness.

"In those early years when I was still naïve enough to believe Antoine loved me, I gave him a great deal of money. But it was never enough and I soon realized that it would not be long before, rich as I was, he beggared me. I decided to withhold what I had left and told him he would never have it. That is why he has kept me a prisoner all these years, hoping to force me into submission!"

Once again she caught John's arm with surprising strength and said wearily:

"I no longer know how long I have been here. But even if I go to my grave carrying the secret of the whereabouts of my fortune, Antoine will never lay a finger upon what is left. He dare not kill me for he knows he cannot hope to discover the hiding place by chance. Do you understand what I am trying to tell you, young man? I am not afraid to die; but I am afraid lest my years in solitary confinement should weaken my mind and I might unwittingly tell him what he wants to know. I see that even now you doubt my sanity and I understand it for there are times when I doubt it myself."

John, however, now believed that his strange companion was rational. Her story, if extraordinary, was not beyond belief.

"If your account be true, I will not leave Boulancourt without you!" he said. "When Antoine returns, I . . . "

He broke off as he heard the sound of footsteps running down the passageway and halt outside his room. Seconds later there was an urgent knocking upon the door.

"Do not open it, I beg you!" his companion cried in a voice of such anguish and terror that John hesitated.

"You have nothing to fear!" he said, keeping his voice low so that he should not be overheard by those outside. "I will protect you!"

She clung to him trembling.

"Do you not understand? If they discover I am with you, they will realize that you know I am a prisoner here. They will certainly kill you!"

"Then I will conceal myself beneath the bed valance," John whispered. "No one need know we have encountered one another. We will let the guards believe you chose this room to hide in by chance. Doubtless if they see you alone, they will not think to look for me for I am thought to be on my way to Compiègne. Neither your guards nor Antoine when he returns will suspect that I know your story. He will not then be forewarned when I confront him with my knowledge of your whereabouts and identity, and will have no opportunity to spirit you away to new prison quarters."

But the continuous thundering upon the door seemed to have demoralized the terrified old woman and John was forced to push her forward. Crying and muttering as if she were indeed the lunatic he had first supposed, she stumbled towards the door whilst John beat a hasty retreat beneath the heavy brocade bed valance. From this dark cavernous interior he was unable to see Antoine's evil-looking servant,

Stefano, burst into the room, pistol cocked, his dark-skinned face contorted with anxiety. The man had little doubt as to his fate were the prisoner to escape from the Château or make contact with the outside world. Regardless of the years of devoted service he had given his master, Stefano knew the Vicomte would kill him for his negligence along with the stupid old crone who guarded the prisoner and who had been careless enough to leave the door of her room unlocked.

His relief upon discovering the Princess alone, unharmed and unresisting, was so great that he gave but a cursory glance around the bedchamber before grabbing hold of his prisoner and marching her back to the tower. Her docility did not arouse his suspicion, for many years had passed since the days when she had been wont to scream and bang upon her door, demanding her release and attacking anyone who approached her. The crazy old lady had become subdued by years of solitary incarceration and only upon the rarest of occasions were her guards surprised by a sudden flare of resistance to her fate.

When all was once more quiet, John emerged from his place of concealment. Moving quickly and silently, he descended the stairs and went out into the courtyard. A stableboy stood yawning in the sunshine, holding the reins of John's horse, patiently waiting for the young English milord to make his appearance. Time was of little consequence to the boy. He rose with the sun and worked till darkness fell. It was not for him to question if his masters dallied and

213

he stood idle for an hour or more. He welcomed the respite from more energetic labors.

With a nod to the boy, John mounted quickly and rode towards the forest. There, in the quiet haven of trees he slowed his horse to a walk and allowed his mind to give full concentration to the recent events.

Alone in the green shade of the giant oaks and beeches, the story the pathetic old woman had told him seemed far less credible. He began to doubt once more that she was truly whom she claimed to be — Antoine's former guardian, Princess Camille.

Yet if not Camille Faloise, *who was she?* And why was she kept a prisoner at the Château? Stefano's behavior in his bedchamber left John in no doubt that the old woman was indeed a prisoner. Nor could he doubt her claim to be an aristocrat for not once had her voice betrayed her as it must have done were she seeking to emulate an educated accent in the hope of lending credence to her story.

Only now did John appreciate the seriousness of her implications. If her account were true in all respects, Antoine de Valle was a married man. And since his wife appeared to be still alive, there was no way that Antoine could possibly marry Chantal even were she to accept his proposal. But would he refute such allegations?

John endeavored to control his impatience, knowing that Antoine would not return from Paris until the following afternoon. He continued upon his way to Compiègne and tried to

214

concentrate upon the beauties of the palace and its gardens.

The palace itself he found cold and bare. He was far from certain that he approved Napoleon's somewhat austere taste. The gardens, however, could not have been more luxuriant. They were exquisitely laid out — the old style of landscape gardening and the new fashion for geometric formality perfectly balanced. The brilliant arrays of flowers were carpet-bedded to give the illusion of cushions of colorful jewels set in lush green velvet grass.

John wished he could identify the many species of flowers. His mother and Chantal would doubtless know their names, he thought. There came to mind a phrase from an old gardening book of his mother's which Chantal sometimes quoted when they walked together through the gardens at Finchcocks. '*Exotic herbage all speckled and pied and ring-straked*' seemed perfectly to describe his present surroundings.

Walnut, beech, oak and chestnut trees formed a perfect backdrop for this blaze of color. Their shade looked inviting for the hot afternoon sun burned down upon his head from a cloudless sky.

He felt an intense longing for Chantal's company. To be surrounded by such beauty without the person you loved to share it with, he thought, was a sadness that was suddenly unbearable. Not wishing to linger in these evocative surroundings he retraced his steps to the palace entrance.

On his return to Boulancourt, he dined alone

with Stefano in attendance and made a point of commenting upon his afternoon's outing to allay any suspicions the servant might have as to his whereabouts during the Princess' brief spell of freedom.

Antoine returned next day in excellent spirits. He greeted John with the announcement that all was prepared for a weekend of great entertainment. If Stefano had already informed his Master of the prisoner's escape, Antoine showed no sign of annoyance nor of suspicion. When John requested a private conversation with him away from the ears of the attendant servants, he said agreeably:

"But of course, my dear fellow!"

Antoine divested himself of his outer garments, ordered wine to be brought to the library and took John's arm in the friendliest of manners.

"It is always a pleasure to return home!" he said.

Seating himself elegantly in a wine-red leather armchair, he motioned John also to be seated.

Watching his half-brother unobtrusively, John felt a little of his self-confidence wane. Face to face with this handsome elegant, charming man, it was impossible to believe that Antoine could in fact be the villain of the Princess' story. Such a rogue must register some sign of his perfidy upon his countenance, John mused. Would there not be a hint of cruelty in the mouth? An expression of ruthlessness in the eyes? A harshness in the voice? But his half-brother portrayed no such traits.

As soon as the footman had served the wine

and left the room, Antoine yawned and putting his slippered feet upon the sofa-table, he said casually but shrewdly:

"Well, *mon vieux*, what preys upon your mind so harshly that you regard me with a scowl rather than a smile? Did my absence appear ill-mannered? Believe me, I . . . "

"My concern is of a more serious matter than you may suppose," John interrupted, his uncertainty causing him to sound more abrupt than he had intended. He paused a moment longer before blurting out the truth. "I have to tell you that whilst you were away, I encountered a stranger within these walls — a woman who told me she was the Princess Camille Faloise and a prisoner in this house."

His eyes searched Antoine's face minutely as he made his announcement, for he was determined upon observing any hint of shock, surprise, dismay or guilt. To his astonishment, Antoine's face remained impassive but for an indifferent smile.

"I hope that crazy old woman has not concerned you unduly, John!" he said, adding with a sigh, "I fear her appearance must have shocked you. I should have warned you of her presence in the Château. But the poor woman is kept under lock and key, and it did not cross my mind that you might encounter her and have your peace disturbed."

With yet another sigh, he stood up unhurriedly and refilled their goblets.

"You realize, do you not, John, that she is not whom she claims to be. The poor old soul is mad. Her story is really quite pathetic. If it would interest you, I will tell you about her."

His conviction now seriously undermined, John was beginning to feel something of a fool. He suspected that he had allowed his imagination to run away with his common sense — possibly, he surmised, because he had wanted to discover something to his half-brother's discredit.

Antoine's voice sounded calm and convincing as he related:

"The woman's real name is Marie Duval. She was once Princess Camille's personal maid and was in her service from the days of her girlhood until her Mistress died. My guardian's death was a terrible shock to the poor woman, the more so because it was so sudden. Camille died in America, you know, from a strange fever she contracted there some few years ago. It was my intention to retain Marie in my employ — perhaps as a housekeeper or laundry maid or some-such. I had hoped she would recover in time from the dementia which followed her Mistress' death."

He paused whilst he pushed the decanter of wine across the table to John. When both glasses had been replenished, be continued:

"Alas, Marie's mind was quite unhinged by her grief. I suppose I could have placed the poor soul in a home for the insane but such places are not very congenial, you understand. So I decided to let her live out her remaining years in such peace as her poor deranged mind would allow. She has never been able to accept the Princess' death and by taking on her Mistress' identity she found a way by which she could continue to believe in her existence. Such twists of the mind are strange, are they not? Yet the physician tells me they are by no means exceptional."

He glanced at John's flushed face and laughed.

"Why, John, I do believe you let poor old Marie hoodwink you into the belief that she really is the late Princess Faloise!" he said. "Next thing you will tell me you also believe the story she is wont to tell that I married my late guardian for her money! Come now, confess you have been duped!"

"I cannot pretend otherwise," John replied awkwardly, embarrassed by his extreme gullibility. "The Princess . . . I mean her maid, Marie sounded most convincing and . . . "

"Do not apologize." Antoine broke in. "I am quite well aware that you came here with your mind poisoned against me, John — a fact which saddens me greatly since I have so few living relatives for whom I can feel affection. It was my hope that you and I would become friends as well as brothers. But I fear that your mother was always intent upon excluding me from her family circle; and whilst I can appreciate her reasons for resenting my birth, it does not seem fair that I should be blamed for my father's betrayal of her. If you will be honest with me, John, you will admit that you have heard no good spoken of me. Yet you have heard no word spoken *by* me to discredit your mother's character."

Seeing the angry rush of color in John's cheeks, he added smoothly:

"I am not implying that your mother is worthy of less than the utmost respect. But there are few people living whose lives are totally blameless. Your mother's intimate relationship with my father never ceased from the time when they were still in their teens and first became lovers until his death. During those years, both were married and deceived their respective spouses. In your mother's case she was unfaithful to two husbands. But you and I and Tamarisk, too, all share one father. 'Tis true that he deceived your mother when he married mine, but neither was your mother blameless. Her past reputation will not bear close scrutiny however conventionally she now chooses to live."

"What is past is no concern of mine!" John said evasively. He had no wish to reveal to Antoine his ignorance of his mother's early life. "I will admit that it came as a great shock to me to learn that I am a bastard and must relinquish to you our father's title."

"By our French Code Civil, you are no bastard!" Antoine interrupted. "Since your mother was unaware her marriage was bigamous, she is deemed to have acted *de bonne foi* and you cannot be made illegitimate."

"In your country that may be so," John argued. "But by English law I am a bastard. Mayhap my resentment of this status has rebounded on you and if this is so, then I see now that it is unfair. I will further admit that I resented your interest in . . . in Chantal. You may already be aware that it is my hope that one day she will marry me. This makes you my rival for her affections and therefore I can never view our relationship dispassionately. Nevertheless I accept that I have felt considerable prejudice against you and perhaps owe you an apology for my mistrust."

"Nobly said! And pray do not apologize. I understand your sentiments perfectly and regret deeply that we are rivals for Chantal's love."

Antoine stood up extending a hand which John accepted but not without a reluctance he would have been hard put to rationalize.

"Let us agree that whilst rivals in love, we can still like each other as brothers!" he said. "I would not want you to feel other than welcome in my house. I hope you will continue your sojourn at Boulancourt for as long as you wish!"

But despite Antoine's clear desire to be friendly and his willingness to forget that John had been ready to believe the worst of him regarding the unfortunate lunatic he was sheltering beneath his roof, John thought it better that he returned forthwith to England. There must be constraint between them following such a conversation and to remain as Antoine's guest was no longer acceptable. Making the excuse that he had promised to call upon the Dubois family on his way home, he informed Antoine that he must curtail his visit. He doubted that Antoine believed his story that he had been somewhat smitten by the charms of one of the Dubois daughters, but the reason sufficed to enable him to make his farewells without further embarrassment to either of them. The

221

verification of Blanche Merlin's marriage would have to await a more favorable occasion.

Riding away from Boulancourt towards the forest and Compiègne, John turned for a last look at the Château. The lightening of his spirits as he had ridden over the drawbridge took a sudden plunge downwards as his eyes were drawn to the windows of the East Tower. There was no mistaking the gaunt outline of a figure waving a white 'kerchief in his direction. Was the mad woman really Marie? Or had Antoine de Valle skillfully lied his way out of trouble? Was the woman with the aristocratic voice after all, truly the Princess Camille?

John was no longer sure.

12

September 1838

FOR three days the wind and the currents drove the longboat eastward further out into the Indian Ocean. On the fourth day, the wind veered nor'westward and the Lascar, observing the stars, smiled for the first time.

He pointed across the empty expanse of blue water ahead of them.

"India," he told Chantal briefly. "Maybe find land perhaps!"

"But when?" Chantal asked, sinking back onto the wet canvas that served as a bed when she was not sitting in the stem sheets watching the Lascar row with slow relentless strokes hour upon hour. "*How soon?*" she persisted when he did not reply.

The sailor managed somehow to shrug his shoulders whilst never ceasing his rowing.

"One week, two! Who know! Mohammed guide us!"

Chantal bit back the exasperation she felt at this Oriental faith in the powers of the Prophet. She tried to smile. She owed her life to her companion whom she called Kaftan because it was the nearest she could come to pronouncing his real name. He was a huge man, immensely strong and seemingly immensely resourceful. She tried to discover if he had been shipwrecked before but he spoke only a few words of English. Most of their communication took place by sign language.

He had allowed her to cry unheeded when *Valetta* had disappeared beneath the waves, but as soon as she stopped crying, he assumed command of their tiny vessel. Pointing to a wooden bowl lying in the dirty water that slopped around her drenched skirts, he indicated that he wished her to start baling. Numbed with cold and shock, it had not occurred to Chantal to disobey the seaman. He had continued to give orders by signs as if it had already been agreed between them that he was the Captain of the longboat and she a member of his crew.

So far Kaftan had proved himself more than able. With his knife lashed to a piece of wood, he successfully speared the fish which his keen eyes seemed to see below the surface of the water when Chantal saw nothing. Having no means of lighting a fire, no suitable place for cooking, he had shown by his example that she must eat the fish raw. Her stomach revolted but soon hunger and familiarity taught her to enjoy the simple repast.

At first there had been no shortage of drinking water for the rain had cascaded from the skies and the Lascar had caught every last drop in whatever container was handy. He rationed it severely, refusing to allow Chantal to wash her face and hands which were now painfully blistered by the wind, salt and water. Although be had retrieved a floating cask of rancid butter from the wreckage of the sunken ship he would not give her any to soothe her parched skin.

"Eat!" he commanded. "Food!"

Only now did she understand why Kaftan was so careful of their few resources — a bag of hard ship's biscuits alive with weevils, dried strips of raw fish, the rancid butter and stale rainwater. He was not expecting to be rescued by a passing boat and his hope of reaching land appeared to be weeks away from realisation.

Tears stung Chantal's lids as her imagination tried to envisage such an eternity of time before they could get off this horrible rocking boat. With the calm weather that followed the hurricane, the effects of seasickness had worn off but the primitive conditions on board meant living in acute discomfort. She could not emulate the Lascar's calm acceptance of the dreadful conditions of their daily existence. At least he turned his back when the demands of nature required privacy. Kaftan had already demanded that she surrender her silk stockings so that he might use them to mend the piece of broken spar he wished to use for a mast. She had feared at the time that he would next demand her torn skirt and petticoats to make a sail; but fortunately he had retrieved for this purpose a piece of canvas sail from amongst the jetsam that covered the water where *Valetta* had sunk.

But the mere need for survival which dominated Chantal's mind in those first days lessened as soon as it became clear that their little boat would survive the remnants of the storm. Her thoughts were now concentrated upon the horror of their recent skirmish with death. She

225

tried to grasp the unbelievable fact that she and the Lascar were *Valetta*'s only survivors; that her beloved sister Tamarisk was dead, as were poor Charles and the two maids. There had been no signs of life in the corpses floating with the flotsam in the sea. It was small consolation that she had not looked upon the dead faces of her sister and brother-in-law. It had been shock enough to recognize some members of the crew and not least, the terrified countenance of poor Elsie.

Kaftan's calm, practical approach to their desperate situation gradually communicated itself to Chantal. It did not occur to her that she had cause to fear this rough foreign sailor against whom any resistance would have been quite useless. His great masculine body with its huge muscles and broad shoulders gave her confidence rather than cause for alarm.

Despite all that Chantal's mind and body had endured, her youthful resilience was such that she watched with fascination and delight when he plunged into the sea and swam easily through the waves to retrieve some object he hoped might mean food or be of use to them. He brought back a bundle of seaweed which first he tasted himself and then gave her to eat. When she spat it out, he held her head as if she were a naughty child and forced some of the evil-tasting sea plant down her throat, ignoring her muffled cries of protest.

"Good, good!" was all he said as tears of mortification fell from Chantal's eyes between each mouthful.

Now on the fifth day, their supply of water was running low. The storm had vanished entirely, giving way to a hot wind and a cloudless sky from which the sun burnt fiercely upon them. Chantal's thirst was tormenting.

Kaftan too needed water. The effort of rowing caused his body to sweat profusely thereby losing precious liquid. He indicated to Chantal that he was going overboard. Taking an empty coconut shell in his hands, he disappeared into the sea. This time he did not reappear as quickly as she had learned to expect when he dived. Anxiously she peered over the side of the boat. There was no sign of Kaftan's brown body.

The Lascar was diving as deep as he could towards the seabed. He knew that the greater the depths of water the less salty it was and if retrieved might be used for slaking the thirst. Having first filled his powerful lungs with air, he forced himself to swim deeper and deeper. When he could go no further, he took his finger from the hole in the coconut shell and allowed the water to seep in. As soon as the shell was filled, he kicked upwards towards the surface, lungs now bursting for the air he had relinquished. Regaining his breath, he climbed back aboard and sampled his prize before offering it to Chantal. As he had thought, it was still very salty but unlikely to harm them too severely.

In such manner the two survivors drifted westward. They had no charts to guide them and no way of knowing how far they were from land. Kaftan no longer spoke of India but of Africa as he indicated their direction.

Sometimes a flying fish landed in the boat to be eagerly caught and killed by the Lascar. On one occasion he caught and killed a turtle. Chantal wept in horror as he stabbed the poor harmless animal to death but although she choked on the raw flesh, her instinct for survival was such that she devoured the savory meat, welcoming this change from their fishy diet. Once they glimpsed a sperm whale. Twice they saw sharks, which were the only occasions Kaftan showed any fear. He left her in no doubt that these sea monsters were man-eaters and that it would be fatal to be caught in the water by one of them.

Somehow the long burning hot days dragged past and restlessly the cooler nights. Chantal slept fitfully, her mind troubled by dreams of death and shipwreck. But worse even than these was when consciousness returned after dreams of home. Such was her longing to be safe at Barre House with her parents and John that she did not know how she could endure yet another endless day drifting in the longboat.

She suffered terribly from sunburn; and from stomach cramps brought on by their strange diet. She was always thirsty; her tongue was swollen and her lips were blistered. The sun was so fierce that it seemed to penetrate even the thick canvas awning Kaftan had erected over her head. Such was her lethargy that Kaftan had constantly to urge her to remain awake. But for him she would have drifted into a sleep from which she had no energy to surface. There were times when quite irrationally she hated Kaftan for his impassivity. He seemed unperturbed when a frigate under full sail passed by them not a mile distant and failed to see their drifting boat.

"We could have been rescued!" she stormed, tears of disappointment trickling down her cheeks. "You do not care, do you? You *like* being Captain of this wretched little boat where you can give me orders and do what you want all day long. It makes you feel strong and powerful! Oh, I hate you. I hate you!"

"Was will of Allah!" came his calm reply.

It was not long before her irrational behavior gave way to a deep feeling of guilt that she had berated the man who had never once failed to do his utmost to keep them both alive; who was kindly and tried so hard to protect her from the worst of their condition.

The lack of water was now their overriding concern. The supplies of stagnant fresh water, replenished only once in a heavy rainstorm after the first week, had now run out. Kaftan dived several times a day. But now that he was physically weaker, he was no longer always successful in his attempts to go deep enough to reach the less salty water that was bearable to drink. More and more frequently he would surface, taste the contents of the coconut shell and tip it back into the sea. Chantal could not fail to see the look of anxiety on his face and she realized that death was the probable outcome for them both.

Kaftan knew even before Chantal that they could not survive much longer. His weakening body frequently refused to obey his will. Diving became more and more of an effort. For the sake of the English Goddess he believed Mohammed had entrusted to his care, he knew he must go back into the sea, however great the risk involved. But Kaftan did not anticipate the manner of his dying.

Unaware that they were drifting towards the coral reef surrounding one of the islands in the Seychelles Archipelago, he gave no thought to the danger of sharks basking in the shallower waters as he dived yet again over the side of the boat. Chantal, lying half unconscious beneath the canvas awning, saw nothing of the dark shadows following Kaftan as he disappeared beneath the surface. It was only when she became dimly aware that he had been absent for a long time that the first hint of disaster reached her consciousness.

All movement now an effort of will, she struggled into a sitting position and peered over the side. At first she could see nothing but the coconut shell bobbing on the surface of the sparkling water. Then she saw red pools eddying in the boat's wake. Slowly her mind took in their meaning and with a stab of fear she caught sight of the thrash of white water twenty yards away as the dorsal fin of a shark cut the surface. Her mouth opened in a horrified scream of protest, but the only sound she made was a strange croak as the parched membranes of her throat remained agonizingly closed.

For a full minute she continued to stare at the terrible evidence of Kaftan's cruel death. Then she covered her face with her hands and sank back in fear and horror from the scene.

Mercifully she was soon overcome by turpitude and the heat and lapsed into troubled sleep. At times she dreamed of England, of her parents, of riding with John through woods bright with streams of cascading fresh water. Once she dreamed of Antoine and experienced again the strange feeling of rapture that had encompassed her when he kissed her. But as always, there were nightmares too, of *Valetta* sinking beneath the waves; of Kaftan swimming for his life with a shark gaining inch by inch upon him as he struggled to reach the safety of the boat; of a mass of seething flames searing her naked flesh as the sun's orb came closer and closer. Only dimly was she aware that night had overtaken day before finally drifting into a deep lasting coma.

When next she awoke it was to see a strange olive-skinned, dark-haired man sitting at a desk, his head bent studiously over a big leather-bound ledger. Chantal lay immobile, watching the man as he turned the pages with long beringed fingers. Certain that she was dreaming, she did not question his strange presence. She decided he was probably an officer of a foreign navy for despite the informality of his open-necked frilled shirt and white drill pantaloons, he gave the impression of being a ship's captain.

Still only half-conscious, her mind wandered from the stranger to the bunk in which she lay. Beneath her she could feel the rocking of a ship at sea. Now she became aware of the creaking timbers and the slap-slap of waves against the sides of the ship as it lay anchored in calm waters.

"Please, sir, will you tell me where I am?" she asked. Even to her own ears her voice barely rose above a husky whisper.

At the sound, the man's head swung round in her direction and he stared at her from the most extraordinary green eyes that she had ever encountered. Beneath the dark, arched brows, his eyes were like emeralds, so compelling that she barely noticed the long aquiline nose, wide mouth and small pointed black beard.

"You speak English!" he remarked, the severity of his face softening into a slight smile as he stood up and approached the bunk in which Chantal lay. So tall was he that he had to stoop lest he hit his head against the crossbeams of the cabin roof. "*Fala português?*"

With an effort out of all proportion to the strength normally required for such an action, Chantal managed to shake her head.

"Very well! We will communicate in your language. What is your name, please?" he asked.

He must have noticed Chantal's attempt to moisten her blistered lips with her tongue for at once he clapped his hands to summon a servant. A native girl came running into the cabin, her African origins at once recognizable by the mass of frizzy hair, the ebony black of her skin and widely splayed nose. Above the colored cotton of her long skirt, her upper torso was bare and Chantal felt her cheeks color with

232

embarrassment as the girl's full pointed breasts swung gently with her movements.

"Señor?" the servant girl enquired, two rows of brilliant white teeth showing in a huge smile.

"*Traga água!*" he ordered. "*E limão!*" As the girl ran off to do his bidding, be added: "Her name is Zambi. I called her so because she comes from the Mozambique coast. She speaks only her own unintelligible language and a little *português* which I have taught her since I took her from a slave ship."

"You mean that African girl is your *slave?*" Chantal asked, deeply shocked. "Surely that is against the law!"

The gaze of the man's brilliant green eyes now seemed to mock her as be replied:

"It is against the English law, yes! But not all the peoples of the world are willing to recognize your rules. However, you need have no fear for Zambi's welfare. She is my devoted servant because she wishes to be. Many of the poor devils aboard the slaver taking her to the Americas had already died when I took possession of the ship. Zambi sees me as her rescuer."

"Please tell me who you are, sir!" Chantal begged for her exhausted mind was fast becoming bewildered with so much that was new to think upon.

"Dinez Guimaraes Paulo da Gama! I am *português* and this is my boat, which I named *O Bailado* because she dances so beautifully over the water." His smile disappeared as he now asked: "And you, Señorita, may I enquire your name?"

"I am Chantal, daughter of Sir Peregrine Waite. I was traveling to India with my sister and her husband, Rear Admiral von Eburhard on Her Majesty's ship, *Valetta*."

She closed her eyes as the memory of the storm at sea flooded back into her mind. A tear, which she attempted to brush away, trickled down one cheek. Her skin, painful and blistered, seemed to he covered with a greasy substance.

"The oil from the coconut!" Dinez da Gama explained briefly as he watched her movements with curiosity.

It was clear to him that this girl had no memory as yet of the two days which had passed since he had come upon the longboat and discovered its single half-dead occupant. So blackened by the sun was the ragged girl that he and his crew had at first assumed she was an escaped slave, although not of African origins, for her hair was too long and straight and her features too sharply defined despite the terrible swelling of her blistered lips and eyelids.

On finding her alive, the men had thrown her into one of the holds, and giving Zambi orders to do what she could for the survivor, began to bargain amongst themselves for the the privilege of being the first to ravish the girl if she lived.

It was Zambi who discovered that Chantal was no insignificant castaway as they all supposed. Not only was the skin beneath the survivor's tattered garments a creamy white, she told Dinez, but around the girl's neck was a gold

234

chain with a ring that Zambi wanted to keep.

Immediately Dinez da Gama went to see the castaway himself. Realizing that she could well be a person of nobility, he had her brought to his own cabin. Such was Chantal's appearance after her weeks at sea, her rescuer had no way of judging whether she was beautiful or ugly; but his keen eyes had taken in the fine bones of her wrists and ankles, the smoothness of her skin and the delicate beauty of her young breasts. He suspected that she might be a virgin and his curiosity increased as hour upon hour he watched the girl lying unconscious in his bunk.

Now that she was awake at last and he could see beneath the swollen red lids the dark beauty of her eyes, he knew that he desired her and that he would claim his prerogative as ship's captain and take her when the right moment came.

Dinez da Gama was twenty-seven years of age and in the full vigor of manhood. The eighth son of an impoverished Portuguese gentleman, he had turned to piracy as an easy means of earning his living, for he had no wish to work like a peasant and his father had no money to give him. In the past five years that he had been at sea, he had plundered ships of all nationalities, appropriating cargoes of great value and carefully hoarding his riches on Coetivy, one of the many islands in the Seychelles Archipelago.

Six square miles of land projecting from the sea, Coetivy was more than two hundred miles from the main island of Mahé and in no danger of exploration by fishermen or traders.

Surrounded by a coral reef, access could be made only in a flat-bottomed boat in which men could row over the reef on the crest of a wave. No man lived there and Dinez was satisfied that his growing hoard would stay undiscovered until he was ready to retire to his homeland, there to lead the life of a gentleman of means. In the meanwhile, the adventure and excitement of his dangerous life at sea pleased him well enough. The handling of his ship and of the rough, tough individuals who made up his crew kept his physical energies engaged and his mind alert.

He would enjoy his life even more, he thought now, if this young English girl became his mistress. She had not yet realized that she was hopelessly at his mercy. He wondered whether she would resist him and felt his blood stir at the thought.

By the time Zambi had finished spooning lime juice into Chantal's mouth, Dinez saw with regret that the girl was once more asleep. He went back to his chair and watched lazily whilst Zambi drew back the voluminous lawn nightshirt covering Chantal's body and gently massaged more oil into her parched skin. The sight of the slave girl's black hands on Chantal's white body excited him further and as soon as Zambi had completed her ministrations, he beckoned her to him.

Smiling, the black girl slipped easily onto his lap and began to caress him. The man took his pleasure of her casually and with selfish indifference. He neither knew nor cared that to this slave girl he was a white god for whom she would happily die if it pleased him. After the nightmare of endless rapings by the French sailors on the slave ship from which Dinez da Gama had rescued her, Zambi bore only love and gratitude toward him. Moreover she was fascinated by the fairness of his skin which she considered beautiful and a privilege to touch.

Zambi had long ago relinquished all hope of ever seeing her family again. Although Dinez had once idly promised that he would leave her on the African coast next time he passed by, she no longer wished to be parted from him. In her simple way, she considered herself his wife and if she felt any sadness, it was that no child had yet resulted from their union. Her uneducated mind had deduced that black and white could not be mixed any more than could the black panther and the white cheetah in the jungles of her homeland.

Dismissing Zambi with a wave of his hand, Dinez returned once more to the bedside. Chantal was calling out in her sleep. He heard the name "Tamarisk" and wondered why this strangely called person should cause Chantal to twist and turn so feverishly as if with fear. Asleep, Chantal's swollen face no longer held the same charm. Dinez shrugged his shoulders and went back to consideration of the chances of landing on the island later in the day.

If Chantal could but have known Tamarisk's true fate, she would not have been haunted by the thought of her sister's drowning.

Tamarisk, in similar manner to Chantal but on the opposite side of *Valetta* had also found the safe haven of one of the longboats. Four English sailors had pulled her from the huge seas in which her life preserver was keeping her afloat. With mountainous foam-capped waves tossing them from trough to trough, neither longboat had glimpsed the other. As the four sailors and Kaftan took up oars to save themselves from being sucked down with *Valetta*, the longboats had set off in opposite directions. Within minutes they were a mile apart and were not to come within hailing distance again.

With far better supplies of food and water aboard and four men upon the oars, the longboat carrying Tamarisk made much greater speed than had Chantal with only Kaftan rowing. After ten days the wind and currents had carried them to within sight of the island of Mahé.

The sailors were jubilant. Although they had no knowledge of their whereabouts, it put fresh heart into all of them to see the sea birds and the dark outlines of thick forest covering the hills on the horizon. But the privations they had endured had brought about a devastating deterioration of their strength. Weakened by the meager rations and scarcity of water, and scorched by the equatorial sun, they were no longer able to row effectively. Although they espied ships to the north of them and surmised that they were in all probability heading for a port, they themselves drifted with the swift currents which carried them westward towards the rocky coastline of the island.

Despite the constant kindness shown her by the sailors and a more than generous share of their small hoard of food and water, Tamarisk was in far worse shape than Chantal, although in similar circumstances. Without the resilience of extreme youth, Tamarisk could not so easily overcome the shock and grief of seeing her husband killed before her eyes.

She worried endlessly about the fate of her children were she, too, to die at sea. Whilst certain that her mother and Perry would assume loving guardianship of the children, she fretted to think that they would become orphans. Moreover, she suffered wretchedly from seasickness and therefore obtained little benefit from the tiny ration of food that was her allotted portion. By the time they were in sight of land, she was too weak to understand why the men were shouting or to appreciate that they were about to face the further danger of being swept to their deaths on the rocks.

This state of semi-consciousness was what eventually saved Tamarisk's life. The longboat was carried inshore by the huge surge of the pounding waves and was dashed against the rocks. Her limp body was tossed overboard into the white foam as the boat splintered and water poured in. The sailors struggled desperately to paddle off the rocks out of danger. But a second wave threw the boat clear of the first outcrop only to dash it with even greater force high up on the rocky beach. The occupants, still clinging to their broken oars, had no chance to save themselves as the boat was dragged back into the sea. She instantly turned turtle and the men were imprisoned beneath the hull.

Tamarisk was kept afloat by the air trapped within her torn but still voluminous skirt and petticoats. The same huge wave that had destroyed the boat carried her like a cork, sideways and inwards and finally rolled her up onto the coral sand. As the wave receded, the tide began to turn and the subsequent waves washed harmlessly against her legs.

Above Tamarisk's unprotected head, the equatorial sun beat fiercely down upon her, drying her hair and clothes and bringing warmth to her inert body. And so she lay for two hours before the Negro found her. She was still unconscious and therefore mercifully unaware of the mutilated corpses of the sailors now littering the water's edge like so much flotsam. She knew nothing of the torn, broken and bleeding bodies covered with huge crabs and flesh-eating fish. Her soft moaning was brought about by the nightmares of her own delirium in which she was to remain for a further ten days.

The Negro bending over her was superstitiously frightened by his discovery that the golden-haired, half-drowned woman was still alive. Nevertheless he carried her twenty yards up the sand and laid her down in the shade of one of the palm trees fringing the beach. Then he took to his heels and ran as fast as his long black legs would carry him through the lush undergrowth towards the plantation where he could be certain of finding help.

240

The man for whom the Negro now worked as a freed slave was seated in a cane chair in the shade of the veranda of his home, the Château Corail. Although small by European standards, it was one of the largest plantation houses on the island of Mahé. Siméon St. Clair was the owner and sole occupant since the death of his father some six years previously.

French by birth, Siméon was the only offspring of a misalliance between his aristocratic mother and a man from farming stock. He had inherited his mother's delicate bone structure, sensitive nature and natural refinement. Fortunately he had none of his father's coarse brutality and were it not for Siméon's instinctive peasant understanding of the natural elements of the soil and its products, there would have been no discernible trait of his paternal origins.

Now but twenty-one years of age, he was striving against all the odds to keep the Corail Plantation viable. It was a losing battle despite the efforts of the few remaining ex-slaves at his command. His relationship with his black workers, both indoor and outdoor, was that of a father with his children. Upon seeing the frightened face of his African foreman, Tobias, he asked kindly:

"*Alors, qu'est ce qu'y a?*"

Despite the change to British rule on Mahé forty-two years previously, the ex-slaves spoke only the French of their masters. Tobias therefore replied to Siméon in his own language, trying with his limited vocabulary and even more limited understanding of what he had seen, to

241

describe the scene upon the beach at Grand Police where he had gone to catch fish for his evening meal.

Siméon listened to the tale of blood and mutilated bodies in disbelief, for rarely was even a living soul to be seen on this southernmost tip of Mahé. The rocky outcrop around Grand Police made it quite unsuitable for fishermen who gave it a wide berth. From most of the sandy, palm-fringed beaches on Mahé, the pirogues could be launched without difficulty and rowed out to sea without danger. Mahé's port, l'Établissement du Roi, was situated on the northeast coast and it was only there that sailors such as Tobias described were likely to be found. For several miles around the Château Corail, as far as Siméon knew, there lived only himself and his workers.

As for the golden-haired, half-drowned female Tobias described, she sounded more like a figment of the old fellow's imagination, he thought doubtfully.

Nevertheless Tobias was clearly terrified by what he had seen, so Siméon gave in to the man's persuasions for urgency and rose reluctantly from his chair. He followed him back down the hill through the cinnamon trees and tea bushes, until the ground leveled slightly. A few hundred yards ahead was the palm-fringed beach of Grand Police.

The first sight of Tamarisk's inert body disturbed Siméon St. Clair even more profoundly than it had affected Tobias. Her hair, like spun gold, was spread across her face and reminded him instantly of his dead mother. It was more than twelve years since Yvonne St. Clair had died and he, a boy but nine years old, had discovered her drowned body upon this very beach. His father, Roger St. Clair had denied absolutely that his wife had committed suicide but Siméon's black nurse had sworn that her beloved Mistress had wanted to end her life. Unwisely she had communicated her convictions to the boy, adding to his shock.

With a sense of *dèja vu*, he bent and felt Tamarisk's neck, searching for a pulse. Tobias looked at his Master anxiously.

"Lady still alive!" he said. "We carry her to the house, yes?"

As if in a dream, Siméon stared once more at the human wreckage strewn across the hot sands, limbs swaying grotesquely as the bodies ebbed to and fro with the movement of the waves. Then he turned back to the living and watched as the great black African picked Tamarisk up in his arms as if she were a child and began the slow upward climb to the Château Corail.

13

September 1838

"PLEASE tell me where I am?"
Even to her own ears, Tamarisk's voice sounded so weak she feared it might be inaudible to her companion. But the young man seated in the chair by her bed replied immediately:

"Do not try to talk, Madame. You must conserve your strength. You have been very ill." His tanned, attractive young face broke into a delightful smile as he continued: "Now you are recovering, *grace à Dieu*, and soon you will be well again!"

For a moment Tamarisk stared confusedly at the face of this stranger. Although he had spoken mainly in English in reply to her question, she realized he was French. By his clothes, voice and finely-boned features, she assumed he was of gentle birth. But she could not imagine who he might be.

As if divining her thoughts, he said:

"May I introduce myself to you, Madame? I am Siméon St. Clair. My home is called the Château Corail and I am the owner of the Corail Plantation which is on the island of Mahé."

He took a glass from the table nearby and held it to her lips. Tamarisk became aware that her mouth was swollen, her tongue parched and that

244

her skin was burning. With difficulty she sipped the cool liquid and sank back once more against her pillows. There were so many questions she wanted to ask but she was too tired. She could not think what she was doing in this strange bed in the house of this strange man or how she came to be on an island called Mahé. Her memory seemed to have deserted her, perhaps because she was ill, she thought.

"Sleep now!" said the quiet voice, infinitely soothing. "Do not be afraid. I will keep watch over you. Try to sleep!"

The gentleness of the young man's voice and his reassuring words relaxed the tension of her confusion. She closed her eyes and drifted back to sleep.

When next she awoke, the room was very quiet. There was a sweet scent all around her with which she was unfamiliar. Golden bars of sunshine crisscrossed her bedcover and she saw that they were filtering through the closed shutters of the window. The room reminded her of the guest chamber she had slept in as a child at Boulancourt. The furniture, imported from France, was mainly antique. Hand-carved, it was meticulously polished so that the walnut glowed even in the semi-darkness of the shuttered room.

On a lowboy near the window was a glass vase containing tall sprays of brilliant yellow mimosa. On the satinwood night table was another vase filled with bright purple bougainvillaea. From outside the window, she could hear a variety of different birdsongs, the occasional bleat of a goat and the clucking of hens.

The door opened and Siméon St. Clair came in. Seeing that Tamarisk's eyes were open, he hurried over to the bed with a look of apology.

"You must forgive me for being absent on your awakening!" he said in his accented English. "I had to give instructions to Tobias. He is my foreman. It was he who found you on the beach at Grand Police."

He stood looking down at her with a shy smile. Now that he had time to observe the features of his guest more closely, her resemblance to his dead mother vanished. There remained only the similarity in the color of her hair. Nevertheless, Siméon was filled with tender concern for this beautiful stranger who had arrived so unexpectedly in his home.

He smiled again.

"Do you feel better?" he enquired solicitously. "I would be very happy to know your name."

"Tamarisk — Tamarisk von Eburhard!" she replied automatically.

At that moment, with the mention of her married name, she remembered Charles. A cry burst from her lips as she recalled the terrifying vision of his death. At once Siméon took her hand and in an attempt to soothe her from whatever horrors were returning to her mind, he gently stroked the delicate skin.

Tamarisk gave way to her grief as piece by piece the terrible memories returned. Gasping and sobbing, she told her silent companion of the cruel deprivations of the days at sea.

Of the final debâcle she remembered nothing, but Siméon was able to give her a probable account of it.

"The bay at Grand Police is one of the most dangerous inlets on the island!" he told her. "The wind and currents are more than capable of carrying a boat onto those rocks and dashing it to pieces. It is a miracle that you survive!"

Tamarisk covered her face with her hands, crying quietly.

"It would have been better if *I* had died with Charles. Chantal, my sister, was only eighteen years old. It will break her father's heart when he bears of her death. And my poor children! They loved their father very dearly."

"You must think only of recovering your health and strength so that you may return to England to comfort them," Siméon said gently. "Try not to grieve for those who are gone, Madame. Now I will send Narcisse to you. She is Tobias' wife and my housekeeper. She has been taking care of you for the past two weeks whilst you have been unconscious. I believe you may very well owe your life to her for I myself have little knowledge of medicine. Narcisse has many remedies, doubtless gleaned from her African tribe. They appear to be most effective. She cures all our aches and pains. She was my mother's slave many years ago but now, of course, she is free."

"You are very kind, Monsieur St. Clair!" Tamarisk said. "I will try not to be too great a burden to you. Please forgive my . . . my lack of self-control. I fear I am still weak from my ordeal!"

Siméon stood up, giving her his shy, gentle smile. Promising to return that afternoon, he bowed gracefully and left her. He felt confused by her words. He was unused to the society of white women for none but the black workers had entered his house since his mother's death. He lived an entirely solitary existence to which he was well accustomed. Until Tamarisk's appearance he had not been aware of his loneliness. She had been in his house for less than a fortnight and yet already she had become the focal point of his day. Whilst he had awaited her return to consciousness he had planned his work so that he was never absent for longer than an hour or two so eager was he to discover who she was.

Now at long last she had awakened. She seemed to him even more beautiful than she had done in repose. Tamarisk! The name had an unfamiliar mystery of its own. Her distress aroused in him the long dormant instinct of chivalry and he wished he could think of some way to alleviate her grief. He tried to imagine the unknown husband, Charles, and the eighteen-year-old sister, Chantal. It might give his sorrowing visitor new heart if he were to suggest to her that the young girl might still be alive. His beautiful lady had herself survived and she had not actually seen the girl drown. When he visited her in the afternoon he would try to cheer her with the thought of such a possibility.

Two hundred miles away, Chantal was even now setting foot upon one of the numerous tiny islands, many still unnamed, that made up the Seychelles Archipelago. Although still very weak, she had persuaded Dinez da Gama to take her with him in the longboat to Coetivy for she desired above all to be away from the rocking motion of the ship and on dry land once more.

Dinez did not need much persuasion. As Chantal's health was restored so had her true beauty revealed itself and Dinez was firmly intent upon her seduction. He would have accomplished this task long since but for the fear of a revolt amongst his crew. The men had already reminded him with sullen scowls that the girl had been promised to them; and moreover, that Dinez already had a woman for his pleasuring. They had always resented it when he refused to sell Zambi with the other slaves, partly from jealousy of his privilege but also because they considered a female on board brought bad luck.

This resentment had been temporarily forgotten due to the extremely successful pirating of a French cargo ship carrying gold and ivory from Africa to South America. The booty, now safely stored in *O Bailado*'s holds, was the richest haul they had ever made and Dinez was able to convince the crew that his nubile young slave had proved lucky rather than the reverse.

Unfortunately the men now demanded that each of them should have a woman with him — an arrangement that would have made life and discipline aboard impossible. They were rough illiterates who argued with knives rather than words. Quarrels over their women would mean fighting on board as it did in port. Dinez was incapable of controlling them when they got drunk on rum pillaged from other ships. He had little doubt that these cutthroats, some of whom had already mutinied and killed one captain, would treat him to a like fate were he to give them a reason for so doing. For the time being, they served under him only because they knew him to be a highly skilled sailor with a superior intelligence that enabled them to outwit their quarries and grow rich on the spoils.

Dinez' method of dealing with his crew entailed an admixture of ruthless punishment for transgressions of discipline and a generous share of the plunder. He had signed them on for a period of five years with the understanding that all the treasures they accrued as they sailed the Indian Ocean would be safely hidden on the island of Coetivy. In due course the entire fortune would be collected from the island, transported to Hong Kong where it could most profitably be sold and each man given his allotted share of the proceeds. Dinez safeguarded himself by ensuring that only he and his trusted first mate, Miguel, knew the actual location on Coetivy where their wealth was hidden. Should any man decide to strike out on his own, he could not lay hands upon his share of past spoils and was therefore disinclined to desert.

But now the sailors were nearing the end of their contract and after four and a half years they were becoming impatient to realize their ill-gotten gains. Dinez was finding it increasingly difficult to maintain order. Common sense warned him that he must use his cunning if he were to appropriate the white girl for himself. After giving the problem some thought, he decided upon a fictitious story of huge rewards that would be forthcoming were Chantal to be delivered back to her family unharmed.

In truth, he believed that this might well be possible since it was clear enough to him that her family in England was of some distinction and that she came from a home of great luxury. He did not need to be clever to note that she never lifted one of her small dainty fingers to assist herself. She was even unaccustomed to brushing her own hair. It had amused him to see how matter-of-factly she received the attentions of the fascinated servant, Zambi, whom she treated much as she might a personal maid. Her own maid, she had informed him sadly, had perished at sea in the foundering of *Valetta*.

But the promise of monetary reward for the return of Chantal *virgo intacta* to her family was no temptation to Dinez himself. His blood was now on fire for the girl as it had never been for the women he picked up in the seaports to amuse him and slake his appetites. Since he had left his home in Portugal there had been no occasion for him even to speak with girls of good family. Chantal's daintiness and innocence fascinated him, the more so because her eyes and body occasionally betrayed a deeply passionate nature hidden beneath her circumspect demeanor.

His ship had now lain at anchor for three days whilst he waited until Chantal was strong enough to be taken to the island. There, he had decided, away from the prying eyes of his crew, he would have his way with the girl. The waiting made the anticipation even more exciting. When of her own accord she asked if she might accompany him to Coetivy, he concealed his exultation beneath a casual nod of agreement. Chantal's smile of happiness — the first he had seen — caused him to catch his breath. Her fascination for him seemed to increase as the half-drowned slip of a girl changed more with every passing hour into a beautiful young woman fashioned for men's desire. He felt his nerves leap in response as she touched his arm in a gesture of gratitude.

"Make haste there," he bellowed unnecessarily at the men who were lowering the strange-looking shallow-draughted boat called a pirogue which was used to cross the coral reef ringing the island. Other members of the crew were bringing up canvas bags from the hold and stacking them on deck. Chantal, having no knowledge that she was aboard a pirate ship, innocently enquired as to the contents of these sacks.

Dinez decided to leave her in ignorance. Instinct warned him that she might have a fearsome loathing of pirates.

"They contain trade goods for the natives," he lied easily. By the time Chantal saw for herself that there was no indigenous population on the tiny island, nor any inhabitant, he would have had his way with her.

Chantal stayed close by Dinez' side on the poop, partly because she could see to better advantage the enticing fringe of golden sand and palm trees not a quarter of a mile away; but also because she feared *O Bailado*'s bearded, motley crew. She could not understand how a gentleman of Dinez' standing could bear to live at close quarters with these villainous-looking men. She could but suppose that the captain of a trading vessel must perforce select his crew for their strength and sailing skills rather than for their appearance or their manners.

Of many different nationalities, the varied collection of ruffians spoke in a dozen different languages Chantal could not understand. What frightened her most was the way they watched her. Whichever way she turned, there were always several faces staring at her with leers or questions in their eyes. Moreover, there was a curious degree of intimacy in their voices when they called to her which proffered little of the respect to which she was accustomed from such people. She assumed that they were greeting her for she could not understand what they were saying. The British sailors on *Valetta* would not have dared even to address her and it required an effort of will on her part not to appear impolite by refusing to nod an acknowledgement. She therefore remained close to Dinez whom she trusted completely.

Physically, Chantal was very nearly restored to full health. The blistering of her sun-scorched skin had disappeared leaving her tanned a deep gold. She had washed her hair and the black girl had curled it skillfully into ringlets. Zambi had proved resourceful in other ways. Using a length of flowered cotton, the African girl had wound it around Chantal's waist to form a skirt. She had cut the sleeves from one of Dinez' frilled shirts, gathering the waist and neckline and fashioned a blouse. Unmodish as these garments were, they were well suited to the climate for every day seemed as hot as the preceding one. Only the slight breeze blowing off the sea gave relief from the constant heat.

In the distance Chantal could see the palms bending slightly in the soft wind and she longed with increasing impatience for their cool shade.

At long last the pirogue was cast off, Dinez sat in the stem with Chantal and the mate, Miguel. Four sailors with massive shoulders and rippling biceps rowed the native canoe towards the island. Dinez had already explained to Chantal that they could not sail *O Bailado* into the bay because of the coral reef surrounding the island.

"We have made the trip many times before," he said reassuringly, seeing Chantal's anxious expression as they neared the white water boiling over the rocks.

Despite the grief that always lay close to her heart whenever she thought of her family or of poor Kaftan, Chantal felt a thrill of excitement as the pirogue cleared the reef on the crest of a huge wave and with a great burst of speed shot towards the beach. Two herons which had been wading by the water's edge flew up into the air in alarm, only just clearing the trees as they made their sudden departure.

The men, barefoot, jumped out onto the white sand and pulled the pirogue higher up the beach. Now Chantal could see that the sand was covered with a carpet of beautifully colored shells. She took off her leather sandals and with a cry of pleasure, leapt ashore. Behind her, Zambi called out a swift warning, her words unintelligible to Chantal.

"She is trying to warn you about the fish," Dinez said. He stooped and picked up a flat, dull brown stone. "Around these islands there are fish that look so like stones you do not see them and if you step upon one, it will poison you and you will die!"

He laughed at Chantal's horrified expression.

"There is nothing to fear if you keep on your shoes," he said. "The men's feet are so toughened by the ship's decks they believe themselves impervious to stings."

Whilst the sailors were unloading the boat, Chantal walked up the sand until she was within touching distance of the first palm tree. High above her head in the cool shade of the fronds, she could see the coconuts. Once again the watchful Zambi called a warning indicating by signs that at any moment a ripened nut might fall on Chantal's head.

But already Chantal's attention was elsewhere. She could see hundreds of great myriad-hued butterflies. She counted a dozen different species

255

in as many minutes and turned excitedly to point them out to Dinez.

But he was otherwise occupied. She could see him disappearing with Miguel into a gap in the lush undergrowth that appeared to cover the whole island. Nearby on the beach, the sailors and Zambi were breaking open coconut husks with their pangas and eagerly drinking the milk.

Zambi wiped her mouth and grinning, carried an opened nut to Chantal.

"Good drink," she said, using two of the few words of English she as yet knew. Chantal was attempting to teach her but such lessons were of necessity conducted by signs since Chantal spoke no Portuguese — the only European language Zambi knew.

Before long Dinez and Miguel returned. Picking up two more canvas bags apiece, they disappeared yet again into the island's interior. Only after their third trip did they rejoin the group. By now the sailors had caught and killed a number of small chocolate-brown birds and were roasting them over a fire made of coconut husks and lit with the aid of an old-fashioned tinderbox such as most of them carried in preference to the new matches.

The smell of the roasting meat was so delicious that Chantal's distress at the destruction of the friendly little birds was soon overcome.

"*Fouquets*," Dinez identified them for her as she went across the beach to join him. "It is good to eat fresh meat."

Zambi, meanwhile, had collected a mass

256

of round white eggs which Chantal guessed correctly had been buried in the sand by a turtle. The hungry sailors now boiled the eggs in an iron baling-can filled with sea-water. Chantal ate with relish. After the diet of salt pork and mildewed biscuits on board, the fresh food stimulated her appetite. But most of all she longed for fresh, clean drinking water. When she asked for it, Dinez said:

"The only water on this island lies below ground. When they have eaten, the men will dig a deep hole and we will find enough water to replenish the ships' casks. Meanwhile you must slake your thirst with coconut milk."

"Did you and Miguel meet with the native people?" Chantal enquired innocently, for she had noted that each time Dinez and the Spaniard returned to the beach, they were no longer carrying the canvas bags they had taken with them inland.

"I will take you to see them shortly," Dinez replied evasively, his eyes resting momentarily on the pointed curves of Chantal's breasts clearly outlined beneath the soft white lawn of her blouse. Although she herself was unaware of it, he knew that his men were as conscious as he of her femininity. He called out sharply:

"It is time to signal the ship. Hurry yourselves, you lubbards. You have more than eaten your fill."

Miguel, grinning broadly, cocked his pistol and fired a shot into the air. At once, hundreds of birds of all shapes, colors and sizes rose in a great cloud over the island, screeching and calling a cacophony of alarm. There was an answering shot from *O Bailado*.

Shading her eyes from the fierce sunlight reflecting off the aquamarine-colored sea, Chantal could discern the figures of sailors lowering one of the longboats.

"The pirogue will row over the reef and meet up with the longboat which will ferry fresh meat back to the ship," Dinez explained. "The pirogue will bring more men to the island to form hunting parties to find food. The crew will be occupied for several hours so I have time now to show you the island if you wish."

"That is indeed most kind of you, Sir," Chantal said, only with difficulty containing her excitement. She was not yet certain if she liked this strange aristocratic Portuguese. At times he could be silent, taciturn and even anxious to avoid her company. But at others be was smiling, friendly and solicitous of her welfare. She owed him her life and she could not deny that he was handsome in a strong masculine way. He would look out of place in a London drawing-room but he looked masterful and competent in his chosen milieu, she thought.

Unaware of Chantal's opinion of him and unconcerned by such irrelevancies, Dinez decided upon the venue for Chantal's seduction. He had in mind a grove where the vegetation was so dense that he knew if a sailor wandered inland from the beach, he would be unlikely to find them. For the most part, Dinez knew that his men would remain close to the shoreline where there were ample turtles, tortoises, crabs, seabirds and eggs to reprovision the ship for weeks to come.

Leaving Miguel in charge of operations, he beckoned to Zambi to go with him, knowing that her presence would reassure Chantal. The black girl was like an obedient puppy with no better purpose in life other than to please him in whatever way she could. With a docility which surprised Dinez, she had shown no sign of jealousy of the English girl upon whom she now lavished almost as much devotion as upon her master. In her halting Portuguese, she even suggested one evening to Dinez that the white-skinned goddess must become his 'first wife' and that according to the customs of her tribe, she would be perfectly content to be 'second wife' so long as he continued to enjoy the pleasure of her body.

In merciful ignorance of such plans for her future, Chantal happily followed Zambi and Dinez as he led the way up the shallow incline from the beach. She was grateful when he turned to offer her a steadying hand. Her legs were still uncertain after the motion of the sea and her balance was precarious.

Chantal's mood was brighter than it had been since the shipwreck. She was finding it impossible to be unhappy on this beautiful tropical island. Impatiently, Dinez was obliged to urge her forward as she stopped again and again to admire a colorful flower, a brilliantly-hued lizard or a gigantic tortoise.

The only discomfort came from the ants

which seemed to be everywhere and were soon attacking Chantal's bare legs. Zambi, her white teeth showing in her ready smile, halted the little party whilst she searched for a particular plant. Upon finding the variety she wanted, she rubbed some of its leaves together between her palms until the green juice ran out. This she smeared on Chantal's legs. It had a strange minty odor which was not unpleasant and which was certainly effective in keeping the tiny stinging insects away.

It was very hot and humid. Soon Chantal's light cotton skirt and blouse were clinging to her damp body and her hair curled into tiny ringlets as if it had been recently washed. She saw that Dinez's shirt, too, was dark with sweat and felt a strange longing to touch his broad, muscular back. How strong he was, she thought as he cleared a pathway for her through the dense vegetation. How perfectly his body was proportioned without an ounce of spare flesh to disfigure it.

Blushing at such immodest reflections, she turned to Zambi who at a word from Dinez, seated herself beneath a giant casuarina tree. Dinez continued to stride ahead.

"Come, Zambi," Chantal said, beckoning urgently. "You will become lost if you remain here. The Señor does not wish to stop here."

Zambi appeared not to understand. She shook her frizzy black head, smiled and settled herself more comfortably beneath the tree.

"Señorita!" Dinez' voice called imperatively.

Chantal hesitated a moment longer and then

ran forward. Dinez stood waiting for her, his hand outstretched.

"The girl is tired — leave her," he said briefly. "We have not much further to go. She can wait for us beneath the tree."

For the first time Chantal felt uneasy. Zambi was never tired. She seemed to have more energy than any white person perhaps because she was accustomed to the climate which was foreign to the Europeans. Hesitating, Chantal reminded herself that Dinez had never failed to be kind and solicitous, since he had rescued her from certain death. Yet she really knew very little about him other than that he was a trader, a ship's captain of Portuguese nationality.

Chantal nearly smiled at the thought that her Mama or Papa would scarce welcome such a man in their drawing-room. But Barre House seemed a million miles away in another world. Her parents could know nothing of the circumstances in which she now found herself. The niceties of social behavior were hardly applicable out here on this desert island and conventions could not be observed even if she wished. She had only to look at her attire to know how impossible it would be to try to live as she did at home.

Partially reassured by her conclusions, Chantal followed in Dinez' wake until suddenly he halted. He had come upon a small clearing in a dense grove of vegetation where the sunlight filtered patchily through the forty-foot-high palm trees. It was cool and inviting and when Dinez indicated that they should sit down for a rest, Chantal gladly subsided onto the soft dry ground. A giant tortoise ambled slowly through the clearing, unafraid of them. Butterflies and birds at first startled by their appearance, soon resettled on the trees and flowers. Chantal lay down on her back, her arms laced behind her head to form a pillow. She smiled at her companion.

"This must be like Paradise itself," she said, sighing with pleasure.

Dinez, who had been about to throw himself upon her, was arrested by that smile. Its total innocence and trusting friendliness was disconcerting. He had expected her to cower away from him; to show signs of fear of what he was about to do to her. But staring down into the bright dark pools of her eyes, he realized that Chantal was without fear because she had no knowledge to forewarn her. He had almost forgotten how young girls of good family were protected and guarded and kept in total ignorance of the facts of nature until their wedding day. This girl would be more likely to fear murder than rape since she knew not what a raping entailed, he told himself.

His body taut, he seated himself beside her and looked at her hungrily. In a strange hoarse voice he asked:

"Has no man ever kissed you? Touched you?"

Chantal sat up and met Dinez' gaze uneasily. The intimacy of his question had shocked her.

"That is no concern of yours," she said reprovingly. "But since you ask me, yes, I have been kissed many times by my brother John and . . . " She paused as a blush stole into her cheeks. " . . . and by my fiancé!" she added defiantly. "Well, he is not exactly my fiancé but I may well marry him when I return to England!"

Despite the urgency of his desire to take the girl and be hanged to this absurd preamble, Dinez was nevertheless amused. Brotherly kisses were not quite what he had in mind.

"Since you are not actually affianced, can you not spare one kiss for the poor, unhappy, lonely man who saved your life?" he mocked. "I think I have earned as much, have I not? There is little harm in a kiss after all, *nao acha?*"

Chantal was confused. A moment ago she had been frightened by his words but now she suspected that he was teasing her.

"You know very well that we are almost strangers and that it would be most improper!" she said with as much dignity as she could muster for even she could sense that this island was hardly a place where the normal proprieties mattered. "Besides," she added, "you promised you would take me to meet the natives."

Dinez' green eyes narrowed. His irritation was overruling his patience.

"There are no natives," he said. "That story was but a ruse to entice you away from the beach where my crew could observe us." He caught her hand and held it against his fiercely beating heart. "Can you really have no idea what effect it has had upon me living beside you in my cabin day after day, night after night. I long for you as I have never before desired a woman."

Chantal tried in vain to withdraw her hand. The passionate urgency in his voice, the outspoken words, renewed in full her apprehension. Yet they had also aroused in her a strange new excitement. She wanted this fierce young man to kiss her.

"*You know that I could take you by force, my lovely Señorita?*"

His quiet emphatic voice belied the flash of fire in his eyes.

Chantal tried to stop the trembling of her body as she held his gaze with a courage she mustered with the greatest difficulty. This time she could not ignore the threat his words implied.

"No true gentleman would force his attentions upon a lady," she quoted her mother primly in what she hoped was an adult tone of voice.

To her surprise, Dinez laughed — a great reboant of laughter that came from his belly. When he had determined upon seducing the girl, he had anticipated only the physical pleasures. He had not expected a conversation such as this, far less that he would enjoy it.

"Thank you for your compliment, Señorita Chantal, but I fear I must disillusion you. I may be a gentleman by virtue of my birth but I abandoned a gentleman's morals many years ago when I took up a life of piracy." Hearing her gasp, he looked at her with wry amusement. "Had you really not guessed as much? Did you really believe that I was a trader and that those canvas bags contained baubles for exchange with native tribes? They contained prizes from other

264

ships I have plundered — valuables of great worth that I have hidden here upon the island. No one ever comes here, for there is no natural port. Does the thought of piracy shock you so deeply?" he added, seeing the horror in her eyes.

Without understanding the reason for it, Dinez felt a sudden urge to justify his way of life to this wide-eyed, horrified girl.

"You do not understand," he said. "You told me you were born into a world of riches. Well I had the misfortune to be born into a family like yours where wealth is a necessity to maintain the customary standards of living — *but without the money to do so.* There is no honest work for gentlemen in my country. So I chose to become a pirate as have many before me. Am I to be condemned for that?"

Somehow Chantal managed to find her voice.

"I know only that it is wrong to take what does not belong to you. Besides, is it not a fact that pirates often kill innocent people when capturing other ships?"

"*Algumas vezes,*" Dinez agreed in Portuguese and seeing Chantal's questioning eyes upon him, said in English: "Certainly I am not an evil man. But in any war there are innocent people killed, are there not? I try to act with mercy when it is possible!"

"Which explains why you are acting mercifully towards me!" Chantal announced with relief. "For it is quite true that you could have taken advantage of me if you so wished — yet you have not done so."

Dinez caught her other hand and drew her closed towards him.

"*There is still time*," he said violently. "Are you not afraid?"

"No, I trust you," Chantal replied, surprising herself as much as her companion. "Besides, if you had really intended to harm me, sir, you would have done so before now!"

Her intuition infuriated and frustrated him. He had been wrong to talk to her in the first place, he thought bitterly. Had there been no exchange of words, he would not now be reconsidering his plan to take her by force. Without understanding how she had done so, this girl had so affected his emotions that he now desired her willing submission to him even more than he desired to ravish her. To take her now would be to steal but half the prize, he decided. If he waited . . . even wooed her . . . it might not be long before she was as eager for his possession of her as was he to lose himself within that slim young body. He sensed that she was far from indifferent to him. The trembling of her hands came not from fear but from her awareness of his proximity.

As if in direct reply to his thoughts, Chantal suddenly lent forward and kissed him lightly on the cheek.

"There," she said as she might have spoken to a child. "That is because you have been so kind to me and because I am very well aware that I owe you my life!"

"And not because you wanted to kiss me?" Dinez asked.

266

A smile trembled on Chantal's lips as she said softly:

"Well, perhaps I did!"

Dinez was suddenly aware of a feeling of tenderness quite foreign to him in his normal behavior with women. He bent his head, and keeping a tight rein upon himself, brushed her lips with his. Then almost angrily, he drew away from her, stood up quickly and said brusquely:

"We have wasted enough time. *E tarde*! The men will be wondering where we are!"

He held out his hand and obediently Chantal stood up. As he strode ahead of her away from the clearing she looked at his rigid back in perplexity. She did not understand his swift change of mood. She was too inexperienced to realize the fight he was having to control himself, or his inability to understand his own confusion.

As he strode furiously towards the casuarina tree where they had left Zambi, he felt humiliated by the thought that the black girl would assume that he had had his way with Chantal, whereas he had nothing but a kiss. He consoled himself with the knowledge that he could alter that situation at a moment's notice; that his ultimate possession of Chantal was but a matter of time.

14

September 1838

BY merest chance John was obliged to interrupt his journey to Dieppe when his horse went lame not half a mile from Beauvais. Being in no great hurry he decided to leave the animal to rest in the comfortable stables of the auberge where he had taken refuge, hire another mount and proceed to the Duc Dubois' Château nearby.

If he had any doubts as to his welcome, they were soon dispelled upon his arrival by the cries of genuine delight of the six girls and the enthusiastic handshakes of their parents. They ushered him into the great stone hall and he was divested of his top hat and surtout by the bevy of pretty daughters all talking at one and the same time.

With a benevolent smile, their father demanded silence until John was comfortably seated in the *grand salon* with a flagon of chilled wine on the table beside him.

"*Alors, mon vieux!* Tell us by what good fortune we are once again enjoying the pleasure of your society?" said the Duc Dubois, adding with a twinkle: "Somehow I doubt if it was my scintillating conversation last week that has tempted you to further our acquaintance!"

John could not help but note how pleased

were the family to see him. Whilst explaining about his horse, he needed little persuasion to agree to remaining as their guest not just for one night but for several days. Immediately the eldest daughter, Fleur, rose to her feet and offered to conduct John to one of the guest chambers. With brief apologies for the shabbiness of the furnishings — and they were indeed threadbare — she led the way to an upstairs room at the far end of a long stone passageway.

"I am afraid we have little enough by way of luxury to offer you!" she said in her charmingly accented English. With a smile, she added demurely: "Only the warmth of our welcome which is of the most sincere!"

John smiled back at the tall, slim, auburn-haired girl. As she crossed to the casement to pull the faded velvet curtains against the hot afternoon sunshine, he found himself comparing her with her younger sisters. Not quite as pretty as they, she made up for this deficiency by the open friendliness of her manner.

The French girl was somewhat voluptuous in build, her features a little too rounded for true beauty; but her hazel eyes sparkled with a tawny glow which John found both attractive and exciting.

"Now that I am to be a guest in your house, I must learn the names of your sisters, Mademoiselle!" he said politely. "With so many of you, I fear I became quite confused on the occasion of our last meeting."

Fleur tilted her head on one side and regarded him reflectively.

"I wonder which one of us has taken your fancy!" she said, her eyes seeming to tease him as if he were a friend of long standing rather than a stranger. "Perhaps it is Rose, who is by far the prettiest. She has blond hair and blue eyes like our mother's. Or could it be Aimée who is petite and dark like Papa? Or maybe Jeanne or Suzanne, the identical twins? Or do you perhaps find Noëlle, the youngest of the family, also the sweetest? She is like a little china doll, is she not, with those big blue eyes?"

"In listing the many attributes of the Dubois daughters, I fear you have forgotten yourself," John said gallantly. "I think your Papa and Mama must be very proud of you all. As for one being prettier than another," he added, returning her smile, "I have yet to make up my mind! But I am in no doubt, Mademoiselle Fleur, that it is you who has the most beautiful hair, if you will allow me to say so."

Fleur gave an exaggerated curtsey.

"When a young man desires to pay me a compliment, no permission is required!" she said. "Now may I take you down to the garden? We follow your English custom and take tea there on these hot summer days."

During the pleasant hours that ensued John had plenty of time to consider the varying attractions of the six young girls, all of whom were vying with one another in friendly rivalry for his attentions. As Fleur had said, Rose was undoubtedly the prettiest. But she lacked the vivacity of her older sister. It soon became clear to John that Rose was the industrious member of the family and that her interests lay largely in her personal adornment. She spoke of little but the new dresses she longed for and those she had skillfully made for herself and her sisters.

John was reminded that not every young lady was as fortunate as Chantal and Tamarisk who could afford to order from a dressmaker whatever took their fancy regardless of the cost. Yet the Dubois family seemed quite resigned to their poverty and made no attempt to conceal it from him.

Aimée's interest seemed to be centered in the gardens where, she told him, she worked long hours caring for the flowers.

"We can afford but one gardener whose time is fully occupied in trying to keep the long driveway, lawns and hedges tidy and trimmed," she explained. "So I must tend the plants myself if the garden is to maintain its color. Were it not for your presence, sir, I would be hard at work now," she told him, adding sweetly, "and for such excellent company I gladly relinquish my labors."

The twins, not yet eighteen years of age, were engagingly mischievous, attracting John's attention by confusing him as to their identities and each pretending that it was the other who was flirting with him so shamelessly. It was harmless amusement and kept everyone laughing, including their good-natured mother, the Duchess Dubois, who sat with them in the shade of the giant chestnut tree.

The baby of the family, Noëlle, at fifteen was still very much a child. With charming innocence she stood leaning against John regarding him with her doll-like, china blue eyes.

"Can you not come to live with us for always, sir?" she enquired wistfully. "It is such a pleasant change to enjoy the company of a brother when one is accustomed only to that of so many sisters!"

Curiously, so it seemed to John, the only silent member of the family was Fleur, the girl who alone with him in his bedchamber had proved herself quite voluble. Yet although she spoke but little that afternoon in the garden, whenever he happened to glance in her direction he found that she was staring at him. Often a strange smile was lurking in her eyes that however improbable the likelihood, nevertheless seemed to imply an invitation. But to what, John asked himself. The Duc's delightful daughters were perfectly brought up with the faultless manners befitting their class. It was inconceivable that one of them should be harboring thoughts that were not of the purest, most innocent coquetry.

Nonetheless the girl consciously or otherwise turned *his* thoughts to desires that were very far from innocent. He felt ashamed for the secret imaginings that kept intruding each time he found Fleur's brooding gaze or provocative smile focused upon him.

Although far from lavish in the number of courses, the evening meal was excellently cooked and wholesome. It was now beyond doubt, John thought, that the Duc's claim to be impoverished was far from exaggerated. The beautiful rugs and chair coverings were threadbare. Rose had told him there was but one gardener and it seemed there were only four indoor servants. Large discolored patches on the wall covering indicated that pictures and tapestries had once hung there and had in all probability been sold. John might have felt more saddened by the undoubted poverty in evidence but for the continued unforced jollity of the family.

It was a happy evening, the girls taking turns to sing and perform upon the pianoforte. Fleur chose to render in a perfectly pitched contralto a song of haunting sweetness, telling the longings of a young girl who would readily give her heart and soul for a moment of love. Once again it seemed to John that she was directing the words of the song at him as she sang: "*Pour un peu d'amour, un peu d'amour, je te donnerai ma vie, mon coeur . . .*"

It came almost as a relief when the Duc suggested they retire to the library for a nightcap away from the "*femmes babbillardes,*" as he fondly described the chattering ladies.

By the time John and his host were ready for bed the ladies had already retired. Not a little drunk on the Duc's cognac, John fell into his big four-poster and despite the heat of the September night, he was almost instantly asleep.

He was unaware how long it was before he was awakened by the sound of his bedroom door softly opening and closing. He stared with alarm at the shadowy figure approaching his bed, still drowsy enough to feel fear at the unexpected appearance of this unknown intruder. But as the figure came closer, he realized with a shock that it was no ruffian intent upon harming him but a female. He sat up quickly.

"Who is it?" he asked in English.

"You are awake then, *mon ami!*" came the reply.

He recognized at once Fleur's husky voice.

"Mademoiselle Fleur!" he gasped in astonishment. "What brings you here? Is aught amiss?"

He heard the girl's laugh as she stepped near enough for him to see her smiling face lit by a shaft of moonlight. She was wearing a loose peignoir in a blue shining fabric trimmed with ruffles of white lace. She had removed her *bonnet de nuit* and her auburn hair gleamed almost golden in the white beam centered upon her. At one and the same time, John was shocked by her presence here in his bedchamber in her undress — and excited. He was also confused.

"Will you not invite me to be seated?" she asked, her voice a low murmur.

Without waiting for a reply she sat down on the edge of the bed. The folds of her peignoir fell open and John felt his pulses leap as he saw that his companion wore no nightgown beneath it. The outlines of her breasts, uncorseted now, were clearly discernible in silhouette against the silvery light pouring through the casements.

She touched his hand and again his pulses stirred. Her body was exuding a strange, exciting perfume he could not identify but which was essentially female.

"You should not be here!" he said, his voice sounding harsh and unnatural even to his own ears. "It is most improper . . . and dangerous!"

Again the girl laughed, the sound unnerving him still further.

"I am not afraid of danger, John!" She lent towards him and now her breasts touched his arm. Desire rose in him so swiftly that he needed all his self-control not to reach out and pull her down upon him.

"Then I must be cautious for us both!" he said as convincingly as be could. "Your reputation . . . your honor . . . if anyone were to find you here, both would be at stake."

"No one will find me here!" Fleur said calmly. "Why else do you think I selected this particular guest room for your use? It is as far from the other bedchambers as it is possible to be."

Before John could anticipate her intentions, she slipped the peignoir off her shoulders and pulling back the coverlet she slid between the sheets beside him.

Astounded beyond words, John lay rigid, his mind awhirl. He was by no means without experience of women. But for the most part they had been women whose standards of morality were governed by the price paid for their favors.

Beside him, Fleur's naked body stirred restlessly.

"Was my instinct wrong and you do not feel any desire for me?" she asked.

John was grateful that she could not see the blush of embarrassment that suffused his face as he said fiercely:

"That question is unnecessary, unfair and

quite absurd! Of course I want you. But I will not seduce an innocent girl and have such ungentlemanly behavior upon my conscience!"

Her laughter came spontaneously and without caution. It was so noisy that disregarding his manners, John quickly covered her mouth with his hand. He drew it away as quickly when she sank her small white teeth into his palm.

"Confound it!" he swore softly. "That hurt!"

Suddenly she was on top of him, covering his face, shoulders, arms with gentle nips interspersed with kisses.

"Dear John! Silly John! Beautiful John!" she murmured. "What must I do to convince you that I am no 'innocent young girl' . . . " she quoted him wickedly " . . . to be bedded for your pleasure. I am no virgin, John, I do assure you. I am a woman who like yourself, is hungry for love. Will you not satisfy that hunger and take me for *my* pleasuring?"

His desire for this extraordinary nocturnal visitor was now overriding his wish to behave in a gentlemanly manner. He made one last effort to keep control of the situation.

"I am your father's guest!" he said. "I cannot betray his trust."

This time Fleur did not mock him with laughter.

"I doubt if Papa would deny me my pleasure!" she said quietly. "He knows very well that my opportunities for fulfillment as a woman are few enough. He must understand that it is most improbable that I shall ever be married. I am twenty-five years of age, John, and I have no dowry. Even if a rich young man were to present himself he would be unlikely to choose me for his wife when he could have Aimée or Rose who are both younger and prettier. But I believe it is better to face the truth and adjust one's way of life accordingly. You are not the first lover I will have had, nor even the second or third. Now that I have told you this, if you still suffer from your conscience, I will kiss you good night and leave you in peace!"

But the farewell kiss she then bestowed upon him was such as to ensure that John would not let her go. As he rolled over on top of her, her moist red tongue found its way between his lips and her hands reached out for his body. He was beyond understanding — or even caring what had brought this aristocratic young woman to his bed. He had no way of knowing if girls of the French nobility were different from their English counterparts; but it no longer mattered. He was now certain of only one thing — that Fleur had been consciously arousing him throughout the afternoon and evening with the deliberate intention of seducing him this night.

He took her with a fierce, quick thrusting of his body into hers. She received him willingly, holding him to her and crying out, whether in pain or pleasure he knew not. It was soon over. As they fell apart gasping, John felt sanity return. He stared down uneasily at the girl beside him.

"I do not understand you, Fleur!" he said.

She reached up and touched his cheek with her fingertip.

"I suppose it must be difficult for you," she replied. "Men do not seem to understand that women are really not so different from themselves. We are all taught that it is unladylike for females to enjoy the pleasures of mating, but I have never understood why it should be impolite for females and not for men to feel desire. You are shocked by my behavior, are you not, John?"

His silence was an admission. Smiling she continued:

"But you enjoyed it, nonetheless!"

"And you?" John countered. "You have not said if I pleasured you."

She moved nearer to him and laid her head on his chest whilst her hands traced the outline of his ribs and hips.

"A little perhaps! But not enough! But I forgive you for your impatience since it was the first time. In a little while we will love one another again, but more slowly, yes?"

The girl was a constant surprise to him, John thought. She could say the most outrageous things and yet by the calm tone of her voice, make them sound quite natural.

"I can teach you many ways to give a woman pleasure!" Fleur said now. "I learned such delights from the man I was to have married. I will tell you about him. He was Spanish by birth, a nobleman considerably older than you and a friend of my father's. His name was Don Giovanni Alfrerez and he was a Carlist. When Queen Christina was made Regent after the infant Isabella was born, Don Carlos was exiled. He had hoped to be made King after the death of his brother Ferdinand and those who believed in his right to the throne, as did Giovanni, were exiled with him. Giovanni lost his estates and when he came to see my father, he was as poor as we were. He fell in love with me. I was twenty years old. We were betrothed and were to be married as soon as be could reclaim his fortunes. Had I had a dowry to give him, we might have been married at once. But as it was he went back with Don Carlos in disguise into the northern provinces of Spain. But my poor Giovanni was recognized by a Christinos and was killed."

"I am sorry!" John said simply. "His death must have been a great sorrow for you!"

Fleur sighed.

"The more so, I think, because he and I had flaunted convention and had become lovers when we agreed to marry. It was Giovanni who instructed me in the art of loving. When I was still a virgin, I thought little about such things but after Giovanni had initiated me into the joys of fulfillment, I discovered that to live without love was to be like a flower without sunshine. When the opportunity came, I took another lover just as I came to you, John, and will go to others if I am in need of loving. Does that seem so wrong to you?"

"I do not know!" John answered truthfully. "I understand your loneliness but . . . but I would not want the girl I love to have enjoyed the favors of other men!"

"You speak as one who intends to marry!"

Fleur said. "As I have already told you, I do not now expect ever to marry. Were I the girl you loved I would want no other man to embrace me; one lover would be enough."

Her words reminded John suddenly and painfully of Chantal. He had not thought of Chantal all day, far less this night! Yet now that her image had come into his mind, he knew that his love for her was as deep and intense as ever. If it could only be Chantal and not Fleur who lay here beside him, he thought with a deep agony of longing. But Chantal would not have come to his room like Fleur, demanding his love. Her interest lay in another man, in his handsome half-brother, Antoine.

"Do not think of her!" Fleur said beside him with quick intuition. "We have a French proverb which says '*Le moineau en la main avaut mieux que l'oie qui vole.*'"

Despite himself, John smiled at the aptness of her proverb.

"A sparrow in the hand is worth more than a goose flying in the air!" he translated. "Ah, Fleur, how practical you are! I feel I am prosaic by comparison."

She bent her head and kissed him.

"You are a romantic!" she corrected him. "But I am not asking for your love, *mon cher*, only your loving. The night has many hours yet before dawn. Put your arms around me, John. Kiss me!"

She drew his head down to her breast and guided his lips to the taut, swollen nipples. Feeling his body stiffen, she began to stroke him until he was fierce with hunger. He rolled over on top of her.

"Slowly, gently!" she whispered. "First I want to kiss you — here — and here! And now you must kiss me. Is that not beautiful, my lover?"

He did not hear her words but only the soft murmuring of her voice as they exchanged caresses that became ever more intimate. Such was the intensity of this second wave of desire that he believed he could no longer withstand the urgent demand for release. But she seemed to understand his body even better than he and after prolonging their mutual pleasure, she brought them both to a wild abandoned crescendo.

Exhausted though he was, John could not sleep. He felt a great tenderness for the girl he held in his arms. She lay relaxed against him. But it was not love he felt for her so much as gratitude. The thought saddened him for he knew himself forever indebted to her for having led him to knowledge of a whole new world he might never have discovered without her. Their loving bore no relation to the selfish, lustful hours he had enjoyed with bought women. With them he had been aware of neither beauty nor joy, but only of an animal satisfaction that was forgotten when he closed the door behind him. This strange French girl had shown him that the greatest pleasure lay in the giving of it.

"Do not be sad!" Fleur said, once again intuitively divining his mood. "If I have no regrets then you should have none either. You will return to your own country and when you lie with the girl you love, you will forget me. But I am not thinking of the future. We have three more days and nights to be together. Let us not spoil them by sadness."

"The girl I love is not in England!" John said. "'Tis possible that by now the ship she is traveling on has almost reached her destination in India. I shall not see Chantal again for at least two years."

"Then you must visit us again at Beauvais," Fleur replied matter-of-factly. "That will make me very happy."

"But what of your other lovers? My presence will not please them, I imagine," John said, only in part teasing her for he was suddenly jealous of the other men who had also enjoyed her favors.

"They are not your concern!" Fleur told him simply. "It is better you should know nothing beyond the fact that they exist. My body is my own, John. I give it to whom I choose and not according to the dictates of another."

Such a concept coming from a young woman like Fleur was too new and startling for him to accept without further reflection. But this was not the moment to challenge Fleur's extraordinary independence, not only of thought but of deed. In one respect at least she was justified — that *he* had no right to dictate how she should conduct herself.

They made love a third time and then Fleur left him to return to her own bedchamber. For a long while after she had departed, John lay awake pondering upon the night's events. He asked himself whether, had Chantal not existed, he might now be considering the possibility of marrying Fleur. It disturbed him to think of so lovely a girl destined to spinsterhood, her beauty fading with the years and with no man to cherish and support her or to give her children. Yet whilst he could believe that he might quite easily have wished to marry her, he could never have felt complacent about her past lovers. A man had a right to expect his wife to come to her marriage bed a virgin.

Sleep continued to elude him. Despite the fatigue of his body, his mind was restless with speculation. Life was turning out to be so much more complicated than he had supposed as he approached manhood. So little time ago, right and wrong had seemed clearly defined and morality and honor easily enough dictated by his conscience. But now Fleur could not be put into the category of a loose woman even though her way of life was indisputably immoral by conventional standards. Nor could he understand why he still respected her even whilst he knew he should not.

His thoughts veered suddenly towards his sister, Tamarisk. Despite the fact that Charles had known she was no virgin, he had still wanted to marry her. It made no difference to him, apparently, that Tamarisk had miscarried the child of a lover and some years later been cruelly raped by another man. John had been told by his stepfather how Tamarisk had nearly died at the hands of the merchant in Genoa. At the time Perry was replying to John's questions as to whether he had ever killed a man.

"Never!" Perry had told him, "although I once came close to doing so."

Briefly, he had recounted Tamarisk's terrible adventure and how he had learned of it from Mavreen on his return to England from Italy.

"It was my intention in any event to go back to Italy to collect Chantal from the Shelleys. I decided to go to Genoa for the purpose of seeking out the rapist and killing him. Your mother and Tamarisk knew nothing of my intent but I was determined such a brute should pay the price for his sins. I came close to murder, for Tamarisk would have died had she not been found by the Romanies on the mountainside where she had been abandoned. But as it transpired, when I reached Genoa I discovered that the man, a Signor Galvanti, had been arrested and flung into gaol. The British Consul in Naples with whom Tamarisk had taken refuge had prevented me and arranged for his counterpart in Genoa to ensure Galvanti was punished. Thanks to him, therefore, I can still claim to be innocent of bloodshed for without doubt I would have killed the man!"

The story had given John a better understanding of the relationship between Tamarisk and her husband. Hitherto they had struck him as unnaturally cool and detached, and lacking the warm, demonstrative affection exchanged by his mother and stepfather. Charles was always solicitous to a fault and Tamarisk was clearly devoted to him, but John doubted if there existed any real passion in their marriage — and certainly not of the kind he had experienced this night with Fleur.

It was nearly dawn when John finally slept, his mind busy with speculations as to how he and his paramour would be able to conceal from her sisters and parents the night's turn of events.

Fleur however seemed to suffer no such embarrassment. In front of her family, her manner towards him was no different in guise than that of the previous afternoon and by the end of the day, John was beginning to wonder if he had only dreamed their nocturnal encounter.

But she returned to his bedchamber that night in exactly the same manner as on the first occasion. She laughed at his perplexity, kissing him provocatively and declaring that he could not find her very desirable if he could so soon tire of her.

Still further perplexed, John said:

"I but mentioned that I was unsure if you would come to my room tonight. I would have been sadly disappointed had you failed to appear."

"But not so disappointed or so desirous of seeing me that you would have made the effort to seek me out in my bedchamber," she countered smiling. "Faint heart never won fair lady, John, and 'twould seem you are indeed fainthearted!"

Thus challenged, John set about proving otherwise. Once again the hours passed quickly and magically until reluctantly, Fleur left him at the approach of dawn.

By the third day of his visit, the Duc and Duchess Dubois were treating John as one of the family, relaxing the few formalities of their day-to-day living and encouraging John to feel at ease within their family circle. John felt it incumbent upon him to tell the Duc that his affections were already engaged elsewhere, and that regretfully he could not proffer himself as a suitor for any of his daughters. His host admitted his disappointment but with good humor, and still tried to persuade John to prolong his sojourn with them.

The promise of further nights with Fleur proved too great a temptation for John and another week passed very pleasantly before his thoughts turned once more to England and increasingly to Chantal. Fond though he had become of the entrancing, seductive Fleur, he never ceased to think of his real love, sometimes even when he held Fleur in his arms. At such moments he felt that he was betraying both of them and that be must steel himself to bid Fleur farewell before the pattern of their life became a habit.

As was the case since their first meeting, Fleur seemed to guess his mood with that sharp intuition so marked in her. It was she who suggested to John that he was finding less joy in their liaison than of yore and that the reason might be that he was troubled by feelings of guilt because of his unfaithfulness to Chantal. Not wishing to deceive Fleur, John did not deny it.

"I think of her constantly," he admitted.

"Moreover, dearest Fleur, I feel that our present way of life cannot be justified despite all the reasons you have given to assure me that you are well content."

Fleur kissed him with fond affection.

"I know that you wish for me a husband, a home, children," she said softly. "That is because you are at heart a conventionalist and you will not accept that I am different from most girls. I do not deny I would have liked to marry Giovanni and to have had children. But since his death I have come to terms with my fate and I have readjusted convention to suit my needs. So do not concern yourself with my happiness, sweet John. I live for each moment as it comes and this is enough for me."

"I shall miss you!" John said truthfully.

Fleur smiled.

"I hope that you will and then you will come back to me. I shall miss you too, John."

He left the Dubois homestead with an admixture of sadness and relief. He knew himself fortunate to have been shown the ways of love by so wonderful a girl as Fleur. But his conscience had troubled him and once the parting was accomplished, he felt a new light-heartedness.

As he rode through Beauvais he was filled with a great urgency to be back in England in the familiar surroundings of Finchcocks where he knew his mother and stepfather would be enjoying the late summer days. It was still far too soon for letters to have arrived from Tamarisk and Chantal who could not hope to reach India before November. Nevertheless he believed it was just within the realm of possibility that if *Valetta* had sighted a home-going ship from the Mediterranean environs, news and mail could have been exchanged and carried back to England.

At worst it would be some comfort merely to be in company where Chantal's name was mentioned freely; at Finchcocks where her presence still lingered in their old nurseries, in the closets where her clothes still hung and in the stables where her white pony would be waiting patiently like himself, for her return.

15

September – October 1838

"IT is very beautiful here!"
Tamarisk broke the companionable silence that was fast becoming a familiar aspect of her relationship with Siméon St. Clair. It was now eighteen days since she had been cast up on the beach at Grand Police. She was sufficiently recovered from her ordeal at sea to be able to lie out in the garden within the shade of the takamaka tree where Siméon had placed a chair for her.

"I am happy that you like my garden," the young Frenchman replied in his quiet, halting English. As always when Tamarisk addressed him, he blushed with nervous shyness, betraying his unfamiliarity with the company of ladies. "My m . . . mother created it!" he added.

Tamarisk had once before noticed that this boy was inclined to stutter when he spoke of Yvonne St. Clair and surmised that her death must have been a great emotional shock.

Tamarisk's eyes wandered to the flowers and trees. Siméon had already identified many of them for her — sweet smelling frangipani, the silvery albizier, scarlet flamboyants and tall pis-pis. There was color in abundance from the rose-pink hibiscus, bilimbo, bougainvillaea and creamy, pink-tinged vanilla. There were

289

exotic creepers too — purple flowered ipomea covering the ground and Marvel of Peru vying with the bougainvillaea to cover the walls of the house. It was small wonder, she thought, that so many birds and butterflies haunted this Garden of Eden.

She had already grown to love this beautiful tropical island. The scarlet cardinals, like the little robins in England, had become so tame that they would fly down, twenty or thirty at a time, from the latania and takamaka trees to sit upon the table by her chair. Sunbirds, which Narcisse called *colibri* in her creole patois, green paraqueets, barred ground doves and magpie robins filled the garden with their incessant happy song. Discovering her interest in the birds, Siméon had pointed out to her the plovers, whimbrels, sanderlings and buff-backed herons flying over the cinnamon plantation.

"Will you tell me about your mother?" she asked gently. "She must have been very artistic to design such an earthly paradise."

Siméon paused thoughtfully, his blue eyes filled with a fierce pride as he remembered the woman he had idolized.

"My m . . . mother was not only artistic but very, very beautiful!" he said quietly. "She was born in France where my grandfather was a soldier of some distinction. He was killed in the retreat from Moscow and our family fortunes declined to such an extent that my mother was obliged to marry a man of considerably lower social standing."

His voice steadied as he continued:

"My father was a well-to-do cotton merchant from farming stock. My mother had no love for him but when he proposed marriage, my grandmother forced her to accept him because he agreed to pay all my grandfather's debts. Maman was but fifteen years old."

"And was she very unhappy in this marriage?" Tamarisk prompted as Siméon paused.

"Unbelievably so!" Siméon replied with bitterness. "My father was a coarse brute of a man with a peasant's crude tastes and manners. Moreover he decided that there was a better life to be had far away on the islands in the Indian Ocean, where the planters were producing the cotton he dealt in. He took no account of my mother's age and reluctance to leave her own country and the comfort of her family. He brought her to Mahé, thousands of miles from her home, purchased this land on the remote south of the island, bought slaves to work for him and began the Corail Plantation. Such was the selfishness of his nature that he planted the first crop of cotton even before he built a proper house for my mother to live in."

"You mean she had no shelter at all?"

Siméon frowned, his voice harshly critical as he replied:

"He built for their use a rough thatched hut similar to those the slaves erected for themselves. For nearly a year they lived little better than animals. My mother said it was not only the lowly habitation that broke her heart but the loss of her beautiful furniture. She had brought with her many valuable pieces given to her by wealthy friends as wedding gifts. But due to the humidity of this climate and the destructiveness of the termites, many of her possessions were ruined before my father would relinquish the slave labor from the plantation to build the Château Corail for her."

Siméon explained to Tamarisk how the wooden house was built on great blocks of coral to prevent the invasion of wood-eating ants. She had noticed these large termites in the trunks of dead trees, the great black mounds that were their nests disfiguring the outlines. Siméon had told her that they were as voracious as locusts and even now they were eating into the old disused cotton press in the shed adjoining the house.

"One forgets in this paradise that there must be some disadvantages!" Tamarisk said sighing. "The imperfections of nature as well as her beauty must flourish amidst such abundance!"

"It was not paradise here in my father's lifetime!" Siméon said harshly. "The conditions endured by our slaves were terrible. My mother did her best for them but my father thought of the Africans only as beasts of burden. The women in particular . . . "

He broke off with such a look of distress that Tamarisk did not press him to continue. Instead she asked how many slaves his father had owned, for she had not seen more than a dozen thatched huts at the far end of the garden.

"There were over a hundred workers when the cotton was fetching a big price ten years ago," Siméon said. "But the American planters started growing it and on a far larger scale. Consequently they could market it at a considerably lower price than we could. Like others here on Mahé my father could no longer make a living out of cotton. Many abandoned their plantations and left the island to live on Mauritius where trading flourishes. But my father had settled down and had become addicted to the island drink, *toddy*. It is made by the natives from the sap of a certain type of palm. The tree is tapped and the juice it emits is fermented. It is a highly potent drink. It finally killed him."

Tamarisk mistook the harshness that crept into Siméon's voice to be an expression of grief. But now, his fair skin flushed with emotion, he continued with a soft violence:

"There was not one among us on the Corail Plantation who was not pleased when he died, I most of all. He had humiliated my poor mother in ways I cannot describe to you, a lady of quality! I am ashamed to have had such a father."

Tamarisk remained silent. She was uncertain how she could best soften such unhappy memories for this sensitive boy who had so clearly idolized Yvonne St. Clair.

"Please tell me more about your mother!" she said finally. "I am sure she must have been both kind and beautiful!"

Siméon flushed again, not from anger this time but from sentiment.

"You remind me of her, Madame. She, too, had the same small hands and feet, the golden hair, the look of a madonna!" He paused before adding softly; "No other woman has been to this house since she died — until you came. I did not wish to . . . how do you say in English . . . *salir* her memory."

"In English we would say 'to sully a memory,'" Tamarisk replied. She glanced at the good-looking young man beside her. "Have you not felt very solitary at times? It is not good for people to live alone. You should be married, Siméon. At your age it is right that you should be enjoying the companionship of a wife!"

"Even were I to desire to wed, there are few white girls on the island!" Siméon said, adding quickly: "But I enjoy my solitude and I have no wish to involve myself with other settlers. I travel seldom to the north of the island. There is no road to the capital, l'Établissement du Roi, and it takes three hours by pirogue, so I go only when it is imperative." Seeing her puzzled stare, he described the native canoe. "I am well accustomed to living alone," he reiterated. "Indeed, I prefer it!"

"Then I must make every effort to hasten my convalescence," Tamarisk teased smiling, "so that I may make my departure and leave you in peace."

Siméon's face was once again red with confusion.

"That would be the very reverse of my wishes, Madame!" he said vehemently. "I cannot tell you how happy I am to have you here under my roof. There are many reasons for this. For example, this morning, as I was leaving to go down to the plantation I heard you singing the French song called '*Vert-Vert.*' It was a song my mother loved to sing to me when I was a child and it brought back such beautiful memories to me. I wondered how you, an English lady, had come to know it."

Tamarisk smiled.

"My mother used to sing it for me, and for my father who was a Frenchman. It had sentimental associations for them both and now for me too. Siméon, shall I ever reach England safely? I am plagued by the thought that my poor children will believe me drowned with their father."

"There is no need whatever for you to worry on that account," Siméon said. "I have already dispatched a letter by one of my Africans to Mr. Wilson, the English Civil Commissioner, telling him that you are safely in my care. I also notified him of the deaths of the sailors who were with you and returned such identification as I could with the names of your ship, HMS *Valetta*. Doubtless Mr. Wilson will send word to England with the next dispatches."

Tamarisk put her hand on Siméon's arm.

"That was most kind and thoughtful!" she said gratefully. "Now that I am gaining strength I will write home myself!"

"First you must rest and allow nature to heal in her own time," Siméon admonished.

It was late October before Tamarisk was fully restored to health. At home the evenings would be dark and chilly, she thought, but here on this magical island it was like an English midsummer's day.

"It is hard to tell the difference in the seasons here on Mahé!" she remarked to Siméon.

They were sitting on the veranda outside the Château Corail. Siméon was wearing cream pantaloons, a white lawn shirt and a nankeen tail-coat; Tamarisk, a pale blue muslin dress that had once belonged to his mother. That it was in the fashion of the turn of the century scarcely seemed to matter as did little else, thought Tamarisk, on this strangely beautiful island. Time moved at a slow pace and was for the most part governed only by the routine of nature herself. Siméon and his workers were only pressed for time when the cinnamon needed harvesting. Otherwise the men went about their duties, moving slowly in the heat of the tropical sun, singing Creole songs whilst their hands and feet moved rhythmically in time with their voices.

In many ways it was an idyllic existence, she thought, although she knew from the many stories Siméon had recounted that in his mother's lifetime, the occupants of the Corail Plantation had been very far from happy. Monsieur St. Clair's cruelty to the then slaves, his drunkenness which led to the raping of the black women and the terrible beatings of the men, had made hell of this paradise. Starved, beaten and despairing, the mortality rate of the slaves was very high. Women, who were not permitted to employ their tribal customs following childbirth, had fallen prey to poisoning of the blood, prolapses and fevers.

Narcisse, who had lived through these times,

had told Tamarisk in her halting French, that old Monsieur St. Clair was a man without mercy who thought nothing of selling a slave, be it a wife, a husband or a child, to another planter if he felt the price was advantageous. Children, in particular, fetched a high sum if they were healthy, for a long working life could be expected from them. For their parents, Narcisse related, to be parted from their offspring was a kind of death to the spirit which caused them to lose the will to live. Many became ill and died from broken hearts.

Narcisse made no secret of the fact that she looked upon Siméon's father as the devil and his son as a god. Siméon had transformed their way of life, she told Tamarisk, treating them with the respect due to human beings, punishing them only when they deserved it. He kept families together and the children born on the plantation could rely on a future there without fear of being sold.

The old black African was a fount of information which she happily imparted to the convalescent Tamarisk. She went about her work in the house, answering all Tamarisk's questions with a toothless smile. The red paste she put upon the wood floors to bring such a beautiful polish to the surface was called *manglier*, she explained. It was made from mangroves growing in the swamps further north on the island. The house brooms were *fataks* made from the reeds which the children gathered from all around them. The heavier yard brooms, used to sweep up outside the house were known as *balaiers coco* and were made from the fronds of the coconut palms.

Tamarisk had slowly become accustomed to the native dialect. The wood used for cooking fires Narcisse called *cedre*. It was not the English 'cedar' Siméon explained, but the casurina tree. Most of the food was cooked with coconut oil derived from the crushed nuts. The Africans fed mainly on the fish they caught, on sweet potatoes and on sugar cane collected from the neighboring plantation. Once in a while they ate turtle meat when one of these huge sea tortoises was caught on the beach. Occasionally a sperm whale was cast up on the shore after a storm and sometimes a goat was killed to vary their fish diet. The men made their own tobacco from the leaves of the plants which flourished like most vegetation, in the tropical climate.

Siméon's only embargo, so Narcisse said showing her toothless gums in a broad smile, was the making and drinking of *toddy*. But the men did occasionally make this highly potent drink in secret. Narcisse suspected that Siméon knew of this but turned a blind eye to these rare lapses.

By now Tamarisk knew many of Siméon's Africans by name. Mathias, Jerome, Fabies, Gasper, Moses Bemba, Figaro, Jolicoeur Justin, Zephir Volant were but some of the men who shared the work of the plantation with Tobias. Azor Lafleur and Babet were two of the women and Narcisse had a daughter by the name of La Rose Printanière. La Rose wished to marry Mathias but there was no priest on the island to solemnize the wedding. All the plantation workers were Roman Catholics and had been baptized at the insistence of Siméon's mother. It was very sad, Narcisse said, that La Rose could not be married by a priest as she wished her children to be baptized and allowed into heaven when they died.

Tamarisk mentioned the problem to Siméon as they sat drinking chilled wine from the Château Corail cellar — one of the few welcome legacies Monsieur St. Clair had left his son.

"I am well aware of it!" he said. "It is a matter of concern to me too that the new generation of my workers should become Christians. I wrote to the Civil Commissioner about this unsatisfactory state of affairs at the same time as I wrote to inform him of your presence here. The reply he sent back with Figaro said that he had made strong representations to the British Government and that there was little more he himself could do."

Siméon had been loath to mention the Commissioner, Mr. Wilson, lest the thought should be put into Tamarisk's mind that it was time she went to l'Établissement to arrange her passage back to England. Now it was too late to withdraw his words and as he had feared, Tamarisk said:

"Do you realize, Siméon, that I have now been your guest here for nearly three months!"

She had written twice to let her mother know she was safe and making a slow but steady recovery. She had no way of knowing that neither letter had ever reached its destination.

The first had been stolen along with some valuable packages from a boat destined for England via Cape Town. The second letter was mislaid at l'Établissement. It still reposed in a canvas bag on the quayside where one of the Commissioner's African messengers had carelessly abandoned it when he could not find the ship to which he was supposed to deliver it.

"I am quite well again now, Siméon," Tamarisk continued, "and I cannot in all conscience further delay my return to my family."

"Do not leave just yet — not unless you must!" Siméon broke in, his voice quiet but intense. "Those who expected your absence from home for two years in India can surely spare you a further week or two! Your health is improving every day but you will need all your strength to undertake the three month journey to England."

Deliberately he omitted to give the true reason why he wished her to remain longer — that he, himself, would miss her gracious companionship to such an extent that he could not trust himself to think about the future when she would not be there. Tamarisk's presence in his home was affecting him deeply — if not always happily. Only now that he had grown accustomed to sharing his home and life with a beautiful and intelligent woman, had he come to realize how lonely his life had been hitherto. He found Tamarisk's feminine ways enchanting and would listen with pleasure to the rustling of her skirt

300

as she approached a room, or watch entranced her dainty artistic movements as her small hands arranged the flowers that now filled his house with color. Her gold hair was brushed until it shone like sunlight, brightening any room she graced. Her voice was soft and melodious and most of all he loved to hear her speak his own language with her charming English accent.

Tamarisk was aware of her young host's admiration and was not unmindful of his ill-concealed adoration. That he might love her did not cross her mind for she was far more conscious than he of the disparity in their ages. There was after all nearly twenty years between them. She had grown very fond of Siméon but her affection was like that of an elder sister for a younger brother.

At first acquaintance Siméon had been reserved and inarticulate in her presence, but as his shyness wore off he had revealed himself to be intelligent and sensitive; and above all, immensely lonely. Tamarisk had set herself the task of bringing a smile to his face whenever she could, and it gave her a surprising amount of pleasure to see his obvious happiness of late.

Her own spirits too had lifted. The first shock of losing both husband and sister as well as poor devoted Elsie began to recede into the past. England, her home, her family seemed to belong to another distant world that she had known long ago.

At first she had believed she would never recover her peace of mind. But only occasionally now did she suffer from nightmare dreams of the sinking *Valetta*. Elsie had always called such dreams '*monsters*,' for her grandmother had told her that '*the black mare of the night*' was a female monster who settled upon people or animals in their sleep, producing a feeling of suffocation. The memory of the loyal, devoted maid she had had since childhood invariably brought tears to Tamarisk's eyes.

But whilst her body was now restored to normality, her mind had not yet fully healed. Perhaps due to her talk with Siméon concerning her return to England, in the early hours of the following morning she suffered a recurrence of the terrible dreams that she hoped had ceased to plague her.

Narcisse no longer slept outside the door of her bedchamber. Tamarisk had been confident that she had no further need of the comfort and solace the old woman's presence had afforded during her convalescence. So now she was alone in the darkness as she twisted and writhed in the grip of a nightmare more vivid than any she had yet endured. It was doubtless intensified by the wild storm that was lashing the palm trees outside the house.

A fierce wind was sending the loose objects in the yard clattering over the stones. Coconuts were crashing down onto the wooden shingles of the roof of the Château. Tamarisk's moans rose to a scream. In her nightmare she was back on board *Valetta* shortly before the frigate sank. Broken spars were falling about her head. Rooted to the wet planks of the deck, she saw one of the spars fall in slow motion, crushing

Charles and sweeping Elsie and Chantal into the boiling white sea.

"Charles, mind out!" she screamed, but her voice seemed to make no sound as she clutched the curtains of her bed in an agony of fear.

"Charles, beware! Beware!" she screamed again and this time her voice echoed around the room.

Siméon, in bed at the opposite end of the house, had already been woken by the storm. Hearing Tamarisk's cries he searched for the *robe de chambre* that lay at the end of his bed.

He could not imagine what could have frightened Tamarisk; she had shown no fear of other such storms which occurred quite frequently on the island. There was little to be feared on this southern tip of Mahé. There were no dangerous animals and the worst that could have frightened her was a *chauve souris*. Occasionally one of these bats that flourished in vast numbers in the thick foliage of the trees covering the island lost its bearings and flew into the house.

It was only as he reached Tamarisk's door and heard her confused shouting that he realized she was once again tortured by bad dreams. He opened the door softly and approached the bed. Tamarisk moaned and he put a hand gently on her writhing shoulders seeking to rouse her.

Barely awake, Tamarisk saw the shadowy figure of a man bending over her and felt two strong arms enfolding her. Were they Charles' arms, she wondered in confusion? Or those of

303

the British sailor who was dragging her into the longboat?

"*Doucement, doucement!*" said a soft voice. Arms rocked her in a gentle embrace as if she were a child. "Hush now, there is nothing to fear. *C'est moi*, Siméon. You are quite safe with me!"

"Oh, Siméon!" Tamarisk cried, relaxing against him as she realized with a vast sense of relief that she was not after all upon the decks of *Valetta* but safe in bed at the Château Corail. But the horror of the nightmare still threatened her. "Do not leave me!" she begged. "I have been dreaming . . . it was so horrible . . . I was so frightened!"

Still suffering the aftermath of fear, Tamarisk pressed herself closer against the strong male body that was her anchor in the darkness. She had no thought for the effect her proximity might have upon the young man who was already half in love with her. She was unaware that her thin night-dress, transparent with the sweat of fear and the damp humid atmosphere of the storm, was clinging to her hot skin, revealing as clearly as if she were naked the curves of her breasts and her dark pink nipples.

A flash of lightning flooded the room. The sound of the thunder reverberated all around them and Tamarisk instinctively pressed her body even closer to Siméon's.

With a small, tortured cry, he buried his burning face against her soft bosom.

They remained so, rocking gently as the thunder rumbled intermittently and the heavy stinging rain cascaded torrentially from the black sky.

Both Tamarisk and Siméon were trembling violently, Siméon from a desire he could no longer control; Tamarisk from a sense of shock. Her dream was forgotten and now she was acutely aware that she was in the arms of a young man she had thought only a friend but who was reacting like a lover. Her sense of unreality increased, for instead of shrinking back from Siméon's embrace — as had been her habit with poor Charles — she found herself wishing Siméon even closer. She could not comprehend why, when she feared all men's desire, she should not also fear this man and wish him as far distant from her as possible.

She touched the fair head laid against her breast and began gently to stroke Siméon's cheek as if it were he who was in need of comfort rather than herself.

"Forgive me!" he murmured. "I heard you call out. I thought . . . "

"Hush, hush!" Tamarisk broke in softly. "I am glad you came, Siméon. I cannot bear to be alone. Stay here with me, *please!*"

She realized from his quickened breathing and from the hardening of his body that his thoughts were no longer concerned with comforting her in her distress but with the desire to possess her.

Her mind was gripped by memories of the past. So many times in her early married life she had submitted to her husband's demands not because she wanted Charles but because she realized with sympathy the extent of his need of her. At such moments she had closed her eyes and tried not to think of what was happening to her; tried not to allow her fear to overcome her willingness to give her husband what he wanted. That fear had never been absent when he invaded her body. It had been one of the greatest misfortunes that Charles could never approach her bedside without she was haunted by the image of the bestial Genoese merchant, Galvanti. Charles had known and understood her horror and he had come only infrequently to her bed to lie with her. After the birth of their last child, he had ceased altogether to enjoy his marital rights. Although she had never denied him and had done her best to conceal her fear of his naked body, he was unselfish enough not to force himself upon her.

Charles' understanding had brought its own rewards, Tamarisk thought. She had loved him more each passing year with a steadfast, if passionless, devotion and of late with gratitude that she need never again relinquish the privacy of her body to invasion.

Now to her incredulity, she felt no hint of apprehension as the boy beside her betrayed *his* desire. She was conscious only of his fear though unaware of its cause.

"Do not be afraid!" she whispered, although there was no one to overhear them. "It is all right, Siméon, I'm not angry with you."

Siméon St. Clair was horrified with himself for harboring such lustful desires for the beautiful woman who had come so unexpectedly into his life. He would rather be dead than have inherited his father's bestial ways, he thought, as he fought against the unbearable temptation to kiss Tamarisk. His mother had been unable to conceal from Siméon his father's abuse of all the women slaves he owned, regardless of their age. There had even been children only just attaining the age of puberty who had been forced to indulge in his drunken orgies, their mothers wailing and crying as they besought their mistress to save their daughters. But Siméon's mother had been powerless against the great ruthless man who thought nothing of killing slaves who disobeyed him, or worse still of punishing them. His favorite method was to tie the culprit to the ground, fasten bundles of sticks to his arms and legs and then set fire to them so that the man burned to death by slow degrees. His head being the last part of his anatomy to burn, the unhappy victim was conscious almost to the end.

On several occasions when his mother had tried to intervene with the boy, Siméon, at her side, her drunken husband had struck them both, warning them that next time they attempted to interfere he would beat them both within an inch of their lives.

Siméon had sworn then that when he grew up, he would prove to his mother that he had no share of his father's blood. So determined had he been never to give way to those baser instincts he knew existed within him, that he had avoided all contact with other white inhabitants on the island. As for the African females, he had never followed the example of other white planters and taken a black consort. He would never so much as lay a hand upon one of them although some of the young girls were truly beautiful.

All Siméon's workers loved him as deeply as they had hated his father. Occasionally one of the girls would encourage him with smiles and welcoming glances, for they were without conventional standards and indulged their bodies as they chose. It was part of Siméon's policy of discouragement that he would only allow Narcisse into the house. She had been his *bonne d'enfant* when his mother fell ill and could no longer care for him. Narcisse was now so old that there could be no fear of misunderstanding in their relationship.

In such manner, Siméon had avoided temptation and when the normal inclinations of his young, healthy body forced him to realize the unnaturalness of his celibacy, he had only to think of his father to renew his determination.

But now not even his childhood memories could subdue the tumult of his emotions.

"I am no better than my father!" he thought in torment.

Tamarisk felt him moving away from her and reached out to detain him.

"Do not leave me, Siméon!" she begged. "If you were to go, I think I might begin to dream again. Stay here a little while!"

"Very well, if you need me. I will stay as long as you wish," he said, his voice husky with emotion.

He reached out and lit the candle on the night table. Only then did Tamarisk become aware of her dishabille. Her nightdress had slipped from her shoulders and bared her bosom, the lighted candle revealing her nakedness to Siméon. She could not guess how young and vulnerable she looked to him with her fair hair in soft damp curls about her wet cheeks, her slim white body trembling still with the aftermath of fear.

"Forgive me for waking you!" she said, suddenly shy as she straightened her nightdress. "It was a terrible dream! You have been very kind. I will be all right now if . . . "

A brilliant streak of lightning flashed across the room, halting her in mid-speech. Almost at once there followed a tremendous crack of thunder and then the storm broke in full tropical fury. For Tamarisk it was as if she were transported back onto *Valetta* in the midst of the hurricane. With a cry of dismay she flung herself once again into Siméon's arms.

Despite the heat of the night Siméon could feel her soft body shivering as she pressed against him. Without thought for the consequences, he lay down beside her whilst the storm raged, then with typical island abruptness, as suddenly ceased.

But the storm within Siméon himself was overpowering.

"*Je t'aime!*" he gasped. "You do not understand. I want you so much, my beautiful, lovely Tamarisk. Oh God, forgive me for my wickedness!"

Now it was Tamarisk who was calm and he who trembled. She felt the shuddering of his body and understood what torment he was

309

enduring. In such a way she had held Charles in her arms in the early days of their marriage knowing that he could not deny his hungry need of her yet unsure of his welcome.

Tenderly she kissed Siméon's forehead. He raised his face and looked at her with blind adoration.

"I cannot hide my longing, my need. I love you. But now you will despise me. I am so ashamed. Forgive me! Forgive me, Tamarisk!"

"Hush, Siméon, there is naught that needs my forgiveness!" she said vehemently. "I am responsible for bringing you to my bedchamber — to my bed. *I understand how you feel*. But have you forgotten my age? 'Tis a young girl you need to love, not me!"

"If you can even think such a thing, then you do not understand," he cried. "You are all that I respect and admire in a woman. And you are lovely beyond words. I love you, Tamarisk. *Je t'aime! Je t'adore!*"

Tamarisk lay quietly stroking his hair, her mind in a turmoil. She realized that she was flattered by the adoration of this young man. When Charles ceased to make his rare marital demands she supposed that with the passing of time she had lost her youthful attraction. Perversely she had wanted her husband's verbal admiration even whilst she welcomed the fact that she need no longer fulfill his physical needs. With Siméon she felt no sense of obligation to assuage his hunger. Nor did he expect anything from her.

Thus was Tamarisk's reaction to her husband

now reversed as she discovered that she wanted to touch Siméon's face, to move her body closer to his, even to encourage his desire.

When still he hesitated, her intuition led her to further understanding. He was not only afraid of his feelings but unsure of his rôle.

"Siméon!" she whispered. "Have you never had a woman?"

He shook his head.

"*Jamais!*" he confessed in his own language. Then with a deep shuddering sigh, he added: "I am no animal, like my father. I am a human being and even if I cannot help the lusts of my flesh, I can control them."

"Oh, Siméon, *my dear!*" Tamarisk said sighing. "I had no idea that your childhood had left such a mark upon you. But I am certain that had your mother lived she would have told you that it is not wrong or bestial to desire a woman. It is a part of man's nature. You are a man, Siméon, and it would only be wrong if you lacked such normal desires."

Without warning, memories flooded her mind of her own youth — of her beloved Perry telling her after her abortive elopement with Leigh Darton that she must never feel ashamed of her body or its needs.

How wise Perry had been!

"Lust without true affection is always ugly!" he had said. "But never if it is enjoyed with mutual respect and affection."

Now suddenly her body stiffened with a longing she had not known since those girlhood days. Bending her head she kissed Siméon's forehead and then his mouth.

"So be it," she thought as she guided Siméon's hands to her breasts. "I will make this, his first experience of love, as beautiful as I can for him."

The rain had ceased and the room was filled with the scent of bougainvillaea. The candle guttered and went out but the full brilliance of the tropical moon poured through the unshuttered casement. The dark sky was studded with huge stars.

"*'This one night shall be a star to outshine all the suns of all men's days!'*" Tamarisk quoted softly as without fear, she removed her nightdress and lay naked before Siméon's eyes.

"Ah, Tamarisk! *Mon amour!*" he cried, covering her face, arms and body with kisses that became increasingly abandoned. "*Coeur de mon coeur!*"

"Heart of my heart!" Tamarisk repeated softly, caught up now as deeply as Siméon in the romantic urgency of the moment. The slim young body of her lover bore no resemblance to that of her rapist and she gave no thought to Galvanti as the boy rolled himself gently on top of her. She stared at him, smiling as she twisted her arms around his neck and kissed him hungrily.

But Siméon's hunger was greater than hers and with a cry, he lifted himself so that he lay above her. Gently she guided him into her and then calm deserted her as they began to move together in natural harmony. She cried out with pleasure and heard him gasp as release came to them simultaneously.

As sanity returned Tamarisk lay immobile with Siméon still deep within her, wondering at the miracle which had just occurred. She had thought only to initiate Siméon into the mystery of love yet in doing so she herself had discovered its beauty. Her body still glowed with the most marvelous of all sensations and she kissed her lover passionately in a surge of gratitude.

He opened his eyes and looked at her with adoration.

"I will never never forget this night!" he said. "Oh, Tamarisk, my beautiful, beloved Tamarisk! How can I thank you?"

"There is no need, Siméon. I too, will never forget this night," she said, kissing him between words. "You will stay with me for what remains of the night? I would be too lonely without you were you to leave me now."

"How can you doubt it?" Siméon said. "I could not bring myself to go from your side even were you to demand it."

"Then let us sleep in one another's arms," Tamarisk suggested softly. "In the morning when we wake we will love one another again if you wish."

"In the morning?" Siméon repeated. "How will I wait so long?"

In the darkness Tamarisk smiled. She had misjudged the youth and strength of this eager lover of hers. His need was her need and she would not deny him.

"Then we will postpone our sleeping!" she said as his arms tightened around her. "Let us talk a little while, and then . . . ”

Siméon stared down at her with parted lips.

“You mean that you will permit me to love you again tonight?” he asked with innocent candor.

He did not need to ask the question a second time.

16

September 1838

IT was Zambi who first detected that there was no sound of voices filtering through the palm trees fringing the beach as they made their way back to the bay. As she paused, tilting her black fuzzy head, listening intently, Dinez spoke sharply to her in Portuguese. The girl spread out her hands in confusion. Dinez turned to Chantal and in a voice full of concern said:

"Zambi insists that the beach is deserted. She *must* be wrong!"

"You mean the crew have gone?" Chantal enquired but Dinez was not listening. Leaving her to follow at her own pace, he ran swiftly towards the bay.

By the time Chantal had caught up with him, Dinez was at the water's edge, shading his eyes with one hand and staring out to sea where the tiny outline of *O Bailado* was silhouetted against the blue sky.

"What is happening?" Chantal asked anxiously. "Are they coming back?"

Dinez turned his head and looked down at her, his expression dark with anger.

"On the contrary, Señorita. They are sailing away as fast as the wind will take them," he said furiously. Fortunately Chantal could not translate the stream of swear words that Dinez

315

let fly in his native language. But she could guess by his face and by the rigidity of his stance that his anger was murderous. Zambi, who had not yet understood the situation, was squatting on the sand swaying from side to side and frowning in bewilderment.

"Wait here!" Dinez commanded without recourse to polite phrases. He strode off towards the trees and as Chantal watched, she saw him retrace the path that he had taken earlier in the day with Miguel. At once she realized that Dinez must now suspect his men had mutinied and before abandoning their captain to his fate, had persuaded Miguel to reveal the hiding place of the pirate hoard. She dared not think what Dinez' reaction would be if he found his treasure gone. She was suddenly deeply afraid.

The fact did not occur to her that she herself was cast up upon a desert island from which there might be no escape, for she assumed that if *O Bailado* could reach the island, albeit by means of the pirogue, other ships could do likewise and that rescue would not be long in coming.

Dinez, however, lost little time in disillusioning her when he returned from his sortie.

"They have taken everything," he said, his green eyes narrowed in fury, his hands trembling in barely suppressed anger. "Miguel, the one man I trusted, has betrayed me and left us to rot here on this outlandish island. If ever we should get off Coetivy which I very much doubt, I swear before God that I will kill him with my own hands. *May the devil take his soul!"*

Although Zambi did not fully understand what had transpired she had by now guessed the salient fact that the ship was leaving them to whatever fate should overtake them. She was by no means as frightened at the prospect as was Chantal. The island terrain was not so different from the African jungle she had lived in all her young life; and survival on nature's resources was as natural to her as breathing. Her sharp eyes had already noted that several of the crew had taken spades and water casks to a patch of ground where the vegetation was greenest, and deduced that they were going to dig a well. Food was in abundance all around them. Dinez was carrying a panga to kill what needed killing and to protect them from hostile natives, if such existed. She feared only the Evil Spirits against which she believed only specific charms were effective and that the Evil Spirits of this island might be different from those haunting her tribal territory.

Dinez da Gama was at first too angry to think of their predicament in such practical terms. But as the futility of his anger touched his consciousness, he began to see what had transpired through new eyes. He alone of the three castaways knew that their hopes of rescue were such that virtually they could be discounted. No trade ships called here and the island had no significance for nations at war or seeking to gain valuable territory. Fishermen from the inhabited islands surrounding Mahé never ventured as far away as Coetivy. For

317

this reason he had chosen Coetivy to hide his plunder. This meant that he and the two women would be alone here perhaps for years.

Suddenly he smiled.

"I may have lost one treasure, but I have of a certainty acquired another!" he thought glancing at Chantal.

But not even the anticipation of the pleasure of Chantal's lovely body could really compensate for the losses he had sustained, his beautiful, beloved *O Bailado* and spoils that would have amounted to a small fortune in gold — the fruits of nearly five years of piracy!

He turned to Chantal and said bitterly:

"Doubtless you feel I had no right to my ill-gotten gains!" He stressed the adjective as if he were quoting her.

"I had not thought in such a manner!" Chantal replied quietly. "But whatever the rights and wrongs of your lost fortune, Sir, I sympathize sincerely with the manner in which it has been taken from you. To suffer betrayal at the hands of your men is a cruel misfortune. Please believe that I am truly sorry!" She glanced at *O Bailado* now only a speck upon the horizon and felt the first glimmer of real anxiety. "How long shall we be here before another ship rescues us?" she asked.

"One year, two, maybe never!" Dinez replied with brutal honesty. He was finding Chantal's calm approach to their plight far more frustrating and irritating than if she had had an attack of the vapors, or at least burst into tears as might be expected of a young girl from her sheltered

318

background. Then he would have been the one to comfort her rather than she to offer him soothing dollops of sympathy!

"That must surely be a very pessimistic prognosis!" Chantal replied, certain that Dinez was exaggerating. "I wager we will be on our way to England within a few weeks at the most."

"To England!" Dinez echoed scornfully. "Do you really have no idea where we are? The nearest civilization is the island of Mahé and that is two hundred miles away. Even though there are British ships in plenty calling there, what reason do you suppose they might come to Coetivy? Just in case a human being has been cast away by some other ship which has left them to their fate?" he added with sarcasm. "Besides we are not on a route to anywhere in the world."

"Are there no other islands?" Chantal enquired. "I most surely remember you telling me that Coetivy was but one of many."

"There are many others, yes! But like Coetivy they are uninhabited!" Dinez told her.

"Then we must build a boat and sail to Mahé!" Chantal retorted.

"Without tools? Sails? And who will build this boat? You? Zambi?"

Convinced that he was deliberately trying to frighten her, Chantal would not allow this dark, angry man to see her gathering apprehension.

"We can help you!" she said quietly. "You are strong, the strongest man I have ever known, except perhaps Kaftan . . . " She broke off, her eyes filling suddenly with tears at this unexpected memory of the brave Lascar who had saved her life.

Dinez was not listening. He was lost in thought, pondering the possibility of building a raft substantial enough to carry them in safety to Mahé. But even whilst he contemplated the feasibility of doing so, he knew that he would never build it. He was a wanted man, wanted not least by the British to whom he was well known as 'The Portuguese Hawk.' The nickname had not displeased him for it was his practice to swoop over the water in his nimble *O Bailado* and grab his prey even before they realized he was upon them. He had five British flags in his cabin, souvenirs of stolen prizes . . . or had had, he thought with a renewed rush of bitterness. There was little doubt that if he set foot upon Mahé, it would be only a matter of time before he was flung into gaol. If his few dealings with the slavers came to light, he would undoubtedly be hanged.

He drew a long breath and let the air dispel slowly from his lungs. It was a sigh of resignation, for no longer could he avoid facing the inescapable facts — they were cast upon this island of Coetivy and must remain here indefinitely, maybe for a lifetime.

"There are worse places to be marooned!" he thought glancing around him. The climate was perfect — seldom less than seventy degrees and at hottest not much above ninety. There was unlimited food and on previous visits they had found adequate supplies of fresh water when they had dug a well.

Slowly a grin spread across Dinez' countenance as he realized for the second time that in addition to nature's blessings, the fates had provided him with a young and beautiful white girl for a wife and a strong healthy black girl for slave and concubine. There must be many men who would consider him to be envied rather than pitied in such circumstances.

"We have wasted time enough bemoaning our misfortune!" he said, his voice sounding almost cheerful. "Now let us be practical. We shall need some kind of shelter for the night." In Portuguese, he said, "Zambi, you must have knowledge of how the men of your tribe build huts. Here is my panga and also I have this . . . "

He took a knife from a ring on the leather belt supporting his trousers — a long, thin-bladed knife called a *navaja*. It had a spring-operated catch to lock the blade in an open position and Dinez had seized it years ago from a Spanish sailor who had tried to kill him with it.

"Please let me help!" Chantal offered. She saw Dinez' eyes on her small, smooth, white-skinned hands and to her irritation she blushed as he replied bluntly:

"I doubt if you can. However . . . "

Chantal heard the note of derision and her embarrassment gave way to annoyance. Her brown eyes flashed with a sudden fire as she said:

"You will see, Señor da Gama. I may look delicate and useless but I am not helpless. Moreover I am not without intelligence. I

321

appreciate your intention to build a shelter for the night, but has it not occurred to you that our need for water is of paramount importance? I will go and search for the well that the sailors dug."

Dinez' eyes narrowed. The girl was right. Water was the first requirement but he was the one who should have thought of it.

"There can be only one captain on any ship, Señorita!" he said furiously. "I will give the orders!"

Chantal drew herself up to her full height.

"In the first place we are not on your ship. Nor is this your island so your title of Captain scarcely applies. In the second place, I live in a country where leaders are chosen and not self-ordained."

Humor now replaced Dinez' annoyance. He laughed.

"I admire your spirit, Señorita. Nevertheless there is nowhere in the world I know of where women are permitted to vote for their leaders. So since I am the only person on this island who has the right to vote, I hereby appoint myself King Dinez of Coetivy. You may now pay homage to me."

Aware that she had been bested but her own humor reasserting itself, Chantal laughed.

"I will pay homage to no man!" she said. "And now Señor Dinez, are we not wasting time as you suggested five minutes ago? 'Tis long gone noon and if we are not to sleep beneath the stars, then you should be about your work!"

Whilst they had been talking, Zambi had been squatting on her heels drawing pictures in the sand with a stick. Glancing down, Dinez saw that they were of a palm-thatched hut in various stages of assembly. Though crudely executed, the drawings gave an excellent indication of how the native girl believed the construction should be effected.

"Well done, girl!" he said. "It appears simple enough. Our first step by the look of it, is to fell a palm tree, which may not be quite so simple. We have only a panga with which to chop it down."

But he went to work with a will, the bare upper half of his torso streaming with sweat as he hacked away at a tall palm on the fringe of the sandy beach. By the time Chantal reappeared with the news that she had found the well and that there seemed to be water a-plenty within it, the tree was lying on the sand and Zambi was chopping at the great palm fronds. Dinez was carrying armfuls of hardwood he had cut for the hut frame.

Surveying the Portuguese pirate and his smiling slave busy about their labors, Chantal had a sudden feeling of total unreality. This past hour she had forgotten that another world existed. Now she was aware of a great surge of homesickness. Beautiful though this island was, exotic and fascinating its wildlife, the sense of adventure that had supported her since the sailors had departed on *O Bailado* now deserted her. She was unhappily conscious of her isolation. These two human beings who

323

were to be her only companions were little less than complete strangers. Zambi spoke barely a word of English and although she seemed sweet-natured, respectful and more than anxious to please Chantal, there were no means other than signs by which she could communicate with her. The girl was still uncivilized however gentle.

As for Dinez da Gama, he too was little short of being a savage, Chantal thought as she stood unnoticed staring at him. He was a pirate, lawless and prepared to kill to gain his own ends. On his own admission he had intended to ravish her this very morning in the clearing to which he had taken her for the purpose. The fact that he had refrained from so doing on that occasion was no guarantee that he would not take her by force in the future, if he so desired.

Despite the heat of the late afternoon sun, despite the friendly chirping of the blood-red cardinals, despite the soft fragrance that surrounded her on this paradisiacal island, Chantal shivered with fear. She felt instinctively that such an attack would be a humiliating violation of mind and body. But there was no escape. She knew that the island covered little more than a few square miles and that were she to hide, it would be only a matter of time before Dinez found her. Moreover she doubted that she could survive alone in such primitive conditions.

Her helplessness had never before occurred to her. It was the first time in her sheltered life that physical strength and self-sufficiency were of paramount importance; her education and breeding irrelevant. Even the slave girl, Zambi, knew more than she. This morning Zambi had demonstrated her knowledge of plants when she found a herb to soothe the insects bites. Now she was instructing Dinez how to build a shelter from the island's resources. No single item of instruction she, Chantal, had received in her classroom at the convent would be of any practical use here!

Remembering her convent, it struck Chantal that there might after all be no need to despair. How often the kindly nuns had reiterated that she had only to put her faith in God to be armed against all life's perils. She and her friends had never been able to match the sublime faith of those women, but nonetheless she believed in a divine protector and had no cause as yet in her young life to doubt that He or her guardian angel would fail her. Had she not had proof of this recently when despite all the odds, God had sent Kaftan to take care of her after the shipwreck? He had let Kaftan live long enough to ensure her survival before Dinez da Gama espied the drifting longboat and rescued her.

Such thoughts were comforting and her spirits lifted as she ran across the warm sands to join Zambi and Dinez.

Zambi greeted Chantal with a smile and showed her how to twist and plait the fibers from the palm into a rope. The task was not difficult but the soft skin of Chantal's hands soon began to blister. Dinez meanwhile had become aware of a severe ache in his shoulders from his vigorous wielding of the panga.

"We will rest a while!" he said, sinking down on the sand and staring with quiet satisfaction at the large pile of palm fronds, some no less than fifteen feet long, he had accumulated. "Zambi has worked well," he remarked to Chantal. "Yet she does not seem in the least tired by her exertions!"

He sent the girl off to collect water in one of the wooden buckets the sailors had intentionally or thoughtlessly left behind. Beckoning to Chantal to sit beside him, Dinez lifted one of her hands and looked closely at it.

"You cannot work longer with those blisters!" he said not unkindly. "It is best if you soak them in sea water. The salt will ensure they do not become infected and though it might sting at first, it will soon soothe the pain."

"I will manage very well, thank you," Chantal replied, withdrawing her hand and meeting his stare with what she hoped was a look of contempt. "Though I am used to a better way of life, I am neither stupid nor helpless. You will find me quick to learn. As for these . . . " she held out her hands " . . . I will bind them with cloth from my skirt and that will protect them!"

Dinez felt a glow of excitement stir him from his state of exhaustion. Chantal's pride, independence and determination not to be a burden in their predicament were unexpected facets of her character that he could respect as well as admire. Many young girls from her background would be swooning, weeping,

326

demanding and complaining.

"*Nao deve fazer esforcos!*" was all he said. "You must not do too much work . . . at least until you become more accustomed to physical labor!"

Now it was Chantal's turn to discover a new facet of Dinez' character. This domineering, threatening, aggressive male was showing himself capable of kindness and consideration. Perhaps she had no real need to fear him — even though he was a pirate, she thought. When he discovered his crew had mutinied and robbed him of his hidden treasure he had not for long raved and ranted. Instead he had put his mind to making good their misfortune as speedily as possible. Working tirelessly, he had ensured that by nightfall the hut would be at least partially built. He had earned her respect.

Zambi's architecture was relatively simple. A strong upright pole was fixed as firmly as possible into the sandy soil. Palm branches, divested of their leafy fronds, were similarly dug into the ground in a circle around the pole, the thin, pliable ends tied together at the top with the rope Chantal had plaited. The whole formed the rounded shape of a huge beehive. Leafless palm branches were then tied around to form circles, each three feet above the other.

Dusk was falling when Dinez and Zambi were finally ready to thatch this framework with the long leafy palm fronds. The fretwork of leaves overlapped one another so that during the tropical downpour of rains Dinez anticipated, they would remain dry inside this rough shelter.

"Tomorrow we will make mattresses for ourselves!" Dinez said to Chantal. "Zambi thinks that the fiber from the coconut husks will make excellent bedding. But now it is too late and we are all too tired to begin fresh labors. Gather up the leaves that are lying in the sand and make some kind of carpet for us to lie down on, Señorita Chantal. I will finish the thatching whilst Zambi goes in search of an evening meal!"

So tired in mind and body was Chantal that she could barely force herself to carry out his bidding. She no longer cared where or upon what she lay provided she could rest her body and sleep. Only Zambi seemed inexhaustible. She soon returned armed with two huge long-tailed fish which she had killed with Dinez' *navaja*. She deposited them outside the hut and went to gather wood for a fire. Half asleep, Chantal lay in the doorway of the thatched hut and watched as Zambi gathered driftwood and lit a fire with the aid of Dinez' tinderbox. The girl then cut four great steaks from what appeared to be the wings of the fish. Spearing one upon the end of the knife which she had bound to a bamboo cane, Zambi held it over the flames.

Into Chantal's tired mind came the memory of an illustration in one of the two books on nature her father had given her for a Christmas present, Gould's '*Birds of Europe*,' and Monro's '*Structure and Physiology of Fishes*.' In this last book was a picture of a stingray — a huge, flat fish resembling a skate — with a tail as long as a hunting whip. She recalled the shiver of distaste she had felt upon reading that the spines of its tail could poison a man were he unlucky enough to be flailed by the whip-like extremity.

But hunger took no account of squeamishness and when Zambi handed Chantal the first of the roasted fish steaks, she ate voraciously, sucking the juice from her fingers in a manner that the governess of her nursery days would have deplored.

Her cooking activities completed, Zambi beat out the embers of the fire and, breaking open coconuts, rounded off the meal with a long drink of milk.

The repast had tasted better than the finest food at one of her mother's banquets, Chantal decided. Too tired even to talk, she wandered slowly down to the sea's edge to bathe her face and hands in the cool water. The sound of the waves lapping gently on the shore was the only noise to break the stillness of the night. She was suddenly aware that the hum of insects and shrill calls of birds that had besieged her ears during the day had ceased. A brilliant white moon had risen behind the palms which were now swaying gently in the faint breeze — like dancers in silhouette, she thought.

But her fatigue was overpowering. She stumbled back to the hut and without thought of where Zambi or Dinez might decide to repose themselves, she lay down upon the carpet of green palm leaves and fell instantly asleep.

The strange sound of coughing woke her some hours later. Although she did not know it, the noise came from a pair of herons roosting some thirty feet above the hut. Suddenly Chantal became aware of the deep breathing of someone lying beside her. With as little movement as possible, she turned her head and gazed into the sleeping face of her rescuer, the pirate, Dinez da Gama.

Moonlight was flooding through the open structure of the entrance to the hut. Zambi's dark head was easily discernible on Dinez's far side. The girl lay curled up facing him, one arm lying loosely, intimately, across the man's body. Like lovers, Chantal thought with a sense of shock.

Her breathing quickened as she became conscious of her own position. She was lying not six inches from a total stranger who but a few hours ago had told her of his intention to force himself upon her. Suppose he were to wake now and carry out his threat, she thought. She would be powerless to defend herself. Would Zambi come to her aid? Instinct warned Chantal that she could not rely on the black girl to counter her master's wishes. If this man intended her harm, she could not avoid it unless she were to kill him or herself first.

In sleep Dinez looked younger and less ferocious than he had seemed when giving orders to his crew or cursing them for deserting him. His mouth above the dark beard was open slightly as if he were about to smile.

Chantal's fear suddenly left her. She did not believe Dinez da Gama was an evil man. He might even prove an amusing companion as well as a tower of strength whilst they waited rescue by a passing ship. Although he had forecast pessimistically that they might never be found, Chantal was convinced that it would prove only a matter of time until they were rescued. Dinez could not be certain that such a day would never come. He must know that if in the meanwhile he molested her, he would most certainly be put to death when she informed their rescuers of his actions. His fear of that day of reckoning should be sufficient in itself to guarantee her safety . . . were it in fact in jeopardy. It did not cross her mind that even if rescue came Dinez might kill her before she could inform on him.

Chantal's thoughts switched to considerations of how they might build a great bonfire on the highest point of the island. When lit, it would emit sufficient smoke to attract the attention of a passing vessel. Even if time rendered Dinez' tinder box ineffective, Zambi would know how to make fire with sticks. She, Chantal, had learned in her geography lessons how natives employed such methods.

It would not be long, she comforted herself, before she was safely aboard a British ship bound for England. Now half asleep, she lay imagining the joy with which her parents and John would receive her; their expressions of astonishment and disbelief when she related her adventure. She thought how worried they would be when they learned of the sinking of *Valetta* and how they would suppose her drowned like poor darling Tamarisk and Charles.

She glanced down at the sleeping man beside her. His body was almost touching hers. Self-consciously, she edged herself further towards the side of the hut in order to put a more modest distance between them. She felt vaguely discomfited at the thought that whilst sleeping, he was at a disadvantage and she should not be staring at him. How shocked her Papa, Mama and John would be if they could imagine her lying here beside a sleeping pirate! The consideration brought a half-smile to her lips. John would regard her as totally compromised. But then he was always overzealous in his concern for her. She knew that his attitude sprang from a desire to protect her but it had the same effect upon her as did the severe discipline of the convent nun — arousing in her a desire to be mischievous.

Chantal felt a sudden sadness that John was not here on this strange island to share the adventure with her. As children they had talked so often of the future when they would be grown up enough to explore the world together. She had taken it for granted that they would never be separated. Even when she had been old enough to start thinking of love and marriage, she had supposed that John would marry her dear friend, Julia, and that it would merely add to their mutual pleasure to be three rather than two.

Only recently had she considered marriage for herself and the consequences were she to wed Antoine de Valle. Whilst the thought of being Antoine's wife had excited her, it had depressed her to realize that John would take no part in that life. His dislike of his half-brother had disturbed her far more deeply than anyone had supposed and was the main reason why she had not given her promise to Antoine to become his wife on her return from India.

Now, with a sense of shock, Chantal realized that she had not given a single thought to Antoine since the shipwreck. She explained away this lapse of memory by telling herself that there had been little time to consider anything other than her own immediate survival. She tried to conjure up his image but it became confused with that of John.

Chantal sighed in deep perplexity. If she were able to transport one or the other here to Coetivy, she thought, it would not be Antoine but dearest John she would want to share her exile. If *he* were here, she would have nothing to fear for he would allow no harm to come to her.

Suddenly Dinez stirred. He moaned in his sleep and flung out one arm so that it lay across her body. Chantal froze at the contact. Unconscious though his gesture was, her every nerve tensed as she became keenly aware of him. Her wayward mind recaptured the moment when she had been following behind Dinez through the undergrowth to the clearing. Her breathing quickened and she lay rigid as she tried to fight against the weakness that seemed to be overcoming her. She was not sure what she would do were Dinez to wake and try to kiss her.

But he slept on, exhausted by the labors of

the previous day. It was only when the shrill chorus of bird-song heralded the dawning of a new day that Chantal was able to sink once more into the innocent world of her dreams. When next she woke the sun was streaming through the aperture in the hut, burning into her arms and face. Both Dinez da Gama and Zambi were gone.

17

November 1838

PERRY glanced over the top of his newspaper at John who was toying with his breakfast.

"The Americans have yet to beat SS *Great Western*'s record of crossing the Atlantic in fourteen and a half days!" he remarked hoping to engage the boy's interest. He was as deeply concerned as Mavreen at John's state of mind. Ever since they had learned from the Admiralty last month that *Valetta* must be presumed lost at sea, the boy had been gripped in a silent world of despair. He had refused to leave the house or to enjoy the company of his friends; and neither Mavreen, the patient Julia nor Perry himself had been able to bring a smile or even a glimmer of interest to John's countenance.

Perry's own deep shock and sense of loss at the probable death of his beloved daughter still tore unbearably at his heartstrings. But he knew it was wrong to give way to grief indefinitely and he fought against it, doing his utmost to cheer himself and those around him. But John was proving inconsolable.

Renewing his attempts to arouse John's interest, Perry continued:

"There is little news concerning France's war with Mexico. 'Tis two months since the declaration and there must have been progress by one side or the other!" He sighed. "This world of ours is never for long at peace. Mr. O'Connell is agitating in Dublin with the whole of Ireland in an uproar since the Irish Poor Law Bill was committed in September. In Canada too there are series of revolts. I suppose we should be grateful that our own country is at peace!"

Mavreen came into the drawing-room, interrupting Perry's monologue.

"I had thought we might take ourselves to the National Gallery in Trafalgar Square," she said in falsely bright tones. She went to stand behind her son's chair and laid a hand lightly on his head. "I am quite ashamed not to have visited the Gallery since it was opened in August," she said. "Will you accompany us, John dear?"

John sighed. He had lost over a stone in weight and he looked pale and unhappy.

"If you will excuse me, Mama, I fear I am not in the mood for Landseers or Turners. I think I shall go down to the Admiralty again to see if there has been any further news."

It was his habit to go there weekly although he had been politely informed that the family would be contacted instantly if there were information of any kind relating to *Valetta*. For the time being nothing was known but that she was overdue at Bombay; that a hurricane had been reported in the environs soon after the ship had sailed from Mauritius and it was feared *Valetta* had not escaped it.

Mavreen glanced anxiously at Perry over the top of John's head. Grief-stricken though she was herself at the probable deaths of her only daughter, her son-in-law and stepdaughter, her concern now was for the living.

"Do you not think, my dear, that you really should begin to take up the threads of life again?" she asked her son gently. "No one would be more distressed than Chantal were she to know that you were mourning her in such fashion. Why do you not go away for a little while? To France, perhaps? You told me how greatly you had enjoyed the company of the Dubois family. I am certain that they would he delighted to see you!"

Remembering his previous visit, John's face flushed. He had given no thought to Fleur since the day he had been told by a heartbroken Perry that Chantal and Tamarisk were probably dead. He had thought he might lose his wits altogether so great was his shock and grief. Even now he could not reconcile himself to the belief that he would never see Chantal again. He was haunted by memories of their shared happy childhood; and by less happy memories of her as he had last seen her, bright, glowing, lovely as she walked into the ballroom, her hand on Antoine's arm.

In his bitterness against fate, John had taken a cruel pleasure in the knowledge that at least Chantal would never marry his half-brother now. Perry had written to inform Antoine of Chantal's death but surprisingly they had received no reply from him.

He drew a long sigh. Perhaps, he thought, his mother was right in suggesting that a sojourn away from Barre House might help him to come to terms with the future which now loomed ahead of him in a despairing void. Perhaps Fleur and her pretty, laughing, happy sisters would liven his mood. It was a possible and better alternative to the idea he had been nurturing these past weeks — namely, to go and fight in the Spanish Civil War in the hope that he might be killed honorably in battle.

So it was that the following week John returned to France and rode once more up the graveled driveway to the Dubois' Château. It looked cold and gaunt in the chill November twilight, the sunshine of his memory replaced by a damp grey fog that lowered his spirits even further. He felt he had been mistaken in coming to Beauvais. But within minutes of his arrival, his mood changed. Massive beech logs some five feet long and one or two whole branches, crackled merrily in the fireplace and sent their hot cheerful blaze into the shabby rooms. The Dubois desmoiselles clustered around him chattering excitedly. Soon the flames and the girls' welcome were warming his chilled heart. Fleur alone was silent, smiling, her expression unfathomable as she removed John's heavy surtout and handed the damp garment to one of her sisters to take to the drying room.

The portly Duc shuffled into the room, smiling benignly as he added his welcome.

"M'wife will be here presently," he said, shaking John's hand. "Hearing of your arrival, she has gone to kill the fatted calf!"

The twins, identically pretty as ever, dimpled at their visitor.

"Have you been ill?" one asked.

"You look so pale!" said the other.

But it was not until after the meal of river trout and roast duck liberally supplemented by the Duc's excellent wines, that John relaxed sufficiently to be able to speak of his recent bereavement. For a few minutes following his announcement the entire family was shocked into silence. Fleur was the first to express her condolences.

"When my fiancé, Giovanni, was killed, a kind English friend wrote to me quoting your poet, William Wordsworth — '*Death is the quiet haven of us all*,'" she said gently. "I realized on reading those words that I was grieving not for the man who had died and was at peace, but for myself. Your loved ones do not need your tears now, John."

He could not trust himself to reply but none seemed expected of him. Much later that night however, Fleur came to his bedchamber whilst the rest of the household slept and spoke once more of his bereavement.

Unlike her manner on his previous visit, she gave no indication that she wished to renew their relationship as lovers. More in the manner of an affectionate sister, she sat on the edge of John's bed and gently stroked the back of his hand. Her silent sympathy unleashed the pent-up sorrow that had held John in its painful thrall for so many long weeks. He found, suddenly, that he could mention Chantal's name to Fleur as he

339

could not to his mother or to Perry, far less to the tearful Julia.

"Perhaps I might reconcile myself more easily to Chantal's death if I fully believed in it!" he cried. "My parents, the kindest of my contacts at the Admiralty, all have told me I must not hope that the ship may yet arrive at some foreign port; that it is too long overdue for such a miracle. I have been told too that were any survivors to have reached the island of Mauritius, they must have done so long since. I know that my advisers must be right and yet deep within me, I cannot believe I shall never see Chantal again. Do not ask me to explain for there is no reason to it. I simply cannot accept that she is dead!"

Fleur's voice was gentle as she replied:

"We have all at some time believed what we wished to be the truth in the vain hope that thinking will make it so!"

John sighed.

"Doubtless that applies now to me. But there are nights when I wake suddenly quite convinced that Chantal is calling to me. I swear it is no dream, no wishful thought of mine."

"In time you will become reconciled to her loss!" Fleur said softly. "You may find another to love. Or if you do not, like me you will adapt yourself to life without your loved one. Will you tell me about her, John? If I am to lessen your sorrow, then I must be able to share your memories!"

For an hour or more, John talked to his quiet companion about Chantal. Encouraged by Fleur's interest he was unaware of the incongruity of praising one girl to another. It struck him as extraordinary the way Fleur always seemed to know instinctively what he needed even when he knew it not himself, and he had needed desperately to talk of Chantal. When at last Fleur said she must depart, he was like a man relieved of a greater part of his pain.

"One often lightens troubles in telling them!" Fleur quoted wisely when he thanked her. With feminine intuition she knew that this was not the moment to try to revive their former relationship. She left him with no more than a gentle kiss upon his forehead.

As on his previous visit, John was made to feel most welcome and was treated with the same informality as if he were one of the family. Although the weather was too inclement for outdoor pursuits, the girls all seemed to enjoy themselves in innocent pastimes, playing chess or backgammon, weaving or embroidering secret gifts for each other for the approaching season of Noël. John helped Rose bring in a fir tree from the garden and they spent a happy afternoon adorning it prettily with tiny wax candles and ribbons fashioned into roses by the girls.

There was a happy bustle about the house and an atmosphere of cheerful excitement. In the evening Fleur and her sisters played and sang carols and derived much amusement from learning new English carols from John. Unbeknownst to John, the entire family were intent upon keeping him well occupied with little time to reflect upon his bereavement.

Before long John was more or less his old self.

Although he did not tell Fleur, he was becoming even more firmly convinced that Chantal was somewhere in the world and that one day be would see her again. In the meantime Fleur had once again stirred his senses and he was newly aware of her strange provocative femininity. In a manner that was totally unobtrusive, the family had 'paired them off.' There was always a place left beside Fleur on the sofa or a chair vacant at the dining table so that he could sit next to her. In their games, he and Fleur were partnered. On the few occasions they drove into Beauvais, it was suggested that he and Fleur ride in the Travelling Coupé, the smallest of the Duc's carriages, allowing room for only the two of them.

The Duchesse treated him like a son as did the Duc. She reprimanded him if he left a muddy footprint on her polished floor and sent him upon errands as often as she did her daughters. Everything she required was always wanted urgently, to the amusement of all her family, who teased her with gentle tolerance as they reminded her to "make haste slowly." John wondered briefly whether there was a scheme afoot amongst this close-knit family to marry him off to Fleur. But the thought seemed unworthy.

Fleur never mentioned the future nor referred to their former relationship. She went each night to John's bedchamber but only to talk for a short while before kissing him goodnight when she was about to leave. There were moments when John put out a hand with the thought of detaining her, his desire for possession of her warm, voluptuous body overcoming his determination not to give way to his self-centered needs. But no matter how convincingly this lovely girl had once argued that she was content to accept their loving without the commitment of love itself, he knew it must be wrong to take advantage of her loneliness: that it was his duty to hold her in greater respect than she held herself.

From eldest to youngest, all the members of the family tried to persuade John to remain with them throughout Christmas. But he knew that he must return to Barre House and his own family. His parents were now responsible for Tamarisk's and Charles' four young children who were living with them and John was greatly attached to his nephews and nieces. Nearer their ages than were the other members of the family, he felt he owed it to the children to try to make this first Christmas without their parents as happy as possible for them.

The night before his departure Fleur came to his room as usual. But on this occasion she was far from exhibiting her usual composure.

"I thought I would make my farewell to you tonight privately!" she said, her voice trembling as she spoke. "I shall miss you so very much, dear John!"

In the soft glow of the bedside candle, John saw tears glistening in her eyes and was shocked. It had not crossed his mind that the quiet, self-contained, independent Fleur could be so emotional.

He put out his hands and took possession of

hers. It was ice cold and shaking.

"Why, you are frozen!" he protested. "Wrap the coverlet around you, Fleur."

She made no move to obey him. Her voice almost inaudible, she said:

"I hoped that I should never be so weak that I would say this to you, John, but my feelings are too strong to contain any longer. I did not want to do so but I must confess now that I love you!"

The tears in her eyes spilled down her cheeks. John, open-mouthed, stared at her white face. He could find no words that seemed appropriate. He was deeply shocked by the discovery that the practical Fleur had been harboring romantic notions about him.

She drew a deep shuddering breath:

"I know that you do not love me — nor ever will," she continued. "I realize that your heart will always remain true to your Chantal and I understand from all you have told me about her why you should treasure her memory. But John, sad though it is, Chantal has gone from your life and you cannot spend the rest of your days with no one to love or care for you. If you would let me, *I* would love you, even though you cannot return that love as I might have wished in other circumstances."

"I do not know what to say!" John answered truthfully. "I am naturally very deeply honored — and touched by what you have told me. But Fleur — my *dear* Fleur, could mere affection ever suffice when it is love you need?"

"Many marriages are arranged without love

344

as a consideration," Fleur said quickly.

"I know!" John answered. "But I believe my mother is right when she tells me — as she often has — that it is only when equal love exists between man and woman that a truly happy marriage can result. I have seen her grow old in the company of my stepfather and it is as if they are one person, each aware of the other's thoughts, needs; each lost in the unselfish caring of the other. And I suspect that even now the mutual passions of their bodies if less ardent are still strong."

John was suddenly aware of Fleur's eyes fastened questioningly upon his face. He flushed, understanding her thoughts. *Their* loving had not been lacking in passion and in this respect they were already proven excellent partners.

He drew her to him and kissed her. Her arms encircled his neck and he felt an instant renewal of all the old excitement at her touch.

"Fleur, my sweet Fleur!" he murmured, weakened almost beyond control by the perfume of her body and the soft silky sweep of her auburn hair as it fell across his face. But even as he reached out to draw her into the bed beside him, his last vestige of conscience gave him the strength to hesitate. If he were to take this young girl now in love, it would be an admission of his need for her and as a consequence an agreement that marriage between them was a possibility. *But he did not want a life partner who was not Chantal.* He had but to close his eyes and it was Chantal's face and body there beside him. It was Chantal's sweetness, beauty, laughter that he needed; Chantal whom he loved.

"Fleur, forgive me, but I have too much respect for you to lie with you whilst I long for *her*. Can you understand? With another woman for whom I had no real regard such a thing might be possible. But I like you too much. *Do* you understand, Fleur? I would be betraying both you and Chantal."

Her face was very white, her eyes larger than ever, as she nodded. She drew a long sigh.

"It is no more than I expected, John. That is why I did not stay with you all night before now as was my custom on your previous visit. But tomorrow you are going away and I . . . I gave way to the call of my heart. I should have let my head guide me. Can you forgive me for being so outspoken?"

"Forgive you!" John echoed. "It is I who must be forgiven! I cannot bear to think I have hurt you when you have been so wonderful a friend to me — far, far kinder that I deserve." He kissed her cheek in fondest affection. "I cannot say I love you because, as you know, I shall always love Chantal and her only," he added. "But if ever I should decide to marry another . . . then . . . "

The fingers she placed swiftly over his lips prevented him voicing the promise he was about to make.

"Hush!" she said. "'Tis better not to mortgage the future. None of us can know what tomorrow or next year will bring. It is enough that you are fond of me — and respect me."

"I will write to you!" John promised. "When

346

the spring comes I will visit you again. And you must come to England to visit my home. I will show you all the places I have told you about — our houses in London and Kingston and The Grange in Sussex. That little manor house was always the home Chantal loved most. You must meet my parents — and maybe we can arrange that all your sisters come too. I will invite some of my friends to meet them and who knows, perhaps they will find husbands despite their lack of dowries!"

"That is a very lovely dream to think upon!" Fleur murmured.

Suddenly John sat up very wide awake.

"'Tis no dream!" he said, as he warmed to his plan. "I am quite sincere in my invitation. Two of you at a time shall come for the season. We have a young Queen upon the throne now, you know and London is very gay in the summer months. Mama could present you to the Queen. She was friendly with King George IV, Victoria's uncle; and my sister, Tamarisk, was a childhood companion of his beloved daughter, Charlotte, who died so untimely . . . "

"John, John, not so fast!" Fleur interrupted. "'Tis true that we might be able to manage the journey to England but we would not have the clothes for the kind of life you describe and . . . "

Now it was John's turn to interrupt.

"That is a simple matter. Mama has an excellent dressmaker and I shall give you and all your sisters bolts of material for Christmas presents. You will not be aware of course, that most of my fortune derives from my grandfather's mills in Yorkshire. I will arrange for samples of their cloth to be sent to you to select what takes your fancy!"

"You seem to have an answer for everything!" Fleur commented. "Nevertheless we could not accept such gifts when we have nothing to offer in return. Papa would never countenance it even if the girls were willing; and Mama will not gainsay my father in any matter."

John pursed his lips thoughtfully.

"Very well! We will arrange a compromise. You shall have my young nephews and nieces to stay here in France to teach them your language. Tamarisk was only recently complaining to me that they are not given a pure accent in their schooling. The children would love it here at the Château and it would relieve Mama of their care — although she has an excellent governess to manage them. Mama has never been enamoured of very young children but she would welcome your sisters. There is nothing she enjoys more than the giving of parties and masked balls and soirées. Your visits will provide her with an excuse to indulge in an orgy of entertainment. By midsummer we shall no longer be in mourning and it will help to liven her spirits. You shall come first, Fleur, with Rose. I wager we shall soon find husbands for you both with no trouble whatsoever."

"I do not want a husband found for me, John," Fleur said gently. "Just now when I invited *you* to marry me, it was only because I wished to remain in your company. I see no virtue in marriage for its own sake."

"Yet you advocated such a marriage for me!" John replied thoughtfully.

Fleur rose from the bed and pulled her peignoir tightly around her.

"I did so only to gain my own ends!" she admitted, smiling. "It was not *any* wife I was advocating to take care of you, John."

"You will come to London nonetheless!" John said, reaching for her hand and holding it to his lips. "If only to please me, Fleur. In the morning I will arrange everything with your father and mother. And I will write to you the moment I have my parents' approval to my scheme. If it were not for . . . for Chantal I could be almost happy at the prospect."

When Fleur had gone, John lay back against his pillows, his emotions too disturbed for sleep to overtake him. It was satisfying to think that he could repay some of the Dubois' kindnesses and their hospitality. But his parting comment to Fleur had been all too true — happiness was impossible for him without Chantal. He tried once more to imagine her dead but his mind could not conjure up an image of Chantal, a wax-white effigy in a long shroud with folded hands and closed eyes. The picture in his imagination was, as always, of a laughing, dancing, sparkling girl — vivacious, teasing, fiery-tempered and sweet in swift changes of mood. But never, ever, could he see her in the stillness of death.

"She *is* alive," he thought with a fresh wave of conviction. "I know she is somewhere in the world and I must find her!"

He was but one day back in London before his restless feet carried him once more down Pall Mall to Admiralty House. He needed no minion to show him the way to the office of the Chief of Staff. He was taken to see Admiral Pentell who received him civilly but with the now familiar shake of his head. There was no news of HMS *Valetta*.

"I understand how difficult it must be not to know the fate of your family," Admiral Pentell said, "but, alas, I cannot offer you any hope. Take a look at this, sir! It might help you to understand the position."

He unrolled a linen chart which depicted the east coast of Africa, the Indian Ocean and the southern tip of India. He pointed to a spot on the chart north of the island of Mauritius.

"This is where *Valetta* would have been when and if the hurricane struck her. We know that the winds and currents in that area would normally carry a drifting ship towards the African coast. Had *Valetta* survived the storm, she would almost certainly have been driven aground somewhere on the east coast of Madagascar. I do not have to tell you that the Navy has made extensive enquiries and no ships or wreckage of a ship has been reported. Neither have any ships on the trade routes reported seeing *Valetta* although our agents have traced most of those who might have been in her line of drift. We do not have so many two decker men-of-war in the Navy that we can afford to lose one lightly, you know."

John looked at the older man despairingly.

"Is there nowhere else *Valetta* could have been driven by the wind?" he asked.

As the Admiral shook his head, the elderly clerk who had been scribbling busily with his quill pen in the background, coughed suggestively. Admiral Pentell turned.

"Well, what is it, Smithers?" he asked, and aside to John, he muttered. "The old fellow makes a point of listening in on all my conversations and that cough he just gave is his way of advising me he wishes to join in the discussion!"

"Well, sir, I seem to recall there being a sailing ship wrecked on some islands a long ways north of Madagascar!" said Smithers.

Admiral Pentell glanced at the man sharply and then turning to John he said:

"Smithers has a memory that confounds us all. And he is never wrong, are you, Smithers? Come along then, what ship was it?"

The old fellow scratched the few remaining white hairs on his pink bald head.

"I recall as it were a three-hundred-and-seventy-five tonner . . . let me see now . . . she was named *Tiger*. Yes, that was her! Left Liverpool sometime in '36 bound for Bombay. Wrecked some three months later, I think. I could look up the records, sir. Shouldn't take too long."

"Will you wait, m'boy?" Admiral Pentell asked John, and seeing John's eager nod, waved the clerk on his way.

"Remarkable old boy!" he commented when

351

they were alone. "You could ask him about practically any ship that ever sailed the seven seas and he will come up with some knowledge about her. Sailing ships are his sole, all-consuming passion. He makes models of 'em all — has hundreds, so I am told. His wife left him because there was no room in the house that was not full of 'em, including the bedroom. Yet do you know, he has never been to sea in his life!"

He looked at John and smiled.

"Got a rotten memory m'self so I cannot afford to ignore old Smithers when he coughs. Never known the old boy to be wrong!"

It seemed that Admiral Pentell's respect for his clerk was well-founded. When the redoubtable Smithers returned, he was carrying a sheet of paper on which he had written several notes in a thin spidery hand.

"Thought you might like the bare facts written down, sir!" he said to John. "If you want more information . . . "

"He has it in his head, so just ask him!" Admiral Pentell interrupted smiling.

"I was right about *Tiger* leaving Liverpool in '36," Smithers said with obvious satisfaction. "Third of May, it were. There was her captain, the crew and some passengers aboard, twenty-one souls in all. All went well with them at first and they reached Table Bay on the second day of July and left again on the twelfth. But from the day they left the Cape, the weather turned dirty — sometimes light winds and calms and sometimes gales." He paused and then asked John: "Is this of interest to you, sir?"

"Very much so!" John replied, for he had already glanced at the notes Smithers had given him and seen that *Tiger* had ultimately been wrecked on one of the islands in the Seychelles Archipelago — lying to the north of Madagascar.

"Luck was running against *Tiger*," the clerk continued. "She lost her fore-top gallant mast and royal in a squall and she was then in a strong southwest wind. The captain had been unwell and despite the care of the ship's doctor and the crew he had become insane and had jumped overboard. With the captain lost, the mate took command of *Tiger* and by the ninth of August, they found themselves off the southeast coast of Madagascar, near the island of St. Mary. There was a French settlement there and the sea was alive with whales spouting and leaping out of the water. The mate decided to turn north — clear of all danger."

Admiral Pentell nodded thoughtfully.

"I now recall *Tiger*!" he said. "The crew were jumpy after the captain's death and at the enquiry swore that they had seen a headless apparition as high as a mast, wearing white trousers and a blue jacket whom they believed was the captain's ghost."

"'Twas only the helmsman saw it!" Smithers corrected him. "By then both chronometers had been found to be faulty. The mate had been hoping to sight Cape Amber on the north coast of Madagascar, but they failed to do so and on the twelfth of August, they were driven onto the rocks on an unknown island which they later discovered to be Astove. Despite the huge waves, the crew managed to reach dry land by longboat and cutter. They also managed to rescue a number of live animals, provisions, charts and books. So their survival was assured and they were finally rescued by the South Sea Whaling Ship, *Emma*, in October."

"So HMS *Valetta* could have met with the same fate!" John cried, his excitement bringing a bright color to his cheeks.

"Steady now, m'boy!" said Admiral Pentell, putting a cautioning hand on John's arm. "If I am not mistaken, there were five months between *Tiger* leaving England and ending up on the island of Astove. It is now getting on six months since *Valetta* set sail. If by a miracle she too, foundered in the Seychelles Archipelago, it will be at least another two months at the very soonest before we can hope to have word of her!"

"But you do not understand, sir, this means that there is hope after all, for *Valetta*'s survival," John cried. "If *Tiger* could end up so far from her destination, then *Valetta*, too, could have done likewise. My sister, her husband, Chantal — *they may yet be alive!*"

"Must not put too much into this m'boy. Not a good idea to raise your parents' hopes either, only to have them dashed again. Dare say they are beginning to adjust to the worst!" muttered the Admiral gruffly. "There is another point you should consider. Astove is only one of close on a hundred such islands in the Archipelago, near all of them uninhabited. Mahé is the biggest and

British owned since we stole it from the French forty years ago. But most of 'em are just large chunks of rock with no life on 'em!"

"You mean people could be shipwrecked on one of them and . . . and never be found?" John asked aghast.

"Suppose that is about the truth of the matter," replied the older man in his clipped manner. "Not much shipping in that area. Only trading is on Mahé — cotton, tea, spices — that sort of thing."

"Then I shall go out there and search *every* island!" John burst out. "I cannot wait here in London for news that may never arrive! There must be a ship going there if this island you mention, Mahé, is British owned."

"It would take months to search all the islands!" the Admiral said, appalled at the mere idea that this impetuous young man had put to him. "And your journey might well be to no purpose. It would be a chance in a thousand if you were to come upon them. We do not have one valid reason to suppose *Valetta* was blown on the same course as *Tiger*."

"But do you not understand, Sir?" John cried. "Now that I know that such a possibility exists, I could not continue to live out each day following my normal pursuits as if there were no such chance of their survival. However remote the prospect of success, I must go. I will charter a ship and search every island in the Indian Ocean!"

Admiral Pentell regarded his visitor anxiously.

"It would cost you a small fortune, young

355

man. You would need a captain, crew, provisions, as well as the vessel. I do beg you to go home and talk this over very seriously with your parents. I fear they will not thank me for being the instigator of this . . . I must say it, *insane* notion! Forgive me if I sound pessimistic but I really cannot condone such an extravagant and pointless plan."

"Please do not feel responsible in any way," John said quickly. "You will agree I am sure, sir, that a long sea journey would not do a young man of my age any harm. As to the cost of such an enterprise, there are far more dissolute ways I could dispense with my inheritance, are there not? Is a sea voyage not to be commended as an alternative to gambling with cards, for instance, or betting upon the horses?"

Seeing the successful effect this argument had upon the doubting Admiral, John employed the same reasoning later that evening with his mother. Somewhat to John's surprise, his stepfather supported him, interrupting Mavreen as she voiced her adverse reaction in the strongest terms.

"It could do no harm, my love!" Perry said to his wife. "At least it would put not only John's mind but all our minds at rest. We would know that we had left no single stone unturned to find our loved ones. May God grant that John is right in his belief and by some miracle they are not dead. I wish that I, too, could share his conviction. You have my blessing upon your scheme, John, and I think when your mother has had time to consider it, you will have hers, too!"

There were tears in Mavreen's eyes as she looked from Perry to her son.

"If go you must, John, then I ask only that you should take the greatest care and run no risk unnecessarily," she said. "For I have lost too many loved ones already and I do not think I could bear it if aught were to befall you too."

As if by mutual consent, the subject was not further discussed that evening. However, Mavreen was far from reconciled to her husband's assumption that such a long voyage would be without danger. Later that night, lying in Perry's arms, she said:

"Do you really believe that we are right to let him go?"

In the darkness Perry smiled tenderly.

"John is a man and we must allow him to travel his own road," he said gently. "One cannot keep one's children protected forever. To do so would be to inhibit their experience of life itself. Think on yourself, Mavreen! You were far younger than John when first you flouted *your* father's dictates."

"You are right of course," Mavreen agreed. "I wonder what makes John so certain that Chantal is alive."

"Perhaps because he cannot yet come to terms with the finality of death," Perry replied quietly. Then he added with a smile:

"Or dare we hope that he has inherited your instinct, my love? Do you recall how convinced you were — and rightly so — that despite all the evidence against it, Gerard was alive during

France's war with Russia? Not even I could convince you of his death, though I never ceased to try!"

Mavreen's arms tightened around Perry as memories flooded back simultaneously to them both.

"You took me by force upon the carpet of the library at The Grange," she accused him with a soft smile.

"And how we both enjoyed it!" Perry said. "I can recall it as if it were yesterday. Ah, Mavreen, my one and only love! Shall we make yesterday today?"

"*You would take me by force?*" Mavreen quoted from the past.

"*Indeed, no, Ma'am, for I would gamble my life that you desire me as ardently as I desire you!*" Perry replied.

"But how did you know?" Mavreen whispered as Perry's arms encased her in an embrace from which she could never escape, nor even wished to. "How could you be so sure when I knew it not myself?"

She could see only the faintest glimmer of his smile.

"The way I am sure now!" he said as bending his head still closer, he began to kiss her with a passion that had not diminished with the years.

18

October – December 1838

TAMARISK awoke from a deep untroubled sleep with a magical feeling of well-being. Sunlight and birdsong filled her bed-chamber as lazily she stretched her arms above her head. Gazing around the room her eyes took in the disordered state of the bed, her nightgown strewn upon the carpet. Memories of the previous night flooded into her mind.

At first she smiled in sleepy contentment, recalling how reluctantly Siméon had left her to return to his own bed-chamber; how ardently he had declared that he could not bear to be parted from her even for a single minute!

Gradually her smile faded as the romantic memory gave way to harsh reality. She, Tamarisk von Eburhard, widowed but three months previously and in her forties, had spent the night in the arms of a boy but twenty-one years of age. What could she have been thinking of, she asked herself, now fully awake and deeply shocked by this tardy awareness of her situation. Her very last intention had been to seduce Siméon. Nonetheless she had fallen prey to passion as readily as he. While his youth and inexperience excused his part in the affair, she should have denied him; done her utmost to discourage him. Doubtless by now he too, was

359

awake and as might be expected of a boy of his age, feeling deeply shocked if not horrified to realize that he had lain with a woman old enough to be his mother.

A deep blush of shame suffused Tamarisk's cheeks. She reached for the pretty enamel-backed hand-mirror on the table by her bed and forced herself to look into the glass. Her hair was as soft and golden as any girl's, she thought. But around her eyes and mouth she could detect the faint lines that would all too soon betray her age. She might look several years younger now than most women in their early forties, but it would not be long before time caught up with her. After bearing four children, although she had given each to a wet nurse to rear, her breasts were not as firm as they had once been.

Siméon had not noticed her advancing years in the darkness of the night, nor compared her body to that of a young girl. But this morning when he saw her . . . Tamarisk pulled herself up sharply, reminding herself that Siméon had known no other female. With a sense of relief she realized that he could make no comparisons.

Tamarisk closed her eyes as if this simple act might shut out the unwelcome thoughts that besieged her. She told herself firmly that it did not matter to her how her young lover thought of her since she did not love him. Only her pride would suffer were he to regret his declarations. It would be better if she faced the fact squarely — the disparity in their ages was irreconcilable. If she was the first to speak of it, she could relieve him of the embarrassing necessity of explaining that his passions had got the better of his common sense.

Tamarisk was still pondering upon the easiest way to broach such a delicate subject when Narcisse knocked upon the door and came into the room.

Her black face was wreathed in smiles.

"Storm all gone!" she announced. "Happy day, Madame! M'sieur Siméon say to give this with coffee and not to stay talking so Madame read letter in peace!"

She placed a breakfast tray upon the night table and put the letter into Tamarisk's hand. The paper was carefully folded and sealed with wax. Tamarisk's heart was heavy as she waited for Narcisse to leave her. She then broke open the seal, anticipating the words she thought Siméon had penned. She believed that in order to avoid the embarrassment of telling her in person, he had found it easier to write expressing his regrets for his aberration and to apologize if he had inadvertently led her to take his words of love too seriously.

But as her eyes scanned the neatly formed script, her cheeks suffused with a color that stemmed not from shame but from pleasure.

'Mon amour!' he had written. *'I wish your day to begin with knowledge of my adoration, my love, my respect for you. I have never before written a letter of love and I do not know how to express all that I feel. I cannot wait to see you and beg you to hurry with your toilette*

so that you may join me quickly. Yes. I want for your sake that you should have as much repose as you need. Are all lovers selfish? I will try not to be, for I want to be as near perfect as possible so that I may please you.

'Tamarisk, *coeur de mon coeur! Do you have any idea how beautiful you are? I suppose many men must have told you so and I am jealous of them all. Do you know why poets write so often of love — it is because they have to tell someone of their euphoria just as I must tell you of mine.*

'My wise and lovely teacher, tell me how I can exist one hour longer without seeing you? Without kissing you? Without touching you? Dare I hope that when you read this, you will not be angry with me for writing such sentiments? I know you will never be able to love me and I would never expect that you should love a dull callow youth who is so ignorant and inexperienced. But I pray that you may feel a tiny spark of affection for me and that you will calm my tortured mind by telling me that you do not regret last night. I could not bear it were you to feel sorrow for something which has given me the greatest of all joy.

'I love you with all my heart.

'*Siméon*'

Tamarisk pressed the letter to her heart where only a few hours ago Siméon's fair head had lain. She was intensely happy and as deeply sad, for she knew that this idyll could not continue. All too soon she would be on her way back to England and her children. The parting with Siméon was inevitable and it would be unfair to him were she to encourage his new-found love for her. Nor was it beyond the realms of possibility that she too, could find herself involved in an untimely, impossible affair of love.

Tamarisk lay back against her pillows trying to rationalize her turbulent emotions. She should be mourning Charles, her kind, adoring, patient husband, she told herself. But the love that she had felt for Charles had never been of the kind that poets wrote about. When she first considered marriage to him, it was in part because she had needed to replace her dream lover, Perry; and in part to give purpose to a life that had seemed empty and meaningless without that misplaced devotion to the wrong man.

Over the years her affection and respect for Charles had grown and deepened. She had always considered her marriage a happy one, and herself fortunate to have such a devoted husband. That their relationship lacked passionate loving was due entirely to the fact that she had wished it so.

Only occasionally had she regretted that she and Charles were not close in the way that her Mama and Perry were. It was not unusual to observe them holding hands when they walked together, or for Perry to kiss his wife on entering or leaving a room. He was forever teasing her with an intimate smile that suggested some hidden meaning for them both.

As for her mother, Tamarisk thought, though a little less fiery than in her younger days, she was still as vivacious and provocative and just as beautiful as she had ever been. Mama might underline her determination to be independent and self-reliant at all times, but those who knew her well were fully aware that in any argument Perry ended up having *his* way whilst making it appear that Mama had *hers*.

Tamarisk rang the hand-painted china bell on her night table. Like so many of the pretty ornaments in the house, it had once belonged to Siméon's mother. Narcisse came hurrying into the room.

"I will take a bath," Tamarisk said, "but do not bring much hot water, Narcisse, for I think it is warmer than ever after the storm!"

The copper bath imported from France by Yvonne St. Clair, being metal was one of the few survivors from the termites. It was hurriedly fetched by Narcisse. Jugs of hot and cold water were brought to fill the tub and soon Tamarisk was soaking gently in the warm water. Narcisse had perfumed it with leaves from the verbena bushes and the air was permeated with their delicate scent.

Refreshed and attired in another of Madame St. Clair's unfashionable but beautiful muslin gowns, Tamarisk went out into the garden where she knew she would find Siméon. Her mind was now firmly made up. For his sake as well as for her own she must leave Mahé before this affair could involve either of them too deeply.

Siméon must have been watching for her. No sooner did she step onto the veranda than he was instantly at her side. Raising her hand to his lips, he kissed it passionately.

"My letter did not cause you offense?" he asked, his blue eyes dark with anxiety.

In the daylight Siméon now seemed to Tamarisk to look younger even than his years. It strengthened her resolve to explain, as gently as she could, that beautiful though last night's loving had been for them both, it must not recur.

Upon hearing her declaration Siméon looked distraught.

Hurriedly Tamarisk gave the reasons for her decision. Whilst she was speaking, his face lost its tenseness and by the time she had finished, Siméon was smiling.

"As if age has aught to do with love!" he said, pressing her hand once more to his lips. "To me you are more beautiful than any girl I could imagine. As for the fact that you have lived more years than have I, I will quote you our French writer, Voltaire, who said, '*La perfection marche lentement; il lui faut la main du temps.*' My mother voiced this wisdom many times to me when making her garden. 'Perfection walks slowly, Siméon,' she would say; 'it requires the hand of time.' I wish not that you were younger, my lovely Tamarisk, but that I were older and thus more worthy of you!"

Somewhere deep within her Tamarisk suspected that Siméon's love for her was related to the adoration he had had for his mother. She realized too that it was enhanced by his previous years of loneliness and by the hitherto unleashed passions of a young man in his prime. Whatever the cause there could be no doubting that he needed her in a manner that was as desperate as it was irrational.

"You cannot leave me yet!" he cried. "If you were to leave me now, I should lose the will to live!"

Despite the emotional extravagance of his declaration, Tamarisk was convinced that *he* believed it.

"Stay here at Château Corail but one week longer!" he begged. "A few more days would not be valued by your family in England as I will treasure them. Last night you swore to me that you had no regrets — that our loving was a miracle for you too. Did you say that only to comfort me? Did you not mean it?"

"Of course I did, Siméon!" Tamarisk said, her cheeks coloring at the memories he had evoked. "I do not want to leave you, but . . . "

"Then it is resolved!" Siméon broke in impetuously. "For one week you will be mine. Promise me, my lovely Tamarisk. One week is all I ask! Is that so much to give me?"

Neither he nor Tamarisk realized when she gave way to his request that she was to remain at the Château Corail far far longer than the promised week.

Having surrendered to Siméon and to her own

366

deep-rooted inclinations, Tamarisk determined to waste no single moment in pointless self-recriminations. Occasionally her longing to be reunited with her children and her guilt at not hurrying home caused her to lie awake whilst Siméon slept in her arms. At such times she determined upon the morrow to be strong and to tell Siméon that the promised week was long since past. But when morning came and her young lover turned to her with his wakening smile of perfect contentment, she could not bring herself to crack the shining mirror of his joy. "*Later*," she would think. "*This afternoon, when we go to the bay, I will speak to him!*" But another day would pass and another night and she became as enmeshed as Siméon in the love they now shared.

She wrote several times to her mother, implying that she was not yet well enough to travel home. But these first indications that Tamarisk was alive never reached England. Had Tamarisk known that her family still believed her dead, she would have succumbed less easily to the temptation to disregard the passage of time.

For the most part she succeeded in avoiding an analysis of her emotions. But once in a while she could not ignore the fact that she and young Siméon St. Clair shared very little intellectually and that the grip he held upon her senses was purely physical. In this respect she was as lost to reason as he.

Their discovery of each other was proving to be a discovery of themselves, too. There were times when Tamarisk was shocked by her own hungry need to be in Siméon's embrace. The adoration and respect he never failed to show her at all other times, was abandoned in the height of their passion. At such moments he would forget everything but his fierce need of her. And she was as abandoned as he — perhaps even more so since she could never forget that she was experiencing this ecstasy for the first and last time in her life. For Siméon, she knew there would be other women and eventually, no doubt, a wife. But she would never again know the wild raptures of youthful desire.

More and more often, she thought of Charles as he had been when they were first married. Such memories left her tormented by guilt for she now realized that he would have been no less ardent than Siméon had she encouraged instead of deterred him. She had denied him this most beautiful and wonderful experience and now it was too late for her ever to be able to remedy her failure. Charles was dead and she could never give or share with the man she had married his rightful desserts.

Sometimes she wondered if such a relationship could ever have been possible. If her mother had not introduced her own lover, Perry, into her adolescent life, perhaps she, Tamarisk, would have desired Charles in the normal fashion a young girl loved a young man. But it had been Perry who had unknowingly fired her mind with dreams of a romance that *he* had never once contemplated. His rejection of her had sent her flying first into Lord Byron's arms to prove herself desirable; and then into the arms of a worthless actor. Her own folly had taken her alone and unprotected to Italy where the terrifying Galvanti had attacked her. By the time she had considered poor Charles as a husband, she was already damaged beyond hope — or so she had always believed until now.

For this restoration of her ability to love, she could never be anything but grateful to Siméon and each time she gave herself to him she was expressing her thanks. That he did not understand the reason for his importance to her was of little consequence.

Her love for him was at its most tender when she saw him in sleep, his long golden lashes lying on smooth unlined cheeks, his limbs perfectly shaped with only a dusting of gold hairs on his legs and chest. She loved to touch him, marveling at the smooth unblemished perfection of his skin.

"You must eat more, you are too thin!" she teased him knowing that he would fill out in manhood and that his litheness was but another indication of his youth. On another occasion she tried to safeguard his future happiness by telling him that when she had gone, she wanted him to find a wife.

"To be so solitary is not good for you, my darling!" she said. "You have no idea how greatly you have changed since my arrival. Then you were very shy, almost morose. Now you laugh and talk a great deal. You have lost your nervousness and you look happy all the time. You used to look so sad and imprisoned in your thoughts. Do you not agree that you need a woman's companionship and that you would do well to marry?"

"*I want no other woman but you!*" was the only reply he would give her. His words were voiced with a furious passion and she realized that the mere thought of her departure frightened him; that he was refusing to contemplate the future without her.

"We should not have grown so close to one another!" she thought. "One day soon, I shall *have* to leave . . . and then what will become of him?"

Or of herself, she wondered. It would not be easy to remake a life without Siméon's tender care, without his absorption with her comfort and happiness, without his ardent passion.

As Christmas neared Tamarisk suggested that they should take the pirogue to l'Établissement so that she might buy a gift for him. But Siméon invented every excuse he could not to go to the island's capital. He feared that once she returned to civilization she would feel impelled to book her passage to England and this he would not contemplate.

"Stay here on Mahé and marry me!" he begged her more and more often. "You said yourself that I should take a wife. Marry me, Tamarisk, for if you do not, I shall never wed!"

"You know that is not possible, Siméon," she told him as gently as she could. "I have four children for whom I am responsible. I could not bring them here to live on Mahé for they have a right to an education and upbringing in their homeland. Richard wants to follow his father into the Navy and soon he will be joining a naval vessel to start his training. And in any event I would not marry you, Siméon. I shall soon be past the years for childbearing and however much you may try to deny my age, I will be old when you are not yet thirty!"

"I do not care!" he cried. "If you will not come to live on Mahé, I will sell the plantation and come to England with you. I do not want children, and if ever I should, *your* children will suffice."

"Siméon, Richard is only eight years younger than you!" Tamarisk said desperately. "You must rid your mind of such folly. I know it is difficult now to think about loving another but you will forget me in time and then . . . "

"Never, never, *jamais!*" Siméon cried, reverting to his own language in his distress. "As long as I live I shall love only you. I will never let you leave me, Tamarisk!"

But even as he picked her up in his arms and carried her to the bed to prove his immediate possession of her, both Siméon and Tamarisk knew that it could only be a matter of time before she must go.

19

October 1838

THEY had now been marooned on Coetivy for over a month. Chantal, who marked a notch on the palm tree outside her hut last thing every night, knew that it was nearing the end of October. In just another month's time it would be her birthday and she would be eighteen years old. It was difficult to recognize the passage of time on this tropical island, she reflected as she attempted to cobble together yet another rent in her already tattered skirt.

Zambi had made a large needle from a fish bone in which she had pierced an eye with the tip of Dinez' *navaja*. With equal dexterity the African girl had woven a coarse thread of fibers from cotton. However, the dimensions of the needle made small embroidery stitches a matter to laugh at in despair. At the present rate her skirt and blouse were disintegrating, Chantal thought sighing, she would soon be faced with the prospect of going around as naked as Zambi. The black girl now wore only the briefest strips of material which hung like tiny aprons front and back and Dinez too, had discarded his hot shirt and breeches in favor of a loin cloth.

The sight of Dinez' bare body was one to which Chantal could not become accustomed however hard she tried. Despite her anger with herself for her weakness, she could not prevent her eyes from straying constantly to his deeply tanned skin, his strong limbs and all too obvious manhood which his loin cloth exaggerated rather than concealed. Furthering Chantal's embarrassment, Zambi seldom lost an opportunity to point out Dinez with simple admiration as he chopped wood or strode across the sands with his homemade fishing rod; or as he lay sleeping in the sun. Zambi was rapidly learning English from Chantal and communication was now possible between them.

"Beautiful man! Very strong! Good husband!" were only some of her admiring compliments. She was totally perplexed by Chantal's attitude to Dinez and no matter how hard Chantal tried to explain that she did not want a husband, however beautiful or strong, Zambi left no doubt that she considered Chantal mad beyond question for rejecting Dinez' advances.

Chantal allowed her hands to lie idle in her lap as sighing, she reflected that English and African attitudes to life were quite opposite. Zambi seemed to live by the very simple philosophy that if something was good, desirable, enjoyable and available, it was silly to refuse it.

"Man need woman! Woman need man!" she said, her expression bewildered when Chantal continued to send Dinez away from the door of her hut. Nor had she understood why Chantal had insisted that she should have a 'home' to herself involving all the disadvantages of having to construct a second hut. As for

Dinez, Chantal thought irritably, he did nothing to lessen Zambi's confusion regarding English conventions. He made not the slightest attempt to hide either from her or Zambi, his desire and determination to possess Chantal. Each night he would sit by the dying embers of the cooking fire trying to reason why she should submit to him.

"When will you accept that we will be spending the rest of our lives on this island, Chantal?" he said, staring at her intently from dark-lashed, fiery green eyes that seemed to search her body and guess at her perturbation. "You think I am lying when I tell you we are not on any trade routes and that the inaccessibility of Coetivy was the very reason why I hid my booty here. I swear before God, Chantal, it is so unlikely we will ever be rescued as to make any expectation of it madness. I want you more than I have ever wanted any woman. I need you. And despite everything you may say, I know that you want me!"

"But I do not love you!" Chantal tried each night to explain her point of view. "You know it would be wrong, Dinez, even if it were true that I . . . I felt as you do!"

Her voice betrayed her at this point, faltering helplessly as she tried to avoid the necessity for referring to the lust of her body that Dinez talked of so freely.

Sometimes he would become angry, shouting that her stupid notions of love and marriage were as irrelevant on this island as the wearing of clothes.

"You are a prude, a silly child, a half-woman who does not have as much intelligence as the black savage who waits on you!" he ranted. "I am fast losing patience. Have you forgotten that I can take you as and when I want? *Que tenho que fazer?* Tell me then . . . " he repeated in English, " . . . *what must I do* to convince you that you are denying us both to no purpose?"

Chantal found it easier to argue with him in such angry moods than when he pleaded. Her convictions were apt to wane when suddenly he stretched himself full length on the sand beside her, reached for her hand and pressed it to his lips.

"Do you really have no idea how beautiful you look in the firelight," he would say in his softly-accented English. "I am so full of love for you, my sweet Chantal! My body aches for you! Have you no pity? Do you really find me so ugly? Do you reject me because you think I am wicked? Ah, Chantal, how shall I persuade you to be mine?"

At such times Chantal could not prevent her body trembling as if with the fever. The palms of her hands would become moist and her heartbeat quicken to twice its normal speed. Not trusting her voice to remain steady, she would stay silent, looking down at the brilliant green of Dinez' eyes. They seemed to beseech her to take pity on him, and yet at the same time, to challenge her to resist him.

Once she attempted to dissuade him from his tireless pursuit of her by talking of her involvement with Antoine de Valle.

"I am affianced to another man. When we are rescued I will be going to France with him!" she said, hoping that Dinez would be more convinced than she by her declaration. For one thing she had no way of knowing whether Antoine would decide to marry another girl if he believed her, Chantal, to have drowned at sea. Nor was she in the least sure that even if she were rescued, she would want to go to France to live. When she thought of returning home, it was always to Barre House, to her beloved Papa, to her stepmother and not least to John.

She tried to tell Dinez about John. But whereas he was prepared to listen, albeit with a disbelieving smile, when she spoke of her love for Antoine de Valle, he would scowl and turn away when she mentioned the special affection she had for John.

"'Tis he you love — not the Frenchman!" Dinez once accused her. He seemed genuinely surprised when she laughed and shook her head.

"I love John only as a brother," she corrected him. "As such I respect and admire him!" she enthused. "He understands me even better than does my Papa!"

But Dinez cut short such eulogies muttering that he had no interest in her past, only in their future. "*Our future*," he would emphasize.

He was like a spoilt, sulky, little boy, Chantal thought with a smile, as she began anew her attempts to repair her skirt. As always the sun was pouring down its beneficial warmth upon her naked body. She had long since abandoned what remained of her underwear. Dinez and Zambi had gone to the lagoon to see if there were any lobsters in the plaited rope baskets they had fashioned for the purpose. These homemade traps had proved most efficient and Dinez rarely returned from his visits to them without at least one tasty offering for their evening meal. Chantal knew that she could count upon privacy for the ensuing hour; that only the eyes of the sea birds, the tortoises and the friendly little fouquets which lived in a colony on the far side of the beach, would be upon her.

The little chocolate-brown fouquets, not much bigger than jackdaws, had webbed feet, hooked beaks and wedge-shaped tails. They made deep burrows in the sand in which they laid their eggs. Like all the birds on the island, they were very tame, knowing no fear of humans; but at night they would emit strange howls from their burrows which at first Chantal found so frightening that she could not sleep.

Now she was accustomed to the noise and in the daytime she loved to watch these strange, friendly, little creatures hopping and flapping over the sand. That they chose to spend most of their time in courtship or in mating hardly surprised her, for on this island nature was without restraint. The tropical climate encouraged rampant growth and reproduction without hindrance.

Her stitching completed, Chantal stood up and became aware by the slant of the sun in the sky, that far more than an hour had passed since Dinez and Zambi had departed. Hurriedly she donned her skirt and blouse; the very last thing she wished was to be discovered with no clothes covering her nakedness. Dinez laughed at her modesty, but despite the possible danger of sharks, sea urchins and stingrays, Chantal always ignored his advice not to go so deep into the water of the lagoon in order to hide her body from his gaze when she went to wash or swim.

"It is carrying modesty too far to risk your life rather than have me catch a glimpse of your beauty!" he said scowling. "I have never known so stupid a female!"

Was she stupid? Chantal wondered as she set about gathering dead branches and coconut shells to fuel the cooking fire in readiness for the return of her two companions. Zambi obviously thought so — and Dinez! But then Dinez was a wild, lawless pirate from whom she should not expect conventional standards of behavior.

As she turned her head, staring out as was her custom to see if there were a ship on the horizon, she caught sight of the evening star. From the latitude of the island, the planet always appeared to be three times larger than it had in England. When she was a little girl, her Papa had pointed it out to her from her nursery window. She would repeat after him:

"Twinkle, twinkle, little star!
How I wonder what you are,
Up above the world so high,
Like a diamond in the sky!"

His beloved voice surged into her memory. Without warning, tears sprang into her eyes. She had felt homesick many times this past month but never accompanied by quite the same degree of despair as now engulfed her. Until now she had steadfastly refused Dinez' so oft pronounced insistence that they would never be rescued; that she would never see her home and family again.

Her sense of loneliness was so overwhelming that when she caught sight of Dinez and Zambi coming towards her through the palm trees, she dropped her bundle of firewood and ran to greet them.

Dinez was carrying two lobster pots, a great clawed shellfish in each. Seeing Chantal flying towards him, he grinned happily, dropped the baskets unceremoniously and scooped her up in his arms.

"*O que é que se passa?*" he asked. "Tears on your cheeks, my little Damascos?"

In Dinez' language, the Portuguese word was pronounced "Dă-mash'koosh." He had translated it into French and Chantal knew that it meant 'apricot.' He had abbreviated it to "Koosh-Koosh" and despite her resolve not to allow too much informality between them, she had been quite happy with the name. She was even flattered when he explained that her skin now tanned by the sun, was golden like the fruit and smelt as sweet.

But now her sense of despair was increased by the unexpected tenderness of his greeting. She did not demand to be put back on her feet but clung to him with her arms around his neck. Giving way to the threatening tears, she sobbed noisily into his shoulder like a distressed child.

Zambi took up the basket of lobsters and showing her white teeth in a broad grin walked away in the direction of the huts. She was humming softly beneath her breath. The sound mingling with the soft wash of the waves on the sand was as soothing to Chantal's ears as Dinez' arms around her were comforting to her spirit.

"What is the matter?" he asked again, this time in English. "You have not hurt yourself? Has something frightened you? What is wrong, Koosh-Koosh?"

"I am not hurt!" Chantal cried. "It is just that I cannot bear the thought that we shall never go home. We will never be rescued, will we, Dinez? And *you* do not care whether we are found or not! You and Zambi are happy to remain here."

He looked down into her tear-streaked face, smiling.

"It is very easy to be happy in this paradise. I, who had thought that wealth was all I needed to ensure contentment, have now come to realize that in a place like this, all one needs is good health . . . and a woman to love!" he added, the smile no longer in his eyes.

"Please put me down!" Chantal said, his words making her once more aware of the intricacies of their relationship. Her tears had ceased to fall and she brushed away those still on her cheeks with the back of her hand. "I am sorry I gave way to despair!"

"*I* am not!" Dinez said shortly. Obediently he put her down but kept one arm around her waist. "I think you are at last coming to terms with the truth, my poor little Koosh-Koosh. There is no escape from the island — or from me!"

Before Chantal realized his intention, he drew her fiercely against his body and pressed his mouth upon hers. For a brief moment she resisted him but the gradual weakening of her limbs and the waves of sweet sensation in her body were too insistent to be ignored. The hands she put against his chest in an effort to push him away now went around his neck and she found herself returning his kisses with a great unbearable hunger.

Dinez was murmuring endearments in his own language. She could not understand the words but his tone was unmistakable. Without warning he drew her down on the hot sand beneath the palm trees where they had been standing. With surprising swiftness the sun dipped behind the sea's horizon and a warm twilight surrounded them in a soft embrace.

"Have no fear, my lovely Koosh-Koosh!" he murmured as his eager hands explored her trembling body. "I will be gentle, I promise. Ah, but you are so beautiful!"

Chantal felt a terrifying weakness as Dinez' dark head bent over her at the same moment as his fingers unfastened the buttons of her ragged blouse. Her body seemed to be on fire as he kissed her breasts with fierce hunger. She tried feebly to lift his head away but in reality

381

she had no wish to do so and her resistance melted beneath his touch. His body, a dark golden brown, smelt of the sea. His mouth when he kissed her was salty against her lips. For several minutes she clung to him returning his kisses and surrendering herself to the waves of desire that were washing over her, sweeping her into a world of sensations that were as new as they were overpoweringly beautiful.

But then Dinez' hands slid down to her waist and began to unfasten the cord that held her skirt. Never ceasing his kissing, he was still murmuring against her mouth:

"You are mine, all mine!"

"No!" Chantal cried, struggling to free herself as she became aware of the enormity of the step she had been about to make. When he made no move to release her and continued to pull at the fabric of her skirt, she beat with her fists against his chest.

"I will not! Let me go, Dinez. Please, I beg you! I do not want you!"

Those last few words arrested him and he let her go so abruptly that she fell backwards onto the sand. He leant on one elbow and stared down at her, his cheeks flushed and his green eyes blazing.

"You give the lie to your body!" he said harshly. "You want me as much as I want you. I know very well when a woman is ready for love . . ."

Desperately Chantal tried to pull the edges of her blouse together so that he could no longer stare at her breasts. She was shocked to realize that the nipples were swollen and that she ached for his touch. She knew then that without doubt Dinez was right — her body was as eager for love as was his.

She looked at him helplessly.

"'Tis true that I . . . that I lied! But Dinez, no matter how I feel, I cannot give myself to you in love. Do you understand?"

"No, I do not!" he said harshly. "Are you afraid of me? Do you fear the act of love?"

As she shook her head, her dark hair fell across her face concealing her burning cheeks. Dinez put a hand beneath her chin and forced her to look up at him.

"Is it that you wish to preserve your virginity?" he pursued relentlessly.

"No, no!" she whispered truthfully. "But I cannot break my sacred oath . . . "

"What sacred oath is this?" Dinez asked. "For the love of God, girl, you have not promised yourself to a nunnery?"

"No, Dinez!" Chantal cried. Despite the seriousness of the moment she nearly smiled at the look of horror on his face. She put out a hand and touched his arm in renewed appeal. "You will doubtless think my true reason pretentious or childish, or maybe merely stupid, but it matters greatly to me."

Dinez caught her hand and pressed it against his heart.

"Then for pity's sake, enlighten me!" he begged. "If 'tis so important to you, I swear I will not ridicule you."

Chantal drew a deep breath.

"'Tis a matter of honor — my honor," she said quietly. "I gave my sacred promise to my mother that I would never lie with a man who was not my husband." She stared at Dinez in desperation. "Were you my husband, Dinez, I would have no wish to deny you!"

All anger left his face and a slight smile hovered at the corners of his mouth.

"So!" he said. "'Tis a matter only of respectability!" He reached out a hand and not without a degree of tenderness, smoothed the dark hair from Chantal's face. "Can you really believe that such conventions matter *here*, on this island?" he demanded. "Only a few minutes ago you were running to me with tears in your eyes because you had finally accepted that we would never be rescued. Chantal, we are alone here for the rest of our lives. I have known it since I first saw *O Bailado* disappearing from view. We have only each other. Can you not understand what a miracle it is that we are both young, healthy and far from uncomely? We make a perfect pair. We can live together as man and wife and have children too if that is what you want. There is no other way!"

"As man and wife?" Chantal echoed.

"'Tis beyond doubt we have no priest to perform the rites!" Dinez said with faint sarcasm but softened by a smile. "Nevertheless we can be married in the eyes of God. Zambi shall be our witness. We will exchange vows before God as if we were in Church. 'Twill be no less binding upon us than is your oath to your mother. What say you, Chantal? Will you marry me?"

Chantal stared back at him, the suddenness of this idea taking her as much by surprise as her own strange yearnings to comply with Dinez' wishes. His fingers were idly tracing the curve of her arm in a way that set her nerves tingling and made it difficult for her to concentrate on the enormity of the decision he had asked her to take.

Dinez warmed to his idea.

"You shall go back now to your hut, tidy your hair and make yourself as beautiful as you can, Koosh-Koosh. I too, will do the same. Zambi shall prepare a feast for us. But first, since you have no bridal gown, she shall pick a bouquet of flowers for you to carry. She can even fashion you a coronet of flowers for your hair!"

For all Dinez' suggestions, it would still not be a proper marriage, Chantal thought. But then nothing that happened on this island could be likened to life in England. If Dinez were right and they were never to be rescued, the alternative to this marriage was to live the rest of her life as an old maid, and this she would not want. Poor Zambi, she reflected, would perforce have to live out her days without a lover. The thought saddened her even as it crossed her mind. For her there was an alternative to spinsterhood — she could become Dinez' wife.

She wanted desperately to believe that it would be a true marriage if they declared their vows before God, despite there being no Church or priest to sanctify the union, Was it possible that she, Chantal Lucia Maria

Waite, was actually contemplating such a step, she asked herself; that she was willing to wed a lawless pirate about whom she knew very little to his credit?

She looked at Dinez helplessly. There was no gain-saying that he was an exceedingly handsome man. On an island such as this, he would make a far better husband and protector than a man like Antoine de Valle, whose delicate beauty and refinement she had all but forgotten. In these primitive conditions strength and resourcefulness were worth far more than intellect and good manners. Not that she could really find fault with Dinez' behavior, for apart from the day of their arrival when he had intended to take advantage of her, he had never since made any serious attempt to do so despite the fact that she remained at his mercy. He had behaved as well as any gentleman in this respect. As for his past career as a pirate, did such lawlessness matter here on Coetivy?

They had made their own laws to suit their circumstances, keeping the little area surrounding the huts scrupulously clean, burying their refuse so that they would not attract termites and scavengers; killing only such wild life as they needed for food and never for sport; sharing food and water in equal parts.

By mutual agreement their work was allotted according to their abilities. Dinez took on any task that required strength, Zambi the fashioning of drinking and eating vessels from the palms, the finding of various plants and herbs to provide them with medicaments for their minor ailments and discomforts. Chantal collected firewood, tore fibers from the coconut husks to renew their mattresses, gathered turtles and birds' eggs, oysters and the little shellfish, tec-tec, to augment Dinez' daily bag of game, fowl or fish. As if it were natural for her, Zambi undertook the chores of cleaning their eating vessels, sweeping out the huts and washing their scant clothing which she dried overnight on the plaited rope washline.

They had created their own civilization, Chantal realized as she reviewed their life during the past month. And as yet not one of them had suffered from boredom for there was so much beauty to be explored on this tiny island. There were thousands of multi-colored, multi-shaped shells of which she was making a sizable collection. There were pools to stare into in which unbelievably colored, ruby, topaz, pearl and sapphire corals grew in profusion. The sea was alive with rainbow-hued fish with no apparent end to the number of their species. Flowers, butterflies, birds, insects flourished with tropical magnitude and profusion. Chantal was making a collection of flowers, pressing them between two flat rocks until they were dried and flat and could be put away in the bamboo box Zambi had made for her in which to keep her few possessions.

Only when it rained was there any disturbance to the gentle soothing monotony of their lives. With unpredictable suddenness, dark clouds would gather in the sky far out to sea and speed towards them. Where a moment before the sun had been blazing down, torrential rain would soak them minutes later, flooding the huts, putting out the cooking fire. No matter how hard they tried to prevent it, the rain would pour through the roof thatch of their meager shelters. There was little to be done whilst the storm lasted but huddle in chilled silence, listening to the coconuts thudding onto the sand and watching the palm tops bending and swaying beneath the savage outburst. Sometimes the wind was so strong that it threatened to uproot the huts. But the supporting poles were dug deep into the sandy soil and were strengthened with rocks. As yet neither hut had collapsed.

At such times Chantal longed for home with a sadness that seemed beyond bearing. But soon the sun shone once more; Zambi's quiet wail became a song and Dinez went whistling across the sand in the best of spirits. Then Chantal was far from unhappy. When they had eaten their evening meal and dusk had fallen, the three of them would sit around the embers of the fire telling stories of their youth — tales as varied by the nature of their individual backgrounds as by the experiences that had befallen them.

Zambi's descriptions of her tribal village were an enlightenment to both Dinez and Chantal. Dinez confessed later to Chantal that he had not guessed the Africans were so civilized in their own code of ethics; and that never again could he condone the usage of black people for slavery.

Dinez himself omitted the more bloodthirsty aspects of his past life of piracy. But Zambi never tired of hearing of his adventures at sea and Chantal was always moved with sympathy when Dinez spoke so lovingly of his beautiful *O Bailado* and her grace and speed. She herself regaled her companions with accounts of her life in London — of the great palaces and cathedrals and the Houses of Parliament which had not so long ago been burnt to the ground and were being rebuilt. Dinez was more interested in Mr. Brunel's tunnel beneath the River Thames and in the life led by London socialites and royalty.

Zambi's grasp of English was still very limited and she therefore missed a great deal of what was said. Nevertheless she listened with an intelligence that often surprised her two companions. Dinez remarked that Zambi had learned Portuguese far quicker than Chantal who had difficulty grasping the language. When Dinez and the girl spoke to one another, it was more often in his language than in English and at times Chantal even felt a little jealous of their interchanges, certain that they were plotting some venture from which she was excluded.

It never once crossed Chantal's mind that Zambi might be Dinez' concubine, ignorant as she was of such relationships. Zambi's outward demonstrations of affection towards her master seemed little different from the gentle, respectful care she afforded Chantal to whom she was as obviously devoted. She had fashioned a comb from the backbone of a fish and she loved to sit combing Chantal's hair, now grown to her waist. When on occasions, Zambi stroked Dinez' face or arm, Chantal supposed that the gesture reflected the same innocent admiration.

"*You have had time enough for reflection Koosh-Koosh!*"

Dinez' voice startled Chantal from her contemplation of her life on Coetivy, bringing her back to the present need for a decision. He reached out his arms and drew her into his embrace.

"This is our fate!" he said. "Why else was your little boat discovered in the vastness of the Indian Ocean by my crew? We were meant to be together here on Coetivy. That is why my crew mutinied. Do you not believe in fate, Chantal?"

She leant against him without resistance as her mind explored the strange possibility that all this was ordained by some power greater than man's will. It was a happier thought than that she had ended upon this island with Dinez by merest chance. If it was God's will, then He must surely condone the marriage Dinez had suggested.

"Very well!" she said softly. "I will marry you, Dinez da Gama, if that is what you really want."

"You know that I do!" Dinez said hoarsely as a thrill of triumph set his heart clamoring. At long last his patience was to be rewarded and this beautiful, aristocratic young English girl would be his. There would be no need now to take her by force. She was giving herself to him of her own free will.

20

October 1838

"**M**AY I enquire if the lady whose name, Tamarisk, you called so often in your delirium, is your wife?" Captain Clifton enquired of the man lying in his bunk on the merchant ship, *Jason*.

Charles von Eburhard turned his head in the direction of the voice which he had grown to recognize after four weeks in the man's company. Fourteen days and nights had passed since he and four of the able seamen aboard *Valetta* had been rescued. Charles was still confused following the blow to his head by the spar which had swept him overboard. Captain Clifton had told him that but for the assistance of the sailors, he would undoubtedly have drowned, for the blow had rendered Charles not only unconscious but blind. The men had lashed him to a floating cask and for thirty-six hours, all five had drifted with the currents, exposed to the fierce rays of the sun and to a raging thirst.

Jason, carrying convicts, was also off course as a result of the hurricane. The look-out had sighted the exhausted survivors bobbing helplessly in the now calm waters and taken them aboard.

Charles' return to consciousness had been

intermittent. He remembered little else of those early days on *Jason* other than the quiet, concerned voice of the kindly ship's captain. Vaguely he recalled receiving several visits from the ship's surgeon-superintendent, a naval man whose duties on *Jason* were to see that the regulations laid down for the carriage of convicts were carried out. Unfortunately, the medical man could not establish the reason for Charles' blindness. He was unable to recommend treatment beyond the necessity for continued rest, and when Charles recovered his full senses, he imposed a strict embargo upon the drinking of alcohol and the smoking of tobacco.

Captain Clifton explained the situation to Charles as soon as he was well enough to take in the facts.

"The surgeon tells me your sight may return, sir. From such details that he could ascertain from your men, you were struck a severe blow on the side of the head. It was this, he believes, that may have damaged the nervous structure of the eye. Detection of the extent of the damage requires the services of an oculist and such a man, I fear you are unlikely to encounter outside Europe."

Occasionally Charles was convinced that he could see vague outlines of shapes and colors in Captain Clifton's cabin. But darkness would descend before he could be reassured that his sight really was returning.

He worried endlessly that he might remain permanently blind. Such a prospect was devastating to a degree. Not only would it mean his dismissal from the Navy on health grounds, but he was tormented by the thought that he would never see his children's faces or his wife's again. Small wonder that he had called Tamarisk's name so often in his delirium, he thought. His despair would be the less if he could only be sure that she had survived. He was not entirely without hope, for he knew that Tamarisk had been wearing the precious life preserver. But having himself been swept overboard before *Valetta* was finally abandoned, Charles could only guess at Tamarisk's fate. There was a slight chance that Captain Anson might have assisted her into one of the longboats if indeed they had been able to launch any of them.

He smiled faintly at Captain Clifton. From the man's voice Charles judged him to be middle-aged or even older. From the heavy tread of his footsteps when he approached the cabin, Charles imagined his rescuer to be of burly stature. From his speech and excellent manners, he knew him to be a gentleman.

"Yes, Tamarisk is my wife's name!" he replied to the Captain's question. "As *Valetta*'s crewmen may have told you, we were on our way with my wife's sister to Bombay where I was to take up the post of Naval Advisor." His smile faded. "If only I could be assured of their safety I am convinced that my own recovery would be the speedier! How soon shall we make landfall? And for which port are we heading, Captain?"

"Our destination is Port Jackson on the east

coast of Australia," Captain Clifton replied. "I have one hundred and thirty-three convicts aboard, half of them women and children. One of the women is about to give birth so I shall have one more human being to deliver to the Colony than we set out with!"

Charles listened with curiosity.

"Forgive me for asking so personal a question, Captain, but what made you choose to take command of a convict ship?" he enquired. "Would you not have preferred a career in the Royal Navy?"

"The answer is really very simple. If it will not bore you I will explain. As a young man, I quarreled with my father and ran away to sea. I applied for work aboard the first ship I could find leaving England and was signed on as a boy in the convict ship, *Surrey*, bound for Australia with two hundred male prisoners. That was back in 1814 and I was a lad of but seventeen years!"

"Then we are the same age!" Charles exclaimed. "In '14, I had just been promoted from midshipman to sub-lieutenant following a battle or two with the Yankees off the coast of America. I must confess, I did not find war at all an agreeable experience."

"Nor indeed was my own experience aboard *Surrey*," Captain Clifton said dryly. "I warrant that our master — a sadistic devil by the name of James Patterson — was one of the most inhumane captains in the entire merchant service. There were never less than one hundred and sixty-five prisoners locked up close together in the 'tween decks throughout the voyage to Australia. The poor wretches had no ventilation and their quarters were awash to such a level that even the rats were drowning in droves."

"Had I not heard this from your own lips, I would scarce have believed such a tale!" Charles commented. "'Twas worse even than life aboard a Guinea-man. I myself arrested one such slave ship and I could not describe the appalling sight of those miserable blacks, starving, sick and chained like animals!"

"As were the convicts!" broke in Jack Clifton, frowning as he recalled the horrors of his first adventure at sea. "Those considered most dangerous were put in irons that would not permit them to do more than stand erect or lie prone. The rest were chained 'tween decks and only twenty at a time allowed out for short spells. 'Twas small wonder that typhoid fever broke out when we were not long out to sea."

"Such an outbreak would soon reach epidemic proportions in the close confines of a ship!" Charles commented.

"Which indeed happened!" said the Captain. "Instead of isolating the sick, Patterson allowed the infected to mingle with the healthy so that the fever spread to the crew. I was lucky enough to escape the disease but by the time *Surrey* was off the coast of Australia, we had consigned to the deep the bodies of two mates, the boatswain, the surgeon, eighteen seamen and heaven alone knows how many convicts. Captain Patterson was dying and the third mate — a likable fellow by the name of Thomas Raine, was in command."

"A most reprehensible state of affairs," agreed Charles. "Was no one brought to account?"

Jack Clifton nodded.

"Though he died before we made port, Captain Patterson and the surgeon were found guilty at the enquiry of causing so many deaths. My tale had a not unhappy ending for Thomas Raine had proved himself a most excellent ship's master and he was given command of *Surrey*. I sailed home with him as acting first mate, and subsequently made two further voyages with him, transporting convicts in very different conditions. Raine proved it was possible to conduct even the most hardened prisoners to their new lives without brutality, relying upon rewards rather than punishment to maintain discipline."

"A method I myself favor!" said Charles.

Captain Clifton nodded.

"Subsequently I obtained my own ship *Jason*, which I conduct on Thomas Raine's lines. When you are feeling stronger, sir, it will be my pleasure to show you how contented my prisoners are. There are classes arranged to teach them reading and writing and they are encouraged to organize for themselves sing-songs and dancing on the deck of an evening. It is a matter of pride to me and my crew that we have never lost a life and as I insist upon good food and lime juice to combat scurvy, the health of my passengers is excellent."

Charles was extremely interested for he

himself was obsessed with the desire to improve conditions for the seamen in the Navy. Over the course of the next three weeks he and Jack Clifton became even better acquainted and even closer friends. When finally they docked at Port Jackson, the Captain insisted upon accompanying Charles and the surgeon to the British Colonial Governor. He wished to ensure that Charles was left in good hands and that word would be sent to England announcing his survival as soon as possible.

They parted company regretfully but with Jack Clifton's promise that he would call upon Charles in London when next he was in the capital.

At long last Charles' sight began to return. The bed rest, peace and quiet afforded him at the home of the Governor quickly proved beneficial. By the end of his first month in Port Jackson, Charles' blindness had become intermittent. For several hours at a time he would see quite normally but then a sudden movement would cause the blackness to return. The physician caring for him insisted that he must wait at least a further fortnight before attempting the long sea journey home.

Charles' impatience to be back in England was nearing breaking point when at last he took passage on a fast clipper bound for Liverpool. The voyage took only a hundred and two days but despite the favorable weather, by the time the clipper sailed into harbor, Charles' sight was once more failing. His periods of vision were now infrequent and occurring less and less often. The ship's surgeon advised strongly against the long arduous coach journey to London and agreed with his patient that the smooth running speed of a railway carriage might be less injurious.

As soon as the ship docked, a stalwart valet was engaged to accompany Charles to London and a first class carriage was reserved for him on the Liverpool to Manchester train. From thence, Charles and his servant could board the train from Manchester to London, paying for an entire carriage to themselves. This consisted of three stagecoach bodies joined together, thus ensuring the space for Charles to lie prone and providing the quiet and privacy he required. A telegraphed message — a new invention for which Charles was extremely grateful — was dispatched to Barre House to forewarn the Waites of his impending arrival.

After resting one night in a comfortable hotel in Manchester, Charles departed for London on the 20th of February, unaware that his brother-in-law, John, was packing his valises prior to leaving London for Bristol to embark upon his voyage to the Indian Ocean.

When the telegraph was delivered to Barre House and John learned of Charles' imminent arrival, he decided to delay his departure for twenty-four hours. Since Charles had announced only his own homecoming, it was painfully obvious to John and his parents that they had no reason to hope for a similarly miraculous return from the dead of Tamarisk and Chantal. Charles would surely have enlightened them had such been the case. Discussing the matter with alternating excitement and despair, they reconciled themselves to the fact that if Charles was bringing with him any intelligence of the fate of their loved ones, it could only be bad.

For this reason it was with mixed emotions that John drove with his mother and Perry to Euston station to meet Charles. For the past two months he had successfully sustained his hopes and good spirits whilst he had pursued his intention to search the Seychelles Archipelago for *Valetta* or her survivors. No matter how frequently Mavreen and Perry had reminded him that he had no real basis for hope that the fate of *Valetta* might be similar to that of *Tiger*, the very momentum of his daily tasks had given him encouragement.

Perry had proved to be his staunch supporter. The first of John's requirements had been to raise sufficient money to finance such a major undertaking. It was Perry who reminded John that he would have very little difficulty in selling his shares in the railways at a vast profit.

When John had been but one year old, his grandfather Sir John Danesfield had died, leaving him sole heir to the mills in Yorkshire. At first the monies accruing from the mills were ploughed back by Mavreen into the privately owned company. New mills and the latest machinery were acquired, resulting in even higher profits. It was Perry however who suggested that some of the boy's capital should be set aside to buy shares in the railways recommended by his friend, Marc Brunel.

Although a great many pessimists forecast that this revolutionary form of transport would never prove acceptable to the public, the very reverse proved to be the case.

"Your shares — and mine," said Perry, "should now be worth at least ten times what we paid for them!"

Perry had sold his house in Harley Street when he married Mavreen. Owing to the development of the street and its environs, he was well rewarded when he disposed of his property. He now offered these proceeds to John to help finance his scheme.

At first John had been reluctant to accept such a handsome gift but Perry pointed out that he too loved Chantal and that if money would help restore his only child to his arms, there was no better way he could invest it.

With the funds he needed now available, John went to Bristol in search of a suitable ship. It was not long before he discovered the small brig, *Seasprite*. The property of a Bristol merchant, the brig had been used as a slaver until The Abolition of Slavery Act put an end to lawful trading. Since then she had lain in disuse and the merchant was only too happy to sell her to John at a low price. John advertised for and found a captain to command his ship. A Scotsman with twenty years' experience of sailing in the east, Captain Hamish McRae professed to know the Indian Ocean as well as any British master knew the English Channel.

"'Tis nae mair than a great big loch wi' a few tiny wee islands pokin' their noses oot

400

the sea here and there!" he told John as they sat drinking together in a Bristol tavern over-looking the harbor. "Ah ken the islands ye call the Seychelles and Ah've visited the one o' them called Mahé. There'll be nae trouble findin' them!"

John soon struck up an excellent relationship with the red-haired, red-bearded Scot. Blunt in his speech, the man was straightforward in his dealings and inspired a feeling of confidence which John believed a first essential in a ship's captain. McRae was cheerfully sarcastic about *Seasprite*.

"She aye stinks o' the puir deils she carried tae the Americas!" he said, "and she's in a bad way. It'll tak a deal o' time and money tae put her in guid shape."

"Money is no problem," said John, "but time is important." He had already explained the reason for his voyage, and the Scot nodded sympathetically.

"Ah'll no' waste time!" he said. "There's ay men wha'll wurk twa the speed fir twa the pay!"

True to his word, within a week he had *Seasprite* in dry dock. Joiners, painters, engineers and repairers were busy about the brig. Sailmakers were stitching a new set of sails. Two coppersmiths were patching the copper keel.

On each of his weekly visits to Bristol, John saw huge progress made and now he and Hamish McRae were busy listing the provisions they would require.

"Fir a' Ah'm a seafarin' mon, Ah'll no' drink

401

anythin' but whuskey!" said the Scot as John wrote down the kegs of rum needed for the voyage. The sailors expected an allotment of grog of not less than two gills a day, but Hamish McRae abhorred all but his native tipple.

"The new iron tank in the hold should carry all the water needed," explained John. "As for your 'whuskey,' Hamish McRae, take aboard as much as you need!"

He spared no expense on supplies of food. Despite the high cost, he put on his list a good quantity of '*bouilli*' — a pressed beef which lasted well on a long voyage since it was put into canisters. Hamish informed him that the Americans referred to this latest method of storing food in tin receptacles as 'canning.'

The list of foodstuffs included everyday items such as fine wheat, flour, rice, currants, sugar, prunes, cinnamon, ginger, pepper, cloves, oil, butter, Holland cheese, old cheese, vinegar, white biscuits and oatmeal. John further listed a dozen legs of mutton to be minced, stewed and close-packed with suet or butter in earthenware pots. Foremost on his list was a large quantity of the juice of lemons to combat scurvy; and not least of all John's purchases was a water still, suggested to him by Mr. Marc Brunel. An inventor himself, Brunel had heard of Dr. Alphonse Normandy's contraption for converting sea water into fresh drinking water.

"It will do this quite reliably at the ratio of six gallons of sea water to one of fresh water," Mr. Brunel had told John. Hamish had not used a water still before although many captains in the Navy did carry one lest they should become becalmed. Since it was possible to be without wind power for anything from fifty to a hundred days, such precaution was entirely sensible. John was pleased to be able to reassure his mother that in this respect at least, he could guarantee his survival.

Mavreen's refusal to encourage his purpose was a matter of distress to John until Perry advised him that it stemmed not from disinterest in the search for Tamarisk and Chantal but from a very natural concern for John's own safety.

"You have always been especially dear to her," Perry explained. "She had given up hope of ever bearing a son and your arrival so late in her child-bearing years seemed like a miracle. Then, when typhus overtook the family, you very nearly died. Now that Tamarisk and Chantal are no longer with us, you are her one remaining child and the more treasured because of it. Do you understand better now why she dreads the thought of the dangers you may encounter?"

So at last John was entirely reconciled with his mother and was delighted to be able to offer her all the reassurance he could.

Now *Seasprite* was entirely seaworthy and "as pretty a wee brig as ever sailed the seas," according to Hamish McRae. A crew had been signed on and the provisions put aboard. But for Charles' sudden return home with who knew what intelligence regarding the disappearance of *Valetta*, he and Hamish would have set sail. John's heart was heavy with misgivings as they drove up the impressive new façade of Euston

Station. He dreaded to hear from Charles' lips that Chantal and Tamarisk were known to have been lost at sea, thus ending his last hopes of finding them.

Charles was unable to disabuse John of his misgivings. There was no doubt that *Valetta* had sunk, he said unhappily, but they had been attempting to lower the longboats so there was still a faint hope that there might be other survivors. He in turn was bitterly disappointed that his in-laws had no word to give him as to the fate of his wife and sister-in-law. As Mavreen settled him comfortably in the great four-poster in the gold guest room in Barre House, Charles gave way to tears of exhaustion.

"I can tolerate the thought of a life spent in darkness," he said brokenly to Mavreen. "But that I may never hold my beloved Tamarisk in my arms again is a prospect beyond bearing."

Mavreen tried to revive her son-in-law's spirits.

"I will not allow you to speak with such pessimism!" she said, stroking Charles' forehead, her eyes alive with a determination that Perry would have appreciated had he been present to see it. "Despite all you tell me, Charles, I am convinced that you will not be blind permanently. You were making an excellent recovery in Port Jackson and the physician there did warn you that the rigors of the voyage home might set you back a little. Tomorrow I will send for the best oculist in London. I believe they now have several renowned specialists who

404

attend at Guy's Hospital. And as for your fears for the fate of Tamarisk and Chantal, we must all continue to hope they are alive. Now try to sleep, dearest Charles."

He felt for his mother-in-law's hand and pressed it warmly.

"You have never lacked for courage," he said to her. "And your convictions give me fresh hope. I fear though that I am a burden on your household and tomorrow I will remove myself to . . . "

"You will do no such thing, dear Charles!" Mavreen interrupted. "Perry and I have made up our minds to keep you here at Barre House with us since your poor Aunt Lisa is ailing. The Baroness is ninety-two as you know and the shock of your disappearance was too much for her at her age. She is now confined to her bed, her wits most confused. When she is stronger and you have recovered from this temporary indisposition, we will break the news to her gently that you are safe and well. Then perhaps you and the children can return home."

Mavreen continued to take charge of Charles' health. True to her word she called in a renowned oculist to pronounce an opinion upon his loss of vision. The eminent gentleman was unable to be very precise but he seemed convinced that the blow Charles had received to the side of his head had in some way damaged the optic nerve.

"We do not yet know how this nerve affects the working of the eye!" he explained to

Mavreen. "But I have personally known a case where the patient fell from his horse and became blind as a result. Complete rest in a darkened room eventually brought about a gradual return of his sight. After six months it was restored completely. Since your son-in-law has already regained intermittent vision, I think we may hope that careful nursing and absolute stillness may have the desired result."

Mavreen repeated the specialist's opinion to John and Perry.

"So there is no advantage to your delaying your departure any longer, John," she said. "Charles would not be able to accompany you even were you to wait a further week or two. 'Tis my belief we should refrain from speaking of your voyage lest his longing to go with you causes him to rest less tranquilly."

"I will speak with Charles in the morning before I leave," John said, "but only to ascertain a small detail he can impart as to the position of *Valetta* when she sank. At least we do have some cause for hope, Mama. Tamarisk had a life preserver and Chantal . . . well, Charles did not see either of them swept overboard and the longboats may have been launched before *Valetta* sank."

Mavreen put her arms around John and sighed.

"I hope you are right, my darling. I do not have to tell you that I shall pray for you as earnestly as I do for them."

When upon the following day John finally

set foot aboard *Seasprite* and Hamish McRae announced that they were ready to sail, it was not his sister, Tamarisk, who was uppermost in his thoughts but the girl who still lived so vividly in his heart — Chantal.

21

December 1838 – January 1839

CHANTAL'S strange, impromptu marriage to Dinez was not destined to take place, despite the fact that he had convinced her of its desirability. It was a chance remark of Zambi's which led to a total reversal of their plans to wed that selfsame evening.

When Chantal returned to her hut and smiling, told the African girl that she and Dinez were to become man and wife, Zambi beamed with the greatest delight.

"Señor good man! Very strong! Very kind! Me very much happy!" the black girl said excitedly in her broken English. "Señor much want Señorita to be wife. Señor happy now. Very much joy!"

"It cannot be a real wedding such as I would have in England," Chantal told the girl. "I know your tribal customs do not require a man of religion to perform such a ceremony, Zambi, but all Christian people are wed by a holy man."

"You have no tribal chief to marry you?" Zambi enquired curiously.

"Only on the rarest of occasions!" Chantal replied. "As, for instance, a ship's captain may marry a couple at sea where they have no recourse to a vicar or priest!"

Zambi considered this carefully, her frizzy

black head tilted on one side as was her custom when she tried to understand Chantal's teachings.

"Señor ship's captain," she said after a few minutes thought. "You say ship's captain can make married, no?"

"I suppose he could!" Chantal agreed doubtfully. The idea of Dinez conducting his own marriage seemed to be stretching the rules more than a trifle. She looked at Zambi affectionately. "I wish it were possible for you to have a husband too," she said kindly.

Zambi looked puzzled.

"Zambi no want second husband!" she said simply. "Tribal law say man have many wives, but wife only one husband."

Now it was Chantal's turn to look bewildered.

"I did not know you were already married, Zambi!" she said. "Is your husband still in Africa? How sad that you should have been separated from him."

"Sprated?" the girl echoed incorrectly. "Not understand word, Señorita." Pointing to Dinez who was building a large cooking fire, she explained: "Zambi have one husband only. Very good man. Very strong. Señorita have many babies, Zambi take good care of white babies!"

Chantal was convinced that somehow she must have misunderstood Zambi's English.

"Señor Dinez is your master, not your husband!" she said patiently.

Zambi scratched her head.

"Señorita explain me, one moon past, when

409

man woman live same hut and make baby, is called husband, wife! Zambi not wife if not make baby?"

Chantal drew in her breath sharply. Now there was no further room for misunderstanding.

"When did the Señor take you for his wife?" she asked, her voice and hands trembling as she awaited Zambi's reply.

Zambi smiled.

"After Señor take me from slave ship. Very kind to Zambi. Other slaves go place long, far far away called Martinique. Señor tell me white man pay much gold for slave but all must work very hard till die. For me very good life on boat. Look after husband and keep happy. Zambi very happy! Señorita be happy, too. Señor good man!"

"*No, he is a bad man!*" Chantal cried. White-faced, she strode through the doorway of the hut. She approached Dinez, her eyes blazing.

"You can stop your preparations for the wedding, Señor da Gama," she said furiously, "because there is not going to be one! I would not marry you now if there were twenty churches and twenty Reverends to perform the ceremony!"

Dinez stood up and stared down at Chantal in total perplexity.

"What is this nonsense?" he asked impatiently. "'Tis but ten minutes since you agreed that . . . "

"*I did not know then you already had a wife!*" she interrupted.

Her voice was sharp and stinging but Dinez

410

looked more confused than guilty.

"Me? A wife?" he repeated. "What put such a crazed idea into your head!"

"Do not lie to me further!" Chantal cried. "Doubtless you will consider me stupid not to have realized for myself that you . . . that you and Zambi were . . . " Her voice trembled as she tried to find respectable words to describe his disgraceful behavior. "Oh, it is all quite clear to me now! You tricked that poor ignorant girl into thinking your marriage to her was sacrosanct in just the same way as you tried to trick me. *And Zambi really believes she is your wife!* Well, sir, since you were the one to declare that what is done before the eyes of God is lawful, you are 'lawfully' married to her and cannot deny it."

To her unutterable astonishment, Dinez let out a great bellow of laughter.

"Of course I deny it!" he said. "The girl is a slave and my concubine. As if I would marry such a girl — or have need to!"

He gave another shout of laughter.

"That is a terrible admission!" Chantal cried. "You admit she is your concubine as if there were no evil in it. You took advantage of her ignorance so that you could have your pleasure of her. And I thought you were an honorable man despite your lawless career!"

The laughter left Dinez' eyes. He reached out a hand as if to lay it upon Chantal's arm but she twisted away from him.

"Chantal, this whole conversation is ludicrous!" he persisted quietly. "I have not behaved dishonorably. You do me an injustice in so

411

accusing me. I have never attempted to deceive you. As for Zambi — can you really be so ignorant of the ways of the world that you do not know that all slaves are the property of their owners and had I not afforded her my protection, the crew would have had their way with her and given her a far worse time than you could imagine."

"You dishonored her!" Chantal said rigidly. "Moreover you dared to speak to me of marriage between us being God's intention whilst you were taking your pleasure with Zambi behind my back! That is sufficient insult for ensuring that I shall *never* speak to you again."

A near indiscernible smile hovered in Dinez' green eyes as he listened to Chantal's indignant, unhappy voice.

"Your innocence is a constant source of surprise to me!" he said gently. "Listen to me, Koosh-Koosh. I am a man like any other. I need to lie with a woman no less than do other men. I wager every bachelor of your acquaintance enjoys a woman's favors before he has a wife — and sometimes after he is wed if his wife proves a reluctant partner! I will give you ten gold guineas for any man you can name who has gone to his marriage a virgin. Were your mother or father here to advise you, they would tell you this is no more than the truth and that not even in the most civilized of societies is it wrong to do as I have done."

The quiet conviction of Dinez' voice unsettled Chantal by virtue of its unquestionable sincerity. Memories flooded through her mind — of

Tamarisk's warning to avoid the lustful temptations that might be put in her way by men who sought to seduce her; of her own father's admission that he had lain with her real mother and begotten a child by her without the sanctity of marriage; of her knowledge of the existence of other children born out of wedlock — even to royalty!

Watching her expression, Dinez sensed her uncertainty and made once more as if to take her arm. But again Chantal twisted away from him.

"Even if you speak the truth, sir, it cannot change my feelings toward you now that I know you have been taking your pleasure with Zambi whilst talking to me of . . . of loving me!"

Dinez' eyes narrowed.

"You have but yourself to blame. You refused me that first day upon the island!" he said. "I would not have touched the girl again had you permitted me to lie with *you*. What else could you expect of me? I did no wrong. As for Zambi, she wanted me no less than I wanted a woman. I could have taken *you* by force — but I did not. I respected your wishes. So do not try my patience too far with this convent-bred nonsense lest I regret the respect I have accorded you and have my way with you without your precious wedding."

The angry flush on Chantal's cheeks died away, leaving her pale and trembling. She raised her head and stared directly into his eyes.

"You threaten me, sir, but do not think you frighten me. 'Tis true you can force me but

413

never doubt that I shall resist you to the utmost; that I shall hate and despise you and that should you force a child upon me, I would kill myself rather than bear it. You would do better to remain satisfied with one 'wife.' I will do everything in my power to make your life here upon this island unbearable if you lay one finger upon me!"

With as much dignity as she could muster, she turned to walk back to her hut. But disregarding her warning, Dinez caught her arm and imprisoned it.

"You may not have realized it as yet, my lovely Chantal, but your objections are not the result of your moral rectitude but of feminine jealousy. Your righteousness stems from the fact that you do not care for the thought that I have lain with another woman."

"I, jealous?" Chantal echoed with outraged scorn. "You think I am jealous of a . . . a black girl?"

Dinez let go her arm, laughing softly.

"And what, pray, has the color of a girl's skin to do with the matter? I do assure you it makes little difference if she is soft to touch, responsive to kisses, willing to give herself freely in the act of love!"

"You are despicable!" Chantal cried, the hot color flooding her cheeks at the picture he had evoked. "But then I should have known better than to expect any kind of refinement of feeling from an outlaw — a pirate! I do not imagine you will have any understanding of my meaning when I remind you that there exists a far deeper relationship between man and woman than the lustful pleasures of which *you* speak. There can be love!"

Now it was Dinez turn to redden.

"You underrate my feelings for you, Chantal. If I did not love you, I would have taken you long since. Think on that when you ponder whether or not you will speak to me again!" With which parting remark, he released her arm and turning, walked away from her towards the lagoon.

Zambi came running to Chantal, her face a mask of distress.

"Señor is angry? What happen, Señorita? No wedding? You not want become chief wife?"

"No!" Chantal said bitterly. "The Señor is a bad man, Zambi, and you would do well not to . . . to . . . "

"Señor not bad man!" Zambi cried. "He good husband. I go now tell him come back."

Without waiting for Chantal's reply she ran swiftly after Dinez' receding figure. Against her will Chantal stood rooted to the spot where she stood, watching until Zambi caught up with Dinez. They were too far distant for her to hear their voices. They talked for several minutes before Dinez walked on leaving the black girl crouching in the sand. He did not turn his head to look back and Zambi made no move to follow him.

The tension that had until now held her in its grip, suddenly left Chantal's body. Slowly she went into her hut and sank down upon the fiber mattress. Her mind was awhirl with thoughts that she would have preferred should remain dormant. But insistently they protruded their ugly meaning until she could no longer ignore them. Dinez was right. She *was* jealous of poor, innocent Zambi. It should have been her, Chantal, he had held in his arms these past hot, sultry nights.

In retrospect it seemed impossible to Chantal that she should have failed to suspect Dinez' relationship with Zambi when they had continued to share the same sleeping quarters. And she, Chantal, had encouraged them by insisting that she had her own hut! Memory brought back a picture of their very first night upon the island and how she had woken to find Dinez' arm around her waist as if even in sleep he must demonstrate his desire for her.

Tears stung Chantal's eyelids and she clenched her fists in confusion. It was time she made up her mind once and for all about Dinez da Gama. Not a half hour ago, she had agreed to marry him and now she was vowing she would never speak to him again.

If only she could decide whether he was a good man or as it now seemed, unscrupulous, immoral and unlawful. There was much to his discredit, not least his life of piracy. Yet in the month they had lived on the island she had also discovered much to his credit. He had set about making their living conditions very tolerable and indeed, his expedience had been equal to Zambi's instinctive knowledge of nature's resources. Alone, she, Chantal, would most certainly have died. She owed him her life when he rescued her from the sea. He was unfailingly good-humored despite the fact that he had been deserted by his men and lost all he had fought for nearly five years to acquire. He could have been excused for bemoaning his misfortune yet had never done so after that first angry outburst as he watched his beloved *O Bailado* sail over the horizon.

Was it possible to love such a man, Chantal wondered? Could she even be certain what love was? She had believed herself enamoured of the romantic, courteous, aristocratic Antoine de Valle — yet she seldom thought of him here on the island. Moreover the sweet sensations she had experienced when Antoine held her hand or kissed her, she now experienced when Dinez da Gama took her in his arms.

Love was a mysterious emotion, she concluded. She could be certain only of loving her Papa and her stepmother and with even greater depth, her dear, kind-hearted John. Memories of their shared childhood flooded through her mind as she recalled the adoration and respect she had always felt for him. Of course she had believed then that John was her brother and it was difficult not to think of him as such. Julia had insisted that John loved her as ardently as any suitor and stated that she herself had given up all thought that John might one day wish to marry *her*.

"If you do not become his wife, Chantal, I believe John will never marry!" she had vouchsafed.

At the time Chantal had laughed away Julia's

remarks. She had not wanted to consider John as a suitor when already her heart was filled with romantic notions about Antoine. She had been totally self-absorbed and only now did she realize that she must have caused John much unhappiness. She recalled her stepmother's privileged old servant, Dorcas, once saying to her:

"You be a right spoilt young madam, Miss Chantal. There b'aint none will deny you your every whim and fancy and that b'aint good for no one. Your Mama and Papa, Miss Julia and most of all Master John let you have your way far too often. And what's more, you don't appreciate it none but just accepts it like it was your due."

Chantal had not taken offense at such impertinence but laughed away Dorcas' criticism. The old woman had adored her for as long as she could remember and spoilt her no less than the others.

"You be the spittin' image of your Papa!" Dorcas used to croon lovingly over the dark-haired, laughing-eyed baby. It had been a simple matter to divert Dorcas from critical observations of herself to tales of her Papa when he was a young man "crazed with love" — as Dorcas put it — for her stepmother.

A sudden sweep of homesickness caused the tears in Chantal's eyes to spill down her cheeks. Zambi had not returned and nor had Dinez. She felt miserably alone. She found herself wondering suddenly whether her two island companions were together, clasped in

418

one another's arms, exchanging kisses. Her tears ceased and her cheeks burned. She did not want to think such shameful thoughts. Yet she could not forget that this was to have been her wedding night and it should have been her, Chantal, whom Dinez was caressing, kissing, loving!

Tears of mortification began to fall again. Her sense of isolation was intense and the years facing her seemed quite intolerable. It was more than an hour before she heard the sound of footfalls. Darkness had fallen. Hating herself for such weakness, Chantal crept to the doorway of her hut and peered out. She had expected to see Dinez with his arm intimately around Zambi's waist. When she saw that Zambi was alone she felt a thrill of relief and satisfaction. Dinez had wanted her, Chantal, and on this night at least, no other girl would do.

Dinez did not return until morning. Giving no explanation he greeted Zambi warmly but only nodded his head coolly in Chantal's direction. For the next few days his manner towards her was distant, remote, disinterested.

Chantal tried not to mind; but she missed their former close companionship as much as she missed his laughter and his provocative conversation. He called her Chantal instead of Koosh-Koosh and spoke to her only when it was necessary.

Zambi too, was far from happy. Alone with Chantal she renewed her declarations that Dinez was a good man and would make Chantal a good husband. Chantal attempted to explain that in her country a man could have but one wife and that Zambi must cease to try to persuade her to flout *her* tribal laws!

The girl did not seem surprised.

"Señor tell me your custom. He say me no more wife for him. At first Zambi very sad. Now understand Señorita not want disobey tribal custom. Zambi no more be wife to Señor. Señorita have many white babies and Zambi take care like own. Very happy!"

Chantal was uncertain whether this was Dinez' idea of a solution or if Zambi, in her simple way, had decided that she would prefer to have babies to mother than a man to love her. It seemed a strange choice until Zambi elaborated in her careful way that babies were necessary for their survival.

"When many moons pass by," she told Chantal, "Señor, Señorita, Zambi, all become too old, too weak and no food, soon die! Need strong children to cut palm trees, catch fish, kill turtle. Señor, Señorita make new tribe on island. Zambi no have babies with white man."

This simple philosophy was unarguable if indeed they were destined to remain on Coetivy for the rest of their lives. But Chantal had not given up all hope of rescue. Every day she went to the highest point on the island and added fresh driftwood to the fire she had built. If ever the miracle should happen and a ship appear upon the horizon, she was determined that it would not sail past without realizing that there were people marooned on Coetivy.

Dinez da Gama knew of the growing pile of

driftwood and kept his counsel. He had no intention whatever of lighting the fire if rescue seemed imminent. For him, if rescue were by a European ship, it could all too easily mean imprisonment. There was not a British, French or Spanish port at which his description had not been circulated. Six foot four inches in height, with jet black hair and piercing green eyes, he could not easily go unrecognized. His daring exploits on the seas had earned him a reputation which brought with it a fame that endangered his life.

Dinez now had time to consider Chantal's reaction to his relationship with the black girl, and soon ceased to worry about it. He was convinced that it was only a matter of time before Chantal would set aside her scruples and give way to the passionate needs of her healthy young body. Nature would see to it so long as they continued to live in such close proximity.

To hasten that end, Dinez had decided to terminate his association with Zambi which at best, had brought him no more than fleeting moments of pleasure. Rightly he guessed that Chantal would welcome such a gesture on his part and the sooner be willing to reconsider him as a husband. He set aside all temptation to force her to succumb to his will. He wanted a responsive, loving girl in his arms, not one who hated him and felt loathing for his body. He could not forget Chantal's sweetness when she had responded to his embrace as they lay on the sand on the eve of that abortive wedding night. She had shown herself all woman, passionate, eager for love, and he wanted no less from her.

Slowly Dinez' policy of remaining aloof began to take effect. He noticed that more and more frequently Chantal's eyes would rest upon him in contemplative study. Whenever she believed him unaware of her, she stole quiet glances in his direction. If she looked up to find him staring at her, the hot color would flood into her cheeks and Dinez realized with satisfaction that she was far from being as indifferent to him as she pretended.

Those next three weeks following the rift between them became increasingly difficult for Chantal. She was prepared to do battle with Dinez, to resist him with every ounce of strength if he made the slightest approach to her. When he did not but remained silent, indifferent, apparently uncaring, she felt strangely disappointed.

Against her will she found herself watching Dinez closely when he was with Zambi. The black girl now had a hut of her own and at night Chantal lay awake fighting the temptation to look into Zambi's hut to reassure herself that she was there and not with Dinez. It gave her some comfort as the days passed to realize that there was no obvious sign of intimacy between them, although Dinez often patted Zambi's curly head with casual affection if she cooked a particularly delectable meal; or fashioned a new utensil for his use.

Zambi seemed quite unconcerned by the loss of her lover. Her one concern was for Chantal to 'marry' the Señor and despite Chantal having forbidden her to mention the subject, she continued to plead:

"Señor lonely! Señorita lonely! Not good! You marry . . . make nice white baby for Zambi. Then all happy!"

It sounded so simple when expressed in Zambi's ingenuous terms. But Chantal was still far from convinced that she should take Dinez for her 'husband' — even were he still willing to have her for his 'wife.'

By now it seemed as if they had been on the island three years rather than three months, Chantal thought unhappily. With the slow passing of every day, with no reminders of home, of England, of her family, it was as if this was the only life she had ever known. She sometimes recalled those long-ago days when she had worn beautiful silk and satin dresses; shoes and stockings; jewelry round her neck and in her hair. She had been barefoot so long on the island that the thought of shoes was abhorrent. Even the brief ragged skirt and blouse frequently seemed unnecessary in the hot, humid climate. She envied Zambi her bared breasts even though she knew modesty would never permit her to emulate the native girl whilst Dinez could see her.

Dinez wore next to nothing. The sun had tanned his skin almost as dark as Zambi's and the continuous physical exercise had brought him to the peak of fitness. His leg and arm muscles gleamed as he cast out a fishing line or swung his panga or lifted a tree branch with effortless grace. More and more often Chantal's eyes were drawn towards him in admiration and her heart felt a swift ungovernable yearning to reach out and touch him.

It was just three weeks after Christmas on the night of the fiercest storm they had yet encountered, that fate played into Dinez' hands and the moment he had waited for so patiently brought its brief reward. As the thunder crashed around their heads and brilliant streaks of lightning lit up the island and the raging sea, the wind caught the fronds of a huge palm overhanging Chantal's hut. The sound of breaking timber was lost in the noise of the storm as slowly the palm bent almost double. The trunk split open and the heavy top crashed onto the roof of the hut.

Within minutes Dinez and Zambi were frantically tearing at the dripping fronds beneath which Chantal now lay buried. Unharmed but for a few bruises, she was nevertheless trembling with shock as they pulled her clear of the debris. Dinez lifted her effortlessly and carried her through the lashing rain to his own quarters.

"Are you all right, Koosh-Koosh?" he asked as he laid her gently on the fiber mattress. It was the first time he had spoken to her other than to give necessary orders for their daily routine; the first time he had reverted to a tender, caring tone of voice; the first time he had called her 'Koosh-Koosh' since the rift between them.

Still suffering from the effects of shock, Chantal burst into tears. Dinez knelt beside her and took her hand.

"*Calma! Calma!*" he said in his own language,

424

his voice soothing, gentle. "There is no danger now! You are not badly hurt?"

Chantal shook her head, her long dark hair falling across her face as she did so. Dinez brushed it from her cheeks.

"The storm is nearly over!" he said. "You are quite safe here with me."

He held out his arms. As if it were the most natural thing in the world, Chantal reached out and clung to him. Dinez' arms tightened around her and bending his head, he kissed her with a fierce, hungry passion.

"I have waited so long!" he murmured against her lips. "Ah, Koosh-Koosh, my beautiful, my lovely girl. This time you cannot deny me!"

Listening to his voice and to her own fierce heartbeat, Chantal realized that the very last thing in the world she wanted was to deny Dinez — or herself. She returned his kisses with helpless despair at her own frailty. Rightly or wrongly she would now surrender herself to him because it was the only thing in the world that seemed to matter.

She felt Dinez' hands tugging gently at the skirt he had wrapped around her naked body when he pulled her from the wreckage of the hut. Every nerve she possessed came alive at his touch as he ran his fingertips lightly over her shoulders, down her breasts and waist until they rested on the delicate curve of her stomach.

"Do not be afraid, my Koosh-Koosh," he said softly.

Such fear as Chantal felt was drowned in the compelling needs of her body as she arched her back, pressing herself closer against him. As Dinez' hands wandered slowly downward between her thighs, she believed she would cry out with despair if he did not soon satisfy the hungry hollow within her. As the blood pounded in her ears she was unaware that the storm had abated and that the only sound filling the leafy hut was Dinez' quick breathing and her own soft cries.

As he took her, instinct lent Dinez a restraint that he had never before employed with a woman. Fully aware of Chantal's abandonment to the delights of his loving and above all aware of her virginity, he curbed his own impatience. When finally he permitted himself to sink into the soft warm depths of her body, she gave one small cry of pain before pressing him even deeper within her.

As the sensations of Chantal's body slowly returned to normality, so did her mind return to full awareness of what had just happened to her. She knew that she should regret it, but the drowsy dream of contentment still held her in its sway. She did not want this man lying beside her ever to leave her. If pain there had been, it was more than compensated by the unbelievable throbbing pleasure that followed after.

Yet she could not forever deny the return of doubt. If only, she thought, she could be certain that she loved Dinez da Gama with the kind of respect and adoration a wife should have for her husband. But before she could ponder the problem further, her eyes closed and she fell asleep with Dinez' arms around her.

426

When she awoke the following morning the sun was streaming through the opening of the hut. Branches, palm leaves and coconuts littered the sand outside — the residue of last night's storm. Chantal's hut lay in a disordered heap.

She turned her head and saw beside her Dinez deep in slumber. Full memory of the previous night returned to her and Chantal flushed at the thought that she was no longer a virgin; that wantonly she had allowed this man possession of her body. Last night her behavior had seemed inevitable, predestined. Now it was only shameful.

Suddenly she felt an urgent need to be away from the tantalizing proximity of Dinez' masculinity. The sight of his naked body only brought promise of further wanton pleasure were he to wake. Slipping silently to the edge of the mattress, Chantal gathered up her skirt and wrapping it around her shoulders, went in search of her blouse. She was relieved that Dinez did not stir and that there was no sign of Zambi.

Finding the ragged garment for which she searched, Chantal hurried down to the lagoon and quickly immersed herself in the warm sunlit water. Careless of the threat of stone fish or even of basking sharks, she lay back until the warm water covered her. She needed to wash away the vestiges of guilt which threatened to assail her whenever she thought of the loss of her virginity. She tried to convince herself that the meaning of chastity was irrelevant here upon this deserted island; that the necessity to remain pure until one's wedding night might have meaning at home in England, where a prospective husband would reasonably demand that his bride should be innocent. But here on Coetivy there was no man other than Dinez to take or reject her on her bridal couch.

If only Dinez had not put himself outside the law, she thought with a fresh wave of uncertainty. Each time he had killed in the act of piracy, he had committed murder. It did not seem possible that she, Chantal, had voluntarily lain with a murderer!

But although she tried hard to do so, she could not envisage Dinez in such dastardly guise, nor bring herself to condemn him as an evil man. Last night he had shown himself tender, kind, considerate as well as passionate. Such attributes belonged to a gentle lover and bore no relation to a man of violence. Yet, pirate Dinez had been for most of his life, taking ruthlessly what he wanted — even Zambi! How could she ever love such a man?

When at last she returned to the clearing, Dinez was about to set off in search of her. He hurried to meet her and with a happy smile put his arms around her. To his astonishment Chantal drew away from his embrace.

"Come now, what is this, Koosh-Koosh? Not even a kiss when last night, you . . . "

"Dinez, I am truly sorry!" Chantal broke in. "But despite anything I may have said last night, I am far from sure this morning that what we did was right!"

Misjudging the seriousness of her mood, Dinez' green eyes lit with a teasing smile.

"So you did not find pleasure in our loving?" he challenged confidently.

Chantal did not return his smile.

"You know very well that I did!" she answered quietly. The honesty of her reply confused him. "But I am speaking now of right and wrong, Dinez, and not of pleasure. I have tried very hard to do so but I cannot put from my mind your . . . your past." Her voice trembled. "'Tis not only your piracy that disturbs me, Dinez, but the manner in which you deceived Zambi."

"So we have come back to that!" Dinez said, his face angry with disappointment. "Now listen to me, Chantal. 'Tis time you ceased trying to impose your conventional ethics upon us. It is true that I was a pirate, but as you well know, those days are over and the 'Portuguese Hawk' no longer exists. 'Tis true also that I took Zambi for my pleasure but though it may offend you to hear it, she was more than willing. Not only did she like me but she had the benefit of my protection. She realized what the alternative would be. Do you really have no conception of the terrible lives led by most slaves sold on the open market?"

"It is illegal to trade in slaves," Chantal argued. "You should have taken Zambi back to Africa to her own tribe!"

Dinez laughed dryly.

"You cannot mean that, Chantal! What, pray, should I have done with the other slaves I had acquired? Illegal though it may be in your country, in mine the trade in slaves is still lawful and flourishes, I assure you. People will continue to sell them as long as there is a market for them! As for my cargo, it was worth its weight in gold and my crew would have considered me insane had I set them all free in their own country!"

By now, Chantal was staring at Dinez with a look of horror.

"You admit to having *traded* in slaves?" she asked accusingly.

"And is that so terrible?" Dinez countered hotly. "They are but savages in any event!"

Chantal's eyes blazed.

"How can you say so when Zambi has proved herself to be anything but savage!"

Into Chantal's mind surged the many conversations concerning slavery she had overheard as a child. Her stepmother had been involved in all the many attempts to abolish the practice and Chantal herself had listened to Mr. Wilberforce speaking with fanatical loathing for this trade in human lives. Without knowing it, she had assimilated her parents' views on the matter and now her mind revolted at the thought that she had willingly given herself to a man guilty of far worse than piracy.

She stared at Dinez in dismay.

"*I can never lie with you again!*" she whispered.

Dinez took a step towards her, a deep frown creasing his forehead. When she drew back he reached out and caught her arm in a fierce grip.

"That is a threat you will *not* carry out!" he said. "I am beginning to know you better than

430

you know yourself, Chantal. You think like a child! You were no reluctant virgin this past night but a woman with passions equal to my own. No matter what your mind tells you to the contrary, you will want me to love you again. If I were to force you now, you would not long resist me! But I shall wait, as I waited before. You are worth waiting for, Chantal."

His eyes seemed to burn into her as they roved slowly over her body. She felt her pulses racing and the sound of her heartbeat was like a drum in her breast. As he strode away across the sand she knew that despite her determination never to let Dinez lay a hand upon her, had he touched her however briefly, she would have melted into his arms; that the victory in this battle between them must ultimately be his.

22

May 1839

"**M**AY DAY!" announced Hamish McRae as he stood on deck beside John watching the crew hoist the mainsail. "Ah've no' been in England fir a May Day in thurty years! They'll be dancin' around the maypoles and gatherin' hawthorn tae decorate their hooses!"

"It was our habit to celebrate the custom at our little country house in Sussex!" John said sighing. "Two years ago Chantal was chosen as fairest maid in the village and crowned Queen of the May. I doubt if Queen Victoria took more pride in her Coronation than my little Chantal!"

"Aye!" Hamish said, stuffing a wad of tobacco into his pipe. He was now well used to John's many references to the girl he loved; and such was the closeness of their friendship, upon occasions he teased him gently with wry humor about his love. "'Tis a strange name for a wee lassie!" he remarked. "Fir a preference Ah'd be choosin' Isobel or Jeanie. Ah mind a braw wee lassie called Jeanie Ah once asked tae wed me. But she'd no' marry a sailor, she said, so that wa' that!"

They had now been at sea for close on three months. They had met with few misfortunes, being becalmed but once and then only for two days. Consequently they were now within a day's sailing of the outer islands of the Seychelles Archipelago.

In Mauritius, Hamish had discussed with other seagoing men the passage of the hurricane over the island before it encompassed *Valetta* some nine months earlier. From Mauritius they had sailed to the island of Astove off the north coast of Madagascar. Secretly John had been nursing the hope that *Valetta*'s survivors might have reached the same haven as those on *Tiger* and only with difficulty did he hide his disappointment from Hamish when their search proved fruitless.

They decided to sail directly to Mahé, a journey of some twelve days, exploring the six or seven islands they must pass en route. At Mahé, Hamish told John, there was a faint possibility that they might obtain chartings of the many islands and islets in the group.

"Ah ken there are forty at the verra least!" Hamish told John. "Mebbe as monie more!"

"We will visit every one!" John replied staunchly although even as he spoke, he realized that they did not have time on their side. The *Tiger*'s crew had had sheep, poultry, a pig and a vast store of provisions to assist their survival, whereas it was doubtful that *Valetta*'s longboats would have carried food enough for a few days, let alone weeks or months.

Now as they approached Mahé, the Scot felt bounden to warn his young employer yet again that there was little chance *Valetta*'s survivors could have traveled so far. He agreed that strong-muscled men aided by wind and currents might have rowed the distance in longboats but reminded John they would have lacked for water and food.

"I will not lose hope at this stage of our journey!" John replied with stubborn insistence.

"Ye'll no' be disappointed, laddie if ye dinna expect ower much!" Hamish cautioned. "We could be on a fool's errand, ye ken!"

But on the charms of the islands themselves the captain could not have been more poetically inspired.

"At least they'll no' be a disappointment tae ye, John," he said. "They're aye like beautiful women everybody wants tae possess. When ye hear the song o' the fishermen and the beat o' their oars upon the water floatin' in frae a distance, 'tis akin tae the beauty o' the pipes when ye hear them frae ower the lochs in bonnie Scotland!"

He went down to his cabin and returned with a tattered piece of parchment which he handed to John.

"There's nae description Ah could give ye that betters the wurds o' an auld Englishmon Ah met, who had settled on the island not lang after the French had been ousted by the British," he continued. "The mon had been a prisoner o' war and when he was freed by his countrymen, he decided tae explore Mahé before gaein' hame. He fell in love wi' the islands and made up his mind to stay. Ah'd nae knowledge o' the place masel' as it was ma first visit there; so Ah asked

434

him tae tell me what he found sae fascinatin'. His wurds moved even me, a hardened auld sea-dog, tae sich a degree that Ah wrote them doon. Ye may read 'em fir yersel', just as he spake them."

John read the few lines with a stir of excitement.

"Take a symphony by Mozart. Add all the hues of the rainbow, dust with sunbeams and surround with a champagne sea. Then you will have a land as God intended it to be — the islands of the Seychelles."

They sailed into l'Établissement du Roi at dusk on May 3rd. The great forests covering the steep hills surrounding the harbor were silhouetted against a purple sky already studded with stars. The port, shortly to be renamed Victoria after the new Queen, was a hive of industry. The building of a vast ship of close on four hundred tons was half-completed and seven others were in various stages of development.

"There's timber tae last a lifetime o' boat buildin'!" said Hamish, as a group of scantily clad Africans came hurrying down the wooden jetty to meet them. Lights glowed from windows in the harbor town. Despite the late hour people of different nationalities and colors thronged the narrow streets — British, French, Chinese, Indian and in huge numbers, the Africans.

"There's no' enow wurk fir them a'!" Hamish explained as his crew made fast the brig. "Monie o' the planters left the island when their slaves were freed and cotton ceased tae be profitable. Noo the puir blacks live frae hand tae mouth, gettin' what little wurk they can around the docks. Yell need tae mind yer belongin's fir they'll steal yer right hand if yer left isna lookin'!"

The hot humidity of the air became more apparent now that they were no longer enjoying the breeze off the sea. As John followed Hamish along the coast road towards the house of the Civil Commissioner, his clean frilled shirt clung to his back and chest and he was forced to remove his tail-coat and carry it.

They were given a warm welcome by the Commissioner, a Mister Augustus Mylius, who was delighted to receive visitors so newly arrived from England. He himself had not long been in the Seychelles, he told John as he instructed his footman to bring a flagon of chilled French wine for his guests. He had no wife or children of his own but his younger brother and family were spending this first year on the island with him, he explained.

"When you, Sir, and Captain McRae have had a chance to refresh yourselves, I will be happy to introduce my relations who will join us for the evening repast," he said to John.

They were given small but moderately comfortable rooms with clean linen upon the beds and African servants to wait upon them. Though the living conditions fell short of those he enjoyed at home, John thought, the mere fact of having a bed rather than a bunk in a tiny cabin was welcome.

So too was the dinner provided by Mistress Mylius, wife of Augustus Mylius' brother, Paul. Served by black servants the meal had been prepared by the Commissioner's two pretty nieces, Janet and Phoebe. Although both girls were fair-haired and blue-eyed, they nevertheless reminded John of Chantal, as he watched them moving about the room in their pretty white muslin dresses, dimpling and coquetting at the unexpected appearance of a handsome young man in their midst. He judged them still to be in their teens.

It was not until the meal ended that John explained the reason for his visit to the Seychelles. His host and hostess did not interrupt whilst he related the ill-fated journey of *Valetta* and his hopes that somehow survivors had reached the islands.

Augustus Mylius scratched his head thoughtfully.

"I cannot recall a report upon such unlikely a happening since I arrived two months ago," he said. "Nevertheless I will study the memoranda given me by my predecessor, Arthur Wilson. I fear I have not yet found time to read the many notes he left me. The climate here is not, alas, conducive to the employment of one's energies and I regret to say that I have not enjoyed the best of health since my arrival."

"Then pray do not trouble yourself until you feel able!" John said politely, although he was in a fever of impatience to know if there was the smallest glimmer of information. "Tomorrow will suffice very well!"

The ladies retired when the Commissioner

insisted John and the Captain should join him in a brandy.

"When the French departed from Mahé, they left excellent cellars behind them!" he said. "Wilson's predecessor bequeathed him a large number of exceedingly good wines and this magnificent cognac. Wilson was good enough to leave me what he had not consumed."

But the cellar appeared to be the only inheritance Augustus Mylius appreciated.

"Had I known of the conditions here, I might well have remained in England," he said. "I was shocked to find such a state of affairs as now exists on the island. There are no churches, no priests, no schools, no hospitals," he told his visitors. "Bodies must be consigned to their graves without religious service of any kind. Houses left by departing planters are rapidly decaying and the estates are returning to weeds. Why, it was reported to me last week that there were pigs in the graveyard uprooting the bodies. I dared not tell my poor sister-in-law or my nieces lest they should be shocked out of their senses!"

"Sae much fir 'the land o' God'!" Hamish McRae said ruefully to John as they made their way upstairs to bed.

Despite this depressing report, the following day was to prove one of the greatest excitement for John. The Commissioner brought to the luncheon table one of his predecessor's reports.

"It could be the very information you are seeking!" he said as he handed the paper to John. "If it proves to be so, you are indeed fortunate

438

to have your hopes resolved so speedily!"

Scarce able to contain his eagerness, John's eyes scanned the flowing script.

'An African by the name of Tobias from the Corail Plantation today brought a letter from the French planter, Siméon St. Clair, saying that he had discovered the bodies of six British sailors washed up on the beach at Grand Police. His letter appended herewith further states that the only survivor was a woman cast up upon the sands who declared herself to be a Baroness van Eburhard. She is from England. St. Clair states that as soon as the good lady has recovered sufficiently, he will escort her to l'Établissement to hand her into my care.

'In view of St. Clair's current hospitality, and as I am hard pressed for time in view of my impending departure for England, I am taking no action to call upon Baroness van Eburhard. She will no doubt present herself to you in due course.'

"The date of this report!" John almost shouted. "How long ago was it, Mister Mylius? The Baroness von Eburhard he refers to is my sister, Tamarisk!"

"I took the page from Wilson's September report!" the Commissioner replied.

"But that is nearly seven months ago!" John cried. "She may no longer be there!"

"Keep calm, laddie!" said Hamish at John's

439

elbow. "'Tis unlikely yer sister wall hae left the island wi'oot Mister Mylius' knowledge."

"The time too corroborates my certainty that this is my sister," John said more calmly. "There can be no doubt about it! Where is this plantation, Sir? Can it be reached easily? I have no knowledge of this island's topography!"

Mister Mylius looked uncertain.

"Grand Police is on the extreme south point of Mahé!" be said. "The quickest route is by pirogue, which would take four hours or so. Or if you preferred you could go overland, crossing the hills to the south of Anse Bougainville, but this would mean traveling in a bullock cart and the journey would undoubtedly take you twelve or more hours at the least."

"And why, pray, do we no' travel in *Seasprite*?" suggested Hamish McRae. "Ah can hae her ready fir sailin' by the morrow. Mister Mylius and the wee lassies could come too, if they fancy a sea-trip."

"Oh, please, Uncle Augustus, may we go?" begged Janet, her delicate white skin flushed with excitement.

"Mama, Papa, we would be no trouble to the Captain!" Phoebe added, placing her cheek in soft cajolery against her father's.

"I see no reason why not — if I am there to keep an eye on you both!" said Paul Mylius. "We would be back before night-fall, would we not, Captain McRae?"

Looking relieved that he need not make the journey as well as his brother, the Commissioner nodded his approval of the plan.

"Ay, we wad that!" agreed Hamish. He looked at John enquiringly. "'Tis fir ye tae decide, laddie!"

John curbed his impatience to set off that very afternoon by whatever means. He confessed to Hamish his fear that Tamarisk must have suffered some grave injury for her to have remained so long at the plantation. Or alternatively, that she might have left the island.

The Captain reminded him that, as the Commissioner had pointed out, Tamarisk could not have left the island without his knowledge. One more day would make little difference to her since she had already been a guest of the planter for seven months. Moreover it would be pleasant to have the company of Paul Mylius and his two pretty daughters who were dimpling most charmingly as they renewed their pleas to be permitted to go with him.

Luncheon over Hamish took himself off to the harbor to reassemble his crew. John, at the suggestion of Mistress Mylius, escorted the girls in their carriage upon a tour of the little town. The afternoon passed happily enough as they stopped at intervals to buy gifts for Tamarisk which the girls insisted she would greatly appreciate since there were no shops within miles of the Corail Plantation. At last, laden with cologne, embroidered slippers, a coral necklace from the Indian traders and a bamboo parasol from the Chinese merchant, they returned to the Commissioner's house.

By now the three young people were on

excellent terms. Their shyness overcome, Janet and Phoebe plied John with questions about his sister, about his home in England, and not least about Chantal. Of an age themselves to be much concerned with the subject of romance, they were deeply impressed by John's declared intention to search the world if need be, to find the girl he loved.

"I fear 'tis unlikely either of us will find so faithful a suitor here on Mahé!" Phoebe told John wistfully. "Most of the white planters have left the island and there is not even a clergyman to pay court to us!"

"But the planter with whom my sister is staying — is he a married man?" John asked. "If not, you may yet find at least one suitor between you!"

The girls could tell John very little about the Frenchman who had reported Tamarisk's presence to the Commissioner. Phoebe's mother had told them he was said to be a recluse. He had certainly not come to l'Établissement to call upon them when their uncle had replaced the previous Commissioner.

Somewhat concerned for Tamarisk's welfare in the company of this stranger, Siméon St. Clair, John's impatience to set out and find her was renewed.

Hamish joined them in time for the evening meal and announced that all was prepared for the morrow.

The following morning *Seasprite* sailed out from the picturesque little harbor, a moderate breeze filling her sails and sending her skipping over the sparkling aquamarine-colored sea at a steady eight knots. The brig was towing behind her a pirogue as well as a dory. Hamish had ascertained that Grand Police could not be too closely approached even in a calm sea, for the currents were very strong and the bay was enclosed by half-submerged rocks. It was his intention, he told them, to anchor *Seasprite* offshore and row in to the nearest sandy beach.

Seasprite and her passengers had a perfect view of the island as they sailed southeastward. The journey passed swiftly and agreeably as they stood on deck staring with fascination at the palm-fringed sandy coves; at the great forests of pine trees sweeping down from high hills to the very edge of the water. And all around them they could espy an unending variety of birds hovering close to the little native fishing boats dotting the sea. The crews were busy helping themselves to the liberal supplies of fish of all kinds thriving in the warm coastal waters.

In little over two hours at sea, Hamish was pointing out the bay at Grand Police. Close by was a tiny cove without a rock visible on its white coral sand. Twenty minutes later the pirogue had landed safely on the beach. Leaving the seamen to guard the canoe, John, Hamish, Paul Mylius and the girls set off on foot in the direction of the Corail Plantation.

Unaware of approaching visitors, Tamarisk moved about the garden cutting fresh flowers for the house. Siméon, stretched out upon a chaise longue in the shade of a huge takamaka

443

tree, was watching her graceful movements with pleasure. In a little while Narcisse would call them for the midday meal, but for the moment they could share their solitude in quiet content. Soon it would be the hottest part of the day and even the birds were silent as they sought the shade of the trees.

It was Tamarisk who first heard the voices. As she paused listening, Siméon too, became aware of them.

"Who can that be, my love?" he asked, for he knew his workers would still be busy on the plantation. Shading his eyes with his hand, he stared in puzzlement at the approaching group of people now just discernible as they came through the albizier trees at the far end of the garden.

Tamarisk stood poised with her flower basket over one arm, motionless as a strange feeling of premonition overcame her. Although she could not have justified her fear, she was suddenly convinced that whoever the interlopers were, they threatened her life with Siméon at the Château Corail.

She was still trying to rationalize this strange notion as the group came nearer and nearer. Now she was convinced she must be dreaming as she became certain that she recognized one of the figures as that of her younger brother, John.

"It cannot be!" she murmured, the color draining from her cheeks and the flowers she had been holding falling to her feet. She turned to Siméon. The look of apprehension on his face changed to one of dismay as she whispered:

"Siméon, I think 'tis my brother, John."

Siméon drew a deep breath as he looked from Tamarisk to the three men and two girls now within hailing distance. If Tamarisk was right and one of the men was indeed her brother, then what he feared most in the world would be inevitable — he would lose the woman he loved.

Slowly Siméon stood up, trusting that he would be able to meet the occasion with dignity. He did not feel guilty in loving Tamarisk — only in so far as he had dissuaded her from returning to her family. He had tried so hard these past idyllic weeks to put from his mind the knowledge that his happiness could not last, that when finally she did return to England he might never see her again. Selfishly he had discouraged her attempts to talk of her children, for he had known that she missed them greatly and longed to be reunited with them. But for them, he believed, he might have been able to persuade Tamarisk to stay here on the island with him forever and marry him.

Silently he waited as the visitors came closer. The youngest of the three men began to run towards Tamarisk, his face full of joy as he called her name. As Siméon watched, Tamarisk threw herself into her brother's arms and they hugged one another with deep affection.

"'Tis like a miracle — finding you alive and well! We all believed you dead!" John cried. "I cannot tell you what joy it gives me to see you, my dearest sister!"

He hugged her anew.

Forgetting all but her pleasure in this reunion, Tamarisk turned to Siméon and smiling happily, said:

"This is my brother, John. John dear, this is Siméon St. Clair who has been caring for me since I was cast up on the beach at the southernmost point of his plantation. I owe him my life!"

John stepped forward and shook Siméon's hand with a genuine warmth lighting up his face.

"I and my family are deeply indebted to you, sir!" he said. "Now may I introduce my friends to you, Monsieur St. Clair. Mister Paul Mylius, and these two young ladies are his daughters, Miss Janet and Miss Phoebe! And this is my ship's captain, Hamish McRae!"

His face impassive, Siméon bowed formally as he shook the extended hands.

"You will have a great deal to talk about, *sans doute!* So please be seated. I will go indoors and advise my housekeeper that you will be my guests for luncheon."

The two girls seated themselves excitedly on the warm dry grass whilst their father, Hamish, John and Tamarisk sat down on the chairs. Unable to conceal their excitement, Janet and Phoebe exchanged whispered comments which Tamarisk overheard.

"Do you not agree, Phoebe, that Monsieur St. Clair is exceedingly handsome?" the elder girl Janet was saying.

The younger sister giggled as she nodded, adding:

"And so much younger than I had supposed!"

Tamarisk felt a sudden chill in her heart. She looked from the two pretty girls in their white muslin dresses, their hair tied with ribbons, to her brother, John. Dark and handsome, he was as young as they. She was conscious as she had not been for weeks of Siméon's age — and her own! These young people were still on the edge of childhood whereas she — she belonged to the same generation as Paul Mylius. The man now sat with a doting smile upon his face as he gazed fondly at his charming daughters.

'*What would he and John think if they knew Siméon and I were lovers?*'

The thought brought a deep blush to Tamarisk's face.

But John seemed happily unaware of her confusion as affectionately he put his arm around her shoulders.

"We have much to recount to one another!" he said. "But of all I have yet to tell you, there is one most important piece of news I bring you, Tamarisk." He looked down at his sister with a smile.

"Doubtless you imagined all lives were lost when *Valetta* sank beneath the waves. But prepare yourself for truly wonderful news."

He felt Tamarisk trembling and held her hand more tightly.

"The day before I left England," he continued, "we received an unexpected visitor at Barre House — a very, very welcome visitor. I fear this will come as a shock, however agreeable. *Your husband, Charles, is alive!*"

447

Had she not been seated, Tamarisk believed she would have fallen in a swoon. The color drained from her face.

"But I saw . . . he was . . . John, I saw him hit by a spar and swept overboard. I saw him . . ."

She broke off as John put a cushion behind her head. She lay back, her eyes never leaving his face as he repeated gently:

"Despite all, Charles is alive and in good health! 'Tis true he was struck by a spar then swept overboard; but several of *Valetta*'s seamen lashed him to a cask and kept him afloat until they were picked up by a passing convict ship nearly two days later."

Seeing that the color was returning to Tamarisk's cheeks, he decided to continue with the less happy part of his story.

"Charles suffered a prolonged bout of unconsciousness after his ordeal and, I am sorry to relate, a loss of vision. But the physicians have assured him that he has every chance of regaining his sight. Naturally he was not in very good spirits when I saw him. Apart from his indisposition, he feared you dead, Tamarisk, although he had not given up all hope. I know that he would have wished to join me in my search for you and Chantal had he been well enough to do so."

"So you have not found Chantal!" Tamarisk murmured although her mind still whirled with the news John had just imparted. *Charles was alive!* As miraculously as herself, he had survived the shipwreck and was safely home in England.

Such a possibility had never once crossed her mind during all the months she had spent at the Château Corail. She had been totally convinced that she was a widow. Now she knew the true facts — Charles, her husband was living. And all the time, she and Siméon . . .

Hamish McRae, who had been watching Tamarisk anxiously, noticed her increasing pallor and interrupting her thoughts, said soothingly:

"Can Ah git ye a glass o' water, Ma'am? Even sich guid news must aye come as a shock!"

"No, no thank you!" Tamarisk replied with an effort. She drew a deep breath as she attempted to regain control of her senses. To know that her dear Charles still lived was indeed great joy. But at the same time, this intelligence and John's arrival meant that there must be an immediate end to her intimacy with Siméon. Tamarisk knew that she was not prepared for so precipitate a conclusion of their shared idyll. The thought that she might never know his embrace again, hear his whispered words of adoration, feel the surging delight as they lay entwined in perfect happiness, was suddenly unbearable.

Hurriedly, to avoid the rush of tears now threatening her, Tamarisk began to question John as to how he had discovered her whereabouts in the Seychelles. She was deeply shocked to learn that her family had received no letter from her. She enquired if Charles had not been able to give any intelligence as to Chantal's fate.

"Alas, no! But your presence here upon Mahé gives us fresh hope!" John explained. "We know that there are vast number of other islands in this group and if you, Tamarisk, reached safety in one of *Valetta*'s longboats, then mayhap Chantal has done likewise. 'Tis my intention to search every island with Hamish to assist me. If Chantal is alive, I will find her!"

Janet now handed to Tamarisk the woven basket containing the gifts John had purchased for her.

"We knew from Uncle Augustus that Monsieur St. Clair's was a bachelor establishment," Janet explained. "So we persuaded your dear brother, John, to buy these few feminine accessories for you!"

Whilst Tamarisk opened her presents, she attempted to tell John in more detail of her rescue and somewhat hesitantly, spoke of Siméon's care of and kindness to her. She was more aware than she had ever been that she had long overstayed her sojourn at the Corail Plantation and she discovered herself making excuses for her prolonged stay.

"I was intending to come to l'Établissement du Roi shortly to arrange for my passage home," she ended her account, stammering over the half truth.

Happily ignorant of Tamarisk's inner turmoil, John replied with a smile:

"But now you will be able to travel home to England in *Seasprite* with Hamish and me. But not of course until we have explored all the islands!"

Siméon now rejoined his visitors with the

450

announcement that luncheon was awaiting them in the house.

As yet Siméon was still unaware that Tamarisk's husband was alive. Believing her to be a widow, he was not conscious of any feelings of guilt for their unconventional behavior. Nevertheless the unexpected encounter with her young brother had caused him to reflect that he and Tamarisk had totally disregarded the accepted standards of morality. He wondered if she intended to keep their relationship a secret from her family or if she would confess to the love they had shared. His eyes rested briefly on Tamarisk's flushed face, but she would not meet his gaze.

The two girls, already on their feet, came over to him.

"I have not yet been inside a planter's house!" said Janet, "and I shall be most interested to see your home, Monsieur St. Clair."

"Are you not lonely living here so far from l'Établissement and other Europeans, Sir?" asked Phoebe.

To his surprise, Siméon did not find himself ill at ease although this was the first time in his life he had ever spoken to a young girl. The pink and white prettiness of the sisters had not escaped his notice. During the meal Narcisse had quickly made for them, he could not fail to realize that both Janet and her younger sister were casting frequent glances in his direction; and that they were vying with one another to attract his attention.

Although he was accustomed now to Tamarisk's

451

compliments upon his good looks and his eligibility were he ever to wish to marry, he had not thought beyond the satisfaction that *she* found him desirable. As far as marriage to anyone else was concerned, he would not discuss the matter so convinced was he that he would never be wed unless Tamarisk herself agreed to become his wife.

"You might change your mind, Siméon, were you to meet and fall in love with a woman younger than I!" Tamarisk had said. But Siméon had not wanted to think about life without her.

Now with the arrival of her brother and her departure no longer a matter for conjecture, he was forced to face the huge void of loneliness her absence would leave. He wished he could dislike the brother who was taking her from him but in point of fact, he found himself conversing with John in easy friendship. Moreover he was pleased and flattered when John in a smiling aside remarked to Siméon that he had undoubtedly made a favorable impression upon the young ladies.

Tamarisk too, noticed the girls laughing and dimpling as they plied Siméon with questions about life on the plantation. Try as she might she could not but feel jealous and guilty. She was jealous of their youth; of their smooth, unlined faces; of their dimples and their laughing, innocent eyes. Even more compelling was her sense of guilt. She had had no right to encourage Siméon to love her or to allow their intimacy to continue for so long that he had come to depend upon her absolutely. As a result she had grown to love and to need him and the thought of the now imminent separation from him was so painful that tears filled her eyes.

She felt guilty too, because ever since John's arrival her mind had been filled with thoughts of herself and Siméon and not of Charles or Chantal. John could talk of little else but Chantal and his love for her. His reunion with her, Tamarisk, had clearly fired his determination to continue his search for her.

Aware of John's impatience to begin the search, Hamish McRae suggested they return at once to l'Établissement so that he could prepare some charts showing the estimated positions of the surrounding islands.

"Wi' a wee bit o'luck we can be ready fir an early start in the mornin'," he said.

John nodded his approval.

"You will return with us, of course, Baroness Eburhard!" said Paul Mylius. "I am sure my brother and my wife will he only too pleased to make you welcome whilst John and Captain McRae are at sea!"

Tamarisk's eyes went to Siméon and read in them a reflection of her own horror at the thought of leaving him so precipitately. Somehow she must find the opportunity to inform him of Charles' survival so that he would not seek to follow her to England as he sometimes threatened.

"I need a day or two to prepare myself for departure!" she said quietly. "I have many people to whom I must bid farewell before I go and to whom I owe thanks. I feel it would be wrong if I were to leave the Château Corail without doing so!"

Siméon breathed a sigh of relief. He had been sick with anxiety lest Tamarisk should fall in with the Captain's suggestion.

"Since Tamarisk wishes to remain a while longer, will you not all stay here as my guests?" he asked impulsively with a courage that surprised him. "The Château Corail has several guest chambers and it would be my pleasure to entertain you within the limits at my disposal."

Whilst the men considered the proposal, the girls showed no hesitation as to their wishes. Clapping their hands they ran to their father pleading with him to accept Monsieur St. Clair's invitation.

Paul Mylius turned to John.

"What say you?" he asked. "I myself, would he happy to remain here."

"Ay can gae by masel' tae l'Établissement tae prepare the charts," Hamish suggested. "Tomorrow Ah can return here tae collect ye and nae time wad be lost."

"Then it would seem a most excellent idea!" John voiced his opinion. He put his arm around Tamarisk affectionately. "We have still much to discuss, have we not?" he said. "I know you must be agog to hear about the children; and of course you will want to know every detail of Charles' rescue and return to England."

Tamarisk knew that Siméon's eyes had turned to her questioningly but she dared not meet his gaze. She had prayed that she would be alone with him when he heard of her husband's survival. She sensed his bewilderment and curbed the poignant longing to turn to him now and take him in her arms.

Fortunately for both Tamarisk and Siméon, their guests were occupied in animated conversation which continued throughout the meal. Their own silence therefore went unremarked. It was a further hour before luncheon ended and they could be alone.

Hamish departed for l'Établissement. John and the Mylius' family were conducted to the guest chambers where they retired for the afternoon siesta. In the privacy of her own room, Tamarisk waited, knowing that it would not be long before Siméon came to her. Her heart was heavy and she felt no joy when at last his knock sounded on the door.

Siméon did not at once take her into his arms as was his custom. He stood young and vulnerable, staring at the woman upon whom he had lavished so much devotion.

"*Dites-moi*, Tamarisk!" he said without preamble. "Did I understand your brother correctly? Your husband is alive?"

Tamarisk nodded, the tumult of her emotions choking in her throat so that she could not speak. Siméon made no move towards her.

"I suppose this intelligence has brought you great joy," he said bitterly. "You are doubtless now filled with regret that you ever allowed me to love you!"

"No, Siméon, no!" The cry was wrung from her as she rose swiftly to her feet. Crossing

455

the room she took his face in her hands. "I shall never regret these past few months, my dearest Siméon. You must believe me when I tell you that they have been the happiest of my life."

Siméon's expression softened as he stared down at her unhappy face. Slowly his arms went around her.

"Then you *do* love me — a little!" he murmured.

"I shall always love you — and far more than a little," Tamarisk replied quietly. "But this is no time for pretence, Siméon, so I will be truthful for both our sakes. I love Charles, too. He is my husband and the father of my children and I owe him very many years of content. Now that I know that he is alive, I cannot in all conscience be unfaithful to him. As you well know, Siméon, I have always believed him dead and although you and I were not lawfully wed, I could see no wrong in our loving. But now I must return to him and to my children."

With a cry of anguish Siméon buried his face in her hair.

"I cannot live without you!" he murmured brokenly.

Tenderly Tamarisk stroked his head. Her expression was not without a trace of bitterness.

"You will find happiness again, dearest Siméon. Now that you are a man and most of all, unafraid to be one, there is no need to return to your former seclusion. You will make other friends and you will not be as lonely without me as you imagine."

She knew that this was neither the time nor the place to remind him of the two Mylius girls, pretty, charming, and intelligent. Both Janet and Phoebe had quite clearly taken a considerable interest in him. She could very well understand how this slim, handsome young Frenchman with his shy charm and perfect manners would appear romantic to a young girl. Even an older woman such as herself had not been immune to his attractions, Tamarisk thought with wry honesty.

Gently she detached herself from his arms, not trusting herself to remain in such close proximity. She fought against the longing to lie with him just once more within the bed where they had discovered such joy together. She knew that for Siméon's sake if not out of respect for Charles, she must not weaken now. Within a very short while she would be leaving with John for England and it would be easier for Siméon and herself were they to face the fact with courage and resolve.

"Siméon!" she said, her tone of voice so changed that he looked at her in surprise. "You must try to understand what a shock my brother's appearance has been for me. I wish now to be quite alone." She turned her head so that he could not detect the lie that came so smoothly from her lips. "I am not as young as you, my dear — a fact I fear you far too often forget!" She added the reproof with great difficulty, knowing that in his own interest she must deceive him into believing she was no longer desirous of his love.

She heard Siméon's tiny gasp of protest; but determinedly she moved still further away from him.

"You have always been very generous in your disregard of my advancing years!" she forced the words from her lips. "And I have tried very hard to hide from you my own awareness of the great gap in our ages. No, do not dispute with me, Siméon . . . " she said quickly as he opened his mouth in denial. "I have loved you so much, my dear, that I attempted to disguise my fatigue upon many occasions. One day you will know that youthful energies do not last forever. You will understand why I have always tried to convince you that the disparity in our ages would not allow us to marry. The fact is, Siméon, I could not have pretended such immunity to my age much longer. So beyond question 'tis best that my departure has been forced upon us."

She would not permit herself to look at Siméon's unhappy, bewildered face. Silently she prayed that she had at last been successful in putting doubts into his mind as to the suitability of their involvement, causing him to wonder if his love had been misplaced. If she could direct his thoughts away from her, he would suffer her loss more easily.

But later that afternoon she saw Siméon take Janet's hand to assist her from her chair and smile down into the girl's bright, expectant face, and her heart ached with sudden jealousy. Fighting her weakness, she knew that she was going to require all her strength of will to carry out her purpose. Whatever the cost to herself, her last gift to Siméon must be to sever the bonds of love that should never have been forged between them.

23

CHANTAL and Zambi were sitting cross-legged in the clearing outside the huts, plaiting palm leaves to make new mats. A giant tortoise which had become remarkably tame and which Chantal had christened George, dozed nearby, his black eyes blinking once in a while as he moved his scaly, wrinkled head into a more comfortable position. As always, the cardinals hopped and fluttered around the two girls, waiting for tidbits and sometimes perching unafraid on Chantal's arm or leg or even on her head. The fouquets bobbed around them too, as bowing, they went about their endless courtship.

Not far away, a young donkey nibbled at the lush vegetation. Chantal and Zambi had discovered a herd of wild donkeys on one of their forays inland for food and the foal had followed them back to the clearing. Dinez suspected that its mother must have died for no adult animal came after the little beast and it was now as tame as any dog and was Chantal's favorite pet.

Finding a herd of donkeys upon so isolated an island had surprised them all and Chantal was greatly cheered by Dinez' supposition that several of the breed must have made their way ashore following upon a shipwreck.

"It proves that at least one other vessel has

passed this way!" she declared.

She turned now to Zambi and sighing deeply, said:

"I have just realized, Zambi, that I am now eighteen years of age. To think that I had a birthday and did not remember it!"

Zambi laid down her mat and counted studiously upon her fingers.

"Zambi eighteen, too!" she said.

Chantal also laid down her work and stared out across the sandy beach to the endless vista of translucent blue-green waters. Beyond that horizon, she thought, thousands of miles away was England.

"It seems so long ago that I can scarce remember my seventeenth birthday party!" she said doubtfully. "It is only five moons since we came to Coetivy — yet already I have all but forgotten there is another way of life!"

Zambi's eyes were bright with amusement.

"Señorita say 'five moons!'" she giggled. "Talk Zambi talk!"

Chantal smiled; and then sighed. It was hardly surprising, she thought, if she was beginning to speak like the African girl since there was no one else for her to converse with. Such conversation as she exchanged with Dinez was minimal and only of practical necessity.

Ever since she had declined to 'marry' him on account of his wickedness, she had adopted a policy of cold detachment towards him which, with every passing day, became increasingly difficult to maintain.

Chantal had good reason to withdraw from

any kind of relationship with Dinez. She feared the power he exerted over her emotions, knowing that she could not trust herself to remain at arm's length were he to be kind, gentle, loving towards her. She hoped that by keeping her distance and appearing coldly indifferent she could discourage him from making any further attempts to change her mind.

Unfortunately Dinez had proved blind to her coldness, or so it seemed. Though he never made any physical approaches he continued to pursue her with his eyes — those strange, brilliant green eyes that followed her every movement as if he were some jungle animal stalking his prey . . . waiting, always waiting for her to indicate her vulnerability.

Chantal had forbidden Zambi to mention Dinez to her in terms of 'marriage' or 'husband.' There was an expression of bewilderment in Zambi's eyes when night after night Chantal retired early to her own hut leaving Dinez alone by the dying embers of the cooking fire; or when she excluded him from their conversation. Ignoring Dinez' presence, she would give Zambi lessons in reading and writing as if he did not exist.

But ignoring Dinez was becoming more difficult, Chantal thought uneasily. Even when he was elsewhere on the island hunting for food for their evening meal, she found herself glancing again and again to the outer perimeter of the clearing to see if he was returning. Sometimes he did not come back until after darkness fell and against her will, she worried lest some harm had befallen him. Yet when at last his strong young body appeared from the palm trees and Zambi would run to him with a glad cry of welcome, Chantal forced herself to turn her back as if she was quite unconcerned as to his welfare. Sometimes she would hurry into her own hut and remain there until Zambi came to tell her "Señor back now!" and that it was time to eat.

Dinez was very far from ignorant of the true state of Chantal's feelings. Indeed, the very deliberation with which she attempted to keep her distance encouraged him in his belief that she dared not trust herself to be near him. As day followed day he watched the telltale signs that indicated her weakening resolve and was able to control his impatience in the certainty that she would ultimately succumb.

Cleverly though Chantal imagined she was concealing her awareness of him, Dinez detected the rise and fall of her breasts as her breathing quickened when he addressed her. Nor could she hide from him the bright color that suffused her cheeks if he touched her hand 'accidentally,' when passing her food or taking from her a cask of water. He knew by the trembling of her hands or the fluttering of her eyelashes that whatever her mind dictated, her body longed for his as ardently as did his for her.

Chantal's determination to remain aloof was finally shattered inadvertently by Dinez on a day early in the month of April. He directed Zambi and Chantal to collect fresh supplies of bananas and *herbe mange tout* — the type of grass that formed a necessary part of their daily diet. Although not yet as hot as it would be the following month, the temperature was nearing ninety degrees and the atmosphere was intensely humid. He intended to go fishing, he informed them. He was tired of the taste of sea birds and had a fancy for something different from the sheerwaters, frigates, fairy and sooty terns that they had been eating these past few weeks.

Late in the afternoon he returned from the far side of the island looking pleased with his day's labor.

"This evening we shall have a dish fit for a king!" he announced as he dumped the plaited basket down in the clearing. "I shall cook the meal myself, Zambi — a potpourri of crabs, prawns, crayfish and other delicacies such as you have not tasted before!"

He set about cracking shells and chopping pieces of fish which he threw into their cooking pot whilst Zambi gathered wood for the fire. Once the stew began to simmer, Zambi's head turned several times in the direction of the steam rising from the iron pot.

"What eat?" she asked, her face expressing her uncertainty.

Dinez smiled.

"It is a surprise!" he told her. For Chantal's ears, he added: "I once dined with a Frenchman who was a chef before he became a pirate. He had learned in his native country the creation of a perfect fish dish which he called 'Bouillabaisse.' You will both enjoy it as much as I!"

When he had tasted the stew several times and declared it cooked to his satisfaction, he ladled portions into the empty coconut shells they used as dishes. Chantal was both hungry and curious, but she delayed testing Dinez' masterpiece lest he noted her interest in his culinary efforts. Zambi, however, lifted the stew to her nose and sniffed noisily. Whilst Dinez watched with amusement she dipped one finger into the stew and licked it.

"Do you not trust my cooking?" he asked laughingly. But with a cry, Zambi threw the shell with its steaming contents into the fire and turning, dashed Dinez' container from his hands.

"Not good! Bad! Very bad!" she cried. Turning to Chantal she rudely knocked her shell from her grasp, spilling the contents onto the ground.

Dinez was frowning as he jumped to his feet. He looked very angry.

"Come now, Zambi, that is enough from you! I took great pains cooking that meal and . . . "

"Señor, not good! Make ill!" Zambi interrupted pointing to the cooking pot still steaming gently on its trivet over the fire. She looked on the point of tears as she cried: "Fish bad, Señor. *Make ill!*"

"It is absolutely fresh, girl!" Dinez argued, his eyes blazing. "I caught and killed everything in that pot not two hours since."

Zambi threw herself at his feet. The tears were now streaming down her black face as she looked up at him pleading for understanding.

"Fish bad!" she sobbed. "Zambi know. Fish kill!"

With a sickening sense of shock, Chantal who had been listening to this interchange now understood what Zambi was saying. Something had gone into the stewing pot that was poisonous — and Dinez had already eaten it!

Dinez was standing perfectly still, staring at Zambi.

"Was there anything in it that we have not eaten before?" Chantal asked, in her anxiety forgetting her resolve not to speak to him.

Dinez turned to look at her, his face drawn beneath the sunburnt brown of his skin.

"There was one fish — a species I had not seen before . . . "

He described it in detail — twenty-five centimeters long with a rounded back, greenish black spots and orange eyes. Its two pairs of fins were orange and greeny-blue. The multi-colored tail had a yellow band in the center.

Zambi, still squatting in the sand and crying quietly, nodded her head, making it clear that she recognized the fish from Dinez' description. Chantal knelt down beside her.

"The Señor did not eat very much!" she said. "He only tasted a little, Zambi. A little will not harm him, surely?" she added uncertainly.

The tears flowed faster down Zambi's cheeks.

"Eat fish and die!" she whispered.

Chantal looked up at Dinez horrified.

"That cannot be true!" she whispered. "It must be an exaggeration, is it not, Dinez?"

He returned her stare with a lift of his eyebrows.

"In truth, Chantal, I do not know. I am beginning to suspect that the fish was a piton — which I had heard of but never before seen. It frequents the waters of the Indian Ocean and Zambi might have come across it on the African coast. I most certainly hope that she does not know as much as she professes. I feel perfectly well."

Zambi now stopped crying and words escaping her, indicated by signs to Dinez that he should attempt to make himself vomit.

"She is probably right!" Chantal said as Dinez hesitated. "If the fish *was* poisonous . . . " Her voice trailed away as Zambi's fear communicated itself to her. "Do as Zambi says!" she said. "Please!"

"Very well, if you insist, Koosh-Koosh!"

His intimate smile as he called her by her pet name caused Chantal to turn away from him quickly lest he should see the sudden tears in her eyes.

Still smiling, Dinez walked off beyond the fringe of palms.

Zambi was crying again and her sobs increased Chantal's feelings of alarm. It was unlike the black girl to be fearful without cause, and, Chantal now realized, she had never before seen Zambi in tears.

"He will be perfectly all right, Zambi!" she said with a conviction she no longer felt.

Dinez returned, professing that he still felt perfectly well.

"Although the sight of your two doleful faces is hardly reassuring!" he added grinning.

"'Tis naught to be laughed at!" Chantal reproved him. "If you had eaten more . . . "

"But I did not!" Dinez interrupted gently. "Besides which, I am still very far from convinced that the fish was poisonous."

But just as they began to congratulate themselves that Zambi's had been a false alarm, Dinez suddenly complained of a tingling of his tongue.

"It is most strange!" he muttered. The tingling spread to his lips and throat and now he complained also of muscular pains and a feeling of nausea. Zambi, usually a pillar of resourcefulness, silently retreated to her own hut and began a soft wailing that brought the first real feeling of panic to Chantal. To Dinez, too, so it seemed, for he said wryly:

"I think Zambi has begun to mourn for me already!"

His hand went to his throat and he looked at Chantal anxiously.

"It is becoming difficult to speak!" he murmured hoarsely. "Mayhap Zambi was right in her diagnosis after all. Would it not be ironic, my Koosh-Koosh, if I who have survived so many dangers in my life, were to die from a fish's poison?"

"You will not die! I will not let you die!" Chantal cried.

She took Dinez' arm as he swayed and supporting him, led him to his hut. He fell across the bed, sweat pouring from his forehead. As

468

Chantal watched horrified, his limbs suddenly twisted into a violent convulsion.

She ran to Zambi's hut and shook the crying girl by the shoulders.

"Señor very ill!" she said. "Zambi get plant to make better. Quickly, Zambi! There must be a herb of some kind which . . . "

"No plant to make better!" Zambi replied, the tears pouring down her face. "Señor die . . . soon maybe!"

With anger born entirely of fear, Chantal struck the girl across the cheek.

"That is a wicked thing to say!" she cried. "He will get better, you will see!"

She ran back to Dinez who was now lying perfectly still. Only by his eyes did he reveal that he was conscious. With a fresh wave of horror, Chantal realized that he could not move, that he was completely paralyzed.

"Oh, Dinez!" she cried, sinking to her knees by his bed and taking his inert hand between her own. "You must not die! I could not bear it if you did. Please try to live. Whatever the poison that is in you, it must wear off in time. And you must fight it with your will. I do not want you to die!"

His green eyes, riveted on hers, seemed to question her.

Chantal was now frankly terrified. Zambi's conviction that the worst was inevitable undermined her own desire to believe Dinez would recover. From his appearance it seemed all too probable that be would not survive the night.

Tears coursed down her cheeks.

"Please do not die!" she wept. "What would become of Zambi and me here on the island without you? Dinez, I beg you, do not leave us. Zambi loves you and I . . . I too, need you. If you will only get well again I will marry you, I promise. Dinez, can you hear me?"

He gave no sign that her wild promise had penetrated his consciousness. His body was racked once more by convulsions and Chantal buried her face in her hands so that she need not watch the tortured writhing of his limbs.

The sound of his labored breathing forced her to look at him again. She was quite certain that he was dying and she began silently to pray; to plead with God to forget his past wickedness and spare his life if only for her sake.

Somehow the long hours of the night passed. Chantal slept and prayed and occasionally wiped Dinez' face and body with a cloth soaked in water. Several times she squeezed drops of water down his throat although she had to force his lips apart to do so.

As dawn broke to the inevitable chorus of the thousands of island birds, she looked helplessly at Dinez' inert figure and was convinced that he had died whilst she slept. Dry-eyed she bent over him, and then with a cry of relief, saw the faint rise and fall of his chest. Barely discernible though it was, his breathing seemed easier.

Feverish with renewed hope, she poured water down his throat and saw his eyelids flutter. His body was cold, covered in perspiration, but his pulses seemed to have steadied and become stronger.

She ran out of the hut and called Zambi. Swollen-eyed, the girl followed her back to Dinez' hut. Bending over him Zambi drew a deep shuddering sigh. When she turned to look at Chantal, there was the beginning of a smile around her mouth.

"Señorita say right. Señor get well!"

"Oh, thank God!" Chantal cried. "My prayers have been answered!"

"You pray white God?" Zambi asked curiously. Chantal nodded.

"White God's medicine more strong than black God's!" Zambi said flatly. "Eat same fish black boy, Zambi's brother, die. Black medicine man not make well!"

Two days later Dinez had recovered his speech and partial use of his limbs. He lay on a mat beneath the shade of the palm thatch outside his hut and discussed Zambi's religious theories with Chantal.

"I would not wish to deny the possibility that God answered your prayers, Koosh-Koosh!" he said thoughtfully. "At the same time, it cannot be forgotten that I ate only the tiniest portion of that fish — perhaps insufficient to kill me as it did Zambi's brother." He smiled at her. "Whatever the truth, I am nonetheless grateful for your prayers for my survival. These past months I had begun to believe that you wished me dead, Koosh-Koosh. It is good to know that you desired so ardently to save my life!"

Chantal smiled shyly. It was impossible to

471

remain unmoved when Dinez spoke with such undisguised tenderness in his voice. He was still very weak but the teasing laughter was back in his eyes as he said:

"I do not think I would recommend a fish stew from Provence even to my worst enemy. The indisposition I suffered was exceedingly painful to say the very least and very frightening!"

"It was frightening for me, too!" Chantal agreed.

"Was it, Koosh-Koosh? You were brave to remain at my bedside. Zambi tells me she had given up hope and saw no point in trying to fight for my life! It comforted me, before I lost consciousness, to know you were there."

He reached out his hand and took hold of hers, carrying it to his lips and pressing a kiss into the palm.

"We are friends again, are we not? For which fact I am glad that I was poisoned if such has been the price of your change of heart."

Chantal shivered.

"Do not let us talk further of your death!" she said. "It frightens me to realize how vulnerable we are on this island with no physician or surgeon when illness or accident befall."

Dinez held her hand more tightly.

"'Tis best not to think of such things!" he said. "Let us talk instead of happier subjects. Tell me, Chantal, am I wrong in my belief that your heart has softened towards me? That maybe now at long last you will consent to be my wife?"

Chantal had been asking herself whether she

would honor the promise she had made at his bedside but had not yet determined upon an answer. Of one thing she had no doubt whatever — namely that she could not again pretend a cold indifference towards him. She had been unable to hide her deep concern for him and it did not surprise her that he had divined her change of heart.

"We have been on Coetivy half a year!" Dinez pursued the matter softly but determinedly. "Do you not agree that I have been very patient, my Koosh-Koosh? You must know by now that I love you!"

Chantal nodded. She did not doubt Dinez' love, yet she was still uncertain of the true nature of her feelings towards him. That he was both important and necessary to her happiness she could on longer deny. But she knew that were they living elsewhere, amongst other people in a civilized world, marriage to Dinez would not have crossed her mind even as a remote possibility. But as Dinez reminded her, they were not living in a civilized world but were alone on Coetivy, on a tropical island where they were like to remain for the rest of their lives. Perhaps, she thought now, she should consider herself fortunate to be cast away with a man such as Dinez. Although she shied away from remembrance of some of his past exploits and most of all from his dealings in the slave trade, she could not but admit that in the light of his background and nationality, his deeds had seemed reasonably ethical to him. Slave trading was a legal occupation for the Portuguese.

"We will talk about it when you are well again!" she prevaricated. But Dinez would not let the subject drop.

"You are not refusing me then, Chantal?" he persisted.

"No!" she admitted. "I am not refusing you, Dinez! But I need further time for reflection."

From then on, Dinez rapidly regained his former good health and strength. Without further discussion it seemed to be tacitly understood by him that they would become man and wife. Chantal made no effort to dispute this assumption. Nevertheless she insisted upon the passage of a further two weeks before their marriage should take place. Dinez did not argue the point. He was not concerned with a wait of a few more days if such was Chantal's wish. With Zambi's help, he set about the task of erecting a new and larger hut to accommodate them both.

"I shall build us a home fit for a queen!" he said laughingly. "For the future Queen Koosh-Koosh of Coetivy!"

Despite her innermost misgivings, Chantal could not help but be caught up in the infectious enthusiasm with which Dinez was planning her future home. She spent hours weaving new mats and roping bundles of latanier to thatch the roof. Although her hands were kept busy her thoughts were free to roam and more and more frequently they wandered to her wedding night. She watched Dinez' golden-brown body as he went about his work and recalled the night of the storm when he had first possessed her. Since then, Chantal had steadfastly avoided such memories and had tried not to think of the cataclysmic effect they had had upon her. She had firmly closed the door on the new world of pleasure and delight into which Dinez had initiated her.

Now, as the day of their 'wedding' approached, her longing to rediscover this new dimension of herself became ever more acute. It was only with difficulty that she kept her hands from reaching out and touching Dinez when he stood close to her. When he addressed her in that husky, tender voice and called her his Koosh-Koosh, her heart melted and the color would rush to her cheeks betraying the effect upon her that he could command merely with his voice.

When at last the day of her wedding dawned, Zambi rose long before Chantal in order to surprise her with a bridal gown. Instead of the beautiful lace and satin Chantal had described as befitting an English bride, the African girl had fashioned a dress of flowers. Each freshly-gathered blossom had been painstakingly threaded into ribbons that hung in strands from a waistband to form a skirt. In similar manner she had woven a tiny bodice and a circlet to crown Chantal's head. Multi-colored and sweetly scented, it was a fairytale gown of such loveliness that Chantal could not bear the thought that it would soon wither in the hot sun and by the end of the day, would have lost its life, color and beauty.

As she thanked the smiling black girl for the lovely gift, she made no mention of her sudden last minute misgivings. Bridal gowns were meant to be kept after a wedding; to be folded, wrapped and stored for a future bride; or to be made into a christening gown. They were made to last, like marriages themselves. If Chantal allowed herself, she thought, she might fear as superstitiously as any native, that her marriage to Dinez would prove no more lasting than the flowered gown itself.

Hurriedly she pushed such unwelcome imaginings to the back of her mind and sat quietly whilst Zambi began to comb her long dark hair.

"This is my wedding day," she told herself. "I will soon be Dinez' wife and then it will be my duty to try to please him in all things."

Her thoughts went like traitors to the new hut where Dinez would carry her that night, to the bridal couch that she herself had made from freshly stripped fibers. All too easily she could envisage the hungry craving of their bodies as Dinez removed the flowered robe from her.

Outside in the clearing, Dinez was singing in Portuguese:

"*Boa noite, Señorita. Ate amanha!*"

It was the same song that he sang every evening when she retired and she knew that he intended the words for her — *goodnight, Señorita. Until tomorrow!* But from now on there would be no more partings to their separate huts. She would fall asleep in Dinez' embrace and wake with his arms still around her.

"I do love him!" she said aloud as Zambi drew the multi-flowered skirt over her hips. "I

476

am certain that I love him!"

Zambi smiled.

"Señor good man. Very strong. Make happy. Make many babies!"

This time, thought Chantal, there was no going back.

24

June 1839

JOHN stood on the mizzen deck of *Seasprite* shading his eyes from the sun's reflection as it danced off the sparkling aquamarine sea. Beside him stood Siméon St. Clair, now a staunch friend and ally after six weeks of close companionship. But for Siméon, John thought, he might by now have given in to the pleas of Hamish McRae, Tamarisk and the Mylius' and abandoned his fruitless search for Chantal.

Siméon alone agreed with John absolutely that there was little point in having searched so many islands if they did not search them all, especially those furthest from Mahé. They had visited Les Amirantes, Desroches, Rémire to the southwest. Now Hamish was heading in a southerly direction.

"I understand how you feel, John!" Siméon had said. "To go back to England without knowing for a certainty that your Chantal is not somewhere here . . . that is to face a life of permanent disquiet!"

There were but a handful of tiny islands left to explore. All those they had so far visited were uninhabited and many were treeless and waterless where no living creature but seabirds could survive.

"'Tis said o' the Seychelles that they're the

peaks o' the lost continent of Lemuria!" Hamish had informed them, "and that ten thousand years ago, before they were engulfed by the sea, they formed a land link between Asia and Africa!"

Sailing in these waters was not always easy. On two occasions there were storms so fierce that Hamish would not put to sea. Conflicting ocean currents, coral reefs and low-lying islets called for the degree of skill which only a man of Hamish McRae's experience could achieve.

Tamarisk had now moved to the Mylius' house in l'Établissement du Roi and spent much of her time in the company of the two girls. Janet the elder, made no secret of her interest in Siméon and Tamarisk was forced to realize as the days passed that Siméon was by no means impervious to the young girl's obvious adoration.

Siméon and John returned from visits to the various islands to enjoy a good meal, a change of attire and a few hours relaxation whilst *Seasprite* was reprovisioned. But now they were venturing further afield and it might be several weeks before they completed their four-hundred mile round trip to the outer island southeast of Mahé.

With no knowledge of Tamarisk's previous relationship with Siméon St. Clair and no reason to suspect it, the Mylius family welcomed the young Frenchman whom they all liked for his excellent manners and shy charm. It soon became obvious to Tamarisk that Janet's parents would not be averse to a match between their daughter and Siméon. Sadly Tamarisk reflected that she herself was the only reason Siméon showed no enthusiasm for such a match. It might have been ideal, he insisted, but for the fact that his heart was still in her keeping.

Knowing that she had no rightful claim to Siméon's love, Tamarisk set about detaching herself from their emotional involvement as determinedly as she could. Her manner towards him became cool and remote. Often she would retire early to her bed, stressing that at her advanced age, she needed more rest than did they, who were so much younger. When Siméon began to argue that it was ridiculous to make herself sound old when she was so far from it, Tamarisk gently reminded him that she *was* a married woman, a mother and nearer in age to Mistress Mylius than to him.

Gradually Tamarisk's remarks began to have their effect. Siméon turned more and more frequently to the starry-eyed, pink-cheeked girl with skin like porcelain and dimples in her cheeks. Despite his former conviction that he could never look at any other woman but Tamarisk with love and desire, he now discovered himself thinking often about Janet Mylius. He questioned whether he might be tempted to unfaithfulness to Tamarisk were Janet to be lying naked in his arms. Such thoughts made him feel guilty and traitorous. But of late Tamarisk had spoken with increasing frequency of her husband, Charles, and slowly Siméon reached the conclusion that she had never really loved him, but that she had been using him to console herself for the loss of her husband. The bitterness aroused by his suspicion gradually gave way to a feeling of relief. He now felt morally free to give less of his attention to Tamarisk and more to the girl, Janet.

John now turned to Siméon with a smile lurking at the corners of his mouth. He had been watching a sperm whale blowing as it surfaced to starboard.

"Are you by chance lost in a dream about a certain young lady called Janet?" he enquired. "'Twould seem you have made no small conquest of her during our brief visits to l'Établissement." He noted the rush of color to Siméon's fair skin and gave him a friendly pat on the shoulder. "I wish you well!" he said. "Were my heart not Chantal's, I might have rivaled you for her affections. Can you believe it, Siméon," be added, "but when we first met, I was silly enough to imagine that you felt romantically inclined towards my sister, Tamarisk! But of course that was an absurd notion, which I very soon realized when I stopped to consider the differences in your ages. One is apt to forget my sister is middle-aged. Do you not agree?"

Siméon was embarrassed by the closeness to the truth of John's remarks, and attempted to turn the conversation from himself.

"Her husband must love her very much!" he said awkwardly.

"Oh, yes indeed!" agreed John. "Charles has always adored her. I recall my mother telling me that he was mad with love for Tamarisk from the day he first set eyes upon her. He

481

was then still a shy young midshipman in his teens. They are very devoted to one another and their four children are quite delightful. Perhaps I can persuade you to make the long journey to England, St. Clair. It would be most agreeable if you were to pay us a visit. My parents, as well as Charles, would be happy to have an opportunity to thank you in person for your care of Tamarisk. She has left me in no doubt as to how good you were to her throughout her long convalescence."

Siméon was silent. A few weeks ago, an invitation to England would have brought him nothing but joy such was his dread of being parted from Tamarisk with no hope of seeing her again. Now he felt both guilty and confused by his abrupt change of heart. It was not that he had ceased to love Tamarisk — he would always do so; but now he saw their relationship in a new light as he recalled Tamarisk's warning to him that they could never reconcile the disparity in their ages. He remembered uneasily how fiercely he had argued that age made no difference. Now he knew that she had been right. Even were she to have been the widow they supposed and free to marry him, he realized that his rightful place was in the company of young people like John and the Mylius girls.

A shout from Hamish McRae relieved Siméon of the necessity for a reply.

"Land ahoy!" Hamish called a second time. "Ah think 'tis the island called Coetivy, John. See it there tae starboard? We'll no be able tae cross that coral reef, that's fir sure!"

John lent over the bulwark and stared across the ridge of white water surrounding the tiny island to the sandy beaches beyond.

"We could git ashore in the pirogue!" Hamish said. They had towed a native canoe behind them for this very purpose on the advice of the Mahé fishermen. "How say ye, John? Is it wurth a closer look?"

John shaded his eyes against the glare, a feeling of hopelessness invading his spirit. There had been so many abortive explorations of so many islands like this one which Hamish called 'Coetivy.' Each search had proved as fruitless as the last as they wandered through lush vegetation or over rocks or sand with only the birds and animals responding to thee shouts.

But suddenly Siméon spoke beside him.

"*La fumée!*" he called out excitedly in French. "Smoke!" he repeated in English. "Do you see, John, where that sandy beach joins the fringe of palm trees? *C'est vraiment la fumée!*"

"God a mercy, 'tis a fact!" Hamish shouted. "D'ye see, John?"

A tiny spiral of blue smoke was winding lazily up through the trees, unmistakable against the bright green of the palm fronds.

"There's a fire sure enow!" said Hamish more quietly. "But it could aye be that o' a fishermon, John. And dinna forget, laddie, that there's still pirates tae be encountered in these waters!"

"But in either event, there would be a boat!" John spoke, his excitement so intense that he had to force the words from his throat. "Get the pistols, Hamish. We will go ashore!"

483

Hamish had added to his crew two Seychelles seamen who were adept at handling the pirogue. These men seemed unafraid of the white surf boiling over the reef and with Hamish and John assisting on the oars, they rode one of the great waves skillfully over the rocks without scraping the flat bottom of the boat on the jagged coral ridge beneath them.

Dinez da Gama was on the far side of the island collecting turtle eggs when the pirogue grounded on the soft white sand. John and his companions therefore saw only the two girls, as they climbed out of the boat, one black, one brown, approaching them hesitantly.

For several seconds John failed to recognize Chantal as she drew closer. The sun had turned her skin a deep golden brown. Her long black hair hung to her waist barely covering the nakedness of her upper body. Her legs and feet were bare beneath the briefest of skirts. So it was not surprising therefore, that he mistook her for a native, an African of a different tribe from the black-skinned girl who stood behind her.

But for Chantal there could be no mistake as to John's identity. When she and Zambi had first sighted the approaching pirogue, she had never once imagined it could be bringing not just rescuers but a member of her own family. It was joy enough simply to know that other human beings were about to land on Coetivy; that she might yet reach the safety of civilization — and home.

Overcome by emotion, she stared at John, half-believing him a figment of her imagination.

But the tall young man gazing at her open-mouthed looked in every conceivable way so like the John she had left in England, that she hesitated no longer and threw herself into his arms.

So accustomed had Chantal become to her lack of clothing, to the color of her skin, the untrimmed locks of her hair, she never considered what a shock it must be to John to see her in such guise. She thought of nothing but the joy of their reunion.

"Chantal!" he murmured, holding her away from him so that he could see her more clearly. "*Is it really you?*"

The sound of his voice — the first English voice she had heard in nearly a year — was sufficient to bring tears to Chantal's eyes.

She became conscious of John's eyes taking in her appearance and she drew back in sudden deep embarrassment. Quickly she lifted her arms and covered her breasts, a deep blush mounting to her cheeks. Only now did she become fully aware of the modesty she had so easily abandoned as Dinez' wife.

Dinez! She had forgotten him in the excitement. She glanced swiftly over her shoulder towards the lagoon and saw with relief that he was not yet returning from his foray. Desperately, she prayed that he would not do so before she had a chance to explain to John who he was and their mode of living.

But was there any way she could explain her 'marriage' to Dinez to these visitors from a civilized world, she thought in sudden desperation? Before she left England, she herself would not have understood her transformation had such a possibility been suggested.

Aware that she had now been standing in silence for some minutes as she and John stared at one another incredulously, she sought for words that would be comprehensible to these strangers.

It was Hamish who now stepped forward to ease the moment.

"'Tis a miracle indeed, lassie, that we hae found ye," he said kindly. "Ma name is Hamish McRae and Ah captain the brig in which John here and me hae been scourin' the oceans fir ye. We had nae mair than a wee hope o' findin' ye. This is Monsieur St. Clair from the island o' Mahé. He's a friend o' yer sister, Baroness Eburhard."

"Tamarisk!" Chantal repeated, forgetting herself once more as happiness overwhelmed her. "You mean that my sister, too, is alive?"

"Ay, and her man! Noo, m'dear, can we no go somewhere tae sit and talk? This sun is ower hot fir me!"

"Of course, I fear I have forgotten my manners!" Chantal cried as she led the way across the white sand to the clearing. "I myself have become well used to the sun!"

Astonished though John had been by Chantal's appearance, he was by now recovering from the first shock. It was more than enough that he had discovered her alive and well. Despite her unseemly state, she was still the dearest person in the world to him and he would have liked to

486

take her in his arms and hug her. But shyness seemed to overcome them both as they walked in solemn file over the sand to the clearing.

"So ye've made a wee hame fir yersel's!" commented Hamish staring at the huts in curiosity and admiration. "Did the twa of ye wee lassies build these shelters a' by yersel's, then?"

Indicating that they should all seat themselves on the plaited mats beneath the shade of the overhanging palm, Chantal too sat down. Silently Zambi handed their visitors wooden mugs of lime juice to slake their thirst. When Siméon addressed her with a few words of her own language, she grinned broadly.

Slowly Chantal became aware that three sets of eyes were fastened upon her as her rescuers waited for her to give an account of her adventures. She knew that she could no longer delay telling them about Dinez who would arrive back at the clearing at any minute. But still she hesitated, for apart from the difficulty of explaining her 'marriage,' she was afraid that if she spoke of Dinez' past piracy, she might place him in some danger.

"I have not yet introduced you to Zambi!" she said at last. "She is an ex-slave, and we both owe our lives to a certain Portuguese gentleman who shares our life here on Coetivy!" She glanced at John's face and read not only curiosity there but an unmistakable look of love — a love expressing the devoted affection he had always lavished on her throughout her childhood.

Realizing how greatly she must now hurt him,

she held out her hands to him in an unconscious appeal.

"You must try to understand what life has been like since the shipwreck!" she said. "I will tell you my story as briefly as I can."

No one interrupted Chantal as she gave her account of the past eight months of her life. She omitted nothing other than the details of the strange, compelling force that had drawn her and Dinez together.

"We truly believed that we had no hope of rescue and that we must spend the rest of our lives here — just the three of us," she said. "It seemed reasonable, after half a year had passed by, that we should make some plans for our future. It was then that Dinez and I . . . " her voice faltered for the first time . . . "we decided to get married!" she ended almost inaudibly.

John was on his feet before her last words had died away.

"*Married?*" he echoed. "To a pirate? Have you lost your wits, Chantal?"

"Steady noo, laddie!" interrupted Hamish in his quiet Scottish voice. "The wee girl had been through muckle that we canna fully ken who've nae suffered the like!"

"But a pirate!" John cried. "A murderous renegade . . . "

"John, I beg of you, do not condemn him out of hand. Dinez regrets his past!" Chantal cried. "He is a good man at heart and . . . and he loves me!"

John's face was now flushed with anger.

"The rogue has taken advantage of your

488

isolation and your innocence!" he cried. He reached for his pistol and brandished it above his head. "Let me catch sight of the fellow and I shall have the pleasure of ridding you of this brute!" He broke off and stared down at Chantal in renewed disbelief. "How could you be married with no priest to perform such a ceremony?" he asked.

Chantal was saved a reply by a cry of warning from Zambi. The girl had sensed John's anger without understanding the cause. Instinctively aware of danger threatening Dinez, she shouted again as she saw him approaching the clearing.

With a horrified glance at John's pistol now aimed at the advancing figure, Chantal jumped to her feet and ran to place herself between the two men. At the same time Siméon stepped forward and quickly removed the pistol from John's grasp.

Dinez had seen the pirogue with its two seamen lying in the shade of the boat. The sound of strange voices as he approached the clearing confirmed his suspicions that despite all his hopes to the contrary, rescue had come nonetheless. For several minutes he had contemplated the idea of finding a place of concealment on the island. But Coetivy was too small to offer any lasting refuge were he to be hunted, and he realized that it would be only a matter of time before he was found. Moreover, he had decided, even were he to lose his life in the attempt, he must try to keep Chantal from leaving the island. He had no hope that once they returned to civilization she would remain his 'wife' even if he himself avoided imprisonment by their rescuers. Not without courage, Dinez faced the fact that his love for Chantal was proving greater than his love of life itself.

As Chantal ran to meet him, he put his arms around her protectively. Tears were pouring down her cheeks as she tried to warn Dinez that one of the three men facing him was a member of her family and that he wanted to kill him.

"Calm yourself, Koosh-Koosh!" he said softly. "You forget that I am well accustomed to defending myself!"

As John fought to release himself from Siméon's restraining grasp, Hamish McRae took charge of the situation.

"There'll be nae fightin'!" he said with an authority which his age commanded. He looked at Dinez and continued: "'Tis clear that this young lady owes ye her life, Señor. But as a Britisher and ship's captain, Ah canna ignore the fact that ye're a pirate and as sich, are in defiance o' the British law. Do ye surrender yer person, sir?"

"You seek to arrest me, Captain?" Dinez asked calmly.

"No!" Chantal cried. She turned to John. "You cannot apprehend him, John. I will not let you!"

"'Tis a matter we mun discuss at length and wi' calmness!" Hamish interposed quickly. He glanced closer at Dinez and said: "Do Ah no' recognize ye, sir? Are ye no' by chance the 'Portuguese Hawk?'"

"To admit it would be to invite my hanging, would it not?" said Dinez with a wry smile. He looked at John and said pointedly: "I doubt if Chantal would thank you were you to assist in my demise! She happens to hold me high in her affections!"

John's eyes filled with bitterness as he turned to look at the girl he had traveled so far to find.

"It is true that you . . . you love this outlaw, Chantal?" he asked. It had not escaped his notice that the man was young and despite his unconventional appearance, exceedingly handsome.

For a long moment Chantal did not reply. Then she said almost inaudibly:

"I am Dinez' wife, John — if not by law then in all other ways!"

There could be no mistaking her meaning. Once again John's hands reached for his pistol which fortunately Siméon still had in his possession.

"What is to be done, Captain McRae?" Siméon asked Hamish anxiously.

"'Tis our duty tae hand this mon ower tae the proper authorities!" Hamish replied in an undertone. "But . . . " He paused as John, unable to bear the sight of Dinez' arm lying protectively about Chantal's bare shoulders, strode away from the clearing down to the water's edge. Hamish sighed deeply and then addressed Dinez. "Perhaps ye wad be guid enow', sir, tae let me talk tae the young lady by hersel'?"

Chantal opened her mouth to protest but Dinez, his eyes thoughtful, nodded briefly and walked away in a different direction from that taken by John. Zambi immediately followed him.

"Noo, young lady!" Hamish said in a fatherly fashion to Chantal. "We mun resolve this awkward situation, sae will ye no tell me yer sentiments? Ah canna imagine that it is yer wish fir us tae leave ye here on this island wi' yer pirate, nae matter what has passed between the twa o' ye."

Hamish's soft, kindly voice broke the tension that had been holding Chantal's emotions in check. Tears filled her eyes as she dropped to her knees and covered her face with her hands.

"'Tis true that I would not have married Dinez if I had believed rescue a possibility!" she murmured brokenly. "Perhaps it sounds unbelievable to you, Captain, but I had resigned myself to remaining here for the rest of my life!" She looked at the bearded Scot in appeal for understanding. "Home . . . England . . . my family . . . they had all begun to recede into a long distant past. It has been another world here, a different life from anything you can imagine. And Dinez . . . "

"Aye, yon Dinez?" Hamish prompted gently.

"He has been so good to me!" Chantal cried. "He had me at his mercy, Captain McRae, and yet never took advantage of my helplessness. When I gave myself to him, I did so voluntarily. John has no right to say that

Dinez took advantage of me. He was not to blame."

"Ah understand verra well!" said Hamish soothingly. "But ye mun gie some thought the noo tae young John's feelin's. It canna be easy fir him after sae lang a search findin' the lassie he loves sae dearly wi' anither mon. D'ye love this Dinez da Gama?"

"I do not know!" Chantal replied honestly. "I . . . I thought I did! I have been very happy here with him despite my homesickness. But now, seeing John again, it is as if this world has become the unreal one, and my longing to be home again with my parents is once more uppermost in my mind."

Unnoticed, Siméon had been listening to this interchange. He understood Chantal's confusion perhaps even better than the kindly captain. Tamarisk, too, had succumbed to the magic of these islands and become involved in a relationship with him that was hopelessly out of keeping with her former existence. John's arrival at the plantation bringing memories of her home and family had changed Tamarisk as surely as it must now be changing this young girl.

"Your sister, Tamarisk, will be happy beyond words to see you again!" he said to Chantal persuasively. "You *must* return with us now to Mahé whatever decisions you may choose to make for the future."

Chantal, her tears ceasing, looked up at the young Frenchman apologetically.

"You must think me most unfeeling to have forgotten so easily the wonderful news that my sister too has survived!" she said. "Will you please tell me how she fares? Is she well?"

Whilst Siméon replied, Chantal looked at him properly for the first time. As she took in his neat, conventional attire, she was once again aware of her appearance. She wished desperately that she had a proper dress to wear. The Frenchman reminded her of Antoine de Valle. With renewed bewilderment, she realized that she had given *him* no thought whatever in many months. Yet she had once believed she might become *his* wife! But now . . .

"I have committed myself to Dinez!" she spoke her thoughts aloud.

"Ye're no' legally married tae him, lassie!" Hamish said gently. "And what has ta'en place on this island need nair be known tae the rest o' the world, ye tak me meanin'? Fir yer ain sake and *his*, it canna be allowed tae be known. This mon has a price upon his head. As yer husband, questions wad be asked and he'd no escape the consequences e'en if *we* a' agreed tae remain quiet aboot his past misdeeds. Yer family, the Commissioner — everyone wad be askin' who was this mon ye'd 'wed' and sooner or later he wad be recognized. D'ye no understand this, lassie?"

He saw the look of horror in Chantal's eyes and added:

"There's mebbe a way by which we can resolve the matter. We could take ye wi' us and leave da Gama here!"

"Leave Dinez here . . . on Coetivy . . . alone?" Chantal cried aghast.

494

"'Twould be a deal better than hangin'!" Hamish said quietly.

"Nor would he be quite alone!" remarked Siméon thoughtfully. "He would have the African girl for company. She seemed devoted to him."

Zambi! Chantal had forgotten her. The Frenchman's reminder was both apt and timely as she considered the Captain's proposal. Before she herself had come into Dinez' life, he had taken Zambi for his concubine. Were she, Chantal, to leave him alone on Coetivy with Zambi, he would of a certainty renew that relationship. Zambi would be happy enough but what of Dinez who loved her, Chantal, with a passion and sincerity that she could not doubt?

"Dinez would want to go with me!" she said thoughtfully, "even were he to put his life at risk!"

"Then can you not persuade him that you do not want him!" said Siméon. "You could tell him that you love John and that it is your intention to return to England and marry him legally!"

"Aye!" agreed Hamish. "That could well be the answer!" He saw the tears welling into Chantal's eyes and said gently: "It'll no' be easy fir ye, lassie, but the mon saved yer life, did he no'? And if ye do as St. Clair suggests, ye can save his in return. Ye dinna want tae stay here wi' him fir the rest o' yer life, d'ye noo?"

"I do not know!" Chantal murmured. But

495

even as she spoke, she knew that John's arrival on Coetivy had changed everything, renewing her desire to be safely back with her family; renewing her misgivings as to her real feelings for Dinez; renewing her longing for books, for music, for her pony, for pretty dresses and friends and dances. Her longing to see her beloved Papa was so intense that for this alone she could not watch John sail away with the Frenchman and the Captain as if they had never discovered her on Coetivy.

But at the same time, she did not know how she could find the courage to tell Dinez that she was going to leave him; nor how she herself could face the fact that she might never see him again — and of a certainty never lie with him again.

Color stained her cheeks as memory brought back to mind the long, hot nights of loving. Dinez had taught her in so many ways how wonderful such love could be. If the union of their minds had never quite matched the union of their bodies, their shared delight in one another had seemed perfectly satisfying. Determinedly Chantal had closed her mind to the knowledge that they were not lawfully wed and she had submitted herself to Dinez without reserve.

Now John's shocked and horrified expression had come like a sword piercing her consciousness; making her painfully aware of her lapse from purity. He had stared at her as if she were unchaste . . . a harlot even. His scorn had both angered and hurt her. She doubted if he would ever understand how long and lonely the days had been at first and how strong the temptation to give way to Dinez' passionate demands.

"There's nae real choice but tae leave da Gama here!" Hamish's voice broke into her reflections. "Ah, fir one, will gie ye ma wurd that Ah'll no mention his presence here, and Ah dinna doot Monsieur St. Clair and John wull aye do the same. As fir the future, who kens but anither boat — Portuguese perhaps, wull stop by and find him and he can return tae his ain country in safety. Do ye no' agree wi' me, lassie?"

The Captain's suggestion did indeed seem the only possible solution, Chantal thought, as she watched John's tall, slim figure returning to the clearing. How elegant and manly he looked. Yet how grim and unforgiving his face! But for all his disapproval, she could not but feel a swift joy at seeing him. She had thought never to set eyes upon him again.

As John rejoined them, studiously avoiding Chantal's abject figure crouched in the sand, Hamish motioned him to be seated whilst he outlined his proposal.

"We canna hand the fellow tae the gallows when he saved yer lassie's life!" the Captain ended with an uneasy glance at John's white angry face. "Let us remember why we are here, John. We hae found the person we were searchin' for alive and well and fir that we should thank God and no' ask fir retribution, d'ye no' agree?"

John drew a deep breath. He was secretly

497

relieved to hear that Chantal was willing to leave the island and her pirate, despite her so called 'marriage' to the villain. Alone with his thoughts and fears this past ten minutes, he had faced up to the fact that da Gama had clearly taken excellent care of Chantal. For all the raggedness of her brief clothing, she showed no signs of malnutrition. On the contrary she looked round and glowing with good health. In truth he had never seen her look more womanly and desirable, John decided. Jealousy took hold of him once more and he was filled with a longing to challenge his rival, and if possible, kill the man who had stolen his love and despoiled her for ever more. Even were Chantal willing, he could never marry her now. The ghost of da Gama would ever lie between them.

Sickened by such thoughts John harkened to Hamish's advice and agreed reluctantly to go along with his suggestion. As Hamish had said the only important question now was to remove Chantal as quickly as possible from the island.

"Then 'tis agreed!" said Hamish. "Wull Ah speak wi' da Gama or wull ye, lassie?" he asked Chantal.

Chantal hesitated. It seemed cowardly to leave Hamish McRae to be the one to break Dinez' heart — yet she doubted if she herself had the courage to go through with their intention were Dinez to plead with her. Were he to look at her from those compelling green eyes and say, "*Koosh-Koosh do not leave me!*" she would be torn in two. Nor would the parting from Zambi be easy either. She could imagine the dark puzzled eyes trying to understand a situation that was beyond her.

"Ah'll gae and find him!" Hamish said, sensing Chantal's indecision. "'Twill mebbe sound better comin' from me!" Without further delay, he set off in the direction Dinez had taken.

Chantal expected that when the Captain returned, Dinez and Zambi would be with him. When Hamish returned alone, she ran to him with a sudden terrible fear clutching at her heart.

"You have not killed him?" she gasped.

The old Scot regarded her with a kindly smile.

"Noo what should put that idea intae yer wee head!" he said. "Tae tell ye the truth, Ah like yon mon fir 'a he's a rogue. He gi'ed me this message fir ye. He said I wus tae tell ye that he wad always love ye; that he had nair been able to gie ye anthin' because on Coetivy he had naught tae gie. But the noo, he could gie ye what ye always wanted — freedom tae gae back tae yers ain country wi' the mon ye love. Ye gae wi' his love and his prayers fir yer happiness! Yon's a gentlemon speakin' for a' he's a pirate!" he added thoughtfully.

He pulled out a 'kerchief and handed it to Chantal as the tears coursed down her cheeks.

"There noo, ma puir bairn!" he said. "Ye'll soon feel better when ye're back wi' yer ain folk. Yer sister will be takkin' care o ye a wee while. Whist noo! Ye're doin' the right thing, lassie — fier yer ainsel' and fir him, too."

499

He was too kindhearted to break the news yet awhile to the unhappy girl that Dinez had admitted to keeping Chantal a prisoner on the island for his own sake; that on two occasions he had seen ships out to sea and deliberately refrained from lighting the fire that would have signaled their presence on Coetivy.

"I saw your ship, too, as you sailed in!" Dinez had told the shocked Hamish. "I was going to run to the clearing, get my panga and kill the first man to set foot on the beach. But . . . " he paused, shrugging his shoulders helplessly. "I have never loved another woman so I cannot say if love always weakens a man as it has weakened the 'Portuguese Hawk.' I knew it would break Chantal's heart to see me kill her rescuers; that I would instantly lose her respect, her affection."

"Ye had tae lose her either way!" Hamish remarked not entirely without sympathy for the fellow. He promised to leave Dinez what provisions were aboard *Seasprite*. "There's baccy and whuskey, rum, flour and cheese," he said. "An'll send one o' ma crew back wi' them in the pirogue and if e'er Ah'm this way agin, Ah'll stop by and see how ye're farin'."

The two men shook hands and Dinez stood silent, motionless as Hamish returned to the clearing.

On board *Seasprite*, Chantal went to the cabin where she wept uncontrollably. Hamish stood on deck watching as two of his crew ferried provisions to the island. He could see no sign of the pirate nor of the African girl, Zambi. But when at last the moment came to hoist sail, he called Chantal to come up on deck, for he could see a thin column of smoke rising from the highest point of the island. Both of them knew it was Dinez da Gama's way of bidding Chantal farewell.

25

August 1839

MAVREEN looked at Perry, her eyes misty with tears, her hands trembling as she held the pages of Tamarisk's letter.

"'Tis clear she has written to us several times previously!" she said. "Unaware that we have not received them, she could not anticipate what shock this letter would give us!"

Perry put his arm about her shoulders.

"But what wonderful news she sends, my love!" he exclaimed. "To think that both she and Chantal are alive. I can scarce believe it!" He broke off as his voice became husky with emotion.

"We must tell Charles presently!" Mavreen said. "But first I must regain my composure lest my excitement communicate itself to him. The physician insists he must be kept calm at all times if he is to continue to make such excellent recovery."

She had scanned the closely penned lines only briefly, too overcome by joy fully to understand the astonishing news Tamarisk related. Now, as Perry seated himself beside her, they read together the lengthy epistle with careful attention. It was dated the end of June.

'I am writing to you from the house of Mr. Mylius, the Civil Commissioner for Mahé. John, Captain McRae, Siméon St. Clair and I were invited here as his guests following upon the miraculous discovery of our dearest Chantal. I have thought many times how I could break this news to you more gently but now I am pressed for time because HMS Grampion is departing for England on the morrow and John has agreed with me that I should advise you of our impending return lest we cause you an even greater shock by our subsequent unannounced arrival.'

"As, indeed, it would have done!" interposed Perry, with a deep-drawn sigh.

'It was suggested by John that Chantal and I might take passage home on Grampion, leaving him to follow next week in Seasprite with Captain McRae. However, Chantal is not yet ready to undertake the voyage for reasons I will presently give you. I hasten to assure you, however, that she is quite well and deeply desirous of being reunited with you both — as, indeed, am I.

'You will know from my previous letters that I was convalescing at the home of Siméon St. Clair. When John and the Captain arrived so unexpectedly, having been told of my whereabouts by the Commissioner, I was already planning my return to England. However, it was John's intention before we

503

came home to search EVERY island in the Seychelles group in the vain hope finding Chantal. He, Siméon, who accompanied him, and the Captain were on the point of giving up hope after they had visited most of the ninety or so islands without result. Then quite suddenly as if by a miracle, they came upon Chantal living on a tiny island called Coetivy some 200 miles from here . . . '

"To think that I attempted to dissuade John from going upon that journey!" Mavreen cried. "But for him, Chantal might never have been found!"

"He held some strange inner conviction that she was still alive — even when we had despaired for her life!" Perry agreed. "I have much to thank John for!"

He and Mavreen resumed their reading.

'As you may imagine, nine months upon an uninhabited island had greatly changed Chantal's appearance and I fear it came as a shock to poor John to find her so. Not only was her skin burned as brown as a native's but she was practically without clothes and living much as do the African workers here, in a palm-thatched hut, her only companions a Portuguese pirate and an African girl the man had once rescued from a slaver. Chantal told us that she believed they would never be found. Coetivy is not on a trade route and it is too far from the main island of Mahé for fishermen to go there. She therefore agreed

after seven months had passed to marry the Portuguese who from all accounts, was well born, exceedingly handsome and deeply in love with her . . . '

Mavreen saw the clenching of Perry's fists as they reached this point in Tamarisk's letter.

"My little skylark, married to a pirate!" he exclaimed in a horrified tone of voice.

"No, my dear, not lawfully married!" Mavreen said soothingly. "Let us read further and mayhap we will understand this situation the better."

'Of course, such a marriage could not legally be ratified and having spoken to Chantal about her so-called wedding, I have ascertained that it was no more than an exchange of vows. However, for the following six weeks they lived together as man and wife. This, of course, has distressed John very deeply although I have no doubt that his love for Chantal is as strong as ever. As for Chantal herself, now that she has returned to civilization, I fear she is very confused. It is quite clear to me that she had a deep affection for this man whom I have promised not to name. He was exceedingly kind and attentive to her and at all times gentle and considerate. Her loyalty to him is deep-rooted — and not without good cause since unquestionably he saved her life . . . '

"A fact you, too, must bear in mind before you condemn him!" said Mavreen gently. His

505

face stern, Perry took the letter from her and read aloud:

"*Nevertheless, the man was a pirate of some considerable notoriety and there was and still is a price on his head. To have brought him back here to Mahé would have meant his almost certain capture and eventual hanging. Out of consideration for Chantal's feelings, it was agreed to leave him and the native girl on the island — this being in his own interest. I think John might have killed him had the opportunity been given him but the Captain and Siméon were fortunately able to ensure that such drastic measures were not called for against the man who had saved Chantal's life.*

"*Chantal remains confused and tearful. Yesterday, she spoke of returning to the island so that her 'husband' would not be left lonely and abandoned, pointing out to me that legal or otherwise, she had made her marriage vows before God and that it was her moral duty to stand by them. It was at this point that I felt compelled to tell her a somewhat unsavory truth I had heard about the pirate. He had confessed to Captain McRae that he had deliberately failed to light the fire that would have signaled their presence on the island to two ships that passed near them on different occasions. He knew that their rescue would probably result in the loss of Chantal and was not prepared*

506

even for her sake to risk such an eventuality. I think I was able to convince her that true love is manifested by unselfishness; that had this man really loved her as she supposes, her happiness would have been more important to him than his own selfish desire to keep her. Since this talk, Chantal has not spoken again of returning to the island and this morning she was expressing her impatient longing to see you both again."

"Thank God!" Perry murmured. "My poor little Chantal!"

"Poor John, too!" added Mavreen. "Tamarisk goes on to say that he is nearly as confused as your daughter!"

"He is trying to hide his love for her from Chantal," Mavreen now read. "He and Siméon spend a great deal of time in the company of the Commissioner's two pretty nieces, but it is obvious to me that John is only flirting with young Phoebe in order to make Chantal jealous. Not entirely without success, I might add, for she has but half-hour since commented that he is making himself quite ridiculous the way he fawns upon Phoebe! Chantal herself has retired to her room where she insists upon remaining. Only I am allowed to see her. She insists that John lacks in understanding and that she knows he despises her for her behavior on the island.

"I hope that by the time we all reach England, the extraordinary events that have overtaken us since last we saw you will have begun to seem like a distant dream to all of us. Nevertheless I know from past experience that no one remains quite unchanged by life's vicissitudes and I hope that this letter will prepare you for such changes as you may find in us.

"I am writing a brief letter to Charles and I am sure I do not need to tell you how much I long to see you all."

Mavreen laid down the letter with a sigh.

"Tamarisk says nothing of her own experiences," she said thoughtfully. "But doubtless she told us of her adventures in the earlier letters that did not reach us. Do you not think that she herself has gained in maturity, Perry? It seems so short a while ago that she was Chantal's age and without a sensible thought in her head!"

"You are forgetting the passage of time!" Perry reminded her with a fond smile. "Tamarisk has passed her fortieth birthday! Now, my love, let us go and inform the children that their mother will soon be home; then we will go and talk with Charles."

Charles' recovery had been slow but steady. His sight was now fully restored and the physicians were contemplating passing him fit once more for naval duties. The news that Tamarisk was shortly to be restored to him was all he required to fill his cup of happiness to the brim.

"I am the most fortunate of men, am I not?" he said to Mavreen and Perry. "Let us pray they are all enjoying a safe journey home!"

The voyage was progressing without mishap, but none of *Seasprite*'s passengers were anticipating their arrival in England with the same joyful enthusiasm as those who awaited them. Tamarisk was grateful that she had Chantal's problems to occupy her time and thoughts, for without them she would have been even more prone to the bouts of loneliness and sadness that followed her parting with Siméon. She reminded herself constantly that at least he had not suffered too severely by her departure, due in a large part to her emotional withdrawal from him. Whilst they resided at the Mylius' house in l'Établissement du Roi he had turned more and more frequently to the carefree company of young Janet. The blow to his pride caused by Tamarisk's apparent indifference was compensated by the girl's obvious adoration.

But Tamarisk herself could not so easily forget those long magical nights at the Château Corail. Nor could she dismiss from her memory her whole-hearted surrender to those passions that should have belonged to her youth but which she had discovered for the first time in the arms of her young lover.

She thought very often of Charles and made up her mind that she must confess her unfaithfulness to him. She tried to convince herself that Siméon's memory would soon recede into the past. Perhaps then, she thought, she might be able to recapture with Charles some of the emotional contentment she had shared with her island lover. Much would depend upon Charles' understanding.

During the long months at sea, John began to come to terms with Chantal's fall from the idealistic pedestal upon which he had placed her. Discussing his emotions with Tamarisk, he admitted his involvement with the young French girl, Fleur Dubois; and Tamarisk was able to point out to him that nature was a very pungent force and not only men but women, too, were easy prey to her dictates.

"There is a world of difference, John dear, between loose-living women with no moral scruples and those who occasionally lapse from that state of chastity men expect of them," Tamarisk commented. "It is often those men who condemn the fallen who tempt women to enjoy their natural desires!"

Fleur had spoken on very similar lines, John thought. He had not condemned *her*! But then he had not loved Fleur as he loved Chantal. He now realized that it was because he loved Chantal so much that the knowledge of her surrender to another man hurt him so deeply. He accepted the logic of Tamarisk's reply when he complained that were he ever to marry Chantal, he feared the ghost of Dinez da Gama would share their bed.

"And would not Fleur's ghost share it also were Chantal to know of that relationship?" Tamarisk had countered.

John's attitude to Chantal softened markedly as the weeks at sea passed in slow monotony. More and more often he sought her out where she stood at the stern gazing across the white-capped waters in silent misery.

They were not regretful thoughts of her separation from Dinez da Gama that brought such an unhappy expression to her dark, tearless eyes. It was regret that she had allowed him to possess her body, and by so doing, ruin for ever her chances to rebuild her life and make a conventional marriage.

Chantal saw in John's revived attentions to her not the love which in fact prompted them, but a pitying kindness. Her pride forced her to reject his advances although secretly she longed to enjoy the comfort of his arms. She now realized that John's loving devotion had encompassed her throughout her life and that she had taken it as much for granted as the air she breathed or the warmth of the sun. It was only now when she thought it denied to her for evermore that she was beginning to appreciate what she had lost.

Her feelings of bitterness towards Dinez lessened slowly as time passed. When first she learned that he had deliberately deceived her by ignoring the passing vessels that might have rescued them, she had wanted to kill him. His betrayal had seemed a total negation of the love he professed to have for her. But now she was coming to terms with the fact that Dinez had never lived by conventional standards; that he had always taken what he wanted without pretense or preamble. She blamed herself for her weakness in not withstanding the temptation to give way to him. She could even admit the truth to herself — that she had wanted to be loved by him; and not least that she had ceased to search the horizon for possible rescue so contented was she in their strange way of life. She knew that by now Dinez would have resumed his relationship with Zambi; that Zambi would be happy. Surprisingly, the thought did not distress her.

Chantal expressed openly to Tamarisk her relief that she had not found herself with child. Zambi too had been childless, Chantal said, and they discussed the possibility that a man, like a woman, might be barren, since there was no other reason they could think of for Chantal's fortunate escape.

"You can now forget your ordeal as I had to forget mine in my youth!" Tamarisk said comfortingly. But Chantal shook her head.

"I will never be able to forget Dinez, the island, or the life we shared. Mine was no unhappy experience as was yours, Tamarisk. I have left a part of myself on Coetivy that I can never reclaim."

"'Tis your childhood you have left behind you," Tamarisk said wisely. "Now you must look to the future, Chantal, as I am looking to mine. I too, have left a little of myself behind me, you know. I grew very fond of Siméon during those months I shared my life with him."

"I suppose you missed your own children very much and Siméon St. Clair was like a son to you," Chantal replied innocently.

Not without a degree of bitterness, Tamarisk reflected that Chantal's words proved what she had always known to be the truth — that she could never have married Siméon even had she been the widow she supposed herself. The world would have seen them as Chantal did — not as husband and wife, but as mother and son.

In London, Barre House hummed with activity as Mavreen prepared for the return of her loved ones. Chantal's bed-chamber was redecorated with a pretty jasmine-flowered Chinese paper. The largest of the guest chambers was turned out, cleaned, polished and refurbished ready for Tamarisk to occupy with Charles. The elderly Baroness was still confined to her bed in a state of senility, making it undesirable for the younger members of the family to return home.

"There is more than enough room for them here!" Mavreen told Perry. "And it pleases me to have them all under our roof!"

With a thoughtfulness that Perry so often remarked in his beloved Mavreen, she wrote inviting Julia Lade to visit them so that Chantal could be reunited with her childhood friend.

"They will have so much to tell one another!" Mavreen said. "And poor little Julia has not been to stay here since Chantal left us over a year ago. The child will welcome the break from home!"

Amongst so much domestic hustle and bustle, Perry sought more masculine company in the person of the convalescent Charles. Over the years they had not spent many hours in conversation with each other, for they met for the most part only at social and family gatherings. Charles had ever tended to be quiet and reserved even after many promotions in the Navy. But with increasing years and responsibilities he had lost much of his former shyness and now the two men found it agreeable to discuss portending events.

Of the two men Charles was the more aware of the changes that they might have to face in their returning loved ones. When Perry vouchsafed that he could scarce wait to hold his little girl in his arms again, Charles commented shrewdly:

"'Tis unlikely Chantal will return to us as a child, Sir. From all Tamarisk tells us, I think we shall discover Chantal a young woman who may well have said farewell to her childhood. Mayhap we should take our cue from Tamarisk and make no prejudgements about Chantal until we know more of her strange life this past year!"

Perry nodded, hiding his surprise at the profundity of Charles' advice.

"You speak but seldom Charles, but when you do, 'tis always with a great deal of sense!" he said. "No wonder you have been raised to the rank of Rear Admiral if you handle your men as you do your women! I do not imagine — and you will forgive me for speaking so plainly knowing how deeply I love Tamarisk — that your married life has always been such plain sailing as your career in the Navy. She was an unhappy child in many ways, as you know, and met with much misfortune. You are to be complimented in achieving so contented a union!"

Charles remained silent, his loyalty to his wife far too strong to allow him to speak of the one part of their marriage that had failed.

No matter how Tamarisk had tried to hide her revulsion of the human passions she unconsciously evoked in him, he had ever been aware of her feelings. Reluctantly he had reached the conclusion that for both their sakes, he must cease to ask of her that side of love he craved. Not very often, but from time to time, he had resorted to the comfort of other women — females whom he could suitably reward with money, and quickly forget. Such encounters were few and very discreet and Tamarisk knew nothing of them. Charles himself sometimes wondered bitterly if she would even care if she did know.

He thought of her homecoming with a deep, silent ache of longing. If it were only possible for him to take her in his arms, show his love for her in the deep, passionate way that would have been natural to him! But he would have to restrain himself; kiss her hand, her cheek with tenderness but with no hint of his need for her.

The man now sitting opposite him could have no idea, Charles thought, how deeply he envied him his relationship with Tamarisk's mother. It was impossible not to be aware in their company of the bond between them. It was even apparent in the warm looks they exchanged; in the tiny intimate caresses that they believed passed unnoticed. A discerning observer could see that even at their ages they were passionately in love.

But as always Charles fought his envy and his self-pity and determined to make Tamarisk's return entirely as she would wish it. Nevertheless when the moment finally came for the great doors of Barre House to open and he saw his wife for the first time in nearly a year, his heart pounded unmercifully in his chest and he knew himself as much a victim of her beauty as he had been the first time he set eyes upon her. She looked astonishingly young and pretty — almost as if ten years had dropped away from her.

Catching sight of him, Tamarisk ran into his open arms.

"My dearest Charles!" she cried, staring up into his face with genuine excitement. "You are quite well again? No, do not answer for I can see for myself that *you* can see me! Tell me, how do I look to you?"

Unable to prevaricate in this moment of emotion, Charles said huskily, "More beautiful and more desirable than ever, my lovely Tamarisk!"

Despite the many people now crowded in the great hall, Charles and Tamarisk seemed to exist in a tiny world of their own. As Chantal, John and the Captain were in turn hugged and greeted by Perry and Mavreen, Tamarisk saw only Charles' face. Her eyes were thoughtful as her ears registered the deep undertone of love in her husband's voice. She could feel the trembling of his arms as he held her and she was aware of the heavy thudding of his heart.

"Oh, my dear!" she whispered as she sensed with a new intuition the depths of his feeling for her. To her own astonishment and his, she made no move to draw back from him but reached up her hand and gently touched his eyes with her fingertips.

"Perhaps you were not the only one to have been blind, Charles!" she said so softly that none but he could hear. "I too have lived in darkness. But now . . . now perhaps everything will be different. We will talk, my dear . . . later. But first I must see our children. Are they not here?"

"They have gone to the Park with their governess!" Charles explained. He could not fully comprehend the change in Tamarisk nor dared he allow himself to hope that her words promised a new kind of marriage for them both. But if it were true he cared not one jot what miracle had brought this about. He would ask no more of life's bounty if not only was his wife returned to him from the dead, but that at long last she would truly be his wife in every way.

Later that night when they were at last quite alone, Tamarisk sat brushing her hair at her dressing table whilst Charles lay in the big four-poster watching her with intense delight.

"You have sat there quite long enough!" he chided her gently. "Will you not come to bed now?"

Tamarisk laid down her hairbrush and drew a deep breath. Her face betrayed her anxiety.

"First I must talk with you, Charles. I . . . I

517

have so much more to tell you of my life at Château Corail than I told the family during dinner. My very last desire is to spoil my homecoming for either of us. It has been so perfect until now, but I cannot deceive you, Charles, and . . . ”

“Come here and sit beside me!” Charles interrupted quietly. “You have no need to be afraid of me, Tamarisk. You know that!” he added as he saw her hesitation.

At once Tamarisk rose and hurried to the bedside.

“I am not afraid of you, Charles. ’Tis rather that I am ashamed and loath to hurt you.”

He reached out and took both her hands in his.

“My dearest, I have not been married to you for nigh on twenty years without coming to know you very well indeed,” he said. “And therefore you have no need to struggle to find words that will not hurt me. I know already what you have to tell me.”

As Tamarisk stared at him in astonishment, Charles went on quietly:

“Each time you mentioned his name . . . Siméon, is it not . . . your voice softened; even your body softened. You spoke of him as being a boy, but not too young, I realized, to have been your lover! It was easy once I had guessed this much, to understand why you took so long to return to England.”

Tears stung Tamarisk’s eyes.

“Charles, I believed you dead!” she cried.

“I know! And not without reason. Tamarisk,

I am not blaming you. From all you told us, I realize that those islands you described must have an atmosphere of love that is hard to resist. Alone with a young man who doubtless fell in love with you, the trappings of society and convention so far away, it does not surprise me that you were tempted to reciprocate his feelings. My only puzzlement is that *I know you have always feared intimacy with men, with me!* What could that boy give you that I could not? I was young too when first we married and I loved you, as I still do, with passionate devotion. Where did I fail, Tamarisk? That is all I want to know!"

Tamarisk turned and put her arms around him.

"My dearest, the failure was not yours but mine. We married too soon after my raping. Each time you came to me, I saw not your need of me but Galvanti's brutish desire. I do not wish to talk of Siméon as I know it must hurt you, yet I have to speak of him so that you may understand. Will you permit me, Charles?"

"I welcome any words, however painful, that will enable us to reach an understanding."

"Then I must tell you that Siméon had never had a woman. He was afraid of himself and the forces within him. In helping him to overcome *his* fears, I forgot my own. You, Galvanti, my past life might never have existed. I wanted only to help him. And suddenly, I discovered that I too had desires, passions that I had not known existed. It was not until then I began to understand how I had failed you. I never

519

knew . . . I never realized . . . I must have made you so unhappy. Yet even now you do not condemn me!"

"For denying me? For your unfaithfulness?" Charles asked. "No, Tamarisk! You tried so hard to be what I wanted, to give me what I needed, and as to your unfaithfulness, I will welcome it for bringing us to this new understanding. Do you not see, my darling, that this can prove the most wonderful blessing for us both? It is not too late for us to rebuild our marriage. Tamarisk, I love you, I have always loved you! I need you now . . . perhaps more than I ever have! I cannot live without you!"

"*I cannot live without you!*" The words brought back a swift stabbing memory of Siméon who had made the same declaration to her. Yet even before she had left Mahé, Siméon was learning to live very happily without her. But Charles . . .

"Oh, my dear!" she whispered. "I pray that this time I shall not fail you. Do you understand what I am trying to tell you? I need you, too, Charles! Perhaps even more than you need me!"

With a glad cry of unbearable excitement, Charles removed the nightrobe from her shoulders and began to kiss her with passionate intensity. Tamarisk closed her eyes, feeling the first stirring of desire stealing over her.

"It is going to be all right," she thought as her last remaining vestige of fear gave way to a now familiar need. Her body arched toward her husband's. Instinct guided Charles as he took

520

her with a boy's impatient determination. He was gentle, caring, yet his insistence brooked no refusal. He gave her no time to pause, to think, to regret, to remember, but swept her along with him on the tide of his own longing until at last they reached together the quiet shores of content.

In the darkness Tamarisk lay beside him, her breathing slowing as coherent thought returned. For a brief moment the ghost of Siméon St. Clair came into the bed and touched her mind with wistful memory. But then he was gone and only Charles remained, his eyes glowing with deepest tenderness as he stared down in perfect happiness at the woman he loved.

26

December 1839

CHANTAL surveyed the light blue flowered silk evening dress which she had worn at a ball given by the young Queen Victoria when the Court moved to Brighton for an autumn holiday in the month of October. The dress had been sent from Paris by Mama's kind friend, the authoress George Sand.

Poor Julia, who had not attended the Ball at the Royal Pavilion, never tired of hearing about the occasion. The Queen, but a year younger than Chantal, had actually complimented her upon the dress which had pleased Mama as well as Chantal and caused Julia's eyes to widen in vicarious excitement.

"I wish you could have been there, Julia!" Chantal said with a deep sigh. "I know that I have so many more of life's blessings than do you and I have no right whatever to be unhappy. You must think me so ungrateful!"

Julia's round, plump face showed her concern.

"'Tis not that I think you ungrateful, dearest Chantal," she replied. "But I cannot understand your reluctance to accept the solution to your unhappiness. You know John loves you with all his heart; and yet you continue to deny him despite his many proposals."

Chantal drew another deep sigh.

"Surely you, Julia, who know John almost as well as I, must realize that a marriage between us could not bring either of us any lasting contentment. If, as you believe, John is desirous of marrying me, then it is not because he wants me for his wife but because unselfishly, he is seeking to rectify the confusion and folly of my life. He has always tried to take care of me ever since I was a little girl and now . . . now I am convinced he feels sorry for me!"

Julia's cheeks colored with indignation.

"'Tis not pity but love that John feels for you, Chantal. I am certain that he has quite forgiven you for your . . . your marriage to . . . to that man!" Her blush deepened as she recalled Chantal's confessions of intimacy with the Portuguese pirate — a daring adventure she was happy not to have been party to.

"But I do not want John's forgiveness!" Chantal cried. "Dinez was a rogue and he deceived me, but he did not force me. It would be unjust to him not to admit that I wanted to marry him, Julia."

The younger girl looked shocked.

"Then you do not regret what took place on that island?" she asked.

"In some ways, yes, and in others, no, by which I mean that I cannot feel that what passed between Dinez and me was evil or wrong. Yet I do regret that John, Papa, people I love like you, must ever regard me now as unchaste, despoiled. I did not need Mama to remind me that I have lost forever that most precious gift a bride can offer the man she is to marry — her virginity."

"But if John has proposed marriage to you, Chantal, he cannot set such store by these matters as you fear!" Julia said thoughtfully. She supposed that like herself, John too, had noticed an indefinable change in Chantal. She seemed now to be far more than two years older than herself and the spontaneous gaiety and innocence which had been so characteristic of her were quite absent. But she was unarguably more beautiful than ever.

"I do not believe that John will ever forgive me — not deep down in his heart!" Chantal said. "I have forfeited his respect and if I cannot have that, I cannot hope to have his love! Let us forget my concerns, for there is much for us to do downstairs!"

It was nearing the festive season of Christmas and the year was drawing to its close. Mavreen had sent out two hundred invitations to a Grand Ball to be held at Barre House, partly in belated celebration of John's coming-of-age, partly to celebrate the miraculous survival and return to the family of Tamarisk, Charles and Chantal.

Five months had passed since *Seasprite* had sailed safely into harbor and the family had been reunited — five months that had by no means been happy ones for Chantal. And John was the cause of her distress.

During the voyage home he had shown her great kindness and attention; but the easy, uncomplicated affection they had enjoyed as children was markedly absent in this new relationship. John had ceased to be the elder brother, authoritative, teasing, fondly affectionate. He was now reserved and restrained in his conversation and the subject of Dinez' and Chantal's life on the island was never mentioned between them.

It was not until the family removed to Brighton to enjoy a short seaside holiday in emulation of the Court that John suddenly and without warning proposed marriage to Chantal.

"I love you! I think I have always loved you!" he said. But he had made no move to touch her, not even to take her hand in his. "I want to spend my life taking care of you, Chantal. Will you marry me?"

To their mutual embarrassment, Chantal had burst into tears and fled from the room. If John had followed her, she wondered now as she preceded Julia down the great staircase into the hall, might she have given way to the desire to accept his proposal? If he had taken her in his arms and kissed her as she longed to be kissed, held her so close that she could feel certain of his determination to keep her near him, would she have ignored her doubts and misgivings as to his real motives?

Chantal had spent many sleepless nights pondering upon the matter. Tamarisk had tried to explain John's feelings to her. He had suffered a great blow to his self-esteem, she said.

"He has always idolized you, Chantal. He had placed you on a pedestal where you reigned supreme, the perfection of his dreams. When he discovered you were no less human than he, he could not at first reconcile himself to the loss of that dream of goodness, purity, innocence. But he has slowly come to terms with the truth, Chantal, and has discovered that he still loves you as deeply as ever. It is not John's love you should be questioning, but your own. Do you not love him?"

The question remained in Chantal's mind to torment her. She did not know the answer. She respected, admired, needed John, and he was dear to her in so many different ways. But she had learned another kind of love on the island of Coetivy. If human passions consumed John, then they lurked unseen in his heart for he never gave them expression. Not even to Tamarisk, and far less to Julia who now seemed like a child to Chantal, could she explain her misgivings when she thought of marriage to John. She knew now that her body had needs and hungers of its own and that to live without passionate love would never satisfy her. Her relationship with Dinez, though limited to mutual bodily pleasure, had been nonetheless totally rewarding in this respect and she could not regret the experience even whilst she realized that she had lost more than she had gained by it.

Were it not for Dinez, she thought, she would readily have agreed to marry John whom she loved with her heart and mind. Secretly she wondered how she would feel were John to take her in his arms, kiss her, love her as Dinez had done. Surveying him across the room, she would trace with her eyes the curve of his mouth, the slim, smooth line of his hips, the delicate grace of his hands and imagine them on her naked body. Her heart would quicken and her limbs tremble with growing excitement. And then ... then John would cross the room and perhaps invite her to a game of backgammon or piquet or enquire if she would like a glass of wine, and the moment would be lost, the magic gone. She asked herself again and again how John could express his love for her and yet be void of desire. Each time the only answer she could find was that John could not bring himself to touch her knowing that she had once belonged to another man.

Tonight there would be dancing in the great salon. Mama had engaged an orchestra and there would be many waltzes played. Of a certainty, John would invite her to dance and would perforce have to take her in his arms. Then perhaps, she would discover his true feelings if, indeed, he were hiding them from her. If he would kiss her but once, Chantal thought with a faint thrill of excitement. She quickened her pace as she and Julia entered the huge room with its great crystal chandeliers. All around stood massive vases and urns of flowers, the arrangement of which the two girls had come to supervise. Tonight she would be wearing another new dress, of white embroidered satin, the sleeves wide and cut open in the latest fashion. The dark coloring of her skin by the sun on Coetivy had long since faded. Her hair was fashionably coifed à la Clothilde — braided in two smooth loops either side of her face and caught in a chignon at the back of her neck. Papa had given her for her nineteenth birthday in November a circlet of diamonds to wear on just such a grand occasion. Chantal knew that she would look like a princess and yet she could not be sure that John would see her so.

Although in Chantal's mind the memories of her life on Coetivy were still vivid and unforgettable, in John's mind they were receding swiftly into a past he was determined to forget. Only occasionally did he see a sudden picture of Chantal, half-naked, barefooted, tanned by the sun, running across the white sand of the island beach. He knew himself deeply jealous and resentful of the tall, strong, handsome pirate who had taken possession of the girl he loved. Yet secretly he did not blame the man, for who could have resisted Chantal's beauty in such circumstances, he asked himself? Such were the primitive conditions of that tropical island, John could well understand how conventional standards had given way to primitive needs.

The memory of Chantal's bared breasts scarcely concealed by her long, dark hair tormented his dreams and filled him with feelings of guilt that he could harbor such lustful thoughts about her. With conscious effort he pushed them from him in her presence, deliberately avoiding any physical contact with her, lest his desire reasserted itself and betrayed him. He was determined that she should see only respect and adoration from him and be in no doubt that he held her in the highest regard unlike the Portuguese fellow who had debased her.

"Give her time to readjust to a normal way of life!" Perry had advised him when he told his

528

stepfather that Chantal had rejected his proposal of marriage. "I am aware of your impatience but do not rush her, John. You are both very young . . . and there is no hurry!"

But it was now eight months since they had left the Seychelles; and John was praying that when he proposed again tonight, Chantal would not refuse him. The magnificent ball his mother had planned would, he hoped, encourage a mood for romantic flirtation. When he held Chantal in his arms as they waltzed around the glittering candlelit room, she must surely realize as he did that they belonged together, not just for one dance, but for always!

But the moment for which, unknown to one another, both John and Chantal were so anxiously awaiting, was not destined to take place. Only the first few guests had arrived and were being received by the family when one of the footmen approached John and discreetly handed him a letter upon a silver salver.

"'Tis marked URGENT, sir!" the servant said. "I thought you might require to read it at once. There is a foreign lad — French, I think, waiting in the servants' hall for your reply!" Nonplussed but curious, John excused himself from the family group and stepped aside whilst he opened and read the letter. The contents were startling enough to cause him to gasp aloud. Hurriedly he went over to his mother and Perry. But by now there were so many guests arriving that a large queue had formed awaiting the opportunity to greet their host and hostess. It was clearly no moment for John to interrupt the line of people passing slowly in front of his mother and stepfather. He saw Chantal's eyes upon him as she curtsied to the elderly woman addressing her and for a moment he forgot the urgency of his purpose. Her beauty overwhelmed him. He had never seen her look more lovely than at this moment when he had no choice but to leave her.

With angry disappointment at his misfortune, he resolutely turned away and slipped quietly out of the room, hoping that his disappearance would not be too noticeable. He dispatched two footmen — one to summon his valet, the other to advise the coachman to have his carriage ready within the half hour. When the valet arrived he ordered him to set out adequate clothing for him to make an immediate journey to Paris.

"If possible I wish to cross the Channel first thing in the morning," John said. "So make all haste, Jenkins!"

Too well-trained to show his surprise or question this extraordinary statement, the valet did as he was told, laying out John's thick waterproof miller beaver cloak made to Mr. Mackintosh's patent, his fur-lined boots and a change of clothing. John divested himself of his evening attire so painstakingly donned but an hour since.

Within ten minutes he was reattired and sitting at his escritoire. With haste he penned note to his mother and enclosed the letter he had received.

"I will leave by the servants' entrance!"

John said to the valet. "I do not wish to embarrass those guests who are still arriving by my untimely departure! See that Lady Waite receives this as soon as possible."

Exactly half-an-hour later he was sitting in his brougham, the bitter cold of the December night penetrating the carriage covering as the coachman urged the big gray southward along the empty road to Dover.

John turned to the lad seated beside him.

"Your name, boy?" he enquired.

"Pierre, Monsieur!" replied the messenger overcome with pride and excitement, for he had never ridden inside a carriage before. He was vastly impressed, not only by the luxuriant comfort and quality of the deep velvet pile of the upholstery, but by the exalted rank of the English milord with whom he was traveling.

"Tell me again exactly how you came by this letter!" John said in French, for the boy spoke no word of English. "Every detail you can recall."

"'Twas given me by *une folle*, Monsieur! I mean no disrespect but her appearance . . . well, I cannot describe to you! Her eyes were filled with madness. Yet strangely she spoke like a lady of quality. She gave me this . . . " Once again, he showed John the gold ring with a falcon engraved upon it. "'Tis real gold. I checked it!" the lad said as if he himself, did not believe it. "And she gave me five gold louis with the promise of five more if I delivered the letter to you, Monsieur. She said: 'Tell the English Milord that it is a matter of life and death!'"

"As indeed it might be!" John muttered.

He had little doubt that the letter had come direct from Princess Camille Falois herself. He could understand why the boy had thought her mad. He himself had been convinced of it — or nearly so, when he had left her to her fate at the Château de Boulancourt. But now he had few doubts left that she was indeed the Princess she claimed to be and not her maid, Marie, as Antoine de Valle had stated.

'Now that I am free from my prison, I can prove my identity!' the letter said. *'Only come quickly, I beg you, for my life is in danger. Antoine will leave no stone unturned to find me. I send my first husband's signet ring as proof of my sanity for had I really been poor Marie and stolen it, I would not now be sending it to you . . . '*

The address she had given was in a Parisian slum, an area unknown to John. But he was satisfied that he would find it with little loss of time since the boy with him seemed to know it well enough. He had promised Camille's messenger a further piece of gold for taking him there by the fastest possible route. The lad was the son of a poor cobbler who plied his trade in the same street where 'the madwoman' was residing, he told John. The house was a shabby rat-infested building of ill repute, the boy said. Women of the street could hire a room there for a few sous and no lady would ever be seen thereabouts. "Unless she was too crazed to know where she was!" he added grinning.

Only upon the rarest of occasions had John thought of the poor unfortunate prisoner at the Château de Boulancourt. His mind had been too preoccupied with his own life for him to concern himself with the misfortune of a lunatic. Now he regretted his indifference to her fate — and indeed, to the whole matter of his half-brother's claim to be the legitimate heir to their father's name and estate. If Antoine were proved a liar regarding Camille, then he might indeed have lied about their father's first marriage.

John felt a swift stirring of excitement as the night drew on. If the Princess Falois could prove her identity and that Antoine had kept her imprisoned, the whole edifice of his half-brother's story was in question. The Princess's claim that Antoine had married her might also be fact rather than a figment of her crazed mind. Were it so, such depravity and dishonor as would lie at Antoine's door could not fail to give credence to John's belief in his half-brother's calumny regarding his right to the title of Vicomte de Valle.

John's impatience to reach Paris increased with every hour. When finally they reached Dover, he was forced to kick his heels in an inn until the packet steamer departed soon after dawn. It was therefore nearing midday before he and the French lad, Pierre, reached their destination.

The dirty, shuttered, crumbling house did not fall short of the boy's description. The rain-swept street looked as deserted as the building itself as John's carriage came to halt outside. Within minutes however they were surrounded by a crowd of ragged urchins with pinched faces and half-starved bodies. Whilst John tugged again and again upon the iron bell-pull, several men joined the group of silent, gaping gamins. When it became clear to John that no one intended to open the door to him, he turned to the nearest man and asked how he could gain entry.

"Madame will not open the door to anyone!" came the laconic reply. "Not after yesterday's goings-on!"

It was some time before John could elicit the facts from the bystanders. They were reluctant to talk until John produced a handful of coins to loosen their tongues. He was then bombarded with information, a great deal of it conflicting. He finally succeeded in extracting the horrible facts. Two days previously — the day upon which Camille had written her desperate request to him for his help — her body had been pulled out of the Seine. Although there had been no papers or means of identification upon her, the neighborhood urchins had recognized her as 'la folle' who had lodgings in the brothel in their street. Madame, the owner of the house, had been taken to the police station to identify the body and had told the *Préfet de Police* of the madwoman's claim to be the Princess Faloise formerly residing at the Château de Boulancourt. No one had believed this crazy story. Nevertheless the *Préfet de Police* had personally driven to Compiègne to interview the Vicomte de Valle. The Vicomte had been able to explain everything to everyone's satisfaction.

Which meant in effect, John realized, that Antoine had given the police the selfsame story he had told *him* — that the woman was not Camille but her maid, Marie.

He felt in honor bound to give the messenger the reward the Princess had promised him were he to bring John to her. In his own mind, he was more than ever convinced that it was Camille who had died, anticipating her murder in the letter she had written him. He regretted that he had left it behind with his mother else he could have taken it with him to show the *Préfet*.

Nevertheless John decided to call upon the Commissioner of Police and state his suspicions that this was no suicide but murder.

The *Préfet* was a small, sharp-eyed man with a red nose on which perched a pair of gold-rimmed spectacles. His manner towards John was respectful enough but implacable. He became visibly hostile when John spoke of his convictions.

"I am entirely satisfied with the Vicomte's explanation!" he said coldly, and looking over the top of his spectacles added pointedly: "And quite frankly, Monsieur, I am surprised that you, a member of the Vicomte's family and a very close relation, should voice such serious accusations. If I may say so, sir, they are groundless and I can see no reason whatever why you should imagine the dead woman was killed. We found no marks on the body and she had clearly died by drowning. Had the Vicomte wished her dead, he has had ample opportunity to dispose of her these past years, has he not?

In any event, I found him at home and his servant verified that he had not been recently to Paris."

With a growing impatience that he barely troubled to conceal, the *Préfet* listened to John's account of Camille's reasons for her continued incarceration — so that Antoine could discover the whereabouts of her hidden wealth. Even before the Commissioner spoke, John knew that the man considered such a possibility as unlikely as murder.

"We made a most thorough search of the room occupied by the dead woman," he said. "There was nothing there — nothing at all! The woman was without a sou to her name. Small wonder that the poor wretch decided to end her life!"

"Nevertheless, *she must have had money when she arrived in Paris!*" John insisted. "She must have paid someone to conduct her to the city, for she certainly could not have walked. Doubtless she would have been asked to pay in advance for her lodgings; and not least, sir, she paid the messenger for his fare and gave him five gold coins and the promise of five more when he returned from England. Such generosity is hardly the action of someone who is down to their last sou!"

The Frenchman shrugged his shoulders, indifferent to John's arguments.

"Who can say what mad people will do? She may have sold her last remaining possession in her crazed determination to convince you."

"Or she may have retrieved her fortune only

536

to have it stolen from her before she was killed!" John said. "You cannot prove otherwise, *Monsieur le Préfet.*"

"It is not for me to prove anything!" the man said with marked indifference. "It is for you, sir, to bring me proof if you wish me to enquire further into this woman's death. I personally am entirely satisfied that it was the suicide of a mad woman who believed herself a person of consequence. The dossier is closed!"

John decided to remain in Paris for the night. He took comfortable rooms in a good hotel in the Champs Élysées and after dining and wining sat down to ponder the enigma of the Princess' death. Calmer than he had been in the presence of the disinterested *Préfet de Police*, he could understand better why the man should hold to his theory of suicide, for he had no reason to discredit the word of the Vicomte de Valle whose character was, as far as anyone knew, unimpeachable.

John could not altogether blame the *Préfet* for refuting his suspicions. He himself had doubted Camille's story when he had first encountered her at the Château, and like the *Préfet* had allowed himself to believe Antoine's explanation. So why now, he thought, should he feel so totally convinced that the letter he had received *was* from the Princess; that she was as sane as he and had been in terrible fear for her life when she wrote it — a fear that had proved well justified.

He toyed with the idea of going to Compiègne to confront Antoine in person. But the longer he considered it, the more futile such an idea seemed. Antoine's story had satisfied the police and John's opinions would scarce be likely to trouble him. There was nothing he could do.

On the following morning however John decided that he could not leave Paris without expressing his suspicions to his half-brother.

'Let him at least know that I am aware of his dreadful act!' John thought as he drew out pen and paper from the escritoire.

His letter to Antoine contained no vague allusion to the possibility of his having killed the Princess for his own gain but expressed in plainest terms his belief in Antoine's guilt.

'Her letter left me in no doubt that she feared for her life and that were she to die, it would be at your hands. I cannot prove my suspicions and therefore I cannot attempt to bring you to justice . . . ' he wrote. 'You can no longer however congratulate yourself on having committed a crime of which no one suspects you. If indeed you are guilty, then may God punish you since the law will not. If you are innocent, then I have wronged you in my thoughts, beyond your forgiveness. Whatever the truth, it would seem obvious that we shall not now, or in the future, be desirous of enjoying each other's company. I would ask you therefore to refrain ever again from calling upon us at Barre House. I am sure that my mother, stepfather, Tamarisk and Chantal will endorse my feelings and that you would not be made welcome under our roof.'

Had John had longer upon which to reflect, he might not have dispatched such a letter to his half-brother. But its composition had been impulsive and the writing of it a measure of relief for his feelings of impotence following upon his visit to the *Préfet*. He gave it no second reading and posted it in Paris before he returned to Calais. Not until it was too late to retrieve it did he realize that he had committed two very serious blunders. He had let Antoine know two important facts of which he had hitherto been ignorant — that Camille had written John a letter casting suspicion upon him and that Chantal was not, after all, forever lost to him as Antoine had until then supposed.

27

December 1839 – January 1840

"**B**ECAUSE Antoine was handsome and fawned upon you, you were always prejudiced in his favor!"

"And you were always prejudiced against him — because he usurped your right to your father's title though it was no fault of his own, as well you know!"

The two voices were raised in genuine anger and Mavreen looked at John and Chantal in surprise and concern. She had not heard them argue so fiercely since they were children.

"Calm yourselves!" she said authoritatively. "If we are to discuss sensibly this whole business of Antoine and the Princess then let us do so without personal feeling intervening."

Chantal's mouth tightened. She walked to the window and stared out into the bare winter garden, her dark eyes stormy. She resented bitterly John's automatic assumption that she still nurtured romantic feelings towards Antoine; that her refusal to believe his wild story was based on loyalty to a man merely because he was handsome and flattered her. John belittled her intelligence, her judgement. In fact he was treating her as if she were back in the nursery and seemed quite to forget that she was a woman now.

540

"You must surely agree with me, do you not, sir?" John appealed to Perry. "Everything we know points to his guilt!"

"Nevertheless 'tis but circumstantial evidence, as Chantal has pointed out!" Perry replied. "And in this country at least, a man is presumed innocent unless he be proved otherwise! We cannot be sure our suspicions are justified, John."

"Let us not forget the unfortunate affair of the unhappy Lady Flora Hastings!" Mavreen said quietly. Seeing John's bewilderment she continued: "Perhaps you and Chantal have not heard speak of it?"

"Julia told me the whole story of the scandal of the bedchamber!" Chantal replied in a more normal tone of voice.

"If ever there were a case of ill-founded suspicion, this was it," Mavreen said. "The matter had political connotations, John. Lady Flora Hastings was one of the young Queen's least favored ladies-in-waiting. Since Lord Melbourne had taken office, of necessity all the Queen's household were Whigs — a matter much to her liking. But she distrusted Lady Flora believing her to be spying upon her on behalf of Sir John Conroy. He, you may recall, was rumored to be the Duchess of Kent's lover. Victoria's dislike of him was a natural consequence of her mother's relationship with this man who had directed their household throughout her childhood. She bitterly resented his domination and as soon as she became Queen she removed herself to Buckingham Palace not only to put herself beyond his power but to avoid the incessant quarreling with her mother, the Duchess. Unknown then to Victoria, Lady Flora was a Conroy sympathizer."

Perry now took up the story.

"In January the unhappy Lady Flora was noticed to have a suspicious swelling of the stomach. You can imagine the scandal and gossip, John, that began to circulate when it was rumored that one of the Queen's household was with child. Her ladies, after all, are supposed to be her moral chaperones! The young Queen believed her guilty but was obliged to reinstate her in her good books when Lady Flora produced a medical certificate to prove she was still a virgin."

"That was in February!" Mavreen said. "The Hastings family wanted redress for the slur upon their name and the newspapers printed their account of the affair. The Queen and the Palace party were viciously attacked and public sympathy understandably went against her."

"On some date in May which I cannot exactly recall," Perry explained, "Melbourne's government fell on account of the Jamaica Bill. Peel accepted office as Prime Minister and tried to obtain the Queen's agreement to change her ladies-in-waiting in order to show confidence in the new Tory government. But the Queen disliked Sir Robert Peel and refused. Without her support, the new government fell and Melbourne was returned to office."

"Which really does not greatly concern Lady Flora," Mavreen interjected. "She, poor soul, became ill once more at this time. In June she was absent from Court and by July the poor woman was dead. Before she died she had requested that a post-mortem should be performed and it was found she had a tumor on the liver. So you see, John, things are not always what they seem to be and there were many who deeply regretted their harsh and unfounded suspicions as to Lady Flora's condition."

"Are you saying, Mama, that you think I am wrong to condemn Antoine? That the letter I received accusing him is but the raving of a madwoman?" John asked, his face revealing his uncertainty. He had been convinced that at least his mother would be as suspicious of Antoine as he, even if Chantal and Perry were not.

"I do not know, John!" Mavreen said quietly. "I agree that the handwriting is that of an educated woman and remarkably well executed for the work of a crazed servant! I do not think, however, that your *Préfet de Police* will have his mind altered by such a minor consideration. You John, will agree that Antoine is plausible and I do not doubt that he has totally convinced the *Préfet* of the truth of *his* story."

"I think it is you who are mad, John!" Chantal broke in. "For your suspicions to be true, it would mean that the Princess — a woman in her forties — had married her young ward then in his twenties. Why should she have done such a thing? She was wealthy and independent, was she not?"

"Perhaps she loved him!" John said quietly.

"You once found him irresistible, did you not?"

Chantal blushed a deep angry red; but before she could speak Perry said:

"I agree absolutely with your mother, John. There is nothing we can do. The Princess . . . Marie . . . whichever she may be, is now dead and cannot be brought back to life. As for Antoine de Valle, I think he is best forgotten by us all. 'Tis unlikely we shall ever set eyes upon him again."

But even had they all been able to put him from their minds, Antoine himself had no intention of being forgotten. To the astonishment of everyone at Barre House he suddenly presented himself there on a bitter cold day in January, two weeks after John's return from Paris.

As always, he was impeccably attired wearing dark blue merino trousers and a matching tailcoat with velvet collar and cuffs. Showing no ill effects from the rough Channel crossing or the chilly coach ride to London, Antoine bowed gracefully over Mavreen's hand as he raised it to his lips.

"You will, I hope, forgive my calling unannounced," he said smoothly. "When I received John's letter telling me that my dear sister, Tamarisk and Mademoiselle Chantal had returned so miraculously from the dead, I could not wait a moment longer before coming in person to offer my felicitations."

He bowed to Perry and turned to Chantal. As he took her hand he stared long and intently into her eyes.

"I find you more beautiful than ever," he said, pressing his lips to her hand. "I cannot describe my happiness when I learned that you had not after all joined the mermaids beneath the sea!"

As Chantal withdrew her hand nervously he added smiling:

"Presently you must tell me of your adventures, Chantal, but first I would like to pay my respects to you, my dear stepmother!"

Mavreen for once was speechless. When the butler had presented Antoine's calling card she had felt instinctively that her stepson must be told she was 'not at home.' Looking to Perry for advice he had sensed her inner reluctance to close her doors to Antoine, and said:

"He is Gerard's son, Mavreen. It is for you to decide if you wish to turn him away."

Much as she might long to do so, she could never forget Gerard's dying request to concern herself with his adored son. He had loved Antoine even more deeply than he had loved her. No matter how greatly she disliked and mistrusted Antoine, he *was* Gerard's flesh and blood.

It did not cross Mavreen's mind as she told the butler to show him in that Chantal might be in any danger from Antoine. She had talked long and intimately with her since her return home and not once had Chantal mentioned Antoine's name, nor expressed a wish that he be notified of her survival. She seemed to have forgotten his existence. It was John that Chantal loved now, she surmised, even if for the moment the two young people seemed greatly to misunderstand each other's emotions. Perry had cautioned her to remain aloof from their problems which he had little doubt would be resolved in due course.

"They need time to readjust to one another!" he said.

It did not occur to her now therefore that Chantal might for a second time succumb to Antoine's charm and disregard John who, fortunately, was absent at this moment.

"I do not wish to be a burden upon your household!" Antoine was saying. "And as it is my intention to remain in London until after your Queen's wedding to the handsome Prince Albert, I have taken rooms once again in the Pulteney Hotel. I hope you will all do me the honor of dining with me there one evening."

"You have news then of the Queen's wedding?" Chantal asked with genuine curiosity. Ever since the Royal Declaration of Marriage had been announced last November speculation had been mounting as to when the wedding to the penniless but handsome German Prince might take place.

"I have it on the best authority that Her Royal Highness will announce her betrothal when she opens your Parliament next week!" Antoine replied. "The wedding will, I believe, follow shortly afterwards. It so happens that on my recent travels I have enjoyed several pleasant evenings in the company of the Duke of Coburg, Albert's father, and through him I am *au fait* with the latest news. I have not had the pleasure of meeting the young Prince since he does not live at home."

Mavreen hid her reaction to this obvious attempt by Antoine to impress them with the importance of his associates. She herself had once met the charming, likable Louise, Duchess of Coburg from whom the Duke was divorced. From Louise she had learned that the Duke was a dissipated spendthrift whose Court was notorious for its profligacy. The poor woman had not been permitted to see her two sons after the divorce but derived some consolation from the fact that the Princes, Albert and Ernest, were being brought up in the house of their tutor, a kindly, learned gentleman by the name of Herr Florschutz. From all accounts he was a far better 'father' to the Princes than the profligate Duke whom Antoine claimed as a friend.

It seemed to Mavreen that she was destined to disapprove of Antoine in every direction. Why was it she could never like him, she asked herself sadly? In looks, he bore such a strong resemblance to his father that she could not help but be reminded of Gerard in his presence. Yet now, as always, she longed for him to be out of the house. She wished moreover that John was at home. Since he was not here to do so, she felt obliged to show Antoine Camille's letter.

She went to her bureau and withdrew the Princess' note from the locked drawer where she had placed it. She handed it to Antoine without explanation, watching him closely as she did so.

Antoine's face revealed no hint of surprise as he scanned the page.

"John wrote to me about this from Paris!" he said calmly. His eyes, as he met Mavreen's, were as wide and innocent as they had been when he had lied to her as a child, she thought.

"Of course it was penned by poor Marie," he continued blandly. "You may remember her, my dear stepmother, from the days when I lived with Camille in London. The relationship that existed even then between mistress and servant was quite unusual. Of course one must not forget that Marie had been with Camille since childhood. In the latter years when we were traveling through the Americas, Camille treated Marie more like a friend than a servant and made her a confidante in most things. Poor Marie never recovered from her mistress' death. Our physician in Compiègne tells me that it is by no means unusual for an elderly, weak-minded woman to confuse her identity with that of a departed loved one. He visited Marie regularly whilst she was under my roof and did what little he could to help the poor woman! But of course, there is no remedy for insanity, though John seems quite unable to grasp this point."

He spoke with great plausibility and both Mavreen and Perry found themselves wondering yet again if after all they had misjudged Antoine. Chantal, who had always been certain that John and her stepmother were prejudiced in their views of him, needed no convincing of his innocence. In a spirit of friendliness, which she believed was the least she could show Antoine in the circumstances, she said:

"You must forgive John's flights of fancy! He

548

does not mean to give offense!"

Even to her own ears her remark sounded ludicrously inappropriate. She was scarcely surprised when Antoine said quietly:

"I think that he does intend every offense!" His face was unsmiling. "Were John not my brother I would have felt obliged to challenge him to withdraw his accusations which are, at the very least, libelous. However I am older and have learned better control of myself than he. Let us hope that in due course he will become less a prey to his emotions. In the meanwhile, for all our sakes, I intend to forget his insults. I have no wish to quarrel with my own flesh and blood, far less with someone for whom I know you care, Mademoiselle Chantal!"

"That is most generous of you, Antoine!" Perry spoke for the first time, the hint of sarcasm in his voice detectable only to Mavreen who knew every nuance of his speech. "I am sure it comes as a great relief to us all to learn that you intend John no harm!"

"As indeed I had hoped to inform him in person!" Antoine said. "Will you be so good as to ask him to call upon me at my hotel at his convenience? It is my earnest wish that we may yet become friends."

"I will give John your message but I am afraid I cannot promise that he will visit you!" Mavreen said.

"I shall continue to hope, Madame," Antoine replied, bowing gracefully as he made his adieux.

Anxious to make amends, Chantal accompanied Antoine to the hall. Whilst she was absent,

Mavreen turned to Perry, her eyes dark with uneasiness.

"I do so wish I could feel less distrustful of Antoine and his motives!" she said sighing. "Why did he come to see us? He made no request to call upon Chantal, yet I sensed that he had lost none of his regard for her."

"And how so?" Perry asked, his voice gently teasing. "What instinct is this which sees things that escape me?"

"You may smile, Peregrine Waite!" Mavreen retorted, "but I could hear a change in his voice when he addressed her — a softness that is not there when he speaks to us. And for what other reason than to renew his courtship of Chantal has he come to London? To re-establish communications with us, his only relatives? Somehow I think not."

"Since he is nought but a worry to you, then let us forget him!" Perry suggested. "I myself see no need for concern. I am convinced that Chantal's heart now lies very firmly with John for all their constant quarreling. Antoine has come back into her life too late. She is no longer the impressionable, gullible child he encountered upon his last visit. She has learned not a few of life's lessons and she thinks far more deeply than was her wont now that she has discovered where her impulsiveness can lead her!"

"Into the arms of an outlaw!" Mavreen said as she stood up and put her arms around Perry's waist and leaned her head against his shoulder. "As did I when I succumbed to the charms of the notorious Gideon Morris!"

"Which thought did not escape me when Chantal told me about her pirate!" Perry agreed. "But he deceived her, Mavreen, as I never deceived you; and it was no love match as was ours!"

"You really believe Chantal will end up married to John?"

"I am convinced of it!" Perry said. "Her very resistance to him only indicates to me how deeply she feels about him! I have not forgotten how *you* resisted *me*!"

Perry's estimation of Chantal's feelings was very close to the truth. Antoine's sudden appearance only served to reassure her in her belief that she had never truly loved him; that those stirrings of emotion she had mistaken for love had been but the awakenings of her body to a first awareness of a man as a potential lover. Ignorant and innocent as she had then been, to be flattered, admired, touched, kissed were excitements that she had mistaken for love. Antoine's beauty had further misled her for she knew now that love encompassed the mind as well as the body. She had learned much during those months on the island with Dinez. Their relationship had always lacked a unity of mind and spirit. Only in the very act of love itself had they been one.

Today, Chantal mused, her heart had not once thrilled to Antoine's compliments; nor had she trembled when he kissed her hand as once she had done. It was her heightened sense of justice, not affection, that led her to support Antoine against her family; and even then it was from loyalty to her own beliefs rather than from a desire to uphold the man himself.

Alone in her bedchamber Chantal studied the note Antoine had pressed into her hand, unseen by other eyes as she had accompanied him to the hall. She would not have attempted to conceal it from her father and stepmother but for Antoine's whispered caution.

"'Tis a matter of life and death and concerns your family!" he had said mysteriously. "*Tell no one, Chantal!* Have I your word?"

She had assumed immediately that such danger as Antoine had implied must threaten John. With no time to consider the matter she had nodded and given her promise.

Antoine's note said little to clarify the mystery.

'*It is imperative that I should speak with you alone, Chantal. I have in my possession a document that could destroy your family. I think you should be told of the background to these events. Please call upon me at my hotel alone, at your convenience.*'

Chantal's first instinct was to consult John. But at once she set the idea aside. Even had she not given her word to stay silent, John's attitude to Antoine was never rational. If as it seemed, Antoine was seeking to save her family from some unimaginable peril, then John's intervention might hinder rather than help the cause.

Her decision to say nothing to John was reinforced when he returned to Barre House.

Upon hearing of Antoine's visit, he became so enraged that even Perry could not calm him.

"I suppose now we shall have him calling upon Chantal and renewing his proposals of marriage!" John cried furiously. "It is not to be tolerated, Mama! You should not have received him. I made it quite clear in my letter that he would not be made welcome here."

Not entirely displeased with this display of jealousy but determined not to allow John to think he could dictate her life, Chantal said coldly:

"It is not for you to decide who shall or shall not be my suitors, John!"

John stared at her in angry misery.

"You care nothing for my opinions, do you, Chantal!" he cried. "Yet there was a time when you respected my judgement. Now 'twould seem you have regard only for renegades such as Antoine and that . . . that pirate!"

The reference to Dinez brought the color flooding into Chantal's cheeks. She had been trying so very hard to forget him and far more importantly, had been praying that John, too, was beginning to forget that episode of her life. Close to tears, she ran from the room.

John stared unhappily at her departing figure.

"It seems I can neither do nor say what is right in Chantal's eyes!" he declared bitterly. "Can she not see that all I want is to protect her?"

"Perhaps she feels that you should place more trust in *her* judgment!" Perry said. "Because she has once behaved unwisely, John, 'tis no cause for you to remind her of it. We men consider females as inferior but they do not care to be treated without respect for their intelligence, even when they have none! 'Tis a fact you would be well advised to learn, John, before you think to enter into the state of holy matrimony! I think 'tis not only Chantal whom you offend but your mother, too."

John's face softened and he went at once to Mavreen and put his arm around her.

"Forgive me, Mama, for speaking as I did," he said. "It is not for me to dictate your behavior regarding Antoine. But I cannot trust or like him."

"Nor I!" Mavreen said. "But Perry is right, John, you must not dictate to Chantal. She is less tolerant of your assumed rights than is your doting Mama!" Chantal's quiet, withdrawn manner that evening and the following morning were attributed by her family to be the result of her quarrel with John; whereas in fact, she had spent a sleepless night worrying about the suspicions Antoine had placed in her mind. Her devotion to her family was absolute and the mere thought that they might be in danger troubled her sorely. By midmorning she resolved to delay no longer but to go at once to Antoine and discover the answer to the riddle. Donning a thick, fur-trimmed cloak and pulling the hood close about her face so that she might pass unrecognized, she slipped out of the house unseen and traveled on foot the short distance to the Pulteney Hotel.

Antoine was expecting her. He had guessed correctly that the contents of his note would bring her hurrying to him.

Even before seeing Chantal again, he was obsessed by his memories of her. When he had been told of her death at sea, he had sought solace in a spate of violent depravity. Believing that Chantal, the only good presence in his life, was forever lost to him, he had decided he might as well give his soul totally to the devil. He added further brutalities to the Roman games in the amphitheatre; indulged in even more bizarre excesses within the walls of the Château until even his associates familiar with the wildness of his behavior were made uneasy.

But the memory of Chantal was not so easily assuaged and he had acquired the habit of eating opium which he imported in large quantities from China. Britain was at war with China in a so far unsuccessful attempt to put an end to opium dealing, so the price was exorbitant since the opium traders now had to run the gauntlet of the Royal Navy.

Only the untimely death beneath Antoine's roof of two young bloods from Paris had brought to a temporary halt the growing addiction which alone helped him to forget the girl he had wanted — the only person in the world for whom he had ever felt any love.

When John's letter arrived telling him that Chantal was alive, he determined that no living creature would prevent him from having her. Given this second chance he would waste no time in petty preambles. If Chantal proved unwilling to marry him of her own accord, then he had an almost certain method of obtaining her consent. He went to the secret chamber where he kept the most private and the most incriminating of his documents. Without difficulty he found the yellowed pages for which he was searching. Though now more than twenty years old, the ink faded and the leaves on which they were written dog-eared, the words were still perfectly legible. Smiling, Antoine put them in his breast pocket and departed for England.

But as Chantal entered the hotel, her hood thrown back, the light-colored fur contrasting with her dark hair, her cheeks cherry-red from the bitter January wind, his cold determination seemed to melt within him. He had underestimated the effect her beauty would have upon him. As he stood up to greet her, his legs and hands trembled and the smile of welcome on his lips seemed to crack and become a grimace.

"I have been waiting for you!" he said as he kissed her gloved hand. "I trusted that you would come without delay. Will you allow me to conduct you to my room so that we may talk undisturbed?"

Chantal withdrew her hand nervously.

"Can we not talk here?" she asked. She wanted no repetition of their last encounter in his chambers. Though she did not share her family's dislike of him, she had no desire to renew the former intimacy of their friendship.

"I think you might prefer the privacy of my sitting room!" Antoine said persuasively. "There is always the chance that we could be overheard here with so many people around us. Do you not agree?"

"Very well!" Chantal nodded uneasily. Although his words gave no indication of his feelings, the tone of his voice and the expression in his eyes gave her instinctive warning that his sentiments towards her had not changed.

She was relieved when he made no attempt to take her arm as they walked up the broad stairway side by side.

But the moment they arrived in Antoine's sitting room, her suspicions were confirmed. Whilst she was still in the process of removing her gloves and coat, Antoine said in a low, vibrant voice:

"I have not brought you here under false pretense, Chantal. I wish you to know that I still want you to become my wife. I love you as I have never loved another human being — nor ever will. No, do not interrupt me . . . " he added as he heard her small gasp of protest. "It is important that you should be aware of my feelings so that you understand the part you must play."

"*The part I must play?*" Chantal echoed. "I am afraid I do not follow your reasoning, Antoine. Naturally I am honored by your sentiments but . . . "

"There can be no 'but,' Chantal!"

Antoine's voice was quiet but utterly compelling as he motioned her to a chair opposite him. He made no move to touch her but waited until she was seated before he continued:

"You see, I know now that I cannot enjoy life without you. When I believed you dead and had no hope, I realized how meaningless my life was.

557

I am therefore in deadly earnest when I say I wish to marry you. It was and still is my hope that you will learn to care for me. But even if that is impossible, it in no way lessens my determination to make you my wife."

"Your presumption astounds me, sir!" Chantal cried indignantly. "You speak as if my wishes are of no consequence!"

"They are of paramount importance to me!" Antoine said, for the first time showing in his expression the latent passion within him. "Chantal, I will give you everything in the world you want. I will live to make you happy. Everything I have will be yours. If you do not care to live at Boulancourt, we will travel the world together if that is your preference. You have but to state your wishes and it will be my pleasure to fulfill them."

Chantal drew a deep breath in an attempt to calm her growing apprehension. Antoine's words were wildly spoken and untimely. Could he not see that she no longer wanted his love? His intensity of feeling frightened her, the more so since he had always seemed so calm and controlled.

"I cannot marry you, Antoine!" she said quietly but firmly. "I am sorry to hurt you for I now realize that you expected to find me in the same frame of mind as when we last saw one another. But since then, Antoine, my affections have been engaged elsewhere. I love John!"

This last declaration had been intended only to deter Antoine's furtherance of his proposals.

558

But as Chantal spoke she knew with a sudden cold clarity that the words were true — she did love John. She had always loved John, but the confusions of their childhood identities as brother and sister had prevented her from seeing the simple truth. It was for John she had longed so many times on the island, wishing to share her adventure with him. It was because of John she had felt so ashamed of her 'marriage' to Dinez. Were John to take her in love with the same passionate need as Dinez . . .

"You will not marry him!" Antoine's voice broke in on her thoughts. His tone was cold and frighteningly convincing. "You see, my lovely Chantal, I am not to be baulked. You will marry *me* because if you do not, *your father will be hanged by the neck until he dies!*"

So shocked was she by these words, Chantal believed her legs might give way beneath her. White-faced, she stared at Antoine in horror.

"Have you gone out of your mind, Antoine? You cannot mean what you say! My father . . . I do not . . . what *is* this crazed nonsense?"

Antoine regarded her almost pityingly.

"I suspected that you would know nothing of the past, Chantal," he said. "It would be natural for your parents to wish to keep you in ignorance of the truth. Nevertheless the moment has come when you must be told the facts. Your father is not, as you suppose, Sir Peregrine Waite. His real name is Gideon Morris and he was once the most notorious highwayman in England. There was a price of a thousand guineas upon his head subscribed by the many gentlemen who traveled the roads and were robbed by him, not once but several times apiece. I have no doubt that many of them are still living and would be delighted to see your father hanged, albeit his deeds were done thirty years ago!"

Chantal's face was so pale that Antoine feared she might faint. But slowly the color returned to her cheeks. She said violently:

"I do not believe this . . . this fantasy. 'Twas not the maid, Marie, who was insane but you, Antoine de Valle, who have lost your wits!"

A faint smile stole across Antoine's perfect features.

"I have never been more sensible!" he said. "You cannot imagine, my dearest Chantal, that I would dare to make such an accusation against your father if I did not have proof of his guilt. You may of course question him if you so wish. But I do not think that is desirable or necessary. May I give you these to read?"

He withdrew from his pocket the two yellowed sheets of paper he had brought with him from France. Over twenty years ago they had been torn from the journal Tamarisk had kept throughout her childhood. When she had eloped so precipitately with Leigh Darton, she had thoughtlessly left the diary in her bedchamber, unaware that the ten-year-old Antoine knew of its place of concealment and had already read its contents.

At that time Mavreen had been married to Gerard de Valle and the boy bitterly resented his father's love for his step-mother. He had reason, too, to hate Gideon Morris who had caught him thieving and beaten him soundly for it. When Mavreen went hot-foot by night after her eloping daughter, Antoine had shown his father Tamarisk's diary. It revealed Mavreen's previous love affair with the highwayman, until then known to her husband only as the dandy, Sir Peregrine Waite. The result of this revelation had nearly broken up the marriage, for Gerard de Valle had been unable to conceal his jealousy of Mavreen's past lover. Innocent though she was of adultery, he believed her unfaithful to him. Tamarisk had bitterly regretted her part in causing the rift between her parents. She destroyed the journal but had never been able to find the pages relating to Gideon Morris and her mother. She was unaware that Antoine de Valle had retrieved them from his father's bureau.

Chantal read Tamarisk's childish script twice over before she spoke. When she did so her voice was nearly inaudible.

"These pages could have been written by anyone . . . " she faltered.

"But they were written by Tamarisk," Antoine interrupted. "You are at liberty to question her as to their validity; and by all means ask your father to confess his villainy."

"Which I shall do!" Chantal cried. "Even if your accusations prove to be the truth, which I do not believe, you cannot mean to make use of this information. What possible reason have you for wishing my father dead?"

"I have no such desire!" Antoine replied calmly. "Nor any intent to disclose his past — unless you force me to it, Chantal. As far as

I am aware, no one but your mother, Tamarisk and I know the truth. The secret has been well kept and no harm can now befall your father except by virtue of these written words. These pages will be my wedding gift to you, Chantal. Once they are in your possession, his secret is safe for ever more."

"But that is . . . . blackmail!" Chantal whispered.

"*Le chantage!*" Antoine agreed. "That is an ugly word, my Chantal. Let us instead call my proposal a part of our marriage settlement."

"I will never marry you!" Chantal cried, jumping to her feet. "You are, after all, as evil as John believes."

Antoine made no move towards her.

"If I am evil, then it must be your task to change me!" he said. "But is it evil to love a woman so much that you would kill for her, destroy the world for her if needs be? No man will ever love you as I do, Chantal."

"You speak of your love for me — yet you would destroy my father knowing how dearly I love him?" Chantal gasped.

"But I shall not have to destroy your father, will I?" Antoine replied with cold logic. "Nor was I ever in danger of so doing. You will marry me, Chantal, because it is preferable to seeing your father's body rotting on the gallows."

He noticed the pallor of her cheeks and added gently:

"I realize that this has been a great shock to you and that you will require a little time to come to terms with the facts. I will wait a week, Chantal. Then you must return here and advise me of your decision. I want to take you back to France with me before the month is out!"

Wisely he made no move to touch her. With a cry of pure horror, Chantal gathered her cloak and gloves and without waiting to don them, ran from the room so that she could no longer see Antoine's angelic smiling face.

28

January 1840

"PAPA, may I talk to you . . . alone?"

Perry looked with fondness at his young daughter. Since her experiences on the island in the Seychelles, she had shown no desire to renew their former close relationship. It had been one of deep affection, often involving them in long heart-to-heart conversations whilst Chantal regaled him with her childish hopes and fears. He had not pressed her for her confidence since her return to England, respecting her desire for privacy. Now he welcomed this first sign that she wished to share her thoughts with him. He suspected, wrongly, that she intended to consult him about her feelings for John.

When they were settled comfortably in the library, Perry in one of the deep red leather armchairs and Chantal kneeling on the thickly carpeted floor with her head resting on his knees, she said hesitantly:

"Papa, you have many times told me how you fought in Italy and encountered my mother and how later, after I was born, you came back to England to marry Mama. But you have never before spoken of your childhood. Or of your own family. I am curious to know about the Waites."

Perry put out a hand and rested it lightly on

Chantal's dark head. He had known that sooner or later his daughter would ask him about his ancestors and he was surprised that she had not questioned him long since about his past life. Her concern had always been with her own affairs. Perhaps because they had all indulged her, she had had little thought for anyone but herself.

It now seemed as if during the long months alone on the island, she had had time to reflect on other lives than her own. The moment had arrived when he must perforce tell her the truth about himself, for he had long since determined that he would not deceive her. He did not fear her condemnation, but nevertheless he worried that she might cease to hold him in such high regard as had been her wont.

"Papa?" There was a note of anxiety in Chantal's voice which he mistook for impatience.

"'Tis not that I am unwilling to satisfy your curiosity, Chantal. It is just that I am unsure where to begin my story!" he said. "You see, my darling, there is a great deal I must explain to you which will, I fear, come as somewhat of a shock. The fact is, my love, the Waites have no more reality than Mr. Dickens' characters. They do not exist and the very name of Waite is a figment of my imagination as indeed is my title. Does this surprise you?"

Chantal nodded, unable to speak for fear of what further admission he was about to make.

"My father was an aristocrat, a good kindly man by the name of Sir Frederick Morris,"

Perry continued. "My mother was his dairymaid to whom he gave a cottage on one of his farms when he discovered her to he with child by him. My father took me into his charge not long after my birthing. I was given every luxury, the very best of educations. But sadly he died when I was thirteen and his wife dispatched me back to my real mother. She was a country woman, with a close knowledge of nature and had learned the usefulness of herbs and plants for the cure of illness. But in those days such remedies were suspected of being the work of witches and my poor mother earned this cruel title. We were hounded, threatened, ignored by the neighbors in the village where we lived. As often as not we were starving. I learned to steal to keep us both alive."

This was a side of her father's past Antoine had not spoken about. Chantal's heart melted with pity as she thought of the poor little boy forced into a life of crime through no fault of his.

"We were fortunate that public opinion was beginning to turn against the burning of witches, else my mother would not have lived as long as she did," Perry continued. "I had had a good education and had learnt the speech and manners of my father. But there I was, a ragged urchin with no shoes and but one set of clothes I had long since outgrown, an outcast and rapidly becoming an accomplished thief, smuggler and pickpocket. We lived by my wits alone. Before I was fully grown I heard stories of the gentlemen of the road and it was my ambition to become one of them. I had no money to buy a horse but I remedied that by stealing one. My smuggling dues enabled me to buy food for the beast. We moved to another village and our fortunes rapidly changed as night after night I would return from a foray laden with rich men's purses."

"Did you ever kill a man?" Chantal asked.

"No, never! There was no need. In any event, my mother in her simple way, had instilled in me certain values, one of which was to appreciate the blessing and sanctity of life itself. The years passed. I was able to buy a small cottage in Sussex for my mother who was now ailing and keep her in comfort. I myself had clothes, pistols, a beautiful black mare which could outgallop any horseman in pursuit of me. I spent little and my careful hoard of money grew until I realized that I had as much as I needed to set myself up in the manner of my father. My mother died, and longing above all for the life of a gentleman of Society, I changed my name from Gideon Morris to Sir Peregrine Waite and bought a house in London."

Unaware of the tiny gasp of dismay that escaped Chantal's lips when he mentioned his real name, he continued:

"To lessen the risk of being suspected of possessing the daring and courage necessary to carry out the deeds that had made me rich, I assumed the rôle of a fop, a dandy. Believe me Chantal, I had much amusement from it! I dressed in silks and satins, bedecked myself with jewels and wore the outrageous modes of the mashers. If I were asked questions about my origins, it was my habit to take a pinch of snuff, wave my lace handkerchief daintily before me and say: 'But my dear fellow, did you not know that I am a country yokel who grew up with the Sussex smugglers and highwaymen and acquired my fortune by engaging in the most terribly dangerous exploits?' Or I might say, 'I do not dare reveal my past for in truth, sir, I am one of the most wanted men in England!' My audience would roll about with laughter at my 'nonsense' for most had seen me jump on a chair like a woman when a mouse ran by and took me for the nincompoop I pretended. Only your mother knew and Tamarisk suspected that I was not the effeminate fool I aped."

Despite everything Chantal smiled.

"Oh, Papa!" she said, "I wish I could have seen you."

Perry patted her head.

"Lest you think me quite unscrupulous," he said, "I was not entirely self-indulgent. I continued upon occasions to return to my former life and to rob the rich, not just because I found such adventures exciting, but because none knew better than I the needs of the poor. I would send the proceeds of my robberies to a friend of your Mama's, Mistress Elizabeth Fry, for the benefit of her poor prisoners for whom she worked so tirelessly."

"Did Mama always know the truth about you?" Chantal asked curiously.

Perry smiled.

"Indeed she did! My first meeting with her

568

was when I held up the coach in which she was traveling to The Grange. Your Mama likes to tell me that I robbed her not of her money but of her heart! Does this story change your regard for me, my poor little Chantal?"

Chantal rose to her feet and flung her arms around him.

"I always knew you were somehow a special person, Papa!" she cried. There were tears in her eyes as she hugged him. "And how could I condemn you when I . . . I too loved an outlaw." She sighed deeply. "Oh, Papa, life is so confusing, is it not? When I was little, good was good and bad was bad and it all seemed so simple. But I learned through Dinez that it is not always so. *He* was not a bad man, although he *had* led a wicked life. But he too had been forced into it by the circumstances of his childhood, though with less cause than you! Nevertheless he was kind and gentle, not only to me but to Zambi, too."

Perry nodded.

"I understand your defense of him and that you bear no grudge against him," he said. "Not only did he help to keep you alive but he gave you some happiness, did he not? All the same, I know that you do not still love him. Your heart is elsewhere, is it not, my darling?"

Chantal walked slowly away from her father. She stood with her back to him staring down at the blazing logs so that he could not see her face. She loved him with such an intensity of feeling that only with difficulty could she voice the lie she must now tell him.

"'Tis true my heart is elsewhere!" she said quietly. "'Tis this I desire to discuss with you, Papa. I fear there will be much opposition to my wishes and I need you to help me."

Perry frowned in perplexity.

"Why should there be opposition, Chantal? Your Mama has long since set aside her worries that you and John are like brother and sister. I can assure you that there is no impediment whatever to your marriage. We would all be delighted to see the two of you wed."

Chantal's cry was wrung from her heart.

"Papa, it is not John I intend to marry!"

"Not John?" Perry echoed disbelievingly. "But then who?"

"Oh, Papa!" Chantal cried despairingly. "Can you not guess? It is Antoine de Valle!"

Perry stood up so abruptly that the decanter on the table beside him tipped over. Its contents spilled onto the carpet. He made no move to right it but stood staring at his daughter's back.

"You are telling me that you love this man, Chantal?"

"I mean to marry him, Papa, no matter how greatly Mama and John dislike him!"

Perry's face was dark with anxiety.

"And if I were to tell you that I too mistrust him? I have made little comment until now because it does not become me to speak ill of him when he is the son of a man your mother once loved and respected. But now I must speak. I beg you to reconsider, Chantal. You know so little about him!"

Chantal drew a deep breath.

"But enough to be certain that I want to marry him, Papa! You are forgetting that even before I left for India, I expressed my regard for him. Now that I have seen him again . . ."

She could not continue the lie further but there was no need, for Perry crossed the room and turned her around so that he could look directly into her eyes.

"You persist in your choice even knowing that this will break John's heart? That it will distress your Mama and me beyond belief?"

Tears spilled down Chantal's cheeks and calm deserted her.

"Yes, I do!" she cried, "I do! I do! And none of you shall prevent me from marrying him. If necessary I shall run away with him. I have to be with him, Papa. Do you not understand me? I *have* to!"

Perry looked aghast at his daughter's desperate face. He could not believe that Chantal really meant what she was saying. She sounded like a spoilt child determined to have her own way regardless of whom she hurt or of common sense; and he had been convinced that she had returned home so much older, wiser!

"In your own interest, Chantal, I cannot give my consent willingly to such a marriage. However, in view of your determination to go to this man despite anything I or your family might say, I will not forbid it. It appears that time alone will convince you of the folly of such an undertaking. When that time comes I wish to be assured in my mind that you will feel able to return home to us. But I cannot condone your decision and can only advise you most strongly to reflect very seriously upon it. As for John . . . you will have to break the news to him yourself for I cannot and will not. You know, do you not, that he loves you? That he hoped to marry you?"

But Chantal could bear the strain no longer and gathering up her skirts, she ran from the room.

The following morning, white faced, dry eyed and utterly determined, she told her family gathered around the breakfast table that it was her intention to call upon Antoine at the Pulteney Hotel.

"I am grieved that you should all dislike Antoine!" she said in a cold, hard voice. "But I do not share your sentiments. I have already told Papa that I intend to marry him and since he is not welcome here in this house, I am forced to call upon him."

Only John was silent as Mavreen, Tamarisk and Charles all spoke at once. Mavreen had been prepared by Perry for Chantal's outburst but Tamarisk and Charles were not.

"You would do this in defiance of your family's wishes!" Charles muttered.

"Chantal, you must not let Antoine's excessive handsomeness turn your head!" Tamarisk cried, believing this the only explanation for her behavior. "It cannot be allowed!"

"You place yourself at great risk!" was Mavreen's quiet comment. "Antoine is not to be trusted."

"Nevertheless I must act as my heart dictates!" Chantal replied, and before she could weaken once more and give way to tears, she fled from the room.

Mavreen looked anxiously at John's white, stricken face.

"Do you not think you should try to deter her, John?" she asked. "Mayhap she will listen to your advice."

"Faint heart never won fair lady!" Charles said, giving John a friendly pat upon the shoulders. "Tamarisk will tell you that I only won her because I would not take 'no' for an answer! Go now and tell the girl how much you love her."

"'Twould be of no avail!" John replied bitterly. "Chantal has never loved me! Of all of you, I daresay I am the least surprised. Antoine charmed her the last time they met and 'tis clear enough that she has fallen once more beneath his spell."

"But we cannot allow her to marry him!" Mavreen cried.

"And why not, Mama?" John asked in the same bitter voice. "As we all agreed on my return from Paris, we have no proof of Antoine's perfidy. If we have maligned him — and I doubt it — but *if* we have, then my half-brother, the Vicomte de Valle, is an excellent match for our Chantal. You would be hard put to find a more eligible suitor than he."

The room fell silent as they pondered upon John's remarks. There *was* no valid reason for objecting to the marriage. They looked to Perry but his face was impassive as he said quietly:

"I have tried but I cannot stop Chantal. Her own desires outweigh her willingness to observe my wishes. And I will not forbid her."

"I will speak with her!" Tamarisk cried, unable to bear the tortured look on the faces of both Perry and John, nor the look of anxiety on her mother's. "Perhaps I can dissuade her!"

But that afternoon when Chantal returned from a brief visit to the Pulteney Hotel, she refused adamantly to discuss Antoine with Tamarisk other than to tell her that Antoine still wanted to marry her despite the fact that she had confessed fully to him her relationship with Dinez.

"You cannot dissuade me, Tamarisk," Chantal said firmly. "As to the future, that is my own affair!"

She seemed to Tamarisk to be concerned only with the past and invited Tamarisk to relate her first meeting with Antoine. Tamarisk told her of Gerard's discovery of his son; of how he had later brought Antoine to London to live at Barre House; and how the boy had proved himself even then a liar and a thief.

Chantal listened quietly, not daring to question Tamarisk about the journal she had kept during those years. Antoine had warned her not once but several times that were her family ever to guess the reason she had agreed to marry him, they would refuse to allow her to 'sacrifice' herself. She must therefore arouse no suspicion.

"Your father, though I like him not, has

574

never lacked for courage," Antoine had said. "He for one would rather be hanged than see you coerced into a marriage you yourself did not wish."

"*You* can say that, yet still persist in demanding I should be your wife?" Chantal had questioned disbelievingly.

Antoine's reply was coldly logical.

"The 'why' matters not to me; I care only that you *should* become my wife!" he said. "You have told me of your involvement with this pirate, Chantal, so I need no longer speak to you as though you were an innocent. Therefore I can tell you that with me you will discover delights that no other man could give you. I am well practiced in the art of pleasuring females and I can assure you, Chantal, that you will learn to love me or at least to desire me."

Chantal could still feel the cold shiver of revulsion that his words had engendered. As her husband, Antoine could claim his marital rights and she knew all too well now what was meant by such intimacy. She reassured herself that it would not come to this. Her willingness to participate in the wedding ceremony was conditional upon Antoine's surrender of the pages from Tamarisk's diary. Once they were in her possession, he would have no proof to substantiate any wild accusations he might in future make about her father and she could return home. Meanwhile she had but to sustain her courage and continue with her pretence to her family.

She was nevertheless deeply afraid. She had not forgotten John's story about the wild woman who had been kept prisoner in the Château. She could now believe all John's suspicions to be well founded and that Antoine might try to keep her too a prisoner. She realized that she must somehow force herself to appear compliant; to soften towards Antoine in order to allay any suspicion he might have that it was her intention to outwit him. She regretted that she had given him her decision so quickly, for Antoine was clearly surprised by it.

"I had not expected to receive your answer before the end of the week!" he had admitted.

"Once my mind was made up, there seemed little point in delay!" Chantal had replied. "If it is your wish, Antoine, I will return to France with you at the end of the month."

She saw the quick unguarded look of satisfaction that crossed his face before it became expressionless once more.

"As you guessed, my family are opposed to the marriage," she added. "'Tis therefore desirable that I leave home as soon as possible. I shall not then be required to listen to their objections any longer than is necessary."

If Antoine was surprised at the ease or speed of his victory, he gave no further indication of it.

"I know at this moment that you are finding it difficult to believe I love you, Chantal!" he had declared, raising her hand to his lips. "But you will learn how great is that love when this is all behind us. In time you will forget the manner of our courtship and be glad that I forced your hand."

The courage that had sustained Chantal throughout the past twenty-four hours now began to desert her. She looked at Tamarisk in despair. Perhaps, she thought, there was still some way to avoid such drastic measures as marriage to Antoine. Perhaps she had been foolish to believe Antoine's threat that her father could hang for misdeeds committed so long ago. She turned to face Tamarisk.

"Tell me," she said, "do you believe that if Dinez had come to Mahé with us, he really would have been imprisoned for his past crimes? Captain McRae said he might be hanged but . . . "

"Do not be under any illusions as to Dinez' fate in such circumstances!" Tamarisk interrupted, surprised to find Chantal still concerned with the pirate. She was, of course, unaware of her sister's true reason for questioning the operation of British law. "If a man had committed a crime in his youth, even if he was not caught until the end of his life, he would still have to pay for his sins. Very few escape the long arm of the law, you know. But even if some go free, like Dinez, they must remain ever at risk of exposure. You must forget Dinez now, Chantal. It is your future that is of far, far greater consequence!"

"My future is already decided!" said Chantal quietly. "I agreed with Antoine that we shall not remain in England for the Queen's wedding, that we leave in two weeks' time for Compiègne!"

She made the same pronouncement to her father and Mavreen. But it was not until the night before she was due to leave Barre House that she could muster sufficient courage to talk to John. Whether by accident or design, they found themselves together in the small salon. They had barely exchanged two words since Antoine's arrival in England but Chantal had been painfully aware of the bitter unhappiness in John's face. She had tried to avoid being in his presence, for the sight of his unhappiness hurt her cruelly and threatened to undermine her resolve. She would have given everything in the world she owned to be able to tell him the truth — that she loved him but that she could not let her father die!

Now that the moment for farewell had finally come, she could not leave him without one word of comfort. She approached him where he was seated by the fireplace moodily poking at the smouldering logs with one of the heavy fire irons. He did not look up although he was well aware it was she.

"John, 'tis I, Chantal! I have come to bid you goodbye!"

Still John did not look at her, although now he spoke.

"So you are determined to pursue this mad course!" he said, no longer troubling to hide his anguish.

Trying to control her tears Chantal knelt down beside him and lent her cheek against his sleeve. She could feel his arm tremble beneath the satin cloth of his tail-coat.

"I have to go!" she said simply, although her reply seemed highly enigmatic to John. "There is no one in the world I wish less to hurt than you, John!" she said huskily. "You . . . and Papa . . . are dearest of all to me and I love you both so much that . . . "

"Love!" John interrupted, turning now to stare at her in bitter anger. "I doubt you know the meaning of the word, Chantal. That you care not for *my* feelings, I can understand. But do you care nothing for your father's? In all my life I have never seen a man more unhappy. Yet you profess to *love* him! No, Chantal, you do not know what love means!"

He seemed to Chantal to be looking at her with scorn and hatred. Unaware of the tears pouring down her cheeks, she gazed back at him speechless in her own defense.

"I thought my life utterly ruined when I believed you dead!" John continued remorselessly. "In fact I could not bring myself to accept that you were lost forever. When Hamish and I found Tamarisk alive and I knew there was real hope of finding you too, I felt that God had indeed blessed me. I loved you, Chantal. I loved you even when I learned the truth about your life on the island. All that mattered was that you were alive and well. I did not speak then of my love because I believed you were not ready for it after your unhappy experience. I waited patiently for you to give me some small sign that you cared for me, unaware that all the time you were nurturing your dreams of a past love. Was Antoine once your lover, too, before your pirate? How blind, how gullible I have been!"

"John, no!" Chantal cried, as roughly he pulled his arm away from her grasp. "I had no thought for Antoine whilst I was on Coetivy. 'Twas of you I thought most of all. I swear it. I . . . I was so happy when I returned home and could be with you and Mama and Papa again. I do love you, John. You must believe me!"

The words were wrung from her despite her intent. But fortunately John misunderstood her.

"You love me as a brother, Chantal, but not as a man you might want to marry. I wish I could tell you that *I* do not love *you*. But God help me, I cannot. Perhaps I always will love you. It matters not. There is a girl who wishes to marry me despite the fact that she knows I love another. I may wed her and in time perhaps forget you Chantal. So do not weep any longer, if your tears are for me. They should be for yourself, for you are the one who will have to endure the degradation of being the wife of Antoine de Valle."

As Chantal fell into the chair he had vacated, sobbing bitterly at the unjust cruelty of John's words, he gave her one last look of despair.

"Better I had left you on the island with your Portuguese pirate than that I should have made such a marriage possible by bringing you home!" he said. "It is my intention never to set eyes upon either you or Antoine again!"

It was no idle threat and one which John fully intended to carry out. But not three days later, Tamarisk came running to him where he was reading in the library. Her cheeks were flushed and her words tumbled incoherently from her lips.

"I know now . . . the truth . . . Perry, you see . . . and we have to stop her. Do you not understand, John?"

"Steady now!" John said, smiling despite the depression that had gripped him since Chantal's departure to France. "So far I have not understood one word you have spoken, Tamarisk. Be seated and calm yourself. Then I can listen to what you have to say. 'Tis not like you to be so close to maidenly hysterics."

But Tamarisk would not be seated although she attempted to regain her composure. She had been supervising the closure of Chantal's room when quite suddenly the pieces of the puzzle had come together and she believed she knew why Chantal had agreed to marry Antoine. Until that moment she had failed to understand how Chantal could have been so quickly convinced of her love for a man she barely knew, that she was willing to leave her home, family, country at barely a moment's notice to marry him. It had seemed even more improbable that she could contemplate a marriage that was not undertaken from her home, without her beloved father to give her away; without her loved ones around her.

Tamarisk looked at John with unconcealed excitement.

"Do you not see, John, that never once did Chantal display the happiness of a girl who had lost her heart so completely that she must be with her beloved at all costs? She was coldly, quietly determined to marry Antoine and would not even listen to our discussions!"

John sighed deeply.

"Whilst that is true, I still do not follow the reason for your excitement, Tamarisk!"

"Nor I the point of Chantal's behavior until I remembered!" Tamarisk said. "John, the day after Antoine's first visit here, Chantal questioned Perry in closest detail about his past."

"Is that so strange?" John remarked. "Chantal may have realized that she might never see her father again. He will never go to France and I doubt that Antoine will allow her to visit her family here in England."

"So Perry thought," agreed Tamarisk. "Chantal's curiosity seemed quite natural to him at the time. But now, since I have spoken to him again, he agrees with me that it might have great import coming at this time."

John was trying hard to keep pace with Tamarisk's reasoning.

"I still do not follow your deductions," he said quietly.

"Because you know nothing as yet of the conversation Chantal had with me, John. She asked me searchingly about the laws relating to wrong-doers. She pretended to me a concern for Dinez da Gama which quite convinced me at the time. But now . . . now I am sure that she had another motive; that she wanted to certain that were the law to catch up with Perry, *his* life would be in danger. What I am trying to tell you, John is that I have little doubt that Chantal

582

is marrying Antoine to save her father's life."

Seeing the look of incredulity on John's face, she said carefully:

"To understand, you must know the part I played in all this. As a girl, I kept a journal . . . "

Slowly, painstakingly, she described how many years ago, the secretive, sly French boy had invaded her room and spied upon her most private possessions; how he had come upon the journal, read all she had written about Gideon Morris the highwayman, who was her mother's lover; how the boy had ultimately shown these comments to his father.

"Antoine is the only person alive who knows of Perry's past — other than Mama, me and dear old Dickon whose loyalty is beyond question. Antoine needed only to threaten Chantal to reveal the truth to ensure that she would agree to his proposal. He knew how dearly she loved her father and gambled upon her willingness to sacrifice her own life to save his. Perry is so convinced of it he is already with his valet packing to go to France to bring Chantal home. Mama is beside herself. I have never seen her in such turmoil. She understands and endorses Perry's fears for Chantal but she fears even more for *his* life."

"He shall not go to France, I will!" John cried. "He must remain safely with Mama. I will bring Chantal home."

"And I will go with you!" Tamarisk cried. "It may need us both to convince her, John, that there must be a better way to safeguard Perry.

It may even be necessary to force her against her will to return home with us. If she has had courage enough so far, she will not now risk her father's life merely because we ask it."

John nodded, understanding very well that Tamarisk's presence might indeed be helpful. Fortunately Charles was away at Dartmouth and Tamarisk was free to leave at once for France.

"Pack as little as you can, Tamarisk!" he said. "With too much baggage, we would be forced to take the carriage, and we will travel faster on horseback if you can endure the weather. Do you think you are strong enough to undertake the journey?"

"I will not hold you up, John dear!" Tamarisk reassured him smiling. "As well you know, to be on horseback is a pleasure and not a matter of endurance for me!"

"If we are fortunate we shall catch the last packet from Dover!" John said glancing at his timepiece. He paused and looked at Tamarisk, his face glowing.

"Let us pray your work of detection proves well founded," he said quietly, "for all our sakes! But most of all for mine. You see, Tamarisk, I still love Chantal and at long last I am beginning to believe that she might love me."

29

THE dress chariot sped smoothly along the streets of Compiègne, passing through the main square where above the magnificent *Mairie*, the little mechanical figures were striking the hour on the huge bell. The carriage passed by the Palace, through the Petit Parc and into the great forest where the trees were still gaunt and bare after the cold winter.

Sitting silently beside Antoine, Chantal was reminded of the time John had taken this same route almost three years ago. With growing fear she recalled his encounter with two of Antoine's woodsmen shooting at a child. She was now convinced in her own mind that Antoine was mad . . . and the more dangerous because outwardly his manner was perfectly normal.

Their journey from England had been conducted in a remote silence that still continued as they neared the Château de Boulancourt. Antoine had seemed lost in thought and had spoken only when necessary to ensure her comfort. His solicitude was as extreme as his possessiveness. He referred to her as 'my bride' when demanding of the packet steamer's captain that she must have the best cabin and the very best wine and food to refresh her. To his coachman and footmen, he referred to her as 'your mistress, the future Vicomtesse de Valle,' and left them in no doubt that they were to observe her every wish instantly and minutely.

But he made no attempt to touch her nor to speak affectionately to her and treated her like a priceless *objet d'art* that must be carefully protected and conducted to his home without mishap. Nevertheless there was an underlying determination in his manner that belied the cold impassivity of his face and speech. In keeping with her mounting fear of Antoine and her uncertainty as to the outcome of her bid to safeguard her father's life was her sense of isolation from her family. Unable to guarantee her strength of purpose in the presence of her father and stepmother, Chantal had lacked the courage to bid them farewell in person but had departed secretly, leaving letters telling them on no account must they attempt to follow her as they could never dissuade her from marrying Antoine.

Chantal knew that many years ago Tamarisk had eloped with an actor and that Mavreen and Perry had followed in pursuit, overtaking them at Gretna Green before the wedding could take place. She was afraid that were they to suspect her real reasons for marrying Antoine, they might attempt the same dramatic rescue of herself. As a safeguard therefore, she added a postscript to her letter saying that she and Antoine would quite possibly marry before leaving England and that they planned a prolonged sojourn in Europe.

'Neither Antoine nor I wish to spend our honeymoon at the Château de Boulancourt,'

she wrote. *'We shall in all probability seek the sun in southern Italy or even Spain now that the Civil War is over.'*

Confident that these lies would circumvent any plan to follow her to Compiègne, Chantal had slipped out of the house during the early hours before dawn and joined Antoine at his hotel where a room had been reserved for her.

He seemed far more concerned than she herself that all the conventions preceding their wedding should be observed and he behaved towards her with the utmost propriety.

In fact, Antoine was obsessive in his determination to have his marriage legally ensured beyond any question. Now that his first wife, the unhappy Camille Faloise, was dead, there was no single impediment to the union he craved so ardently. He knew that once Chantal was his wife, the law would not allow her to leave him. Divorce was obtainable only by mutual consent and he would never, never consent to it. On the brink of realizing his heart's desire, he would allow no loophole for escape.

As far as the pages of Tamarisk's journal were concerned, Antoine had not the slightest intention of handing them to Chantal as a wedding gift as she so naïvely supposed. He had given the promise of their return only to ensure her compliance. She had believed him, the very innocence that had attracted him when first he met her, leading her like a helpless fly into his web. He regretted her ultimate disillusionment but consoled himself with the belief that once in his arms she would soon forgive his trickery as she succumbed to his magic.

With a sardonic inward smile Antoine silently thanked his father for having placed him as a boy in Camille's guardianship. Through her and her friends, he had quickly learned all the ways of pleasuring a woman. Until his marriage to Camille, he had continued to exert his charms with every woman who showed interest in him, but always for the rewards that followed and never out of affection for them or even to please himself. From Chantal he would seek no reward beyond the perfect satisfaction of seeing her weak with love and desire, a prisoner to the delights he alone could give her. He did not believe that she would retain for long her bourgeois notions of romantic love for his youthful, inexperienced half-brother. Her childish adoration for John, he assured himself, would soon be swept away by the sensual passions of her awakening body.

Mistakenly Antoine discounted the influence Dinez da Gama might have had upon her. Chantal had confessed to him that she was no longer a virgin, hoping that he would lose interest in the proposed marriage. But upon hearing that the man was a pirate, Antoine assumed that the renegade had forced himself upon her. Her reluctance to speak of da Gama or of her experiences on the island confirmed Antoine's supposition that she had suffered miserably at the hands of her seducer.

Chantal's belief that Antoine was mentally

disturbed was not far from the truth. When John's fateful letter arrived from Paris stating that Chantal was alive, he had attempted to cease the habit of opium-eating. But by then he could no longer control it and now he was again indulging in the practice. As a consequence he was subject to moods of high elation followed by periods of depression. The cold, clear logic that had been characteristic of him since his childhood was markedly absent. It had been in one of the periods of excessive mental stimulation that he had dispatched Stefano to kill Camille. His orders had been to dispose of her first and then ransack her quarters. It was not until after his servant had carried out the orders that in changed mood, Antoine realized he had defeated his own main objective in keeping the miserable woman prisoner for so long. Stefano had found nothing in her room and now she could never tell him the whereabouts of her fortune. With a lack of foresight totally uncharacteristic of him, he had failed to take into account the fact that on reaching Paris Camille might not immediately withdraw her jewelry from its hiding place.

But now Antoine was once more in a mood of euphoria as seated beside Chantal they drove over the drawbridge into the courtyard of his house. He no longer cared about the loss of Camille's fortune, he thought. He had beside him the most precious jewel of all — the girl he loved. It mattered not that he had had to blackmail her to achieve this moment. His joy and satisfaction were intense.

He made no demur when Chantal declared she wished to retire to her room and remain there for the following day in order to recover from the rigors of the journey. He had much to occupy him in preparing for the wedding. Within hours of his return, the Château hummed with activity. He vacated his own luxurious bedchamber and ante-room in order that they could be entirely redecorated and refurbished as the bridal suite. He dispatched a note to the local Curé informing him that he would be required to officiate at the Vicomte's wedding in the Chapel of the Château one week from the date of the letter. Another servant was dispatched to Paris to bring back lengths of the finest satin and lace for Chantal's bridal gown and a Parisian *couturier* with her assistants to design and stitch the dress.

"You shall have a wedding gown no less beautiful than that of your young Queen Victoria!" he had promised Chantal. Warming to the idea of a royal similarity, he declared that they would be married on the selfsame day as the Queen.

Chantal did not welcome the proposed delay.

"Can we not be married at once?" she asked, believing that the sooner the wedding day arrived, the sooner she would have possession of the fatal document and could make her escape to England.

Antoine was agreeably surprised by what he hoped was Chantal's change of heart. Nonetheless he insisted upon at least a week in which to make adequate preparations.

"I want you to be fully recovered from your fatigue, my dearest Chantal, before our wedding night!" he said pointedly.

Lying in the huge four-poster in Antoine's guest chamber, Chantal shivered at the memory of those words. She felt miserably alone and deeply apprehensive. She wished desperately that she had poor Dorothy with her to attend her. A thin, gaunt greying servant in her fifties had been appointed by Antoine as her personal maid, and although the woman smiled often, the smile never reached her eyes and there seemed to Chantal to be a hint of cruelty in her expression.

Although this female attended to Chantal's every need with the utmost care and precision, it was not long before Chantal began to feel as if the woman were not her personal maid but her wardress. Such thoughts brought to her mind yet again John's strange story of the mad prisoner and Chantal wondered fearfully if Antoine had allotted her one of the Princess's gaolers. The servant said her name was Marianne, yet Chantal began to doubt it, for more often than not she had to call her several times before the woman answered.

Her feeling of apprehension deepened. The evening after her arrival, when Marianne left the room to arrange for Chantal's evening meal, she decided to leave the safe haven of her bed to discover for herself whether Antoine were in fact keeping her a prisoner in her bedchamber. The door was unlocked and she made her way unmolested along the cold draughty stone

591

passage to the top of the main stairway. Far below she observed a liveried footman. He went through the great hall from the kitchen quarters, carrying a silver tray on which was a decanter and glass goblet which she presumed was intended for Antoine. From the direction of the small salon, lights glowed with cheerful normality.

Chiding herself for such lack of courage, Chantal hurried back to her bedchamber and awaited the return of the forbidding Marianne. Since Antoine seemed set upon pleasing her, she thought, she would speak to him tomorrow and inform him that she would prefer that a younger servant attended her, even if such a girl lacked Marianne's experience.

The following day she rose, dressed with care and joined Antoine for the midday meal. He greeted her warmly and at once acceded to her request.

"Although it may take a day or two to arrange for a suitable girl to be sent from Compiègne!" he said with apparent regret that he could not at once oblige Chantal. "I am sorry that you do not care for Marianne. This is of course a bachelor establishment and as you will discover, I have few female servants. As soon as you are my wife you shall engage whomsoever you please!"

So Chantal was forced to endure the ministrations of the daunting Marianne. Despite her discouragement, the woman continued to touch all her belongings, fingering them in a way she found distasteful — as if she were a dog trying to sniff out the scent of an unwelcome stranger, Chantal thought.

By the third day she could stand her presence no longer and dismissed her cursorily. The woman departed without any sign of distress.

"I admit that I may be behaving quite unfairly to her," Chantal told Antoine, for she did not want the woman punished in any way since she had not committed any offense. "I found no fault with the way she carried out her duties. If anything her services were too frequent but always perfectly executed. I simply do not like her personality and I do not care to have her near me."

She thought she caught a glimmer of anger in Antoine's face but if it were there at all, within seconds it was gone. Bowing in graceful acknowledgement of her remarks, he said:

"You know that your happiness is more important to me than anything in the world. You have but to tell me your wishes and I will ensure they are fulfilled."

Chantal looked up quickly.

"If you mean that truly, Antoine, then you have it within your power to make me the happiest girl in the world. You cannot fail but appreciate my deep concern for my father's safety. Will you not give me the extract from Tamarisk's journal this very day, so that I may be free of my anxiety?"

To her unutterable astonishment, Antoine smiled his perfect smile, saying:

"But of course, my lovely Chantal. I had no idea that you still feared I would make use of those papers to harm your father. How could you think me capable of such a terrible deed now that you are here at Boulancourt with me? I have put the pages from your sister's journal in a safe place here in the Château for the very purpose of safeguarding your father. I will find them for you this very afternoon. If you will honor me by dining with me this evening, it will be my pleasure to hand them to you."

"Thank you! *Thank you*, Antoine!" Chantal cried, adding quickly: "Such a kindness on your part will raise you immeasurably in my eyes!"

"And in your heart?" Antoine enquired, no longer smiling. Quickly Chantal turned away so that he could not see her expression.

"You know that I need time to readjust my emotions!" she prevaricated. "I am sure I shall soon have further occasion to appreciate your true worth and already you have given me reason to be most grateful, Antoine!"

But Antoine had no intention of handing Chantal the papers she wanted, for only by retaining them would he be certain of retaining her. Nor did he intend to engage the maid he had promised her. The woman she had supposed a servant in his household was his own mother, Blanche Merlin, who had adopted the name of Marianne lest any should guess her real identity. She was invaluable to Antoine in that she kept him informed of all that transpired within the Château, for none knew of their true relationship with the exception of Stefano.

Twenty-five years ago, Gerard de Valle, true to his promise, had provided generously for the farm girl who had borne him the son he wanted.

He had purchased for Blanche a small farmstead in the south of France and provided her with sufficient means to survive there in moderate comfort for the remainder of her life.

Antoine was unconcerned by the separation from his mother. Brought to England by his father as a boy of but five years of age, he even then had been concerned only with his own advancement. He had little love for the woman who had slaved and sacrificed herself to feed and educate him in order that one day he might be recognized by his aristocratic father. During his childhood in England he had not once enquired what had become of his mother. Even when he had returned to France to live at Boulancourt, he had neither written to her nor visited her. But when he realized that he must have some woman upon whom he could depend absolutely to guard his wife, Princess Camille Faloise, he remembered her.

Blanche Merlin was more than happy to be reunited with the son she had once idolized. She soon saw that he had totally fulfilled all her wildest ambitions for him and within a very short while, both realized that they shared the same unscrupulous nature. It satisfied Blanche's bitter revengeful mind that she, a farmer's daughter, should be placed in control of a Princess; that she could degrade the *aristo* as she had once felt degraded; wield power over her in any way she chose short of hastening her death.

It did not strike Blanche as being in the least immoral that her handsome, beautiful, talented son should have married this elderly aristocrat for her money. No less avaricious than she had been thirty years ago, she was willing to assist Antoine in every way possible to obtain Camille's fortune. Antoine had promised her a generous reward, well aware that her loyalty to him would thus be reinforced.

The Princess' death was a matter of deep concern to Blanche — not just because there could now be no pecuniary gain but because she realized that her son had erred in his judgment. She knew of Antoine's habit of opium-eating and she worried about this, too, attributing to it his irrational adoration of the English girl he wanted to marry. Blanche had reason to resent his choice. She knew that Chantal was related, if only in marriage, to the woman, Mavreen — the woman Antoine's father had loved so obsessively and who had ultimately borne him a son, John. That son threatened Antoine's rightful heritage and only Antoine's clever scheming had circumvented his young half-brother from usurping the de Valle title. Blanche herself had obtained the forged certificate 'proving' her marriage to Gerard.

But now the English girl was under Antoine's roof and Blanche feared the strange power Chantal had over him. She had never before seen him anything but indifferent to a woman's charms and she had believed him immune from such influences. She could not understand why Antoine should wish to marry a girl who clearly had no love for him and no dowry to tempt him. Realizing that she could no longer trust her son to be rational, she designated herself as guardian of his happiness and well-being, and mistrustful of Chantal, watched her like an eagle.

Blanche was hardly surprised when Chantal took an instinctive dislike to her for she had not been able to pretend any warmth of feeling. But she regretted her coldness when the stupid girl went running to Antoine with her complaints. Antoine, in the privacy of his room, had rounded upon her, his mother, telling her that she must either grow to love Chantal as he did or else she must return at once to her farm where there would be none of the luxuries she now enjoyed.

"Keep out of Chantal's sight from now on!" he ordered harshly. "And if you do encounter her, then try to be pleasant. If you cause her one more minute of anxiety, you will pay heavily for it!"

Blanche knew better than to plead with him that she was his mother and that he owed her some respect. She knew that her son was like herself, ruthless and merciless. Her jealous hatred of Chantal increased and she continued her espionage at a discreet distance. Her eyes and ears missed nothing.

The arrival at the Château of Gerard de Valle's legitimate son, John, and his sister, Tamarisk, was therefore known to Blanche even before word reached Antoine. As the footman opened the doors to the weary travelers, her keen peasant instinct for danger sent her scurrying to the servants' quarters to don mobcap and apron. Thus disguised as a cleaning maid, she could move in the regions of the *grand salon* where

Antoine would receive his unexpected visitors.

It was not long since Antoine had partaken of a liberal quantity of opium. He therefore faced the new arrivals in a mood of extreme confidence, despite his assumption that they were here to 'rescue' Chantal.

"Be seated, *je vous en prie!*" he said, making an elaborate bow to John and raising Tamarisk's gloved hand to his lips. "You have come doubtless to see Chantal and I will send word to her presently. But first I think it best we should talk alone, do you not agree? You see, I fear your journey will prove quite pointless. I can assure you that Chantal will not change her mind."

John's relief on hearing that Chantal was within call and seemingly unharmed outweighed his anger at Antoine's cool effrontery.

"That remains to be seen, Antoine!" Tamarisk said quietly. "But by all means let us discuss the situation whilst Chantal is absent."

Despite the gravity of the occasion she discovered herself admiring Antoine's immaculate appearance. He looked the height of elegance in his jade green velvet tail-coat and darker toned, close-fitting trousers. "You may as well know," she continued, "that John and I have guessed the measures you must have used to persuade Chantal to come here to France with you."

Antoine smiled, unperturbed.

"Then you will also know, I presume, that your sister has agreed to marry me!"

"That will never happen!" John cried, jumping to his feet. Tamarisk quickly drew him back to the seat beside her. It was already agreed that she would speak for them both. "You are far too personally involved to remain as cool-headed as may be necessary," she had cautioned him.

"What John means, Antoine, is that we cannot allow Chantal to marry you in such circumstances," she said quietly.

Antoine took a step towards Tamarisk and stood looking down at her, his eyebrows slightly lifted, his mouth distorted by an undisguised sneer.

"I seem to recall, my dear sister, that there was a time in your life — in your youth, should I say — when you yourself would have made any sacrifice necessary to save your beloved Perry's skin!"

The color burned Tamarisk's cheeks and her eyes blazed.

"Do not think you can humiliate me by such remarks, Antoine!" she said bitingly. "'Tis clear that you are not very well acquainted with Chantal's father else you would know that he would rather be dead than that his daughter should suffer on his account."

"And who is to provide him with this choice?" Antoine asked coolly.

"'Tis already made!" Tamarisk retorted. "If you will not agree to release Chantal at once, Antoine, I shall return home and inform her father. I would not care to be in your shoes then for if Perry must die in the end by your betrayal, he would of a certainty kill you first!"

To her consternation and John's, Antoine merely laughed.

"Then perhaps I should instruct my footman to have your coach prepared for your immediate departure," he said, "for I have not the slightest intention of allowing Chantal to leave the Château!"

"You cannot keep her here by force!" John cried, once more upon his feet.

"Nor have I need to!" Antoine replied calmly. He walked away and tugged on the bell rope. As soon as a servant appeared, he gave orders that Chantal was to be requested to join him in the library at once.

Chantal had been unaware of John's and Tamarisk's arrival and as she entered the room she turned a deathly white when she saw them.

"Oh, no!" she gasped. "No! I did not want you to come here!"

Tamarisk hurried across the room to her and took both her hands.

"Dearest Chantal!" she cried, "you cannot go through with this marriage, not even for your Papa's sake. He does not want his life at such a price. John and I have come to take you home."

"Perhaps Chantal does not consider the price too high!" Antoine said confidently.

Chantal was looking at John. With all her heart she longed to run into his arms; to beg him to take her home at once, away from this dreadful house; far away from this man she hated and feared. But better even than John and Tamarisk, she knew that Antoine would not fail to carry out his threat to expose her father if she left him now. They knew nothing of Antoine's promise to surrender the incriminating papers on their wedding day.

"John, Tamarisk, *trust* me!" she begged in a low urgent voice. She turned quickly to Tamarisk. "You must believe that I know what I am doing!" she said. "I am no longer a child, Tamarisk. You know that I am older, wiser than I was. You yourself have said so. I have weighed up the situation — every aspect of it — calmly and clearly and *I know what I am doing*. You must leave me to make my own decision."

In Antoine's presence she could not explain to Tamarisk that she never intended to live with him after the marriage. She could only hope that Tamarisk understood her implications. Tamarisk's eyes searched Chantal's face as if she were trying to assess her reasoning. Then she turned to John and said:

"Chantal is right, of course. We have overlooked the fact that she is no longer a child and that it is for her to decide her own future. We have no right to interfere in Chantal's plans, John."

"How very sensible!" Antoine remarked without troubling to conceal his sarcasm. "I am happy to see that you, Tamarisk, have grown wiser with the years!"

Tight-lipped, John faced the three of them.

"I would not want to kill my own brother, but I would commit fratricide rather than see Chantal married to you, sir!" he cried.

"You speak in hot blood!" Antoine said. "But when reason reasserts itself, John, you will realize

601

that you do not have the upbringing or the character that would permit you to commit the crime you suggest. Nor would Chantal approve, would you, *ma chère*?"

"Antoine is right!" Chantal cried. "You cannot harm your own brother, John. Besides which I am acting of my own free will, can you not understand? Although I deplore the manner in which Antoine used threats to obtain my consent to our marriage, I now know that he never intended to carry them out. I think I might enjoy being mistress of such a beautiful home and I am quite reconciled to the idea of marriage to Antoine."

The look of total incomprehension on John's face gave way to another as it dawned on him that Chantal was acting out a charade; that she would never have forgiven Antoine for threatening her father, no matter what the purpose.

"Let us calm ourselves and try to forget the angry words we have exchanged!" Tamarisk interposed quickly. "I for one, wish only Chantal's happiness as does John, too. We have no further need to concern ourselves, John, now we know that Chantal is acting of her own free will. Now tell me, please, has the date for the wedding been arranged?"

Lulled into a false sense of victory, Antoine replied triumphantly:

"A week from today!"

"Then we must surely stay to attend the ceremony!" Tamarisk said. "You would wish us to be present, would you not, Chantal?"

Chantal returned Tamarisk's gaze. She was certain now of Tamarisk's divination that she had no intention of offering herself as a willing sacrifice to the slaughter.

"That would be a great comfort to me, my dearest sister!" she replied. "If Antoine will agree, then it would indeed make me very happy!"

She forced herself to cross the room to stand beside him. She looked up at him with a carefully contrived innocent appeal. "You have told me so many times that you will do anything that brings me happiness. I would feel so much less lonely with a female relative beside me. Tamarisk can advise me about my wedding gown. My dress is to be even more beautiful than the Queen's, Tamarisk!" she added, her manner so prettily childish that Tamarisk knew at once it was false. "Antoine has sent to Paris for the materials and he has promised me a Parisian *couturier* to design and stitch the gown for me. She arrives tomorrow and I am so excited!"

Because his sense of caution was dulled by opium, Antoine was both beguiled and deceived by Chantal's words. More than anything in the world he wanted her as charmingly and sweetly enthusiastic about her wedding as she now appeared to be. If having her sister present was instrumental in bringing about such a happy state of affairs, he was willing to comply with her request. He looked with less assurance at John. John, like Tamarisk, knew Chantal too well to be taken in by her childish exhibition but he was astute enough to realize that he might arouse Antoine's suspicion were he to change his attitude too quickly.

"I shall never reconcile myself to Chantal's marriage to anyone but myself!" he grunted. "I cannot believe that you intend to go through with this . . . this mockery of a wedding!" he added to Chantal. "But then I never did understand you very well, did I? I never guessed you would stoop so low as to 'marry' a pirate! Well, we shall see if this time you are in earnest. I for one, will not be convinced of your desire to wed Antoine until I see with my own eyes the rites performed. Or is this marriage, too, to take place without church or clergy?"

"I advise you to guard your tongue if you wish to remain beneath my roof!" Antoine said furiously. "If it were not for Chantal's wishes, you would be shown the door for far less insult than this last abuse of her. Fortunately for you, sir, I have long been aware of your jealousy and I am now aware, too, of your bitterness towards Chantal. But I caution you to remember that you are no longer addressing your sister but my future wife, the Vicomtesse de Valle, and whilst you are my guest you will afford her due courtesy. I hope that is understood!"

John muttered beneath his breath but gave the appearance of being chastened. He caught Tamarisk's eye and with a swift surge of excitement he was at pains to conceal, he realized that he had guessed correctly that a plan was afoot to defeat Antoine.

Chantal came running to him, all smiles and dimples.

"Oh, John!" she said sweetly. "Is this not turning into a merry adventure? I am quite giddy with excitement now that I know you and Tamarisk are to join in the festivities. You and Antoine must now forget your past disagreements for my sake. I want you both to be friends as well as brothers. And really, John, you do not need to be concerned for me. Antoine has promised me anything in the world I want, so I shall lack for nothing that I desire. Is that not sweet and kind of him?"

Antoine smiled, well content. He would honor that promise in every respect but one — he would never give her the papers that would guarantee her father's life, thus ensuring that she remained by his side.

30

February 1840

ANTOINE made no demur when Chantal declared that Tamarisk must be quite exhausted after so long a journey and that she would accompany her to one of the guest chambers where she might rest. He did, however, instruct a servant to go at once and find Marianne to attend Tamarisk.

"Whilst your room is being prepared, you may refresh yourself in my bedchamber," Chantal said.

As Tamarisk followed her up the great stairway, she whispered:

"I trust you will like the odious female, Marianne, better than I do. I dismissed her from my service. Although she was good enough at her tasks, I am convinced she was spying upon me."

She did not speak again until they were alone in her room. Then she flung her arms around Tamarisk and hugged her.

"You cannot believe how happy I am to see you and John!" she cried. "But your arrival could have proved a disaster, Tamarisk. Papa is in great danger and . . . "

"I think I know all the reasons why you left England!" Tamarisk broke in. "Brave and laudable though they were, you should have told at least one of us of your plan. But Chantal, what possible way have you conceived to defeat Antoine in his purpose? From your conversation downstairs I assumed that you have no real intention of marrying him?"

Chantal led Tamarisk to the chaise-longue at the foot of her bed and when they were seated, their arms around each other, she said excitedly:

"Antoine has promised to give me the pages from your journal as a wedding gift, Tamarisk. So even if I have to participate in the ceremony itself, I need not remain here one moment after he has handed them to me. As for my marriage to him, I am convinced that if made under threat it would not be considered valid in England. And even if it were, Tamarisk, it would be a small price to pay for Papa's life. Antoine could not force me to live with him."

Tamarisk looked at Chantal pityingly.

"My dear child!" she said, "have you not considered that Antoine may never give you the pages of my journal as he has promised? What possible reason have you for supposing he will keep his word? He is quite without scruples and 'tis my conviction now that everything John suspected of him is true. He might well seek to imprison you as he did the poor Princess Faloise!"

Chantal shivered involuntarily.

"I did wonder if he might betray me!" she said quietly. "But I have discounted such misgivings because I do not think he really wishes to harm Papa. His threat to do so was merely ruse to

607

obtain my consent to the marriage. Once he believes I am his, he will have no further use for those pages."

"Unless it be to force you to remain beneath his roof!" Tamarisk replied shrewdly. "He cannot have overlooked the possibility that you will try to return to England!"

Chantal drew a deep breath.

"I know! But it is a chance I have to take. I may not have the opportunity to speak alone with John so it is important that you relay to him what I am about to say. In these few remaining days before the wedding it is my intention to convince Antoine that I am succumbing to his charms and that I have no further interest in John. John would doubtless be deeply distressed by my manner were he not made aware of the truth. Please tell him that I love him dearly but that he must pretend jealousy of my manner towards Antoine. At the same time, he must not provoke Antoine too far lest he angers him and puts himself in danger. And Tamarisk," Chantal added sighing, "no matter how genuinely John disapproves, if I am obliged to take part in the ceremony, *he must not try to prevent it.* It may be our only chance to save Papa's life. If John really loves me, he cannot insist at such a cost that I remain free to marry *him*. Once I am safely returned to England, I will live with him as his wife if he so wishes, for I will never consider myself married to Antoine even if I am legally declared so."

Tamarisk nodded.

"I do not approve this wild scheme!" she

said thoughtfully. "Nor do I think will John. Nevertheless I can see no better alternative if we are to make this last attempt to save Perry. I will do my best to assist you in any way I can. Somehow I will persuade John, too, to comply with your wishes."

John was far more perturbed than Tamarisk at the terrible chance Chantal was taking. His happiness at knowing she loved him was greatly diminished by the extent of his concern for her. He believed they might all be in serious danger and his instinct was to take Chantal away from Boulancourt as speedily as possible.

But knowing she would not leave without the fatal documents that could incriminate his stepfather, John determined to search for them. He supposed that Antoine had concealed such private papers somewhere in the Château but the size of Boulancourt was so immense and its places of concealment so many, that he feared he might need five months rather than five days to find them. As he set about his prodigious task his frustration mounted, for wherever he went, there always seemed to be a servant not far away keeping observation upon his movements. He was certain that Antoine had guessed his intent and determined to circumvent it, had set spies upon him.

As it transpired it was not John but Tamarisk who by merest chance two days after their arrival, happened upon the hidden door of the secret chamber where Antoine kept the most private of his documents. He also kept there his supply of opium. Tamarisk's visit to the library was for the most innocent of purposes. She was seeking a book to read to help pass the time whilst Chantal was being fitted for her wedding gown. As she reached upwards to one of the higher shelves, her foot slipped upon the polished floor. She fell sideways, bruising her shoulder against the cornice of one of the stone columns framing the fireplace.

At first Tamarisk did not notice the set of bookshelves to her left opening slowly inward. But as she regained her feet, the gaping aperture became immediately apparent. Too astonished to be cautious, she hurried forward to see where this unexpected doorway might lead.

The room beyond was windowless, dark and musty. Tamarisk could see only that it was very small, circular and that tin boxes covered the uncarpeted floor. She realized at once that no further exploration of this cleverly concealed room could be carried out without the aid of a candle. She knew that secret chambers such as this were often to be found in mansions in England. They had been used in the main by smugglers as a stronghold for their booty, or as a safe hiding place for religious or political refugees fleeing from their persecutors. The existence of this room did not therefore surprise her but she was curious and intrigued to know how she had inadvertently touched the spring, if such it was, that had caused the door to open.

Since she had fallen against the fireplace, it seemed the obvious place to begin her search, but as her fingers traveled over the carved stonework of the cornice, the door of the library opened and a woman came into the room.

It was Blanche Merlin who in accordance with Antoine's command, should have been keeping a watchful eye upon Tamarisk's every movement but had only now discovered her whereabouts. At first the woman did not notice the door of the secret room as Tamarisk's hands reactivated the spring and it swung slowly back on its hinges. But as the door clicked shut, Blanche realized with shocked dismay that somehow Tamarisk had discovered its secret.

Instinct lent her caution.

"Were you looking for something, Milady?" she asked, her voice as expressionless as her face.

"I came to find a book!" Tamarisk replied guiltily like a child caught stealing sweetmeats. "But as I reached up I slipped and fell. I must have hit my head on the stonework for I lost consciousness and have only just this minute recovered my senses! See, here is the mark upon the floor made by my shoes as I fell!"

She, too, had heard the door close and now she could but hope that the servant would believe her tale that she had been unconscious and had seen nothing of the secret chamber.

"If Milady would like to lie down for a while?" Blanche's voice gave no indication of her true feelings of anxiety. "I will bring Milady a little cognac. It will help you to recover from the shock of your fall."

Reasonably confident that she had indeed averted suspicion, Tamarisk made pretence of a return of faintness and allowed herself to be helped out of the room and upstairs to her bedchamber.

Once satisfied that Tamarisk was, for the the moment anyway, safely in her bed, Blanche Merlin went slowly downstairs in search of her son. She was trembling with fear, for she could be in no doubt of the mood in which Antoine would receive her. His fury with those who failed in their duties was well known to her and she dreaded the effect her confession would have upon him when she told him she had failed to see Tamarisk leave her bedchamber.

She paused, hesitating as she reached the top of the stairway. She realized that Antoine would have to be told that his secret room had been discovered; that if he were not made aware of it, his life as well as her own would be in danger. But equally she realized the repercussions that must follow. Her admission that she had allowed Tamarisk to roam the Château unobserved and with such disastrous consequences, would be of a certainty mean that she would be banished forthwith and made to return to the lonely, uneventful life of her modest farmstead.

Blanche hated her own home. The airs and graces she had assumed when first she went to live there had aroused the mistrust of the peasants who were her neighbors. She had had neither the money nor the appurtenances to pass for a woman socially acceptable to the noble families in the environs. But here, at the magnificent Château de Boulancourt, she had everything in the world she wanted. It did not trouble her that Antoine had forbidden her ever to let it be known she was his mother. She herself disapproved of any action that might undermine his authority here as the Vicomte, the *aristo* — a position for which she truly believed he had been destined. It was enough for her that she was the chatelaine, the housekeeper whom all the servants but Stefano must obey without question.

That her son showed her no filial affection, Blanche accepted without question. Of an evening, if he were not entertaining his Parisian friends, he would come to her sitting-room where it amused him to discuss with her his thoughts and plans and exchange opinions with her on the respective merits of the prisoners in the dungeons. He trusted her absolutely.

But if she confessed her negligence concerning Tamarisk, she thought, that trust would be instantly withdrawn.

Blanche shivered. Since he had begun to eat opium, Antoine's moods were unpredictable, often violent to the extreme when he denied himself the drug. She knew him to be ruthless when his will was thwarted and she knew the degree of obsessional love he had for the girl, Chantal. If he were to lose Chantal by virtue of *her* carelessness, who knew but that he might turn upon her, his poor mother, for revenge; that he might even kill her!

Her mind, ever shrewd with peasant cunning, was working furiously on a way out of her predicament. It was not many minutes before there occurred to her an alternative to confession. Gradually a smile replaced the grim

613

concentration on her gaunt face. She turned and retraced her steps along the stone passageway. Pausing outside Tamarisk's door, she tilted her head as she listened. From within came the sound of a second voice which she recognized instantly as John's. It was as she thought! Plainly Tamarisk was losing no time in regaling her brother with details of her discovery of the secret room.

"So both must go!" she thought. Their deaths would not be difficult to effect. But she must take care that the girl, Chantal, remained unharmed. To hurt one hair of her head was to court Antoine's certain retribution instead of the thanks she might expect for ridding him of two potential enemies.

Her first instinct was to use chloroform — a chemical substance discovered three years ago which Stefano had used most effectively on the Princess before drowning her in the River Seine. He would know where it could be procured. But Stefano was heart and soul his master's man and would report her request to Antoine. An alternative method was to put poison in the food, but Blanche feared its ingestion by others at the dinner table — by Chantal, or even worse, by Antoine himself.

Blanche was convinced that she could extricate herself from the necessity to confess her carelessness without risk to Antoine. She returned to her vigil in the small room adjoining Tamarisk's from whence she could ascertain her movements. She did not doubt that with a little thought she would soon light upon a clever, subtle method of safeguarding her son.

Tamarisk was uneasy. John had pointed out that it was unnatural that Marianne had not questioned her about the open door and she was now convinced that the ugly old woman knew of her discovery. Neither she nor John doubted that the servant would report the matter to Antoine. Yet the afternoon and evening passed without him referring to it and his manner seemed in no degree changed. At breakfast the following morning when there was still no mention of it, John took Tamarisk to one side and said:

"I am beginning to feel we have been worrying unduly and that the woman believed your story. In any event, we can delay no longer. Tell Chantal to devise some means of keeping Antoine away from the Château this afternoon — a visit to Compiègne, perhaps. But do not tell her of our intention lest Antoine questions her and inadvertently she appears less innocent than must be the case if she is truly ignorant of our plan to investigate the secret chamber at our leisure!"

Tamarisk nodded. It was simple enough for her to talk to Chantal alone but Antoine watched John like an eagle whenever he so much as glanced in her direction.

After luncheon, at John's suggestion, he and Tamarisk became engrossed in a game of chess in the library and were so engaged when Chantal and Antoine came to bid them farewell before departing to Compiègne.

"Doubtless we shall still be battling when you

return, my dear!" Tamarisk told Chantal, her words intended for Antoine's ears. He, however, seemed quite disinterested in their pursuits and if he had reason to suspect them he gave no sign of it.

In point of fact, Antoine was delighted that Chantal had sought out his company and expressed the wish to go alone with him to the town. He cared little how his half-brother and sister chose to pass their afternoon.

When finally Tamarisk and John felt confident that they were quite alone, they made certain that the door was firmly shut. Then Tamarisk hurried over to the fireplace and began eagerly to trace the patterned stonework of the cornice. John waited silently, his excitement and impatience mounting with every minute. At last Tamarisk's fingers found the piece of moulding that operated the hidden door. John watched in fascination as one whole section of the bookcase swung slowly inward. Hurriedly he lit the candle with which he had equipped himself and preceded Tamarisk into the dark interior of the room.

Mindful of Tamarisk's description of the tin trunks, John had also provided himself with a mason's chisel. His heart beating fiercely with anticipation, he knelt on the dusty stone floor and set about prizing open one of the lids.

As he had suspected, the trunks were locked. The iron hinges did not yield easily to John's forcing and so engrossed was he in his labors that neither he nor Tamarisk heard the quiet opening of the library door nor the soft footfall on the deep-piled rugs. It was not until the heavy book-lined door slammed shut that he and Tamarisk realized they must have been observed.

White-faced, Tamarisk stared at her brother. "We are prisoners!" she gasped.

Equally unnerved but anxious not to let Tamarisk see his apprehension, John held the candle aloft and peered intently around the room. It was small, circular and to his dismay, he saw that it was windowless. There was no possible means of escape for the walls were built of great blocks of stone as was the rounded ceiling. Not even with his chisel could he hope to make any impression on them.

"There must be some method by which the door can be opened from the inside!" he said as confidently as he could, for he could see none. "We have but to search long enough, Tamarisk, and eventually we shall find it."

Calmed by this sensible suggestion Tamarisk breathed more easily.

"I will feel the wall to our left; and you go to the right, John!" she suggested. "Then we cannot overlook the release point if such exists."

The trunks forgotten, they began their search. They moved steadily around the room towards one another until John dropped the candle and they were plunged into darkness. He felt for his tinderbox and quickly re-lit the candle.

"'Twill not last a great deal longer!" he remarked uneasily. "Perhaps since we came for the purpose, I should make use of the light we still have to investigate the contents of the trunks whilst you continue to search the walls.

Even if we do not find a way out, someone will come for us sooner or later, and by then I am determined to know what is hidden here. It must be of consequence to be so well concealed."

Tamarisk made no demur although her own curiosity had now been effectively replaced by her mounting fear. She controlled it, reminding herself constantly that Chantal on her return to the Château, would demand to know their whereabouts; and that no matter what Antoine intended to do with them he could not mean to leave them here to die.

Her curiosity returned once more when John, quite forgetting their predicament, gave a sudden shout of excitement.

"Tamarisk, these are the very documents I am seeking!" he cried. "Here is the paper stating that Antoine did in fact, marry the Princess Faloise in New York in eighteen-thirty." He shuffled through the papers eagerly. "There is no such document relating to my father's marriage to Antoine's mother! But here — here is my father's last Will and Testament!" he cried. "The past is all here, Tamarisk. Father speaks of Antoine as *'My first son'* and then of me as *'My legitimate son, John, who is the rightful heir to my title.'* And Tamarisk, he makes provision for *'the woman, Blanche Merlin who bore my first son.'*"

He continued to read aloud:

" . . . that my son, John, shall consider my obligation to this said Blanche Merlin as his own, and bearing in mind that she has no

618

rightful claim upon me, that as long as she lives it shall remain a matter of honor for him to discharge my obligations."

"So 'tis written down, Tamarisk. He never did marry her!" John cried.

"Which only proves more clearly that Antoine is without honor or scruples if he could so deceive us!" Tamarisk said warningly. "John, 'tis not only our lives and Perry's that would seem to be in jeopardy whilst we remain here, but Chantal's too. And have you considered that if we do not live to tell her, Mama will never know that our father did not after all, betray her. We *must* find our way out of here!"

But in the brief remaining time that the candle burned, neither she nor John could find the way by which the door might be opened. As the tiny flame flickered and finally went out, they realized that the means of escape no longer lay in their hands. Not only were they without food or water, but John feared that air too might be lacking; moreover that now they knew the contents of the hidden documents, it was doubtful if Antoine would be in any hurry to release them from their tomb.

As he sank to the floor beside Tamarisk and put his arm about her shoulders, he tried to bolster her spirits by reminding her that Chantal would surely find a way to effect their release. But even as he spoke, he remembered that she knew nothing of their whereabouts, or even of the existence of the secret room.

At first Chantal was not concerned by their

absence when she returned from Compiègne. Aware that John and Tamarisk were upon some secret mission of their own devising, she supposed them somewhere about in one of the innumerable rooms of the Château. Antoine, however, was openly curious as to their whereabouts and Chantal's main concern was that he would come upon them in some place where he did not wish them to be.

When neither Tamarisk nor John returned to their bed-chambers to change their attire for the evening meal, she felt the first stirring of real anxiety. Much as she disliked the maid, Marianne, she rang the bell in the hope of discovering from her some indication of Tamarisk's movements. But the bell remained unanswered and there was no sign of the maid in the passageway.

Chantal made her own toilette as was now her custom and hurried downstairs to the *grand salon*. Antoine was already there. His face lacked its customary expression of affection and admiration and a coldness underlined his voice as he invited her to be seated, adding:

"I understand that my dear brother and sister are not to be found in the Château. Perhaps you would care to inform me of their whereabouts!"

"*I* . . . tell *you*!" Chantal cried, her cheeks pink. "But it was my intention to enquire of you if *you* knew . . . "

"I know nothing!" Antoine interrupted. The lie came easily from his lips. "I consider their behavior most discourteous to say the least. As guests in my house it behooves them to keep me informed of their movements. Dinner will be delayed, of course. It is to be hoped that they are not too far away."

"And has no one seen them?" Chantal enquired. "Surely with so many servants about . . . " Her voice trailed away uncertainly for she knew that whatever John's purpose, it was of a secret nature and he had not intended to be observed.

Antoine crossed the room and seated himself beside Chantal. He was still unsure from her manner whether John and Tamarisk had told her of the secret room and their intention to go there. He suspected that her request that he should accompany her to Compiègne had been a ruse to remove him from the Château. Yet her anxiety for her brother and sister appeared to be genuine. If she knew of the secret chamber she would surely now speak of it, he thought.

He allowed the evening meal to be delayed an hour whilst he sat watching her anxiety grow. Every five minutes or so she would glance at the ebonized bracket clock on the mantel-shelf and ask him anew if he could not suggest where they might be. He pretended ignorance.

When he had learned from his mother on his return from Compiègne that she had locked John and Tamarisk in the secret room, he had been furiously angry with her for her failure to circumvent their discovery of its existence.

Blanche had been prepared for his wrath.

"You yourself suspected nothing when you left the two of them in the library playing chess!" she

621

reminded him. "I followed your instructions and kept as close surveillance as was possible through the keyhole. One of them must by chance have happened upon the way to open the door but as they were not in my line of vision, I did not at first suspect it. Only when I heard them forcing open the lids of the tin boxes, did I realize what was happening. With great presence of mind, I crept into the library and shut the door upon them, knowing that you would not wish me to allow them to go free with so much knowledge of your affairs."

Seeing that Antoine's first bout of anger was abating, she had continued:

"I took great care that they did not see me, Antoine. If you now wish to release them, it is possible to do so without arousing their suspicion. You can tell them the door is self-closing."

Antoine quickly realized that his mother's instinct was right — he could not allow John and Tamarisk to go free now that they had had access to his documents. They would have to die. But first he needed time to consider how he might allay Chantal's suspicions. The deaths of his half-brother and sister were of little concern to him personally, but the thought of her distress made him distinctly uneasy. He genuinely did not want her to be unhappy. Yet there was clearly no alternative. As threats to his own life, theirs must be forfeit, and there was no way he could spare Chantal the unhappiness this would cause her.

He regarded her with something akin to pity.

"Please try to enjoy the repast!" be said gently. "I do not doubt there will be a satisfactory explanation before long!"

Chantal ate little, her mind too confused and plagued by anxiety to concern itself with victuals. Antoine's concern seemed genuine enough — yet she was convinced that he was associated with John's and Tamarisk's disappearance. For the most part the long drawn out meal was eaten in silence.

By the time it was over Antoine had decided upon an explanation he believed would satisfy Chantal — at least for a short while. He was determined at all costs to keep her from any precipitate action before the wedding in three days time.

"If you will be seated in the salon for a short while, Chantal, I will go personally to make further enquiries. I cannot bear to see you so worried!"

"Thank you, Antoine!" Chantal replied. "I fear some harm *must* have befallen them, for both John and Tamarisk would have anticipated my anxiety and advised me had they intended to be absent so long."

Within the quarter hour Antoine returned, and addressed Chantal with false bonhomie.

"You were quite right in believing your brother and sister would not have left you ignorant of their whereabouts!" he said, sitting down beside her and taking her hand in his. "I have just now dismissed from my service one of the under-grooms for not relaying a message to you from Tamarisk."

He felt Chantal's hand trembling and continued to lie smoothly:

"It seems that she and John received word by messenger from a certain family called Dubois in Beauvais. John, as you know, became acquainted with them some time ago and was their guest on several occasions. As far as I can ascertain from that half-witted groom, the Duc Dubois died very suddenly yesterday. Knowing that John and his sister were here, the Duchesse called on his assistance in her time of bereavement. John and Tamarisk decided to leave at once with the messenger in his carriage to see if they could be of comfort to the poor lady and her many daughters. Doubtless they have been detained at the Dubois' Château! It seems Tamarisk's message to you warned of the possibility that they might remain away a night or more but that they would most surely return in time for our wedding!"

Chantal breathed a great sigh of relief. On first hearing, Antoine's explanation was plausible enough and for a little while she did not doubt it. John had spoken of the Dubois during the voyage home from the Seychelles, describing their charms and their poverty and expressing the wish that now she, Chantal, was safe, he could honor his promise to the family to invite the girls to London. She had understood that he was on excellent terms with them and that they all treated him as a member of the family.

But later that night when she retired to her bedchamber, she had time for further reflection. A brief search of Tamarisk's powder-closet had

624

shown that she had taken no clothes with her upon her visit to the Dubois. Moreover her fur-lined cloak and bonnet were still hanging in the garderobe. The February weather was bitterly cold and Chantal knew that Tamarisk would not have ventured outside without such garments.

Her apprehension returning in full force, she lay awake pondering upon the many weaknesses she could now see in Antoine's story. It was unlikely that a messenger from the Dubois would have come in a carriage and not upon horseback. Moreover, how did the Dubois know that John and Tamarisk were at Boulancourt? If they had taken the unlikely step of calling upon the family when they had followed her, Chantal, posthaste to Compiègne, they would surely have mentioned it. Chantal's anxiety increased as she considered that the Dubois must have relatives, neighbors and far closer friends than John whom the Duchesse could call upon in her bereavement. Even if she had asked John for assistance, it would have been quite unnecessary for Tamarisk to accompany him. Tamarisk believed her, Chantal, to be in danger and would not have left her to comfort a strange family.

Chantal was now certain that Antoine had fabricated this story for her benefit. It followed that he must know the actual whereabouts of John and Tamarisk else he would have had no need to lie to her. She chided herself for her gullibility. It was most improbable that one of Antoine's grooms would have failed to relay so important a message. It was equally improbable that the servants within the Château would have been unaware of a visitor or of John's and Tamarisk's subsequent departure.

She re-lit her bedside candle and sat up, hugging her knees whilst she tried to recapture in her mind the last conversation she had had with Tamarisk.

"I have made a most important discovery this morning in the library."

Tamarisk's words returned to her memory as clearly as if they had just been spoken.

"I have told John of my discovery and he agrees with me that we may be on the verge of solving our difficulties. I will give you no further details now because were Antoine to question you, 'twould be best if you were ignorant of the truth. 'Tis enough for you to know that John and I require several hours quite undisturbed and for this purpose, you must find some way to distract Antoine . . ."

Tamarisk and John must have been detected as they pursued their plans, Chantal decided. Where were they now? In the tower where Camille Faloise had been kept prisoner? Or somewhere far below ground where Antoine had told her were the huge wine cellars and the dungeons used in bygone days for incarcerating prisoners? If she were to demand to search the Château from top to bottom, would Antoine permit it?

"If only Tamarisk had told me what she and John were about!" Chantal thought with a shiver of fear.

Tears filled her eyes as she considered her helplessness. No longer could she count on John and Tamarisk to protect her. For a moment she contemplated making her own escape — taking one of the horses and riding through the night to Beauvais. The Dubois would lend her assistance. They would facilitate her journey to England where she could call upon her father to take control of the situation. He would know what to do.

But even as this avenue of escape occurred to her, she knew that she could not take it. If John and Tamarisk were in fact Antoine's prisoners, he might wreak his vengeance upon them if she were to leave him now, besides which she still did not have the pages from Tamarisk's journal and her father's life would remain in jeopardy.

"'Tis time I began to show a little courage!" she remonstrated with herself. For too long she had relied on others to cherish and protect her, she thought. She was no longer a child. If Mama could brave the dangers of Russia and Tamarisk survive the rigors of Italy, then she, Chantal, could surely summon sufficient fortitude to overcome her loneliness and her fear here in France.

31

February 1840

ANTOINE'S mood was momentarily overconfident. He believed that Chantal had accepted his story that John and Tamarisk were visiting the Dubois family in Beauvais. He thought it unlikely that she would question their absence until the day preceding the wedding. By then he would have forged a letter from the Duchesse Dubois stating that Tamarisk was mildly indisposed and therefore she and John would be delayed a further few days. Chantal would have no way of verifying the truth or otherwise of the letter before the wedding.

Blanche Merlin, however, did not share his confidence in the situation.

"It may be three days before they die!" she reminded him forcefully. "Were they to escape . . . "

Antoine regarded his mother impatiently.

"They cannot do so!" he interrupted her. "You know as well as I that there is no means by which the door can be opened from the inside!"

The woman's face twitched with emotion.

"It would be safer to dispose of them, Antoine. Why will you not do so? If you have no stomach for it, then Stefano . . . or I . . . "

628

Antoine's smile never quite reached his eyes. "In truth, my dear mother, I have always considered *myself* merciless but you . . . you have fewer scruples even than I! Have you forgotten that we are speaking of my half-brother and sister? I doubt that the Curé would give me Absolution on my death-bed were I to confess to fratricide!"

Blanche concealed her surprise. She had not supposed her son to be in the least concerned with religion although she herself retained a superstitious fear of a righteous God who might demand revenge on Judgment Day.

"You think that to leave them both to die from privation is not the same as ordering them to he killed?" she asked with genuine curiosity.

"A moot point!" Antoine said carelessly. "I prefer to leave nature to take its course. After my wedding the bodies will be discovered and not even Chantal will be able to lay blame at my door. The fools went into the room of their own accord and for very obvious purposes. I shall be able to speak with the conviction of truth, will I not, when I tell her I had naught to do with their deaths."

Blanche nodded, admiring as she so often did, her son's cupidity. It was small wonder that he had risen so far in life from his humble origins, she thought. Nevertheless her instinct warned her that until John and Tamarisk were dead, Chantal might yet bring about his downfall. Antoine's love for the girl was his only weakness — other than the hateful drug, opium. But despite all his reasoning why the prisoners must not be killed, it disturbed her to think of them still alive.

"The door of the secret chamber is not proof against sound!" she said warningly. "If the girl were to hear their cries . . . ! At least lock up the library, Antoine, so that she cannot go near, I beg of you."

"And at once arouse Chantal's suspicions?" Antoine retorted irritably. Then he relaxed and smiled. "You have given me an idea, nonetheless, my dear mother. I think it might be a suitable time for me to arrange to have my valuable books catalogued. That would make the library a most unsuitable room for reading or meditation. Send Stefano to me! He can arrange for one of the better educated servants to act as bibliographer. The fellow can begin his task this very morning!"

Had he considered this plan more carefully he might have forseen the danger of placing a man who was very far from being a scholar in the rôle of a bibliographer. It proved to be a serious mistake.

Later that morning Chantal went once again to Tamarisk's bedchamber in search of any clue that might throw light upon the mystery of her disappearance. On the bed table she came upon the book Tamarisk had taken from the library — 'Monsieur de Pourceaugnac' by Jean Baptiste Molière. It was so strange a choice of reading matter for Tamarisk who preferred the Italian language to French, that Chantal studied the book more closely. She looked carefully through the pages, hoping to find a mark that might draw her attention to a special phrase or meaning. But she could find none. She decided to return the volume to the bookshelf in the last vain hope that Tamarisk had left a note or sign that would have significance and perhaps explain her excitement after her last visit to the library. Chantal might have been less hopeful had she known that Tamarisk, when she saw that she was being observed by the servant, Marianne, had but taken the book nearest to hand.

Chantal made her way to the library only to find herself halted by a footman who stood outside the closed door.

"There is a bibliographer at work within, Mademoiselle!" he said. "I have orders that he is not to be disturbed!"

"I will not disturb him!" Chantal replied. "I have but to return this book. It will take only a moment!"

Ignorant of the real reason why his master wished to keep anyone from entering the room, the footman assumed that it could do no harm to let the young lady go in. He opened the door for her and stood aside.

At the foot of a set of library steps stood a burly middle-aged man whose face was unknown to Chantal. He was staring at her with a look that was far from welcoming.

"*Bonjour Monsieur!*" she said politely. "I regret if I am disturbing you but I wish to return this book!"

The man muttered some reply which Chantal failed to interpret. But as he came towards her, his hand outstretched for the book, she stepped backward. There was something in his manner and appearance which made her uneasy. When her mother had had the many books in Barre House catalogued, the man who came to perform the task was a most scholarly gentleman, refined in speech and manners. This man had the large hands and coarse-grained skin of a peasant.

"I will replace it myself!" she said, holding tight to the book. "If you will be so good as to direct me to the right shelf? It is Molière's *Monsieur de Pourceaugnac*."

There was a look of total incomprehension on the man's face. He stared at her blankly, fidgeting from one foot to another.

"I assume this volume comes from a set of Molière's work!" Chantal said. "It should not be hard to find!"

"I am unfamiliar as yet with the cataloguing arrangements!" the man said gruffly. He took a step nearer to her. "Give me the book, Mademoiselle. I will replace it!"

But Chantal had ceased to listen to him for she had become aware of a strange noise. It sounded like a piece of metal striking continuously upon stone. She supposed that somewhere a mason must be at work on the walls of the Château. But before she could identify the direction from which it came, Antoine entered the room. He looked very angry.

"I gave orders that no one was to disturb the bibliographer!" he said in a cold, hard voice. "Please leave the man in peace at once, Chantal!"

Irritated though she was by the peremptoriness of his tone, Chantal decided to appear ignorant of anything untoward. She followed Antoine docilely from the room. His anger had only increased her suspicion that something strange was occurring in or close to the library. She was determined to investigate the sounds she had heard and without much difficulty persuaded Antoine to take her for a brief walk in the fresh air.

"It is too cold to go far!" she said. "But I would enjoy a short perambulation around the Château if you will accompany me, Antoine! Since I am not permitted to take a book from the library, I need other occupation."

Once outside she pretended an interest in the architecture of the Château, inviting Antoine to tell her which walls had been rebuilt after the Revolution. Thus she could observe without arousing his suspicion whether in fact there was a stone mason at work on the exterior. There was none.

Their walk completed, Chantal allowed Antoine to persuade her to go with him into the small chapel. In preparation for the wedding in two days' time, candles had been placed in their holders and vases stood ready to receive the hothouse flowers that were being sent by carriage from Paris. Antoine, his complacence restored, took Chantal's hand.

"You will not regret your marriage to me!" he said, his tone now as ardent as a short while before it had been peremptory. "I know that you are coming to this marriage under duress but I swear before God you will be glad that I forced you to it. I will make you happy, my lovely Chantal!"

"If only I could believe that!" Chantal replied quietly. "Will you not give me proof of the love you profess for me, Antoine? If it is truly my happiness and peace of mind you desire, will you not give me now those pages which incriminate my father?"

Antoine released her hand, his eyes narrowing as he smiled slightly.

"That would be foolish of me, would it not? After all, Chantal, they are my only guarantee that you *will* wed me the day after tomorrow!"

"But you have promised them to me, Antoine, as a wedding gift!" Chantal persisted.

"You shall have them after the ceremony!" Antoine replied quietly. "Come now, Chantal. 'Tis cold in here. Let us return to the warmth of the house."

Chantal was fully occupied that afternoon with the *couturier*, an appointment she could not cancel without arousing comment. But in the hour before dinner she found the long-awaited opportunity to return to the library which she hoped to find vacated. A new footman now stood by the door and she dared not contravene Antoine's orders a second time.

As soon as the meal was over she pleaded a headache and retired early to bed. From her window she could see the lights from the *salon* glowing in the darkness far below her. It was clear that Antoine was not intending to retire early. She waited with increasing impatience for the lights in the Château to go out. It was after midnight before all was in darkness and she felt it safe to leave her room.

She dared not light a candle lest the grim Marianne was concealed somewhere in the shadows, spying upon her. Trembling with cold and fear she felt her way along the stone passage until she was at last at the head of the stairway. The darkness was intense and she clung to the balustrade, trying to subdue her quick, gasping breaths. Fortunately she now knew her way about this part of the Château and she could locate the library without difficulty. At this hour there was no guard outside the door.

She paused, listening. In the garden an owl hooted eerily. Another answered and its call was followed by the peculiar cry of a nightjar. Chantal's fear mounted. She had the feeling that somewhere in the darkness surrounding her, eyes were watching her movements. But as she pushed the library door inward, no voice spoke and the silence remained inviolate.

She stood listening. No sound came from the walls. Not daring to call out lest she be overheard, she moved toward the window. A faint light shone through the chink in the window hangings. Outside, the courtyard was bathed in brilliant moonlight. Chantal opened the drapes a further inch so that she could see clearly the contours of the room. She crossed to the fireplace.

Picking up one of the heavy fire-irons, she banged it lightly down upon the hearth. There was no answering noise. She knocked again and at her third attempt, she heard the chink of metal against stone. Trying to still her own fierce breathing, Chantal listened intently. The noise continued. She knocked once more upon the hearth and then moved towards the answering noise. It seemed to come from the bookshelves adjoining one side of the fireplace.

"John? Tamarisk?"

Her voice sounded shrill even to her own ears. She waited with beating heart for the sound of footsteps approaching the library, but there were none. Gathering the remnants of her courage she called out once more. This time she was certain that she could hear muffled cries. She put her ear against the bookshelf and now she was in no doubt that one or more people were calling to her. Their voices were muffled and so indistinct that she was only in part convinced that she had located John and Tamarisk.

Close to tears of frustration and anxiety, she knocked yet again on the hearth and heard the reply. She now assumed that it must be they, since no one else would have been awake and knocking on the walls at this post-midnight hour. She ran to the window and drew the curtains further apart. Returning once more to the bookcase, there was now sufficient light for her to read the titles of the books on the shelves. At shoulder height, her eyes were drawn to a leather bound collection of Molière's works. The discovery brought a flush of excitement to her cheeks, knowing that she herself now stood where Tamarisk must have stood to select her book.

But slowly her confidence waned as she glanced around her and found no further clue to the problem facing her. Behind the bookshelves, she supposed, was the ante-room adjoining the big dining hall. But she knew that this had only the one entrance door and if John and Tamarisk were imprisoned within, their cries would have been heard by any passerby.

With a shiver, she realized that wherever they were incarcerated they had been there for more than a day. She hoped that they had food and water as she began feverishly to search along the bookshelves for a hidden doorway. None was to be seen. She was now convinced that there must be a chamber concealed behind the fireplace. There was a priest hole at their own country house, Finchcocks, where, like the Château, the thickness of the walls made it possible for a large cavity to exist within the framework of the stones.

The knocking had ceased but on the instant that she banged upon the hearth, it was renewed.

At least, she thought, if it were John and Tamarisk trying to communicate with her as she now firmly believed, they would know that she was aware of their predicament. But how was she to effect their release? Antoine had told her that they would he back from Beauvais the day before the wedding. Was it therefore his intention to release them on the 'morrow? He must realize that John and Tamarisk would tell her of their imprisonment and his lies. It seemed far more logical to suppose that he intended to prevent their return until *after* the marriage when there would be no risk of her abrogating her promise.

For a further hour Chantal searched for an entry to the chamber she was now quite convinced was situated somewhere behind the fireplace. Her search was to no avail. She could think of no solution to the situation and was close to despair when suddenly she became aware of a new noise — the sound of footsteps approaching the library door. As her skin prickled with fear, she ran to the window and concealed herself behind the drapes. The door opened and a woman came into the room. Dressed in a thick woolen nightrobe, a nightcap upon her head, the woman was not at first recognizable to Chantal. As she crossed to the fireplace and held her lighted candle aloft, Chantal saw that it was the servant, Marianne. She bit back the cry that rose to her lips and shrank even deeper behind the dusty drapes.

Blanche Merlin had no inkling of Chantal's presence in the library. She had come here for no other reason than that she had been unable to resist the sadistic urge to gloat upon the two 'aristos' concealed in the chamber. For the past twenty-seven years she had lived with the hatred of Mavreen close to her heart. That hatred was second only in intensity to her resentment of Gerard's mother, Marianne de Valle, whose name she had taken, delighting in the twisted belief that she was reducing the grand Vicomtesse to the status of a servant.

As a child of the Revolution, Blanche Merlin had grown up in violent and secret opposition to her father who, simple farmer that he was, remained loyal to the de Valles. Blanche's seduction of the handsome young officer, Gerard, son of the late Vicomte, had been deliberate. The bearing of a child by him she had calculated would raise her from her humble environment since it was customary for noblemen to pension off the servants who bore their bastards. But Blanche had not foreseen that Gerard would return immediately to the wars after a short leave from the army and that it would be a further six years before she could tell him of the existence of his child.

A decade later, her son Antoine was acknowledged as the new Vicomte de Valle and everywhere accepted as being a true aristocrat. Thus Blanche's desire for compensation for her early suffering was fulfilled. Fate had turned the tables and it was now she, the farmer's daughter, who held power over Gerard de Valle's son and daughter by the English milady, Mavreen. Blanche was more than ready to kill John and Tamarisk before she would allow them to harm one hair of Antoine's head; and only his direct order prevented her from doing so. She wished, nevertheless, to be certain of their deaths and to gloat over the manner of their dying.

She reached for the secret knob and the heavy door with its facing of bookshelves swung slowly open on its hinges. In one hand Blanche held the candle; in the other a cocked pistol.

As the door opened, Tamarisk struggled weakly to her knees. Her disappointment was no less intense than John's when she saw the armed servant at the doorway. Like John, she had believed it to be Chantal knocking outside the room and their hopes had soared. John, too, saw the pistol and dared not try to rush past their gaoler — if such she was.

He and Tamarisk were already suffering acutely. They had now been without food or water for over a day and the resultant parching of their throats had become increasingly painful. He shared Tamarisk's conviction that they were to be left to die. He was comforted to know that at least it would not be from suffocation, for he had felt a cold draught entering the room from beneath the door even when it was tightly closed.

Throughout the long day they had heard noises from the library. Sometimes they heard voices but their cries and knocking had remained unheeded. With no light, John could not tell the time and he was uncertain as to the duration of their incarceration.

For Tamarisk's sake he now lowered his pride and pleaded with the servant.

"I beg you to bring a little water!" he said. He withdrew his gold time piece from his pocket and held it out. "See, this is real gold! I will give it to you if you will bring some food and water!"

A sneer twisted the woman's face.

"You think I value *that*!" she said scornfully. "Why I can have all the gold I want from Antoine!" She looked from John to Tamarisk, her lips curling. "You think me a servant, do you not?" she said. "But I am the mother of the Vicomte de Valle — yes, I am Antoine's mother!" Her voice rose shrilly. "You think me lowly born and to be scorned for it, but long after you are dead and forgotten I shall be living here at the Château de Boulancourt like a queen. I shall have beautiful clothes and jewels and all the luxuries my son can give me. Think on that whilst you rot here like rats, my fine *aristos!*"

With a last gloating look at John's and Tamarisk's horrified faces, she withdrew from the room, and pressing the protruding stone on the cornice, waited with pistol cocked whilst the door swung to.

Chantal paused only long enough to be certain that Marianne had had time to return to her bedchamber before she ran to the fireplace and felt feverishly up and down the cornice. Within seconds the door once more swung open and she was in John's arms.

"Thank God I was hidden in the library when that vile woman came in!" she gasped, half laughing, half crying. "I had been searching for hours beforehand and might never have found my way to you had I not seen her movements. Hurry now, before we are discovered!"

She kissed Tamarisk's white, exhausted face.

"It is all over now. I have found you!" she said comfortingly. But John broke in:

"Since I first heard you knocking I have had much time to think of the possibilities of escape, were we fortunate enough to be released by you, Chantal," he said. "But with so many of Antoine's servants about, I do not think we could remain concealed within the Château for very long once it was found that we were

641

missing from here. And you, Chantal, are the only person who could have effected our rescue and might even be tortured to reveal our hiding place."

"Can we not escape to the woods on foot?" Tamarisk faltered, her voice hoarse and strained. But even as she spoke her legs gave way and she sank back to the floor.

"We could not walk halfway to Compiègne in this weakened state!" John said. "Moreover there is the matter of your father's life still to be considered, Chantal."

He explained briefly the importance of the documents they had discovered and how they incriminated Antoine.

"*But the pages of Tamarisk's journal were not amongst them,*" he ended unhappily.

Chantal stared at John in an agony of indecision. She loved both him and her father. Must she now choose between them? Tamarisk's life, too, must be taken into account.

John was looking at Tamarisk.

"Do you have strength enough to bear this terrible imprisonment a while longer?" he asked quietly. "If we could remain here, Tamarisk, at least until the wedding, Chantal might yet recover those pages which can condemn our stepfather to the gallows. However much we may doubt it, 'tis not impossible that Antoine will keep his word and give them to Chantal!"

"I could bring you food and water!" Chantal said thoughtfully. "A candle perhaps and a tinderbox. But the library is guarded in the daytime by a man who professes to be a

642

bibliographer. I could come to you only at night!"

They stood discussing the possibilities a while longer. Tamarisk agreed to fall in with whatever John felt best.

"I, too, will abide by your decision, John," Chantal said finally. "But I cannot risk your life and Tamarisk's on no more than a faint chance of saving Papa's. I love you, John!"

John looked down at her white anxious face with deepest tenderness. Her declaration thrilled his heart but he knew this was no time to speak of love.

"It behooves us to show a courage equal to your own, Chantal," he said quietly. "It now seems certain that you will have to go through with the marriage ceremony. But afterwards — then it is up to you to use your wits to obtain those pages from Antoine. Once that is done, you can reveal our plight to the Curé and bring him here. Antoine will not dare to have us killed in front of a priest and we can all leave Boulancourt under the Curé's protection."

Tamarisk's spirits revived.

"I think John's plan a most excellent one!" she said. "If you can conduct the Curé here our lives will be assured, but if we were to leave now with you, Chantal, *all* our lives would be endangered, including Perry's!"

Chantal nodded thoughtfully.

"I will go to the kitchen quarters at once and try to find food!" she said. "But I must shut the door upon you when I go. I dare not leave it open lest that horrible woman returns!

Is it really possible that Antoine can have such a mother?"

"'Tis more than likely!" Tamarisk said dryly. "For of a certainty he did not inherit such villainy from our father. Go now, Chantal, for I think I shall expire if I do not soon have water!"

Chantal's sortie to the kitchens required further summoning of her courage, for with its many daytime occupants absent, the huge room was alive with rats. Their great hairy grey bodies scampered over the rushes covering the flagstone floor, squeaking as they ran in fright from the unexpected intruder. Chantal could see little but the red flash of their eyes and her skin prickled in horror as she forced herself to tread amongst them.

She found food aplenty — ham, cheese, bread. The water she carried in a tall copper jug which Tamarisk would have to conceal beneath her skirts if the woman who called herself Marianne visited them again.

Returning undetected to the secret chamber, she watched whilst John and Tamarisk drank eagerly from the jug. She had taken two candles from one of the candelabra in the hallway, trusting that their absence would not be noticed. She handed John her own tinderbox.

"We must use them sparingly," John said, "lest the air become stale and the smell of candlewax be detected."

Chantal shivered.

"'Tis cold in here, John!" she whispered. "And with only the stone floor to sleep upon . . . if I were to bring at least one cushion for Tamarisk, it could be concealed in one of the trunks if Marianne returns."

"One only then," John agreed, "for she can rest her head on my lap! Do not worry about us, Chantal.'Tis you who must take care, for upon you all our lives now depend. You must continue to ask Antoine as to our whereabouts, do not forget!"

Chantal smiled.

"He has informed me that you are with the Dubois family in Beauvais!" she said. "He says you will return in time for the wedding. I shall be interested to see what lie he next tells me!"

John could not return her smile.

"Be on your guard, Chantal!" he said urgently. "Though he be my half-brother, I am certain now that he is mad and very dangerous . . . "

He put his arms around her and for a moment they clung to one another fiercely. But then Tamarisk cautioned:

"All the while Chantal is here, we are at risk. She must return now to her bedchamber!"

Reluctantly Chantal left them. She was convinced that she would never sleep with so much to think upon. But barely had her head touched her pillow than the exhaustion of the night's events overcame her. She gave but one deep sigh as she imagined poor John and Tamarisk trying to sleep in their cold prison. Then her eyes closed and she fell into a dreamless sleep.

645

32

February 1840

E VERY servant in the Château de Boulancourt was aware that at eleven of the clock their master, the Vicomte de Valle, was to marry the beautiful young English girl who had left her home and defied her family to become his bride.

The Chapel was ablaze with flowers and candles. Downstairs in the huge kitchens, an elaborate feast was being prepared for the wedding luncheon to follow the ceremony. There had been much gossip in the servants' hall concerning the absence of guests, for no one had been invited other than the Curé who was to perform the rites. However, the Vicomte had sent word that his entire staff of one hundred and twenty-six servants were to be present in the Chapel to witness the marriage — a state of affairs so unusual as to generate intense excitement and much speculation as to the Vicomte's motives.

It was generally agreed by the upstairs servants that since their master had become enamoured of the foreigner, he had altered a great deal in character. His moods were less predictable and far more extreme. Only Stefano and Blanche Merlin knew of Antoine's opium addiction and that this was the true reason for the change in his personality.

Excitement had mounted as the wedding day approached, penetrating even down to the dungeons. There, two prisoners had been awaiting for the past four months for the day when they were to compete for their lives and fortunes in the Vicomte's Roman games.

Each man was locked up by himself in one of the dungeon cells that had existed in the twelfth century when the Château was first built. Not even the great fire which had reduced Boulancourt to a shell during the Revolution had touched the dungeons which were below ground level. The moat which flowed beneath the Château passed by the very edge of the cells' doors, causing such dampness in the stone walls that the flames had been unable to take a hold.

Two of these dark vaults had been converted into reasonably comfortable quarters for the men who lived there whilst awaiting Antoine's requirement for their services. Like their predecessors, the men now living in these cells were society's outcasts — miserable wretches who had been flung into a debtors' prison in Paris with no hope of reinstating themselves; nor of being able to raise the money to pay their debts and secure their release. Antoine's intervention had seemed to each of them like a heaven-sent miracle. Like those before them, they never considered refusing the offer he made to them.

The offer was but one example of Antoine de Valle's shrewd understanding of human

647

beings. He had given many careful hours of thought to its conception. His idea was simple but totally effective. Never less than two prisoners at a time were interviewed by him in the prison Governor's office. They were selected by the Governor to meet Antoine's demands — namely that they should have already spent a year or more in gaol; that they were between the ages of twenty and thirty; that they were basically strong, healthy men weakened only by months of meager prison fare and not by physical deformity; and were of low intelligence.

Antoine, having bribed the Governor discreetly but handsomely, conducted his interviews in private. The prisoners were permitted to observe one another whilst they were informed that their unknown benefactor was prepared to buy their release. From then on, each man was informed separately of the conditions attached to his acquisition of freedom.

"You will be lodged in quarters in my Château!" Antoine told each in turn. "You will be well-treated and fed upon the most nourishing of victuals. You will be given wine in moderation and facilities for exercising in the open air. Once you are restored to full health and strength, and only then, you will be required to fight your fellow prisoner. He will at all times be lodged apart from you so that he cannot see what food you eat or how strong you are becoming. Do I make myself clear?"

"Not entirely, your Honor, your lordship, your Grace!" was the reply, for it was hard to believe in such good fortune when the future had but

648

an hour since seemed without hope. But by now the man had taken the bait and assumed that he alone of the two prisoners would receive special treatment, his fellow prisoner being kept unaware of his growing strength. "In what manner will I be required to fight?"

"With short swords — and to the death!" was Antoine's brief reply. And before the man could fully comprehend his own shock, he added: "There will be a full purse of gold louis for the victor — sufficient to make a new start in life wherever he may chose to live."

"And the victim? I'd not want to be guillotined for murder. I'd rather rot in gaol than have me head lopped off!"

"The victim's death would not be murder!" Antoine stressed the word. "'Accidents' can happen when men fight with swords. As for the victim's body — it would be my responsibility to see that it disappeared without trace. Now make your decision, man. Are you game for such sport?"

"*Sans doute!* But if I were not? If I were to tell the Governor that you are not employing me to labor for you but to kill another man?"

Antoine's expression betrayed only scorn.

"You really think the Governor would believe such an improbable tale? The word of a scoundrel such as yourself would scarce carry weight against the word of a Vicomte, my poor fellow, and I would, of course, deny every word you say. My story would be the easier credited, I think — for I have maintained that I am here for the sole purpose of acquiring men to work on my estate."

The alternative was too grim for any prisoner to turn down this hope of ultimate freedom — and wealth. Each man believed he must inevitably win any contest against the other — left, so he thought, in a skeletal state. It was rare for such interviews to last more than an hour before the prisoners gathered their few ragged possessions from their cells and followed Antoine out to his carriage, their ankles chained together lest they should attempt to escape in the streets of Paris.

Once at the Château de Boulancourt, neither prisoner saw his companion again until they met in the arena for the mortal combat for which they had both been prepared. By then, both were in superb health, their bodies filled out so that their massive frames rippled with muscular strength and their senses were as alert as their none too intelligent minds allowed. By the time they realized they had been tricked into believing their opponent would be no stronger than when he had left the prison, it was too late. They were in the arena and with no alternative but to fight.

The guard who had been detailed to remain on duty on the day of the wedding grumbled bitterly to his prisoners that because of them, he alone of all the servants would be denied the honor of seeing the Vicomte wed. One of the men, Pierre Lavant, grinned and shrugged his shoulders indifferently. Despite the guards occasional bouts of brutality when for no good reason they would hit out with a baton and cause a nasty bruise or two, Pierre was perfectly content to pass the days in his cell in idleness. The excess of good food and the comfort of his quarters had fattened him to the point of grossness and this condition had brought about a laziness of both body and spirit. Gone was the aggressiveness of his youth when he had roamed the streets of Paris starving and ready to kill for a loaf of bread. He was in no hurry to fight his rival in the cell next door for he supposed him to be as thin and skeletal as when he had last viewed him on their way to imprisonment at the Château; and that his victory in the contest was therefore ensured.

His rival, François Noyer, however, was far from content. Now that his body had recovered its full stength, his dulled mind had also begun to function. Of immense stature, François in infancy had lacked the nutriments to feed both brain and body. His early childhood had been spent in doltish misery whilst he remained the butt of his street companions who jeered and abused him for his simple-mindedness. But gradually his physical superiority manifested itself and he discovered that he could keep his torturers at bay with no more than a well aimed hefty blow of his arm or foot. His mental powers remained those of an adolescent and his inability to control his emotions inevitably led him into trouble with the law. He came close to killing a man in a bistro, who had been taunting him for his foolish manner and had ended up in the Paris prison where Antoine had discovered him.

During his incarceration at the Château de Boulancourt, François had grown to hate his guards with a simple but violent hatred that he could not have concealed even had he been intelligent enough to do so. The guards feared him for his strength and never ventured too far inside the cell.

Comfortable though he was, the confines of his quarters began to prey on François' mind as his now healthy body demanded more exercise and freedom. Apart from these he lacked nothing other than a woman, and his lustful cravings now dominated his limited powers of thought. He understood well enough that he must first fight the other prisoner before he could regain his freedom and he waited with growing impatience for the day of the contest.

When François' guard entered his cell grumbling about the festivities he must miss on the morrow, François at first misunderstood the reasons for the gala occasion. Mistakenly he supposed that the promised day of the Vicomte's Roman games had at long last arrived.

When he realized his error, his disappointment was matched only by his anger. He would have strangled the guard had the man not beat a speedy retreat.

Throughout the remainder of the day and night, François pondered the injustice of life. Next day, he thought, the rich *aristo* who had promised him freedom was to be wed. He would have for his pleasuring a comely young woman, soft-skinned, perfumed, a ripe peach for the plucking; whilst he must languish here alone for God alone knew how many more weeks, months before he was free to buy himself a woman!

By morning François' frustration had seriously affected his few claims to rationality. He gave no thought to the possibility that if he should manage to escape by overpowering his guard, he would still have the gauntlet of other servants to run; that were he caught, he would undoubtedly be killed. He knew himself to be in the very peak of condition and he believed that brute force would overcome any problem he might encounter. He was not capable of forming any plan other than to overpower his guard when breakfast was brought to him. He had often considered how easy this would be if he could entice his gaoler far enough into the cell.

Giant that he was, it was not easy for François to conceal himself, but somehow he managed to squeeze his great bulk under the iron bed and pull the duvet so that it draped over the side of the mattress and hid him from view. The stone floor of the dungeon was bitterly cold and damp but he lay there happily enough waiting for the sound of the guard's footsteps and the heavy clang of his keys as he unlocked the cell door.

The guard was still in a sullen mood. Upstairs in the kitchens where he had gone to eat his own breakfast and collect that of the prisoners, the atmosphere was like a carnival. The kitchen and scullery maids were running to and fro, decked in their Sunday clothes and regaling one another with descriptions of the beautiful wedding gown the bride was to wear and the

653

magnificence of the Vicomte's attire. Even the grim-faced Stefano was close to grinning as he slapped the guard on the shoulder and promised him a flagon of wine and a sumptuous repast later in the day.

"And there's to be double pay for all at the week's end!" Stefano added by way of consolation.

Partly mollified, the guard carried the tray of food down the long dark passages to the dungeons. Lulled by the prospect of extra wages, he unlocked the door of François' cell, calling out cheerfully:

"*Venez manger, mon vieux!*"

He could not at first believe his eyes when he saw the room was empty. Still holding the tray, he stared at the rumpled bed in utter astonishment. François was usually ravenous and already seated at his table as he awaited his food. Muttering, the guard took a step towards the bed.

He never knew that it was François' hand that caught his leg in an iron grip and threw him over on his back. The hot black coffee scalded his face as it spilled from the bowl. He knew a single moment of agony before the full force of François' weight fell upon his chest, knocking the breath from his body.

It had not been François' intention necessarily to kill the guard. He wished merely to make his own escape. But now that he had the man at his mercy he could not resist the animal impulse to put his great hands around his victim's throat and strangle him. It took but a minute or two

654

before the guard ceased to struggle. Without haste François removed the heavy ring of keys from the body. He then sat down to enjoy what he could retrieve of his *petit déjeuner*. Having eaten all the food he could find, he went through the open door of his cell and found the tray awaiting the second prisoner. Once more without haste, he stuffed the bread and cold pork eagerly into his hungry mouth and washed them down with coffee. The basic needs of hunger and thirst now satisfied, he turned his slow-moving thoughts to his other requirements.

By now all the servants were assembled in the Chapel. Had François found a kitchen or scullery maid lurking in the passageways, his needs might have been quickly slaked with one of them. But the great Château was silent and as far as he could ascertain, empty of people.

François had never before in his life been in a house of such grandeur. His mission was temporarily forgotten as with childlike curiosity he wandered from room to room, staring in awe at the magnificence and opulence all around him.

In the banqueting hall the wedding feast lay spread out in preparation for the bridal couple. François crammed his mouth with the delicacies as if he had not just eaten his breakfast. Still munching be wandered into the adjoining *salle des preaux*. Over thirty-foot long and with heraldic coats of arms, weapons and flags decorating the walls, the sight of this room was impressive enough to bring a gasp from

655

François. But then he caught sight of the long rows of knights in armor, lances held upright as if on parade, and he gave a cry of fear. It was some moments before he realized that these were not servants in a strange metallic livery but empty shells of armor plating, eye and mouth holes eerily gaping at him.

He grinned, and walking over to one of the figures, removed the lance and stood upright as if on guard. But this posture soon became tedious and he spent a further few minutes lunging with his newly acquired weapon. Only then did it occur to his sluggish brain that he was now well-armed if anyone should try to apprehend him. He remembered that it had been his intention to find himself a woman and realized that he knew exactly where he might do so. His mind pictured the Vicomte's bride, her young virginal body be-decked in white as she stood in the Chapel beside her groom.

Breathing heavily with mounting excitement, François conceived the possibility that he and not the haughty Vicomte should be the one to enjoy the wedding nuptials. He was taller, stronger and infinitely more powerful than the Vicomte. To him, François Noyer, should go the spoils by virtue of his superior strength and physique, he decided. Had not the Revolution been fought to establish the rights of the common man? He had been reared on stories of the storming of the Bastille and the Palais de Versailles; of Madame Guillotine and the heads that had rolled bloodily into the baskets. "*A bas les aristos!*" They had played such games of re-enactment in the streets in his childhood. Now he could play the game in verity.

Still carrying his lance, he set off in search of the Chapel.

The wedding ceremony had already begun. Chantal stood quietly beside Antoine, determined not to give way to the nightmarish horror of the occasion. She kept her eyes fastened on the box reposing upon the altar, for in there, Antoine had sworn to her, were the pages of Tamarisk's journal that could destroy her father.

Chantal had had perforce to allow the grim Marianne to dress her. The woman's compliment that she did indeed look beautiful in her magnificent wedding gown only increased her distaste for the charade she must shortly enact. She was finding it increasingly difficult to play the rôle she had designated for herself. When Antoine had told her that John and Tamarisk would not be returning in time for the marriage, only with the greatest difficulty had she simulated disappointment. The strain of her secret nightly visits to the hidden chamber had also begun to take its toll. Her nerves were strung so tight that she knew if she relaxed for one instant she would give way completely and never find the strength to do what must be done. It concerned her deeply that Tamarisk had looked near the point of collapse when she had visited her last night. John had regarded her anxiously.

"There can be no danger to your person, Chantal, provided you remain always in the

Curé's presence," he had cautioned her emphatically.

But the Curé, when Chantal first saw him in the Chapel, looked old and feeble and seemed to fawn upon Antoine as if fearful of incurring his disfavor. It was Antoine who directed the procedure, stating that he wished to dispense with the lengthy Mass which would complete the ceremony. He brushed aside the Curé's objections to the fact that Chantal was not of the Catholic religion.

"I do not pay your living in order to hear your objections to my wishes!" he said in a peremptory tone. "Now proceed with the service lest I lose patience and send for another priest to oblige me!"

On the verge of achieving his obsessive desire to make Chantal his wife, Antoine's patience was wearing thin. Despite Chantal's seeming docility, he sensed she was no more eager for this marriage than she had been when she first left England. He could not lay a finger upon the exact reason for such belief but instinct told him that the girl was too passive, too acquiescent. She had not even demanded that the wedding be postponed when he had told her Tamarisk and John were further delayed in Beauvais. At the same time she had continued to demand the return of the pages that incriminated her father and he did not doubt that his promise to give them to her as a wedding gift was the only reason she was complying with his wishes.

But reluctant though his bride might be, Antoine told himself, it would not be many hours more before he could conduct her to the bridal couch and reap the rewards of his patience. He smiled as he stared down at the fairy tale figure beside him. A veil hid her face from him but it would not be long now before he could lift that delicate lace covering and kiss his bride — his *wife*! His possession of her would be the culmination of his life's achievements, for never had he desired to own anything more intensely than the young girl at his side.

Stefano stood close behind Antoine holding the ring that would seal the marriage contract. Behind Chantal stood his mother, her face impassive as she gripped the bridal bouquet in her bony hands. The rear of the Chapel contained the gaping-faced servants who were trying to grasp the meaning of the Curé's Latin intonations as the ceremony proceeded.

All eyes were centered upon the bride and groom and none, therefore, observed the stealthy opening of the Chapel door as François Noyer peered inside. The man paused, staring at the spectacle of flowers and glowing candles with childish admiration. Then he caught sight of Chantal and with a hoarse cry, he lunged forward up the aisle, the lance he was holding poised to fend off anyone seeking to bar his way to his goal.

The Curé broke off in mid-sentence as he saw the great giant of a man bearing down upon them. He shrank back against the altar in undisguised fear. Simultaneously Stefano turned to see what was causing the commotion behind him. But he was too late to take any effective action. As he stepped forward to halt the crazed interloper, François raised his arm and with a single blow pierced Stefano's heart with the lance, killing him instantly.

Horrified, Antoine stared at the great fountain of blood that poured from his servant's body as François withdrew the lance. Instinctively he raised his hands to protect himself but the madman ignored him and grabbed at the white folds of Chantal's gown. Several of the menservants stepped hesitantly into the aisle with the intent of going to their master's rescue. But the sight of Stefano sprawled on the altar steps, his life's blood pouring from him, arrested them.

Shocked and sickened, Chantal struggled frantically to free herself from the man's handhold upon her gown. The lace fabric of the dress tore in one great rent as she moved. Thwarted of his prey, François lunged again towards her but now Antoine managed to interpose himself between them.

"Lay one finger upon her and I will have you killed!" he called out, forgetting in the confusion of the moment that neither he nor any man within the Chapel was armed.

"*A bas les aristos!*" shouted François crazily. He was enjoying to the full this burst of freedom after all the months of inaction and solitude. He gave no thought to the danger he might be in. Lifting the lance which was still wet with Stefano's blood, he aimed it at Antoine.

With unflinching courage Antoine stood his ground. He was afraid that were he to step aside to avoid the blow, the lance must inevitably strike Chantal. He knew no other fear as it hit him, entering his armpit and piercing the brachial artery. He felt no pain as he sank slowly to his knees, the lance pinioning him by his shoulder blade so that he could fall no further. His attacker stood watching him with impersonal curiosity.

Behind François, Blanche Merlin screamed again and again. Her hand reached into her corselet and she withdrew a small jeweled dagger. She did not yet know that Antoine was dying — only that he was injured. With no thought for the incongruity of a frail elderly woman such as herself attacking so vast and dangerous a man, she ran forward and drove the dagger into François' back.

Like a wounded bull he bellowed in pain and swung round as Blanche stabbed him yet again. This time her blow caught him at such an angle that the knife glanced off one of his ribs and pierced his lung. Gasping with pain he fell on top of her, crushing her beneath him. The horrified servants took courage as the madman fell and ran forward en masse to overpower him.

Chantal, too, had been standing immobile, frozen in horror at the spectacle that was being enacted before her eyes. Now as Antoine groaned she ran forward and knelt beside him. She realized that without doubt he had just saved her life and all other considerations were forgotten as she tried to ease his terrible posture.

"Chantal! *Mon amour!*" he whispered, his face ashen with pain.

Chantal looked frantically around for assistance. The sight of Antoine pinioned by the lance appalled and sickened her.

"*Aidez moi!*" she cried wildly as she endeavored to support Antoine's body in her arms. Blood was seeping from around the point where the lance pierced his armpit. It covered her white bridal gown, staining it a brilliant red.

One of the senior footmen stepped forward and took hold of the lance. With one great wrench, he pulled it from Antoine's body. As Antoine sank to the floor, his face twisted in agony, the terrified Curé crept to his side.

"It is a mortal wound!" he whispered to Chantal, crossing himself. "Come away, my child. 'Tis no sight for your eyes!"

"Do not leave me, Chantal," Antoine said with difficulty. His head fell back against her shoulder. Her arms tightened around him as he groaned once more with pain, the blood now spurting from his gaping wound. She tore off her veil and vainly attempted to staunch the flow. Suddenly Antoine smiled — a smile so beautiful that Chantal forgot the dreadful evil within his soul and tears sprang to her eyes.

"Not quite . . . the wedding . . . I had planned!" he said. "I love you . . . so much, Chantal! At least *you* live!"

The Curé knelt down beside him.

"Your confession, Monsieur le Vicomte. There

is not much time!" be begged.

Despite the pain and the certainty of approaching death, Antoine's lips curled in a cynical smile.

"I doubt God has the stomach to hear my sins!" he said.

The Curé's face blanched and he crossed himself.

"Monsieur le Vicomte!" he cried. "I cannot give you Absolution if you will not make your Confession! God will forgive you if you repent!"

Antoine drew a deep sigh but the movement caused him a further terrible stab of pain and he gasped as his fingers clenched around Chantal's hand.

"Antoine, I must know one thing," she pleaded. "Were you intending to give me those papers concerning Papa?"

For a long moment Antoine did not reply. Then he smiled again.

"I think you already know that I could not have kept my promise to give them to you. I was afraid you would leave me once they were in your possession. But now . . . " be said, his voice faltering once more, "now it is I who am leaving you. Try not to hate me, Chantal!"

"You saved my life, Antoine!" Chantal said. "I will never forget that!"

The Curé pressed forward again.

"Monsieur le Vicomte!" he persisted, holding out both hands in appeal.

Antoine shuddered as another great spasm of pain engulfed him.

"Send them all away!" he whispered as he caught sight of the circle of frightened faces of his servants staring down at him in awe. As they moved slowly backwards, he added: "They look like ghosts who have come to greet me in Hell!"

Tears filled Chantal's eyes. She added her pleas to those of the Curé.

"Will you not make your Confession, Antoine? Then your soul may rest in peace!"

"I think perhaps I was born without a soul!" Antoine whispered. "There are many who have proclaimed me heartless! But I am not without a heart, Chantal, for I love you . . . as I have never been able to love my fellow men. It is strange, is it not?"

The Curé who had been listening intently, now said:

"God is merciful, Monsieur le Vicomte. He will forgive you if you will but confess and repent your sins!"

Very slowly, for he was weakening rapidly, Antoine turned his head to look at the old man.

"I do not think I repent in any degree!" he mused as if he were unaware that he was very near death as the last of his life's blood ebbed away. "If I have any regret, 'tis that John and not I was my father's legitimate son. Had I been so, then my early life might have been very different!"

His face was now so white that already he looked like a corpse. Once more the Curé lent over him urging:

"If you abstain from Confession, you will never know God's peace for eternity!"

But Antoine never heard this last desperate appeal. His eyes closed, his breathing slowed and his lips turned blue.

Blanche Merlin had been knocked unconscious when François' huge frame had fallen upon her. But now she had recovered her senses and she stumbled to her son's inert body, wailing hysterically. Dragging him from Chantal's arms, she rocked him to and fro in an agony of grief. She had aged ten years and she looked like a wizened old witch, her grey hair straggling over her frantic eyes.

But it was only a matter of minutes before her grief gave way to a bitter fury as she rounded on Chantal.

"I warned Antoine that you would bring him no good. Until he met you he was never in danger. You killed him . . . *you killed my beloved son!*"

Chantal stood up. Her legs were trembling and she was shivering uncontrollably with delayed shock. Nevertheless, she felt a brief moment of pity for the pathetic creature who was accusing her. Antoine's death was a merciful release to her, Chantal, but to the old woman, virulent and cruel though she might be, it was the greatest tragedy life could have inflicted upon her.

The Curé was still kneeling, his voice rising and falling in a monotony of prayer. But Blanche now rounded on him.

"You think your prayers can help him now?" she cried. "God never helped him in his lifetime.

It was I who helped him rise up from his miserable start in life and Antoine himself, who by his cleverness and scheming, achieved what was due to him. What good has God been to him!"

The Curé ceased praying and crossed himself quickly.

"You blaspheme, woman!" he said. "Remove yourself from this holy place. You are in the house of God!"

But Blanche now seemed to have lost all control. She screamed abuse at the Curé until two of the shocked servants still remaining in the Chapel stepped forward to restrain her.

Realizing that with Antoine dead, there was now no one to take control of affairs, Chantal forced herself to do so.

"Take her to her room and lock her in!" she ordered the servants with quiet authority. "And send a messenger post-haste to fetch a physician. Women will be needed also to attend to the dead. The bodies can remain here in the Chapel. Monsieur le Curé, will you please come with me? There are two people imprisoned within the house and I am by no means sure if I can trust the Vicomte's servants not to harm them."

The old man was not as surprised by Chantal's remarks as she might have supposed. Rumors that all was far from right at the Château de Boulancourt had circulated among the surrounding farms and villages for many years. But the Vicomte had paid him handsomely for his services, given him a house upon the

666

estate, and his duties had been few and far between. He had shut his ears to the gossip and since the Vicomte never attended Mass or Confession, he remained ignorant of the evil that was perpetrated within the walls of the Château.

He turned now with relief to the young English girl who appeared to have assumed control. Meekly he followed her from the Chapel, his hands clasped around the silver cross he held as if he were aware that this alone would protect him from any further evil he might be about to encounter.

At the door of the Chapel, Chantal paused. Her eyes went to the altar, still blazing with the bright glow of the candles. She had almost forgotten the box containing the incriminating papers. She could not have imagined, she thought, that three people would die before she could gain possession of them. She still did not know who the huge man was who had tried to assault her and could feel no more regret for his passing than for the deaths of Antoine and his servant Stefano.

As she turned to retrace her steps to the altar she knew that it was not the dead who must occupy her thoughts but the living . . . her Papa, Tamarisk and her beloved John.

33

July 1840

"**I** HAVE it on the best authority that our young Queen is with child!" Mavreen remarked to Perry as they walked arm in arm towards the ballroom in Barre House. The melodious strains of a waltz reached them as they drew nearer. They bowed and smiled as they passed various of their many friends who had come to enjoy the evening's entertainment.

"Then soon all England will be rejoicing — just as we are!" Perry said, smiling down at Mavreen as he pressed her arm closer against his body.

Mavreen looked up at him happily.

"Is it not a miracle that all has turned out so well!" she said softly. "Are you not proud of Chantal, my love?"

Perry nodded.

"It must have been your influence upon her that enabled her to endure so much," he replied. "She told me that it was the thought of your courage and Tamarisk's that sustained her when she was most afraid!"

"Nevertheless she is *your* daughter, Perry, and I truly believe she has inherited your derring-do!"

"There is no doubt that I owe my life to her!" Perry acknowledged. "And to John and

Tamarisk, too. I must confess myself truly delighted that Chantal has at last agreed to marry John. The announcement of their betrothal this evening will surprise many of our friends!"

"I doubt if anything could now surprise our friends; they have long since ceased to expect any members of our family to live quiet, conventional lives!" Mavreen said, with a glint of amusement in her eyes. "Nor would I care even were they to disapprove the marriage. If John and Chantal are happy, then I am well content."

As they entered the ballroom John and Chantal swirled by them, oblivious to everyone but each other. Chantal's face was radiant with happiness and excitement, John's flushed with pride and love as he waltzed his future bride around the great room. When the music ended, he took Chantal's hand and drew her to one of the window recesses. Uncaring of any eyes focused upon them, John raised her hand to his lips.

"You are so very beautiful!" he said breathlessly. "I still cannot believe that you truly love me, Chantal!"

"I love you so much I could positively die of it!" she said. She glanced around the room, her eyes searching for the tall, dark Junoesque figure of Fleur. "Are you certain, John, that you do not have any regrets that it is not Fleur to whom you are betrothed?" she asked. John had but recently told Chantal of his relationship with the French girl in order to lessen her own feelings of guilt regarding Dinez. Chantal had felt a tinge of jealousy when John had asked that all the Dubois daughters should be invited to the Celebration Ball.

"She is very pretty, of course!" he teased now, and then added quickly: "But less so than her sisters or you, Chantal! I do not think it will be long before all of them find husbands, judging by their popularity with my friends. Not one of the girls has been partnerless this evening!"

He was delighted to see this happy outcome to his plan to assist the kindly Duc and Duchesse Dubois, for he owed them much. Following upon the dreadful events at the Château de Boulancourt, it was the Dubois family who had taken Tamarisk and Chantal under their wing and nursed them both back to normal good health and spirits. He himself had felt obliged to remain at the Château for a few weeks. He now knew beyond doubt that he was the rightful heir and owner and recognized that the responsibilities were likewise his.

There had been a great deal to put in order, little of it in the least agreeable. The *Maire*, the *Préfet de Police*, the Curé had all with John been involved in an attempt to piece together the terrible details of Antoine's life.

It was not until after Antoine and Stefano and the dead prisoner has been decently buried that the awful facts began to emerge. The second prisoner had readily betrayed the macabre details of Antoine's Roman games, but John had not been able to bring himself to reveal to his family the sordid method by which his half-brother had disposed of the losers of these mortal combats. Their bodies had been thrown into the deep moat surrounding the Château, where the giant eels put there for the purpose, had quickly consumed the remains.

Servants at the Château confessed to the knowledge of the wild orgies that had taken place there when their master's degenerate friends had visited him from Paris. Although they had been forbidden to enter the room where these parties took place, several admitted to having spied upon such occasions and to have been eye witnesses to the most shocking depravities.

Finally, the brokenhearted Blanche had confessed that the madwoman who had been in the tower was Antoine's wife, Princess Camille, and that Antoine had ordered Stefano to kill her when she escaped to Paris. Aware that the Law could not touch Antoine now and caring little that she was incriminating herself, Blanche bragged wildly to the *Préfet* that her son had been so clever he had outwitted even the Chief of the Paris police. Inevitably she had been arrested as an accomplice to the murder of Camille, and only John's pleas for clemency on the grounds of her state of near insanity had saved her from immediate imprisonment in Paris. He had requested that she be placed in an asylum, convincing the *Préfet* with his argument that no sane woman could have connived in such evil.

It was several weeks before all the enquiries ended. John dismissed the indoor servants as one by one the rooms of the Château were covered in dust sheets and locked up. He retained only a nucleus of outdoor staff to tend the gardens and the horses. It would be a long while, he knew, before he could bring himself to return to his father's home. His last task before he had driven away was to watch whilst a stone mason blocked up forever the doorway of the secret room where he and Tamarisk had been entombed for three terrible days and nights.

On his return to England John had at once given all his father's papers to Mavreen.

He smiled as he remembered his mother's joy at the discovery that Gerard had not after all betrayed her; that her marriage had not been bigamous and that John was, as she hoped, their legitimate son.

"With such intelligence and the knowledge that Perry's life is no longer in danger, there can be no happier woman than I!" she said.

John drew a deep sigh of contentment. He must of a certainty be the happiest of men, he thought, as he glanced at Chantal. He was on the point of asking her to dance with him again when he caught sight of a burly, red-headed figure approaching them. It was Hamish McRae.

"Yer sister said Ah'd find ye both in the ballroom!" the Captain said, a broad smile covering his bearded face as John rose to greet him. "And a wee bird told me congratulations were in order!"

Chantal laughed and standing on tiptoe, kissed the old Captain's rugged cheek.

"I am so happy to see you!" she said. "I fear I never did find the occasion to thank you properly for all you did for me when last we were together!"

"Whist noo!" said Hamish. "Ye were too distressed fir sich niceties, Ah dinna doot, lassie. But Ah can see those memories nae longer hurt ye so Ah'll gie ye a wee bit o' news. Yon pirate we left tae his fate on Coetivy," be said smiling. "Wull, the mon's nae langer there!"

Seeing the young people's look of astonishment, his smile broadened.

"A munth past Ah wus in the port o' Madrid and Ah heered that a sairtain rogue by the name o' the 'Portuguese Hawk' was on the high seas once mair."

"Not . . . not trading in slaves!" Chantal cried.

Hamish shook his head.

"I no heered *that!*" he said. "But pirating, aye! Stealin' ships as dinna belang tae him, the villain! And doin' verra wull fir hissel', too!"

Despite the dubious expression on John's face, Chantal laughed.

"I cannot pretend I am sorry — even if he is wicked!" she said. "Would you wish me to regret he is free again, John?"

"Not if it makes you happy!" John replied indulgently.

He was rewarded by Chantal's glowing smile.

"*I* have some intelligence for *you!*" John said to his old friend. "We have staying with us a young Frenchman well known to you, Hamish — Siméon St. Clair."

Hamish looked suitably surprised.

"The lad's heer, in England?" he asked.

"Aye!" replied John, imitating the Scot. "He and Janet Mylius are to be married. The Mylius' have returned home from their appointment in the Seychelles, Mr. Augustus Mylius being far from well, as you know. So Siméon decided to come to England with them in the same ship. He and Janet are to be wed next month and then they will return to Mahé to the plantation."

"And that is not all!" Chantal said happily. "Mr. Paul Mylius has been offered a diplomatic post in Quebec. Perhaps if you have been at sea, you have not heard that Upper and Lower Canada were united last month?"

She turned to smile teasingly at John. "In the few days since they have been staying here as our guests, Phoebe has become exceedingly friendly with my very best friend, Julia Lade. When we were children, we all expected John would marry Julia!"

"With the exception of me!" John reminded her, laughing.

"So, with Janet about to marry Siméon, Mr. Mylius felt Phoebe might like a companion and they have invited Julia to go with them to Canada," Chantal continued. "Julia has never been out of England and she is so excited at the idea that I think she has quite forgotten her passion for John. Mama has promised her a complete trousseau so it only remains for Julia's Mama and Papa to give their agreement. I am so happy for her!"

"That's guid news!" said Hamish. "And Ah couldna' be better pleased fir Siméon and the wee Janet. It's nae guid fir a mon tae live by himsel', eh, John?"

John nodded, his mind elsewhere. He had long nurtured the suspicion that Siméon St. Clair had entertained a feeling for Tamarisk that went beyond mere respect and liking; and strangely enough, when he and his sister had been incarcerated for so long in the secret chamber, Tamarisk had once or twice slipped into delirium. In such state she had several times mentioned Siméon by name in such a tone of voice as to suggest that he had been a lover rather than a friend.

Now he was convinced that he must have been mistaken. Siméon and Janet seemed quite inseparable and Tamarisk and Charles appeared more devoted than ever before. They could be seen quite frequently to hold each other's hands and look into one another's eyes as if in some secret communication. If aught had ever been amiss, clearly the marriage was on a solid footing now.

"Dare I hope to be as happy as they? As Mama and Perry?" John asked himself. He still found it hard to believe that Chantal loved him. Since her recovery from her ordeal at Boulancourt, she had been his shadow, just as she was when they were children. It was as if she could not rest happily if she were not in his company. But then he, likewise, could not be happy unless she were there close behind him.

Love was the strangest of emotions, he thought. No human being seemed able to avoid its embrace — not even a man like

Antoine de Valle whom he had once believed heartless. In the last resort, Antoine had given his life unquestioningly for the girl he loved — a fact John tried to remember when he considered his half-brother's perfidy.

He shivered. Such memories were best forgotten. He could not endure to speculate how close Chantal had come to marrying Antoine. It was as if God had been watching the tangled weaving of their lives, knowing that in the end He could intervene and save them from destruction. It mattered not how it had come about — only that he and Chantal were free now to marry each other.

When Hamish wandered off to see if he could find Siméon St. Clair amongst the several hundred guests, John turned to Chantal.

"I know that you have lost all the bitterness you once felt towards da Gama," he said uneasily. "But are you quite certain, Chantal, that you have lost all feelings of affection for him?"

Chantal took one of John's hands in hers as if by way of reassurance.

"I do think of him sometimes!" she admitted softly. "When I am lonely or hungry for love, I remember the passion of his kisses, his embraces." She saw the look of pain in John's face and smiled tenderly. "But it is not Dinez' kisses or embraces that I long for, John!" she whispered. "My thoughts turn always to you and to how it will be between us when we are wed. Do I shock you, my darling John, with such admissions?"

It was all John could do not to take her in his arms in the midst of that crowded room.

"On the contrary, my love, for I too am impatient for our wedding night. Do you think I will make a worthy lover, Chantal?" he asked, but confidently.

Her large dark eyes widened suddenly in laughter.

"Aye!" she said with Hamish's soft burr. "Ah hae nae doot aboot it! Oh, John," she added sighing, "we are going to be so very happy!"

"Aye!" agreed John. And this time he could not resist the temptation of her softly parted lips. Oblivious to the world around them he bent his head and kissed her.

As Chantal's eyes closed, it was not the sound of the orchestra's violins she heard, but the cry of seabirds as they landed on the coral sands, the rustic of palm fronds, Zambi's soft chanting and Dinez' voice murmuring beside her:

"Koosh-Koosh, I love you. You belong to me!"

Then the room was filled once more with the strains of the violins. It was John's voice she heard, John's mouth pressing against hers.

"I belong to you, John!" she said softly.

The sound of the wind in the palm trees faded, and she could no longer hear the soft whisper of the waves on the island shore.

CHINESE ALICE
Pat Barr

The story of Alice Greenwood gives a complete picture of late 19th century China.

UNCUT JADE
Pat Barr

In this sequel to CHINESE ALICE, Alice Greenwood finds herself widowed and alone in a turbulent China.

THE GRAND BABYLON HOTEL
Arnold Bennett

A romantic thriller set in an exclusive London Hotel at the turn of the century.

SINGING SPEARS
E. V. Thompson

Daniel Retallick, son of Josh and Miriam (from CHASE THE WIND) was growing up to manhood. This novel portrays his prime in Central Africa.

A HERITAGE OF SHADOWS
Madeleine Brent

This romantic novel, set in the 1890's, follows the fortunes of eighteen-year-old Hannah McLeod.

BARRINGTON'S WOMEN
Steven Cade

In order to prevent Norway's gold reserves falling into German hands in 1940, Charles Barrington was forced to hide them in Borgas, a remote mountain village.

THE PLAGUE
Albert Camus

The plague in question afflicted Oran in the 1940's.

THE RESTLESS SEA
E. V. Thompson

A tale of love and adventure set against a panorama of Cornwall in the early 1800's.

THE RIDDLE OF THE SANDS
Erskine Childers

First published in 1903 this thriller, deals with the discovery of a threatened invasion of England by a Continental power.

WHERE ARE THE CHILDREN?
Mary Higgins Clark

A novel of suspense set in peaceful Cape Cod.

KING RAT
James Clavell

Set in Changi, the most notorious Japanese POW camp in Asia.

THE BLACK VELVET GOWN
Catherine Cookson

There would be times when Riah Millican would regret that her late miner husband had learned to read and then shared his knowledge with his family.

THE WHIP
Catherine Cookson

Emma Molinero's dying father, a circus performer, sends her to live with an unknown English grandmother on a farm in Victorian Durham and to a life of misery.

SHANNON'S WAY
A. J. Cronin

Robert Shannon, a devoted scientist had no time for anything outside his laboratory. But Jean Law had other plans for him.

THE JADE ALLIANCE
Elizabeth Darrell

The story opens in 1905 in St. Petersburg with the Brusilov family swept up in the chaos of revolution.

THE DREAM TRADERS
E. V. Thompson

This saga, is set against the background of intrigue, greed and misery surrounding the Chinese opium trade in the late 1830s.

BERLIN GAME
Len Deighton

Bernard Samson had been behind a desk in Whitehall for five years when his bosses decided that he was the right man to slip into East Berlin.

HARD TIMES
Charles Dickens

Conveys with realism the repulsive aspect of a Lancashire manufacturing town during the 1850s.

THE RICE DRAGON
Emma Drummond

The story of Rupert Torrington and his bride Harriet, against a background of Hong Kong and Canton during the 1850s.

FIREFOX DOWN
Craig Thomas

The stolen Firefox — Russia's most advanced and deadly aircraft is crippled, but Gant is determined not to abandon it.

THE DOGS OF WAR
Frederic Forsyth

The discovery of the existence of a mountain of platinum in a remote African republic causes Sir James Manson to hire an army of trained mercenaries to topple the government of Zangaro.

THE DAYS OF WINTER
Cynthia Freeman

The story of a family caught between two world wars — a saga of pride and regret, of tears and joy.

REGENESIS
Alexander Fullerton

It's 1990. The crew of the US submarine ARKANSAS appear to be the only survivors of a nuclear holocaust.

SEA LEOPARD
Craig Thomas

HMS 'Proteus', the latest British nuclear submarine, is lured to a sinister rendezvous in the Barents Sea.

THE TORCH BEARERS
Alexander Fullerton

1942: Captain Nicholas Everard has to escort a big, slow convoy . . . a sacrificial convoy.

DAUGHTER OF THE HOUSE
Catherine Gaskin

An account of the destroying impact of love which is set among the tidal creeks and scattered cottages of the Essex Marshes.

FAMILY AFFAIRS
Catherine Gaskin

Born in Ireland in the Great Depression, the illegitimate daughter of a servant, Kelly Anderson's birthright was poverty and shame.

THE EXPLORERS
Vivian Stuart

The fourth novel in 'The Australians' series which continues the story of Australia from 1809 to 1813.

THE SUMMER OF THE SPANISH WOMAN
Catherine Gaskin

Clonmara — the wild, beautiful Irish estate in County Wicklow is a fitting home for the handsome, reckless Blodmore family.

THE TILSIT INHERITANCE
Catherine Gaskin

Ginny Tilsit had been raised on an island paradise in the Caribbean. She knew nothing of her family's bitter inheritance half the world away.

THE FINAL DIAGNOSIS
Arthur Hailey

Set in a busy American hospital, the story of a young pathologist and his efforts to restore the standards of a hospital controlled by an ageing, once brilliant doctor.

THE COLONISTS
Vivian Stuart

Sixth in 'The Australians' series, this novel opens in 1812 and covers the administration of General Sir Thomas Brisbane and General Ralph Darling.

IN HIGH PLACES
Arthur Hailey

The theme of this novel is a projected Act of Union between Canada and the United States in order that both should survive the effect of a possible nuclear war.

RED DRAGON
Thomas Harris

A ritual murderer is on the loose. Only one man can get inside that twisted mind — forensic expert, Will Graham.

CATCH-22
Joseph Heller

Anti-war novels are legion; this is a war novel that is anti-death, a comic savage tribute to those who aren't interested in dying.

THE ADVENTURERS
Vivian Stuart

The fifth in 'The Australians' series, opens in 1815 when two of its principal characters take part in the Battle of Waterloo.

THE SURVIVOR
James Herbert

David is the only survivor from an accident whose aftermath leaves a lingering sense of evil and menace in the quiet countryside.

LOST HORIZON
James Hilton

A small plane carrying four passengers crash-lands in the unexplored Tibetan wilderness.

THE TIME OF THE HUNTER'S MOON
Victoria Holt

When Cordelia Grant accepts an appointment to a girls' school in Devon, she does not anticipate anyone from her past re-emerging in her new life.

THURSTON HOUSE
Danielle Steel

At forty four, Jeremiah, a mining baron was marrying for the first time. Camille was a captivating eighteen-year-old girl. But can money buy happiness, a family . . . or love?

THE FOUNDER OF THE HOUSE
Naomi Jacob

The first volume of a family saga which begins in Vienna, and introduces Emmanuel Gollantz.

"THAT WILD LIE . . . "
Naomi Jacob

The second volume in the Gollantz saga begun with THE FOUNDER OF THE HOUSE.

IN A FAR COUNTRY
Adam Kennedy

Christine Wheatley knows she is going to marry Fred Deets, that is until she meets Roy Lavidge.

ONCE IN A LIFETIME
Danielle Steel

To the doctors the woman in the ambulance was just another casualty — more beautiful than most . . .

AUTUMN ALLEY
Lena Kennedy

Against the background of London's East End from the turn of the century to the 1830's a saga of three generations of ordinary, yet extraordinary people.

LADY PENELOPE
Lena Kennedy

Lady Penelope Devereux, forced to make a marriage of convenience, pours all the affection of her generous nature into her children . . . and her lovers.

LIZZIE
Lena Kennedy

Tiny, warm-hearted but cruelly scarred for life, Lizzie seems to live only for, and through, her burly, wayward husband Bobby.

GOING HOME
Danielle Steel

Gillian and Chris pledged their love for always, their happiness seemed complete. Until a moment's infidelity broke the bond they shared . . .